PENGUIN CRIME FICTION

WHO DROPPED PETER PAN?

Jane Dentinger is the author of *Murder On Cue*,
First Hit of the Season, *Death Mask*, *Dead Pan*, and
The Queen is Dead (all available from Penguin).
She lives in New York City, where she is also an
actor, director, and teacher.

WHO DROPPED PETER PAN?

A Jocelyn O'Roarke Mystery

Jane Dentinger

PENGUIN BOOKS

PENGUIN BOOKS
Published by the Penguin Group
Penguin Books USA Inc., 375 Hudson Street, New York, New York 10014, U.S.A.
Penguin Books Ltd, 27 Wrights Lane, London W8 5TZ, England
Penguin Books Australia Ltd, Ringwood, Victoria, Australia
Penguin Books Canada Ltd, 10 Alcorn Avenue, Toronto, Ontario, Canada M4V 3B2
Penguin Books (N.Z.) Ltd, 182–190 Wairau Road, Auckland 10, New Zealand

Penguin Books Ltd, Registered Offices: Harmondsworth, Middlesex, England

First published in the United States of America by Viking Penguin,
a division of Penguin Books USA Inc. 1995
Published in Penguin Books 1996

10 9 8 7 6 5 4 3 2 1

THE LIBRARY OF CONGRESS HAS CATALOGUED THE HARDCOVER AS FOLLOWS:
Dentinger, Jane.
Who dropped Peter Pan?: a Jocelyn O'Roarke mystery / Jane Dentinger.
p. cm.
ISBN 0-670-86070-0 (hc.)
ISBN 0 14 02.4554 5 (pbk.)
1. O'Roarke, Jocelyn (Fictitious character)—Fiction.   2. Women detectives—United
States—Fiction.   3. Actresses—United States—Fiction.   4. New York (N.Y.)—
Fiction.   I. Title.
PS3554.E587W48   1995
813'.54—dc20   95–6768

Printed in the United States of America
Set in Adobe Minion
Designed by Virginia Norey

For RICK KASE (1947–1994)

Like Karen in All About Eve, *he was "of the Theatre by marriage." And, while no performer himself, he was the best possible audience an actor could have—and the best possible friend.*

ACKNOWLEDGMENTS

Great thanks for all the great fun to John Courtney Pollard, Marc Castle, Lora K. Powell, Thomas Brennan, and Steven Yuha$z. Also, my deep appreciation to Veri Lee Krassner, Simon Brett (and Charles Paris—natch!). And, as always, a special nod to Dr. Mark Dentinger and Dr. Russell Menkes.

WHO DROPPED PETER PAN?

1

"What can I get you, miss . . . Miss?"

The roly-poly Jewish guy behind the busy fish counter at Zabar's wondered why the brunette standing before him had tears in her eyes. Then she looked up with an ear-to-ear grin on her face and he saw they were tears of joy.

"Uh, okay—let's see. Okay, I'd like a half pound of Scotch salmon—no, no, make that the Nova. And—aw, what the hell—a quarter pound of Beluga."

Beluga caviar was a mad extravagance for an out-of-work actor waiting for her first unemployment check to come through, but Jocelyn O'Roarke didn't care. She was back home, she was back at Zabar's, her favorite food mecca, and all was right with her world.

Contrary to popular myth, not all actors have "the gypsy" in their soul. Some do, of course; primarily musical theatre folk who jump for joy when they land a six-month national tour—unless it's a bus-and-trucker, which requires youth, stamina, and a soupçon of masochism. But a first-class tour of, say, *Guys and Dolls,* with long layovers in major cities and a hefty per diem to boot is often regarded as a busman's holiday and, given the scarcity of jobs on Broadway, a consummation devoutly to be wished.

Many working actors, even the less nomadic by nature, spend part of the year (pilot season) in L.A., where, even if they don't land a job, they can at least fantasize about being discovered while ambling around the Farmers' Market sampling great Mexican food. Others, who would rather be on a stage *anywhere* than not on a stage at all, traipse off to do regional theatre, summer stock, or even, God help them, dinner theatre.

By showbiz standards, therefore, Jocelyn was something of an anomaly; she was a one-town woman and that town was New York. Oh, yes, she would pack her bags if the role was great or the money was good but, after a week or two, she would start itching to get back home.

O'Roarke had been itching for nearly a year.

A trip out to the Coast had turned into a prolonged stay thanks to a powerhouse agent named Gabby Brent who, grateful for Josh's help in the solving of her husband's murder, had set up a whirlwind schedule of auditions and interviews that had kept O'Roarke busy and gainfully employed for months. When Gabby headed off to Europe for a much-needed vacation, Jocelyn had headed home, only to be detoured upstate by an old director friend who had just lost his leading lady. Once that job was over, it had been time for O'Roarke to visit her family in Saratoga before they completely forgot what she looked like. While she had relished playing Auntie Mame to the hilt with her horde of nieces and nephews, by the end of her stay she was breaking out in homesick hives. The little gypsy in her soul had long since given up the ghost.

After a morning spent prowling her old neighborhood to see which restaurants had closed and what new ones had opened, she had browsed through the new, huge Barnes & Noble on Broadway. O'Roarke was amused to find that it had become the epicenter of the Upper West Side singles scene, giving a new spin to that old saw: Read any good books lately? But, upon consideration, Jocelyn thought it was more informative to know if a guy reads Henry Miller than if he drinks Miller Lite. Still, amidst all the changes, she was comforted to find Zabar's just as it ever was—overcrowded, overstocked, and fragrantly fabulous. And she was so damned glad to be back there, she didn't even mind the usual everlasting wait in the checkout line; that is, not until she got out the door and checked her watch.

"Aw, crud! It's after four. I told P.J. to come at six," she muttered aloud, then smiled to see that no one around took the slightest notice. Another thing that hadn't changed while she was away. Hurrying up West Eighty-second Street as quickly as two bulging grocery bags would allow, Josh told herself not to worry. Pasta alla Mama took almost no time to fix and her buddy, Peter James Cullen—P.J. to his friends—would be happy to wait as long as the wine kept flowing.

Normally Jocelyn's first homecoming dinner guest would have been her old friend and mentor Frederick Revere. But Revere, a legendary actor still much in demand, was in England wrapping up a Merchant-Ivory film. Her sometimes paramour, sometimes pal Phillip Gerrard of the N.Y.P.D. was also out of town, on loan to a Chicago Police unit working on a very hush-hush homicide case. So O'Roarke, who keenly felt the need to get back in the thick of things theatrical, which meant, of course, getting the most news and gossip in the least amount of time, had immediately called Cullen, an up-and-coming young stage manager whose motto was: "Work hard. Play hard. And always get the dish." If you wanted to know what show was going to fold, which new production was in trouble, or who was doing what to whom or was about to, P.J. was your man.

They had met several years back when Jocelyn had stepped in to replace an ailing director in a summer-stock production of *Steel Magnolias*, which P.J. was P.S.M.ing. Before rehearsals started, they had arranged a lunch meeting, ostensibly to discuss production details, but the real purpose was to check each other out. When you're trying to get a show up and running in ten days' time, the director and the production stage manager have to work as closely as Siamese twins. By their second Bloody Mary, P.J. and Josh had joined at the hip. Jocelyn had sensed this when P.J., who hailed from Texas, had slapped his empty glass down on the table and declared, "Yup, I grew up a lone homo on the range. Tell ya, it takes guts to produce a drag show in San Antone but I did it."

He also did a bang-up job on *Steel Magnolias*. During a final dress rehearsal fraught with tech troubles, P.J. had soothed a nervous cast by constantly cooing, "Thank you for enduring, ladies." And he had won Jocelyn's eternal gratitude as well, in return for which she had introduced him to Peter Morrance, Broadway's leading P.S.M. and Josh's old comrade in arms. After that, Cullen never had to work summer stock again. So P.J. was more than happy to accept O'Roarke's dinner invitation. Not only had he missed Josh during her long absence, he had missed her cooking. Their friendship was founded on three firm pillars—love of theatre, gossip, and food—though not always in that order. P.J. was looking forward to the meal. Josh was looking forward to the dish.

Only later, much later, would O'Roarke realize that, if her soul's gypsy hadn't croaked, she might have had the prescience to see what disaster lurked ahead.

2

"Oh, no, you're too much, girl. You found a *straight* hairdresser in LaLa Land?!" P.J. Cullen slapped a jean-clad knee and poured himself another glass of pinot grigio. "Wait—shouldn't we call the *Guiness Book of Records*?"

Lifting a pot of linguine off the stove, Jocelyn poured the contents into a colander, then rinsed it under the faucet. "Well, Jack's not doing much cutting these days. Now that westerns are back in vogue, his horse ranch has really taken off. Did you see *Geronimo*? Those were some of Jack's quarter horses."

"Really? I'm impressed. They gave better performances than some of the actors."

As O'Roarke tossed the pasta with the egg and cream sauce, P.J. snuck a cube out of the ice bucket and dropped it in his wineglass. Josh heard the clink of ice against glass and gave him a sorrowful look. He stuck out his tongue in defiance and went on the counteroffensive. "What I don't get is—you find this cute guy who has horses *and* gives great head—I'm talkin' hair, a' course—and you just up and left! Why?"

"I told you I got homesick," Jocelyn said, dishing the linguine into separate pasta bowls. Her black and white butterball of a cat, Angus, who had been left behind when his mistress went out West, defended her decision by ferociously attacking the tip of Cullen's cowboy boot. "Get the garlic bread, will you."

"Sure, uh . . . Can you detach the cat, please?"

"Angus—off! He's just happy to be home."

"Then I don't want to be around when he's feeling sad." P.J. sniffed as he removed the bread from its foil wrapper and brought it to the table. "So how did our Mr. Breedlove take it when you did a bunk?"

"Oh, he wasn't thrilled but I don't think it was a shock. Frankly, the last month or so, I was not a joy to be around."

"No? Gee, I just can't picture *you* cranky."

"Shut up and eat. Anyhow we parted on good terms and I think, deep down, he was a little relieved to see me go. But we still keep in touch. He's a great guy."

"Uh-huh. But I just wonder—" P.J. paused to take a bite of salad. "Whoa! You put crushed garlic in this dressing, huh?"

"Too much?"

"Are you nuts? There's no such thing as too much garlic. . . . What was I sayin'? Oh, yeah—you sure it had nuthin' to do with ol' Robocop breaking off his engagement?" Robocop was Cullen's nickname for Phillip Gerrard, whom he had never actually met but disliked on general principle. Twirling pasta around her fork, Jocelyn made a face at her friend.

"Noo, it did *not*. All right, so Phillip came up to visit me when I was working in Corinth. I didn't invite him but he did. And it was good thing, too, or we never would've got to the bottom of that awful Tessa Grant business."

P.J. watched Josh refill her wineglass and take a long sip, and knew better than to press for details of what had obviously been a painful affair for her. Instead he asked, "So how do things stand with you and Robo these days?"

Smiling despite herself, she assumed a prim tone. "By the time I got back to town, Phil had already left for Chicago. He'll probably be gone for a while. So for now we're just—"

"Just-good-friends." Cullen grabbed his throat and made loud gagging noises. "Oh, barf me! The cliché from hell. From you of all people—tsk, tsk. You don't *deserve* to have a love life, O'Roarke."

"Well, that's fine," she sniped back. "You screw around enough for both of us."

Reddening, P.J. grinned and dropped his head in mock shame. "True. 'Tis pity I'm a ho—but at least I'm having fun!"

Another thing that hadn't changed while she was gone was Cullen's rabbitlike sex life. Having sown her share of wild oats in younger days, O'Roarke wasn't judgmental about such things, simply concerned, as she was for most of her gay friends. Pointing her fork at him, she said, "Well, carry on wayward son . . . as long as you're being *safe.*"

"Ah, here we go again!" P.J. tossed his napkin in the air with a shake of the head. "I swear, you sound like La Olivier in *Marathon Man*—'Is it safe? Is it safe?' Hey, I may be trashy but I'm no mow-ron, honey chile."

"Really? So the glazed look and the drool cup are just to throw us off track then?"

"Bitch."

Josh made kissy sounds and wrinkled her nose. "Missed you, too, asshole."

Over coffee and cannoli, Cullen gave a loud satisfied burp. "If we were Eskimos that'd be a great compliment, you know."

"If we were Eskimos, you'd be eating whale blubber, fool."

Comfortably back on old ground, P.J. poured a little Martell's into each coffee mug as Josh lit a cigarette and wondered why he hadn't yet told her what show he was working on. Ambitious as a beaver, Cullen was usually chomping at the bit to fill her in on his latest career move. He caught her speculative gaze and waggled his eyebrows wickedly, saying, "Hey, let's play the game."

"What? Oh—Cast in Hell? Sure!"

Cast in Hell was something P.J. had invented one lunch hour in stock when Jocelyn was frothing over the fact that the damn hair dryers hadn't arrived yet. The game succeeded brilliantly in distracting her, and became an instant favorite of theirs. You named a Broadway show with a star who was about to leave the cast, then proposed the most grotesquely wrong actor you could think of as a replacement. There was always a certain degree of irony involved, since there was also the very real chance that the producers might make an even more horrific choice. P.J. started the ball rolling.

"Okay, ummm, Vanessa Williams is about to leave *Kiss of the Spiderwoman* to be replaced by . . ."

He held out a hand as Josh's cue to finish. Without missing a beat, she answered, "Sheena Easton."

"Ooo! Ouch! That's good. Haven't lost your touch." He writhed in pleasurable pain, then paused. "That's too scary—they could *do* that! Your turn."

"Okay. Uh, Charlotte d'Amboise's going to leave *Damn Yankees*." She hummed a few bars of "Whatever Lola Wants, Lola Gets," then asked, "Who'll fill her shoes?"

Scrunching his face, P.J. pondered a second, then shouted out, "Debbie Boone!"

O'Roarke cackled with glee, causing Angus to leap from her lap disgruntled. Then Cullen suddenly changed the rules, saying, "Okay, I got a real one for you. The Peakmont Playhouse is about to do *Peter Pan*. Who's going to play Peter?"

This was a toughie and Jocelyn's face corkscrewed in concentration. Less than an hour from Manhattan, the Peakmont Playhouse was a large, prosperous L.O.R.T. theatre, which meant it paid well above union minimum, very well if you were playing a lead, and its proximity to the city was a big plus since actors could commute to work—and still get reviewed by the *Times*. While the playhouse didn't often attract big Broadway names, its boards had been graced by many fading luminaries, ex-TV stars, and popular soap actors who wanted to hone their stage skills. This made for a large pool of potential Peters.

"Gimme a hint," O'Roarke begged. "Just a little one, like—is Richie directing?"

"Oh, yes indeedy." Cullen nodded and smiled like Angus after a big meal. Rich Rafelson was a former Juilliard graduate who had briefly tried his wings on Broadway as an actor-singer and then flown off to direct in regional theatre. Several years back he had found a permanent nest at the playhouse as its artistic director. Jocelyn wasn't surprised that Rafelson was directing *Peter;* his stock-in-trade was remounting grand old American musicals, like *Oklahoma, Carousel,* and *South Pacific,* in the style they were once accustomed to, i.e., with large casts, huge sets, and enormous budgets, something very few theatres could afford to do anymore. His productions, large on spectacle, small on substance, were not O'Roarke's particular cup of tea. But the blue-haired ladies, who made up a great part of the Peakmont audience and didn't seem to care that the character comedian wasn't very funny, that the ingenue had all the sex appeal of a prison matron, or that the leading man couldn't act his way out of a paper bag, loved them. This blanket approval, while not always shared by the New York critics, gave Richie a lot of room to indulge his casting whims.

"Hmmm. Rich casts about as well as I *knit.* Uhh, let's see." Josh stared into her mug as if it were a crystal ball, then, in the spirit of the game, said, "I got it! LaToya Jackson. I can see the ads—Peter's back and she's black!"

Shaking his head, Cullen gave her a pitying smile that said she had gotten a little rusty. Then he whispered one word. "Worse."

"Christ! You're scaring me now, P.J." And he was. Shutting her eyes in dread, she mewled, "Please, please God, not . . . Bonnie Franklin?"

P.J. shook his head again and Josh sighed with relief. But again he whispered, "Worse."

"Aw, come on! You can't be serious." O'Roarke smacked the table in frustration. "There is no worse!"

Very gently, preparing her for the blow, Cullen reached over and took her hand. "Think back, hon. Couple years ago, when he did *Dolly*—who played Barnaby?"

"Richie did. He was a little long in the tooth for it but at least he could still hit the high note—" Jocelyn choked mid-sentence and stared at Cullen as the light broke and horror dawned. She shook her head, tried to speak, failed, and shook her head again. P.J. nodded yes and they went on like two mismatched metronomes until she finally croaked out, "No."

" 'Fraid so. I think we've got a shot at makin' *Ripley's Believe It or Not* with this one."

Simultaneously finding her voice and her outrage on behalf of all talented, deserving actors who were out of work, O'Roarke roared, "Sweet Jesus! The man's past forty. He's too old, too tall, and not a *woman!*"

"Least he's gay," Cullen offered weakly.

"P.J., it's—it's unholy!"

"Yuh, I gotta admit it's kind of shaken my faith in the Lord. I know He works in mysterious ways but this is just *too* strange. . . . What I can't believe is Tony's letting him get away with it."

"Well, he always has," Josh said sadly. She knew Anthony Romero, the producer of the Peakmont Playhouse, from his days as a casting director. Over the years he had called her in to audition for the one or two nonmusicals they did each season, but Rafelson, who once told a mutual friend that he found her "too Dorothy Parker for *my* tastes," had never cast her. Romero, an elegant man in his mid-fifties, knew how to charm his board of directors—hadn't he gotten them to build a bigger and better facility after the old playhouse had burned down five years earlier?—and how to woo his ladies' auxiliary. But he had never seemed to know how to curb his artistic director's over-weening ego.

P.J. and Jocelyn now shook their heads and sighed as one. Adding more Martell's to their mugs, O'Roarke muttered, "Tell you one thing—it's gonna give a whole new meaning to the 'Clap if you believe in fairies' speech."

"Ah-*haaaa!*" Cullen brayed his unique rendition of a Texas

mule in stitches. "Can't *wait* to tell the guys on the crew that one!"

"On the crew? You mean you're working on *Peter?*"

"Can't afford not to. It's the big fifth-anniversary show—since the fire, you know? And they've offered me A.S.M."

"Oh, baby," was all Josh could offer in return.

"I know. It's a bitch but I need the money. Thing is . . . I'm kind of worried."

"About what? The reviews?" she asked. "Well, sweetie, they're gonna *cream* it, of course, but that's not your faul—"

"No, no, that's not it. . . . You know, there's a reason why Peter's always played by a woman."

"Yeah, like the songs being written for a *soprano*. Hell, you can only transpose music so much—"

"I'm talking about the *flying*, Josh," he broke in. "It's much easier to fly a woman than a man 'cause the center of gravity's different, see? Flying is tricky, even with a small woman. Mary Martin, Sandy Duncan, Cathy Rigby—they're all petite and they still got banged up a bit . . . and their crews *liked* them."

"Oooh . . . I see." And she did. Rafelson, who fancied himself a latter-day Ziegfeld, only more demanding, was notorious for the hell he put his tech crew through in rehearsals. Apparently P.J. was worried that some of the guys might think it was pay-back time. Josh scoffed, "Aw, get real. You don't really think they're gonna bounce him off the walls or anythi—"

"Uh, let me put it this way." He was all in earnest now. "From the first day of rehearsal, they've been calling him *Splat* Rafelson. Okay?"

3

"A *guy* doin' Peter Pan," Sergeant Thomas Zito groused. "Shit, sounds un-American if you ask me."

"I'm sure you're right." Jocelyn refrained from mentioning that the role had been written by a Brit as she drew him toward the backstage door of the Peakmont Playhouse. Zito, Phillip Gerrard's comrade in arms, had had scant—which is to say zilch—interest in theatre before he met O'Roarke. Now, however, he read the trade papers, frequented the TKTS half-price booth, and fancied himself the true voice of the blue-collar audience. And on the whole, Josh was usually far more interested in what Tommy had to say about the latest plays than in what the critics wrote—which is why she had dragged him out to Peakmont for the first preview performance of *Peter Pan*. She, jaded and skeptical in the extreme, was expecting a turkey; Tommy would let her know if it really gobbled.

"Hey, Rocky, why're we going backstage *before* the show?" he asked. "Isn't that bad luck?"

"No, Tommy, you're thinking of weddings." She squeezed his arm reassuringly; for all his Italian bravado, Zito was shy around show folk. "I have friends in this show. I want to tell 'em to break a leg."

"That is somethin' I have never sussed," he said, dragging his feet. " 'Break a leg.' Why's that good luck? In Brooklyn, we take it as a threat, you know?"

"I know, I know," she laughed, delighted to be back in his company again. "It's just another theatre superstition, Tom. If you tell somebody to have a great show, they'll go out and suck eggs. So you say the opposite."

"Jesu and Maria, you folks are weird," he said with grudging affection. "That's like me telling a rookie goin' out on night patrol—'Hope ya get shot!' "

"No, it's different. Here the bullets can't kill you. They can only kill your career. . . . What in the world?"

O'Roarke stopped short as they entered the scene shop. The shop itself, which was huge and high-ceilinged, looked much as she remembered it, but the people in it had sure changed. Except for an actor here and there in a dressing gown or partial costume, everyone else was in uniforms. Uniforms? Jocelyn was used to seeing the crew in worn jeans or chinos and a vast array of T-shirts ranging from tie-dyes to ones sporting rock group logos to the plain black ones worn by those crew members who shifted sets or struck props in view of the audience. Tonight, however, they all wore identical dark blue coveralls with "Peak-mont Playhouse" stitched in yellow over the front pocket; they looked like grease monkeys at a formal affair.

It took her a moment to locate a familiar face, then she waved and called out, "Hey, Big Al, how ya doin'!"

A huge bearded man wearing a heavy tool belt over his coveralls waved back at O'Roarke and lumbered over to give her a bear hug that almost obliterated her from Zito's view. Lifting her off her feet, he grunted, "Good to see you, girl," then deposited her back on the ground. Smoothing her rumpled dress, she looked him up and down and asked, "What's with the mechanic's getup?"

The big man snorted in disdain, jerking a thumb upward. "Orders from the Big Cheese. Sez it's less distracting to the audience. I say, if the house is watching the crew, it's cause the show sucks."

"Well, at least it's your color," Josh teased as she turned to Tommy. "This is Al Brenner. He's the master carpenter. Al— meet my friend Tom Zito."

The two men shook hands. Zito barely came up to Brenner's shoulder, but something in his face made Al break the hand clasp and step back. Tommy watched him shove his hands in his back pockets as Josh asked, "Where's P.J.?"

"Uh, I—I think he's on the deck checking harnesses. I'll tell him you're here." With that he did a fast about-face and headed out the door. Frowning slightly, Zito tapped Josh's shoulder.

"What's the deck?"

"The stage. Techies have their own slang for certain things. To actors, it's the stage. To them, it's the deck."

"Uh-huh," Tommy grunted, then asked, "Brenner an old buddy of yours?"

"Not really. I met him through P.J.—he's a good guy though. Hell of a carpenter." Catching something in his look, she said, "What is it? What's bothering yo—"

Before she could finish, P.J., in the same grease-monkey outfit as the others, marched into the scene dock like a toy soldier that has been overwound. She introduced him to Zito and, as they shook hands, even his arms seemed to have a mechanical tick to them. O'Roarke knew it was just an overdose of adrenaline. Rubbing the back of his neck, she said, "How was the run-through today?"

"Don't ask. Just do *not* ask," he hissed through clenched teeth. "I can't go into it now. Lemme just say—the man is a *flaming* asshole!" He cranked up the volume on the last two words and heads turned their way, though no one looked particularly startled. Dropping his voice back down, P.J. added, "Let's have drinks after—many, many drinks—and I'll give you the whole poop. . . . Nice to meet you, Tom." He nodded to Zito, then turned abruptly to a young girl with a ring in her right nostril who was passing by with an armful of small wooden swords. "Rhea! Don't forget to preset the shadow and the soap."

Without breaking stride, she hollered back, "I did, I did! Lighten, will ya?"

Cullen followed her out the door, hectoring all the way. "And don't forget to count those damn swords! We had one weaponless Lost Boy today."

An atmosphere of choreographed chaos was building and the air was charged with purpose and panic. Jocelyn smiled and soaked it in but Tommy, who didn't know this was the norm for a first preview, was beginning to feel like Olivia de Havilland in *The Snake Pit*.

"Um, Josh, shouldn't we, like, get the hell outa here now?"

"In a sec. Come with me." She drew him out to a hallway lined with dressing room doors. "I have to say hi to Captain Hook."

"Ah, jeesh! *Another* old pal?"

"Not of mine. Of Revere's," Josh answered absently as she checked the names on each door. "I've never met him but I promised Freddie I'd send his regards. Won't take a sec."

She stopped at a door with MANVILLE GREER stenciled on it. From within came a sonorous rumbling. "The strongest always plays Peter. They make the *baby* play Hook. Bicarbonate of soda! That's where the canker *ga*-naws!" Tapping lightly on the door, she was answered by a stentorian "Enter!"

Popping her head in, she smiled at the figure who posed before the mirror in his Mr. Darling costume and full makeup. Greer had come up through the acting ranks the same time as Frederick Revere had, though without ever achieving the latter's star status. Still he had worked steadily, often as Revere's understudy, and the two men had become good friends. To Jocelyn, he looked like a faded copy of Freddie; a little shorter, a bit less broad-shouldered, without the effortless élan Revere exuded, but nonetheless, a fine example of that dying breed, the Gentleman Actor.

"Mr. Greer, I'm Jocelyn O'Roarke, a friend of Freder—"

"Of *course* you are, darling!" He strode across the tiny room with hands outstretched to clasp hers. "Freddie's talked about you for years. We meet at last!"

Tommy, always amazed at how touchy-feely show folk are, watched the old actor embrace O'Roarke like a long-lost daughter, kissing her on the cheek and leaving lip-prints behind. Jocelyn smiled up at him warmly. "I won't keep you but Freddie would have my head if I didn't come back to say break a leg—or a broadsword, in this case. In his absence, we're your rooting section."

His eyes lighting on Zito, Greer exclaimed, "Ah! Is this your consort—the renowned Lieutenant Gerrard?"

Embarrassed, Tommy shook his head and stuck out a hand. "No, no, I just work with Phil . . . Tom Zito."

"Well, good of you to come, Tom," Manville replied but Zito caught a subtle look that said, "Thank God." He didn't mind; he knew, by theatre standards, he was a second banana while Phil would always be a headliner, and that was fine by him.

Seeing that he had smudged his lip liner, Greer snatched up a pencil to retrace it but his hand started to shake. With a quick "Let me," Jocelyn took the pencil from him and deftly redrew the lines, joking lightly, "Girls are just better with lipstick. It's one of those things that requires two X chromosomes really." Manville chuckled gamely as she handed him a tissue and commanded, "Blot!" Laying her hands on his shoulders, she met his eyes in the mirror and winked. "You look darling, Mr. Darling. Knock 'em dead."

As she whisked Zito out the door, he was struck anew by this paradox in her nature; as sarcastic and downright ornery as Josh could be with her peers, she was unfailingly respectful and kind to her elders. She would knock his block off if he ever said so, but Tommy chalked it up to the good little Catholic girl that lurked somewhere in her cynic's heart.

Rushing down the hallway, they heard P.J.'s voice on the intercom calling, "Fifteen minutes to places, ladies and gentlemen. Fifteen minutes."

The hallway jogged to the left. Turning the corner, they came upon a man in a curly-haired wig, green tights, and doublet who was whispering urgently to a fawnlike young woman in a nightgown, staring down at the floor and holding a hankie to her mouth. Zito didn't need a program to know these players; it had to be Peter and Wendy.

O'Roarke stopped so fast she nearly toppled Tommy. The guy in the Harpo wig looked up with an angry scowl, which he quickly smoothed into a bland smile.

"Is that Josh O'Roarke? I thought you'd left us for Tinseltown!"

"Guess again. Hi, Rich . . . nice wig," she lied through her teeth. Rafelson was the one person she had not wanted to run into. Desperate for a diversion, she turned to the unhappy girl in the nightie who was now twisting the hankie into a corkscrew, and said, "You have to be Wendy, right? You look absolutely *perfect!* Like you could fly without the wires. . . . Have a great one, you two!"

With a wink and a nod, O'Roarke was off, propelling Zito before her. As soon as they got outside, they paused like sprinters for a gulp of air. Then Josh hustled toward the front of the theatre with Tommy on her heels, gasping and rasping, "*That's* the guy? *He's* Peter-fuckin'-Pan? I'm tellin' ya'—it's un-American!"

4

"Come on, Wendy, Michael, John—think *wonderful* thoughts!"

As Richie Rafelson encouraged the Darling children to bliss themselves into free flight, O'Roarke covered her eyes and tried to do the same. She conjured up her six-year-old self sitting enraptured in front of a small black and white Motorola, watching Mary Martin glide through the children's bedroom window and land light as a sparrow. It had been her first taste of theatre magic.

When Coleridge wrote of "That willing suspension of disbelief for the moment, which constitutes poetic faith," he hadn't been thinking of kids. A six-year-old, at least in Jocelyn's day, had very little disbelief to suspend. Josh had had none, and "more imagination than sense," as the good sisters had often said. For weeks afterward, she had kept climbing up on the furniture and, in a truly blind leap of faith, throwing her little body into the air. Rug burns and bruises hadn't discouraged her, but her father, after catching her coming off the top of the refrigerator in full trajectory, finally had. Sitting her down and putting Mercurochrome on the newest scrape, he had patiently explained the workings of flywires and body harnesses in his best Mr. Wizard manner, wrapping the lecture up with, "So you gotta cut it out, Joshie—at least till you can afford the right equipment."

She had nodded obediently but still believed, in her heart of hearts, that she just hadn't been concentrating hard enough. She had still wanted the magic.

And she still did—but she wasn't getting any so far.

Things had gotten off to a rocky start when Rafelson had caught his foot on the windowsill on his entrance, and landed like an albatross. The guy working the Tinkerbell spotlight seemed to be having an attack of palsy. Little Tink was shimmying all over the set like a demented firefly. Rich would turn to the stage right mantel, where she was supposed to be—then the spot would pop on stage left. Titters ran through the audience after the second of these goofs, and Peter was getting pissed off at his fairy girl. Then someone behind Josh muttered, "He probably can't see her without his glasses," and another chorus of choked laughter followed. Zito looked over his shoulder, then at O'Roarke, whispering, "Tough house."

"The toughest."

At first previews, the audience, for the most part, is an invited one; friends of the cast and crew, a few of whom are family or loved ones but most of whom are fellow professionals . . . and usually out of work. If the show is good or at least looking like it will *get* good (no one expects perfection at a first preview), they'll cheer it on with an ardor above and beyond its merits. A hit is good for business, everybody's business. But if a production is looking lame or downright wounded, it triggers a showbiz version of Darwin's survival-of-the-fittest theory; the weak must be destroyed so the strong can flourish. And the house gets ugly.

At the moment, the natives were merely restless. They had liked Greer's turn as Mr. Darling, even though he had gone up on a line or two. And Amy St. Cyr, looking fully recovered from whatever had been ailing her backstage, was truly charming without being sappy. But once Rafelson had tripped onto the set, things got tense. Josh fancied she could hear the gnashing of teeth coming from every young female actor in the house, and she couldn't blame them. Good roles are always scarce, and Peter Pan is one of the great "breeches" parts for women and has been since the days of Maude Adams. In O'Roarke's eyes, there was a very good reason for this that went beyond mere theatrical tradition; for an audience, there is something deeply satisfying in watching a girl be "all boy" onstage. Peter brags and swaggers like a peacock, and when a girl does it, it's a delight and a kind of secret joke between actor and audience.

When a fortyish man does it, however, it's rather desperate and depressing. The story ceases to be about the joys of eternal youth and becomes more a case study in arrested development. But what Jocelyn found truly bizarre was the degree of *girlishness,* in the stereotypical sense, that Rafelson brought to the character. He pouted at Tinkerbell when he should have upbraided her. He flirted with Wendy, which is a big no-no. He was coy when he should have been cocky. The "I Gotta Crow" number, an exuberant paean to pure chutzpah that Josh dearly loved, sounded like "I Gotta Simper" when Richie sang it. She told herself she was being overcritical and a plain bitch. Then Tommy nudged her and muttered, "If he was my daughter— I'd spank him."

Still there was a spectacular moment, thanks mainly to the set designer, Rex Strauss, when the Darling bedroom broke away and melted into the wings at the end of "I'm Flying," as Peter and the children streaked across a midnight sky for Never Never Land. In front of her, a tech director sighed in admiration, then said, "That little effect cost a fortune. That's Peakmont for ya—when in doubt, throw money at it."

Once in Never Never Land, the audience discovered that the Lost Boys had become, in Rafelson's directorial interpretation, the Lost Children of both genders. O'Roarke guessed he had done this as a sop to any irate feminists around, but it didn't work for her. Wendy and Princess Tiger Lily, representing

J. M. Barrie's yin and yang of girlhood, were only undercut by it.

But then Manville came on in full sail as Captain Hook, and the house sparked to his droll rendition of "The Poison Cake Tango," welcoming it as a salty antidote to Richie's saccharine. Their spirits rose, then fell again as Rafelson led the Lost Kids in building a home "For Wendy," a number that played like a rerun of *This Old House.*

The first-act curtain fell and the house plunged as one toward the bar, like lemmings toward the cliffs of welcome oblivion. Zito, however, headed toward the long line to the men's room and O'Roarke ducked outside for a much-needed smoke. Drifting toward the back of the theatre where she knew the crew would be, she ran into Arthur Freed, Rafelson's assistant. She had met him at her last fruitless audition, nearly two years ago, and was surprised to find him still on board. Rafelson's assistants usually had a very short shelf life. A tall, slim man with a shock of dirty blond hair, Freed reminded her of the Cheshire Cat; he had an enormous ear-to-ear grin that was so blinding you almost lost the face behind it. When she had first met him, his attitude toward Richie had been one of wry deference, which had led her to suspect that he found his emperor not exactly naked but in need of better threads. Tonight, however, he seemed as antsy as a mother hen.

"Jocelyn! I thought you were still away—but you're here."

"Right. I'm not and I am. . . . How're you, Artie?"

"Uh, oh, okay—so? What do you think? How's it going?" He danced around her in a tight circle, practically panting for some kind of reassurance.

"Crikey, Arthur, take it easy. It's only the first preview."

"I know, I know. But it's my first co-director gig, see?"

Having gotten to her seat too late to read the program, she hadn't known. No wonder Freed was all in a tizz—and all in denial. This show was his baby, so he didn't sense it was about to go out with the bath water. Jocelyn squirmed and wished her British pal, Charles Paris, were about; he was brilliant at coming up with oblique compliments at moments like this. She recalled going backstage with Paris after a truly dreadful performance of *Timon of Athens* and watching him embrace his friend, who had just butchered the title role. Paris had then exclaimed, "*Good* isn't the word!"

Whereas O'Roarke, no slouch at slinging bull herself, was incapable of lying when it came to the quality of the work. The best she could offer Freed was a shrug and "It, uh, needs some work."

"Oh? Oh, right! I see what you mean. Like the pacing's too slow in the opening. And Nana the dog is *all* wrong."

No, like you've got Aged Lord Fauntleroy playing Peter, she thought, but said, "Yeah, maybe. . . . Hey, where's Tony? I thought he'd be around."

"He is, he is. I mean, he's not *here*." Freed pointed his forefinger toward the ground, then upward—"He's there"—indicating the second story of the theatre, which housed the administrative offices. "He's in a meeting with the Ocelot."

"The who?"

"The Ocelot—oops! I mean Nan Semper," Arthur censored himself. "Head of the board of directors . . . nice lady. Just wears too much eyeliner."

"Oh, I think I saw her when I came in." Scooting through the lobby, past the bar, she had caught a glimpse of a woman ordering a gin and tonic, wearing expensive jewelry and Liz Taylor's Cleopatra look. "She about yea high? Hair streaked and tipped for days?"

"Yes, that's our Nan." Freed peered anxiously into the lobby. "She and Tony watched the opening, then went up to his office. I thought they'd be down by now."

"Well, if you see him, tell Anthony I said hi, okay?" She patted Arthur's arm and hightailed it toward the back of the building and relative safety. She was comfortable with techies because she didn't need to bullshit them. Unlike directors, producers, and all the other people who work out front, the crew is always the first to know if a show stinks. And since they know, they, mercifully, don't ask for your critique.

Coming around the corner of the building, Josh spotted Al Brenner leaning against the scene dock, drawing on a fat cigar.

"Got a light, meester," she asked à la Dietrich. Brenner obligingly flicked open an old Remington that flared up like a blow torch. O'Roarke lit up, then jumped back to avoid singeing her eyebrows. "Where's P.J.?"

"Checkin' the harnesses."

"Again? Well, he was always into leather," she quipped, eliciting a grunt and the ghost of a smile from Al. It could just have been the night air, but Brenner seemed to have cooled toward her considerably. Tipping his head back, he blew a series of smoke rings just over her head, then squinted down at her from his towering heights. For a moment, she felt like Alice meeting the Caterpillar and half-expected him to ask, "Ah-whooo ah-re youuu?"

Instead he said, "That guy you came with . . . he a cop?" Al spoke in a monotone but the last word came at her like a rock out of a slingshot.

"Yes, he is. How'd you know?"

"Just did . . . you can smell it." Raising the cigar to his mouth, he lapsed into a moody silence.

It was a fact of life that some people simply did not care for cops. It was a sort of inchoate bias that Jocelyn understood since she herself had once been subject to it. Usually it was based on bad press, sometimes deserved, more often not, and the average American's fear of Big Brother. But looking at Al, she sensed his was a more personal prejudice. He was clearly *offended* that she had brought Zito into their midst, and seemed to expect some act of contrition from her. The hell with *that,* she thought as the end-of-intermission lights began blinking. So they exchanged curt nods and went their separate ways.

When she got back to her seat, Tommy was leafing through his program with keen interest. He loved reading actors' bios and finding out which ones he'd seen before on TV or in movies. Without looking up, he asked, "Where'd you go?"

"Out back. I had a smoke with Al—you know, the master carp."

Still studying his program, Zito nodded, "Oh, yeah, the con."

"Con! What're you talking about?"

Closing his *Playbill* with a patient sigh, he turned to her. "The guy's an ex-con, Josh."

"No!"

"*Yes.* Jeez, I thought I taught you better. Didn't you see—after we shook hands—how fast he stuck 'em in his pockets? Know why?"

"No."

"Didn't want me to see the tattoos on his fingers. He didn't get those in no parlor. Those're prison-made."

The light dimmed and O'Roarke's jaw dropped just as the curtain went up.

5

"Oh, please, *please* clap for Tink. Clap if you believe in fairies!"

As O'Roarke had predicted, Richie's interpretation put a whole new spin on this famous speech. Peter's plea for the languishing Tinkerbell's life, and the applause that followed, was, in most productions, a high point; the audience's vociferous vote for make-believe. But Rafelson's ham-fisted fervor garnered not only applause, but a goodly amount of hoots and hollers as well. Poignancy went down the tubes and high camp reigned supreme.

"Christ, how could you *not*," someone in the fifth row cackled.

Clapping dutifully, Tommy leaned toward Josh and whispered, "Is this *suppose* to be funny?"

"No." Unable to watch, she shut her eyes and made a mental apology to the late, great Mary Martin, wherever she was. "Lord, Lord," she prayed, "he must know by now this was a *mistake*." But deep down she doubted it; she had seen unchecked egos like this before. Tonight, after the performance, he would be upset by the fiasco. By tomorrow, he would be blaming it on everyone and everything but himself—the Tink spot was off, the house was catty, the other players were slug-gish, whatever. Did Napoleon listen when they told him not to march on Russia? No. It took Waterloo to convince him he'd overplayed his hand. It would take something equally cataclys-mic to convince Richie.

So far the only one of Rafelson's numbers that had remotely rung true was "I Won't Grow Up"—since it was so patently the case. He suffered from what Jocelyn called Dick Clark Syn-drome, common to actors whose boyish looks allowed them to play twenty-year-olds through their thirties and thirty-year-olds, with the aid of diet, exercise, and a nip and tuck here and there, through their forties.

Still it was fascinating to Jocelyn, when she could bear to look, that so much of the production worked. Manville and young Amy sparkled, as did Lois Hart as a feisty Princess Tiger Lily. And the large ensemble numbers had verve and brio. The battle on board Hook's ship was a fun, frenzied slugfest, which Josh guessed owed much to Arthur Freed's invention. Basically, the parts where Peter wasn't talking or singing were fine. And the house, taking pity on the other players, softened somewhat in the second act.

The final scene, where Peter returns to the Darling home only to find Wendy grown up and "too old" to go back to Never Never Land with him—a scene that had purely broken Josh's heart as a child—pained her in a different way now. Richie's Peter curled a lip and dismissed her as past her prime without any of Barrie's sweet regret for lost innocence. When Wendy sent her daughter Jane off with Pan, Jocelyn wasn't the only woman in the house who wanted to stand up and shout, "Don't be a sucker twice!"

Then came the curtain call, something Rafelson loved stag-ing. He pulled out all the stops now. The lesser players came on en masse and took their bows. Then Tiger Lily came on, dancing up a storm, and got a big hand. Manville was brought on stage in a litter, carried by the pirates and preceded by Mr.

Smee, bowing and scraping and getting a lot of laughs. When Greer sprang from the litter with sword pointed at the house, he received a rousing welcome, which trebled when the ticking crocodile slithered on from stage left in search of Hook's other hand. Hamming it up royally, Manville cowered and sprang to the right just as the three Darling children flew onto the set; Michael and John first, followed by Wendy.

Saving the best for last—and for himself—Richie flew onto the set. He touched down front and center, without tripping this time, and made a deep bow. The audience, many of them feeling like Hook's crocodile and in search of blood, applauded in a measured, ticking rhythm.

But Rafelson wasn't done with his big finish. He dashed into the wings to get his harness hooked to a different fly line. Coming back on, he bowed again, then threw both arms up wide and was lifted from the stage, up and over the house. Despite themselves, the house gasped in awe. Rafelson flew back to the front of the stage for a full company bow. And how could you not applaud? He was milking this cow for all it was worth. Then the company exited into the wings as Richie flew out *again*. It was a solo flight, just for him and his shadow as it were. He soared above the orchestra seats, straight toward the balcony. He came so close, people in the first row of the mezzanine gasped as he nearly brushed the rails. Triumphant now, he pivoted around to fly back to the stage.

That's when Josh heard the sound—a dull groan followed by a sharp rip. She craned her neck and saw the travel spot still on him like the sun. For an instant, Rafelson hung suspended above the house, arms and legs flailing wildly. There was another tearing sound, then he fell, like Icarus, down and down. His right side hit the end of row L and he bounced off it into the aisle and lay splayed like a starfish.

There was a single horrified gasp from the house, drowned out by the oblivious orchestra, which kept playing and kept the crowd frozen, disbelieving what they had just seen. Tommy and

Jocelyn, however, were instantly out of their seats and dashing up the aisle. But Anthony Romero got there first.

Cradling Rafelson in his arms, with tears pouring down his face, he urged over and over, "Wake up, Richie, wake up. Come on, look at me! Just wake up." Behind him stood the Cleopatra clone, Nan Semper, wide-eyed, slack-jawed, and rooted to the spot. Jocelyn poked her into life and barked, "Call 911!," then knelt by Romero.

"Tony, Tony, don't move him, okay? We're getting an ambulance."

Romero looked at her as if she were the angel Gabriel and, ever gracious, whispered, "Oh, yes. An ambulance. Right, right. Thank you, dear, thank you."

Gently but efficiently Zito eased Richie out of Romero's embrace and went to work on him: checking his pulse, listening for a heartbeat. Then he whipped off his suit coat and started administering C.P.R. Tony, the lapels of his suit streaked with pancake makeup, looked up at Jocelyn anxiously.

"It's okay," she soothed. "He knows what he's doing."

But Rafelson wasn't responding. His skin was turning a chalky gray. The audience, roused from their shocked stupor, rose from their seats but obediently followed the ushers' instructions to clear the house and leave by the side aisles. A hushed buzz filled the air around them as Tommy did his damnedest, chanting softly, "Come on, come on, *breathe*, you mother."

Richie's curly auburn wig had slipped sideways on his head, revealing a faint bald spot under a crown of thinning blond hair. Jocelyn reached over to remove it but Romero stayed her hand. Tenderly he slid the wig back in place, explaining sweetly, "Someone might see . . . he doesn't like it to show."

"Sure, sure. Sorry," she apologized lamely. Her chest was tight with fear, not just for Rafelson, but for the man beside her, who looked as if his life, too, hung in the balance.

Finally Zito squatted back on his heels, breathing heavily as he angrily wiped the sweat from his face. Jocelyn knew what a fighter he was, how much he hated losing, and her heart ached for him as well. But Romero didn't realize the battle was over. Gazing down at the still face, then up at Tommy, he asked hopefully, "Is he coming round?"

6

"Just wait a damn second, will ya? I need a *drink,*" O'Roarke growled at her fat cat, who was past due for his late-night snack, as she sloshed some merlot into a wineglass.

For once in his greedy-guts life, Angus paid heed, stopped his meowing, and plopped down docilely by her feet. Dumb animal or no, he sensed when his mistress was at the end of her tether. By way of a peace offering, he rolled onto his back, exposing his furry black and white belly. She bent down and rubbed it, taking comfort from his purring warmth.

"Thanks, sport," she murmured, then reached into a cabinet, grabbed a bag of dry food, and shook some of it into his bowl. Instead of pouncing on it in his usual manner, he politely rubbed her shin before partaking. Lighting a cigarette, she watched him chow down as she sipped her wine and thought, not for the first time, that life was like an ant farm—those glass-sided ant farms your folks gave you as a kid where you could watch the colony build their intricate tunnels and roll their food from one tier to the next, laboring like Egyptians on the Great Pyramids. Inevitably disaster always struck; somebody would bump against it and a tunnel would collapse at the top, suffocating a whole work crew. But at the bottom, the rest of the colony, unaware and unaffected, went about business as usual.

In the cab coming uptown, she had watched people on the streets, nocturnal ants, strolling home from a movie or a friend's home or a bar, seemingly safe in the belief that their own particular tunnel would hold firm. Why not? We have to believe bad things only happen to *other* people or we couldn't step out the door in the morning. Richie Rafelson, she felt sure, had never doubted for an instant that his own little colony would soldier on and build the pyramid of his dreams.

Plopping down on the sofa, she saw the light on her answering machine blinking rapidly. Shaking her head, she lit another cigarette and sighed, "Not tonight, Irene." Whoever or whatever wanted her attention would have to wait till morning. Right now her head was too filled with the images of disaster: Nan Semper, her cat's-eye makeup running, frozen by the flashing light of the ambulance; Anthony, shaken and sobbing, insisting that he be allowed to accompany the body. Backstage had been a shambles: Amy St. Cyr in hysterics, Manville Greer gray as a ghost, and the crew—that had been the worst. While none of them had been wildly fond of Rafelson, they all possessed a fierce professional pride. It was their job to make sure things *worked*. And when they didn't, when it resulted in bodily harm or, in this instance, much worse, they felt it keenly and to a man. When the police had come to take away the broken harness, a stricken P.J., propped up by Jocelyn's supporting arm, could only repeat his mantra: "I checked 'em. I checked 'em. Swear to Christ, I checked 'em."

Too tired to move, too wound up to sleep, in the grip of that profound loneliness that follows in the wake of death, she sat staring into space. Angus burped, then jumped up onto her lap and rubbed his head against her chin.

Then the phone rang. She couldn't imagine who it could be at this hour and was about to let the machine pick up, but with the faint hope it might be Phillip, the one person she could bear speaking to just then, she reached for the receiver.

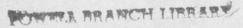

"Hello."

"Hey, good-lookin'. What ya got cookin'?" Jack Breedlove's greeting was so blithe and breezy she laughed until her voice broke roughly. Possessed of a sharp ear, he said, "Hey, what's wrong? I've been trying to reach you all night. Where've you been?"

"Uh, at a show . . . Didn't go too well," was all she could manage.

"A bomb, huh? Friend of yours in it?" he inquired carefully. "Sweetheart, I know you hate to see a pal wipe out but, now, don't fret. It can't be *that* bad."

"Oh, it is, Jack, it's *that* bad. And he wasn't even a friend."

"Well, tell me."

Somehow knowing Jack was five thousand miles away, in a safer part of the ant tunnel as it were, made it easier for Jocelyn to recount the night's events. Her throat tightened now and then, but Jack waited patiently and drew the whole story out of her with gentle proddings. When she finished, he sighed. "Oh, you poor kid."

"Don't! Don't be so sweet," she snapped irrationally, partly furious because his comforting was so dear but so distant. "I can't take it right now."

"That's 'cause you're alone . . . and you're scared. I would be, too."

"Yeah, maybe," she admitted. "But I'll live."

"Aw, crap! Stop trying to be such a toughie . . . I'm coming up there."

"Oh, don't be silly," she said, mis-hearing him. "I don't want you jumping on a plane and—"

"Hey, I've already jumped—I'm *here*, Josh."

"Here? Where?"

"At the Rihga Royal. I got in this afternoon—for the horse show at Madison Square Garden. Look, I'm getting in a cab now."

"Jack, no, you don't have to—"

Then the line went dead. Jocelyn jumped up from the sofa,

poured another glass of wine, and paced the room, fuming and trying to sort out her feelings. Breedlove's arrival was totally unexpected. Why hadn't he let her know? She didn't like being caught unawares. He knew that. And tonight of all nights, when she was on such shaky ground. It wasn't fair. She wasn't up to it. She would have to tell him, quietly but firmly, to go back to his hotel until she had time to regroup.

Before she knew it, her buzzer buzzed and Jack announced his arrival. Throwing open the front door, O'Roarke planted herself on the landing with arms on hips, just like Yul Brynner in *The King and I*. Then Breedlove bounded up the stairs, two at a time, tall and tan with that familiar laconic grin on his puss, and stopped on the last step in front of her.

"Don't be pissy now, Josh. I know you—you're hurtin'."

The withering rejoinder she had ready quivered and died on her lips. The present, full-blooded fact of him overwhelmed her. Witnessing death, especially one so sudden, leaves a lingering chill in the bones and a deep wish to deny mortality.

Jocelyn frowned, sighed, and shook her head. Then she flung both arms around Jack's neck and, letting all the pent-up tension go, sobbed like a baby. Knowing a thing or two about loss himself, Breedlove scooped Josh up in his arms and carried her inside.

"Maybe, baby, I'll have you." Jack's clear baritone voice rose above the hiss of the shower and bounced off the tile walls of O'Roarke's tiny bathroom as she rooted around the icebox trying to find something that resembled breakfast. Her usual morning fare consisted of a banana and a cup of yogurt, but Breedlove, whose eating habits rivaled those of the horses he raised, would require something more substantial. Behind a wilted head of lettuce, she discovered a half carton of eggs and pulled it out. Jack emerged from the bathroom, with a bath sheet wrapped around his waist, toweling his hair vigorously. One fat drop of water flew through the air and hit Angus in the left eye. He batted it away, then crouched low to make a leap at Jack's naked leg. Josh handed the eggs to Jack and turned swiftly to catch the cat midlunge. Angus looked up at her aggrieved.

"Hey, you've *had* your breakfast," she scolded, then added by way of consolation, "At least wait till he's got his jeans on, okay?"

"Nice kitty." Breedlove followed this wry observation with an insinuating glance at the fresh scratch marks on his right shoulder. "Like mother, like son, huh?"

"Very funny," O'Roarke mumbled as she deposited Angus on the sofa, then fidgeted with the belt of her kimono. She had woken up many mornings with Jack Breedlove, but she had never woken up with him in *her* apartment and had never really expected to. Unlike herself, he was a disgustingly cheerful riser, and his easy expansiveness suited his airy ranch house. But in her one-bedroom brownstone it was too much of a muchness for Josh; it made her feel as edgy and awkward as a freshly deflowered virgin. Which was ludicrous, she knew, but there was no help for it. Skirting around him, she started opening cupboards and prattling. "Well, I've got eggs but no bacon. I dunno . . . maybe we should go out or somethi—"

"No sweat," he said, coming up behind her to plant a kiss on the nape of her neck. "I can whip something up." She jumped away from him just as the phone rang. Ignoring her involuntary reaction, Jack gave her a gentle shove, saying, "You answer. Me cook. Ugh."

Telling herself to stop being such a ninny, Jocelyn took a long breath before picking up the phone—and nearly choked on it when she heard the voice on the other end.

"Josh, it's me, Tom. . . . Did I wake you?"

"No, no. I was already up," she answered loudly, trying to mask Jack's lusty rendition of "Come a Little Bit Closer." Had she been in full command of her faculties, which clearly she was not, she would have expected this call from Zito, but it caught her off guard and off kilter. The spot on her neck where

Jack had kissed her burned like a hot brand as she asked, "What's the news?"

"Huh? I can't hear you. You got the radio on?"

"Yeah, yeah. Hold on a sec." She made a mad grab for a throw pillow and lobbed it across the room, hitting Breedlove on the top of the head as he pulled a box of taco shells and a jar of salsa out of the pantry. Waving her hands for silence, she repeated her question.

"It's good and bad," Zito said somberly. "Let me give you the good part first. The investigation's being handled by a buddy of mine, Michael Flynn. We went through the academy together. He's solid, Josh. I mean, he's no Phil. Hell, who is, you know?" The undercurrent of pride and admiration in his voice made O'Roarke wince and rub the back of her neck hard. "But Mikey's a good cop."

"Gotcha . . . now what's the bad bit, Tommy?"

"It ain't no accident, hon."

"You mean the harness didn't just . . . break?" It was a stupid question but then she was feeling quite stupid and all she could think was, None of this should be happening. Jack shouldn't be here fixing eggs rancheros in my kitchen. Richie shouldn't be dead. And, sweet Jesus, Tommy shouldn't be telling me it was murder.

But he was.

"Nah. It was cut—the leather waist strap was sawed half through. That second swing out over the house was what tore it."

"I see, I see." The awful irony of it finally pierced her fog of unreality. "So if Richie hadn't milked his curtain call, he'd still be alive."

"Yeah. Ain't that a kick in the head?" Zito gave a mirthless chuckle, then added, "Jeez, I remember you goin' on about always leave 'em wanting more. Too bad you never told that poor schmuck, huh?"

"He wouldn't have listened anyways. It was never his style."

Jocelyn slumped down in the rocking chair as Jack came over with a plate of eggs and a worried look on his face. With a sorry smile she waved the plate away. Her appetite was gone, but her curiosity was whetted. And she knew in her gut that Tommy hadn't told her the worst yet. "So does your friend Flynn have any leads?"

"Uh, no, not really. But he's heard . . . some stuff." Zito was beating around the bush and that wasn't like him.

O'Roarke straightened up in her seat and demanded, "What stuff?"

"Look, it's not hard evidence or nothin'—but seems there was a big blowup during the rehearsal yesterday."

"Well, it wouldn't be a Rafelson production without one," she quipped. Now that her intuition was back in gear she knew the other shoe was about to fall. "So who did Richie go after this time?"

"Actually it's who went after him." Tommy sucked in air, then dropped the bomb. "It was your pal, P.J."

Zito held the receiver away from his ear, expecting a roar of outrage from O'Roarke. Instead she asked calmly, "What was the fight about?"

"Safety. Dig that. Seems Cullen thought Rich was rushing the crew. Said they needed to slow down to get all the cues right, even if it meant they wouldn't get through the whole show. Then Rafelson said—"

"Let me guess." It didn't take much imagination since Jocelyn had heard countless such stories. "He said something like—'Either we get to the end of this sucker or you go to the head of the unemployment line.' Right?"

Impressed, Tommy whistled, then said, "Pretty close. Man, Josh, it's like you've never been away!"

"No, it's just that this shit's been going on for years. Richie went through stage managers faster than I go through panty hose. . . . So what did P.J. say?"

"Uh, basically, he told him to go fuck himself six ways from Sunday. That it was in Rafelson's best interests for them to take it slow. Called him a 'flaming asshole' and said if anybody got hurt, he would personally report him to Actors' Equity."

"Uh-huh. Well, I'd do the same if I were in his position," Jocelyn said as she watched Jack share his eggs rancheros with Angus. It was an oddly comforting sight and it soothed her enough that she could ask, "So does Officer Flynn think P.J. cut the strap to prove his point? 'Cause that's plain crazy, Tom."

"Yeah, yeah, I hear ya. But you gotta look at it from Mike's end, Josh. Right now, that's all he's got. That and the fact that . . . P.J. *was* the last person to check the harnesses."

"How can Flynn be sure of that?"

"He can't. But that's what your friend's been telling him all morning."

"What?" Jocelyn jumped to her feet so fast Angus actually stopped eating for a second. "You mean they're already interrogating him?"

" 'Fraid so. And from what Mike told me, Cullen's not helping himself much, either. He hasn't even called a lawyer. Said he doesn't know any."

"Oh, that little *twit!* What's he using for brains?"

On the other end of the line, Zito nodded sympathetically as O'Roarke ranted on about P.J.'s mental shortcomings for several minutes. From the number of four-letter expletives she used, he could tell how fond she was of the little guy. He knew, too, that she was going to go to bat for Cullen. This was just her way of warming up for the game.

7

———

"Always expect the unexpected. Yup, that's gonna be my motto for this whole trip," Jack Breedlove muttered from the backseat of a beat-up Ford Escort that was being driven, at hair-raising speed, by a short, plump redheaded woman he had just met twenty minutes ago. "Maybe for my whole life."

"You say something, Jack?" O'Roarke twisted around in the passenger seat to face him.

"Me? No, just talking to myself." He flinched as the redhead zoomed off the entrance ramp onto the thruway with nary a glance in her rearview mirror. "You two get on with your business. Don't mind me."

Taking him at his word, Jocelyn turned back to her companion, leaving Jack to wonder why it was that every time he met up with O'Roarke all hell broke loose. Of course, the hell that had broken loose last night in her apartment had been pretty damn nice, he had to admit.

After his arrival and after Jocelyn had cried herself out, she had blown her nose, wiped her eyes, and then given him a concise description of Rafelson's performance, right up to his dramatic demise. By the end she had started to well up again, moaning, "I just wish I hadn't been so spiteful about it."

"About what? His performance?" Assuming a clinical tone, he had asked, "Well, did he *really* stink up the joint?"

"Oh, God, yes," she had answered without a thought as she lit a cigarette. "We're talkin' major stench— Shit! There I go again! I'm such a bitch."

"Nah, you're not, Josh." Putting an arm around her sagging shoulders, he had drawn her close. "I've seen you lie yourself blue in the face to spare someone's feelings. But you never lie when it comes to acting—because you can't."

"Yeah, I guess," she had murmured wearily, taking comfort from his words and the feel of his soft denim shirt against her cheek. Then, faintly, she had added, "I saw him die, Jack. It's an awful thing to watch. So final, so scary. And it leaves you so . . . cold inside."

"Well, let me warm you up," he had said, rubbing her arms with his hands. He had only meant to soothe her, maybe help her drop off to sleep. But somehow his comforting hands had generated more heat than either of them expected. Then that heat had turned to flame and, before he knew it, they had catapulted past the point of no return. While never a passive partner, Josh had stunned him with the naked urgency of her desire. Even as he had torn off his shirt and pressed his body against the length of hers, his mind vaguely realized her hunger had little to do with him per se; it stemmed from a primal need to deny death—and his body, pleasured beyond reason by her stroking hands and beckoning mouth, was all for it. At the moment of final release, he had heard a low, long growl and hadn't known if it had come from her, him, or the cat.

In the morning, he had woken to find Jocelyn already up and skittish as a high-bred filly. That was no surprise. He had expected a certain degree of postcoitus constraint and was prepared to jolly her out of it. But then Zito's call had come; an accident had become a homicide and a friend had become a suspect. And O'Roarke, in that mercurial manner he had never quite got used to, had ceased being a blushing bedmate and become an androgynous whirling dervish.

As soon as Zito had hung up, she had grabbed her plate and wolfed down cold eggs while punching in a number.

"Who're you calling?"

"A lawyer. P.J. doesn't have one—the stooge!"

"He needs one?"

"Damn straight he does." Shrugging off her kimono without a shred of self-consciousness, she had walked into the bedroom with the cordless phone and started dressing.

Forty-five minutes later they had been picked up by Judith Kravitz on Central Park West. Waiting for Kravitz to arrive, Josh had repeated for the tenth time, "Look, you don't have to do this, Jack. Go to the horse show. I'll call your hotel as soon as I get back."

"No. I told you, they're doing dressage today," he had assured her. "If it were the jumping competition, that'd be different." The truth was Breedlove liked dressage but he had fallen prey, once again, to the foolish fancy that he might somehow extricate O'Roarke from the mess she was about to get herself into.

That was before he met Judith Kravitz, criminal defense attorney and driver from hell.

To be fair, Josh had tried to warn him. On the way out the door, she had given him a quick profile. "I met her at an AIDS walkathon when she'd just left Legal Aid and gone into private practice. She's very P.C.—but she's smart, she's tough, and she works her ass off 'cause she has to."

" 'Cause she's a woman?"

"Yes—and a royal pain in the ass. But she's good."

Once inside the Escort, the interior of which resembled a very messy handbag, Jack had realized how good Kravitz must be for Jocelyn to call on her services, since the two women were as simpatico as Tonya and Nancy. After making introductions, Jocelyn had reached into her purse for a cigarette only to be forestalled by Judith's protest. "Please! I don't want secondary smoke in here, okay."

"Sure," O'Roarke had replied obediently, but couldn't keep from glancing back at the fumes from Kravitz's faulty muffler and observing, "Guess it's okay if it's *outside* the car."

Ignoring the gibe, Judith had taken an orange-glazed cruller from the Dunkin Donuts bag beside her and bit into it. After dabbing at the sugar flakes on the lapel of her lady lawyer's suit, she had paused to lick her fingers and demand, "So tell me, your boy do it or not?"

"Not."

"*Tsk.* Too bad. He'd be a first-time offender. Always easier to plea-bargain 'em than to go to trial."

Breedlove had fully expected Josh to rip the squat broad's head off. But, after years of listening to Phillip Gerrard wax poetic and profane on the subject, O'Roarke had learned a thing or two about criminal lawyers. To Jack's surprise, she had replied evenly, "You're here to see it doesn't get that *far*. The cops have nothing—not even circumstantial. It was P.J.'s job to check the fly harness for chrissake! And they've been questioning him all morning without benefit of counsel, Judith."

"But he had a fight with the deceased that day, right?"

"A professional disagreement, that's all. When was the last time you went through a day without an argument?" Jack had watched O'Roarke pause for effect, then heave a doubtful sigh. "Jeez, a Boy Scout with a dull pocket knife could cut through this crap."

In the backseat, Breedlove had mentally applauded Josh's ploy; she had waved the red cape and Kravitz, nostrils aquiver, had charged right in. "Hey, don't sweat it. If these country bumpkins haven't gone by the book every step of the way, I'll have your pal out of there faster'n you can say Ernesto Miranda." Then she had gotten down to business, making O'Roarke recount the previous night's events in chronological order and exact detail.

Now, as she pulled off the thruway onto a tree-lined street,

Judith started quizzing Jocelyn on Cullen's background, both professional and personal. But Breedlove was only half listening as they drove by a mini-mall decked out like a Tudor village. Boutique town, he thought as they turned onto a residential street with large houses and two-car garages surrounded by lush lawns that would do a country club proud. Boutique town with bucks. Christ, the landscapers must make a fortune.

Then Kravitz broke in on his thoughts by observing, "So Cullen's gay, huh?" With a satisfied nod, she added, "That's good."

"Why?" Though Jack had already decided to have as little direct contact with Kravitz as possible, he was too curious not to ask. To his horror, she caught his gaze in the rearview mirror and gave him a girlish wink.

"Possible ammunition. Most cops are major homophobes, you realize. Things get dicey, I can always holler gay-bashing." She cooed happily, "They just *hate* that."

He saw Jocelyn stiffen in her seat but say nothing, though he thought he heard the faint sound of teeth grinding. Then she sat up and pointed to a red-brick building coming up on the right. "Jude, slow down. I think that's the police station."

"Ju-*dith*, if you don't mind," Kravitz sniffed as she turned into the parking lot without signaling. Shutting off the engine, she pointed to two cement tubs filled with flowers flanking the side entrance. "Jesus, what're those? Goddam *geraniums?*" Tossing her car keys in her purse, she popped open the door, snickering, "Why it's Mr. Rogers' station house. Oh, boy—this could be fun!"

"*Fun?*" O'Roarke asked in a strangled voice, but Kravitz was already out of the car. Shoulders squared and head lowered, she trundled into the building like a small steamroller. Twisting around in her seat, Josh demanded, "Did she say *fun*, Jack?"

"Easy, sport, easy," he said, squeezing her hand. "She doesn't have to win our hearts and minds—she just has to be good at what she does, right?"

"Right, right." Jocelyn nodded, struggling to regain perspective, then growled, "And she damn well better be."

And she was.

Twenty minutes later P.J. Cullen emerged from Flynn's office, looking drained and disheveled, and stumbled across the waiting room toward Josh. With a wild-eyed look, he clutched her sleeve and, jerking his head toward the office, croaked hoarsely, "That woman is freakin' *amazing*. . . . Where did you find her?"

"Never mind that. Did she straighten things out with Flynn?"

Just then Judith's voice rose above Flynn's and rattled his glass door.

"I think they're getting straighter by the second, yeah." P.J. rubbed his eyes with a fist and let out a long whistle. "I mean, shee-it, those guys were all over me like flies on a cow pat. Then she walks in and—zip-a-dee-do-dah! I'm a free man."

O'Roarke felt her shoulders loosen and her jaw unlock. "So there are no charges?"

"Nope . . . and I think I'm getting a gold star for bein' so 'cooperative,' too." She wasn't so sure about that. It was all too likely that Kravitz had merely secured her client a momentary reprieve, but Jocelyn wasn't about to burst his bubble. Instead she filled a paper cup from the water fountain and handed it to P.J., who took a small sip, then tossed the rest in his face. Shaking off the droplets, he gave her his old shitkicker grin. "Thanks. I needed that."

"You need your head examined is what you need," she barked. Now that the crisis was, for the moment, over, she felt herself working up to a good scolding. But Jack, who saw the poor guy cower under O'Roarke's harsh gaze, intervened. Unfurling his six-foot frame from an orange vinyl sofa, he came up behind Josh and chided, "Where *are* your manners, missy? You haven't even introduced us." He stuck out his hand and gave Cullen an oh-these-womenfolk grin. "Hi, I'm Jack Breedlove."

"You are?" The color came back to P.J.'s face as he clasped Jack's hand and looked him over head to foot. "Yeah, you *are.* You're the cowboy coiffeur. Hot damn! Nice to meet ya—sorry 'bout the circumstances."

"Not your fault. Shit happens."

"Man, ain't that the truth." Butching it up for all he was worth, Cullen shrugged and stared down at the linoleum floor. Catching sight of Breedlove's footwear, he exclaimed, "Hey, cool boots! Where'd ya get 'em?"

"Houston. You can only get good boots in Texas, right?"

"Oh, for sure." The topic of men's fashion brought P.J. back to life and back to type. Placing a hand on Jack's arm, he added excitedly, "I know this *fabulous* store in San Antonio that has the best—"

A cackle of mad laughter burst out of O'Roarke and kept bursting. The bemused stares of Cowboy Mutt and Cowboy Jeff only accelerated her hysterics until tears rolled down her cheeks. Wiping her cheeks, she gulped for air and grasped Cullen's wrist. "P.J., honey, you're in a police station. You were nearly arrested. And you're—" the absurdity of the moment overcame her again and she chuckled breathlessly—"and you're talking *footwear?* You're certifiable, sweetheart, you know that?"

Before Cullen could beg to differ, the door of Flynn's office flew open and Judith Kravitz stepped into the hallway, breezily calling over her shoulder, "Of *course* my client will be available for further inquiries. Just remember, Mikey—play nice next time." Then she strode up to P.J. and poked his back. "Okay, cookie, you and I are gonna have a nice long chat now. Over lunch—you're buying."

Hooking her arm through his, she hauled him toward the side door. Looking over his shoulder, he beckoned Josh with urgent eyes. But when she and Jack started to follow them, Judith spun around with a forbidding face. "Sorry. Two's company, four's a violation of client confidentiality. Right, J.P.?"

"Uh, it's P.J.," he mumbled, then mouthed to Josh, "Come. She's scary."

Before O'Roarke could object, Kravitz said, "We'll swing by here after lunch and pick you two up—if you're done, that is."

"Done? Done with what?"

"The man." Pointing toward Flynn's office, Judith gave Jocelyn a smug smile that made her want to scrape the freckles off that little pug nose. "I did my bit. . . . He wants to talk to *you* now. Bye."

Watching Kravitz waltz P.J. out the door, Jack shook his head and said, "Well, I'll be a son of a—"

"Bitch," Josh hissed.

"Where did you find that broa— uh, lady?" Mike Flynn shook his head as he filled two Styrofoam cups with coffee. "She's hell on wheels."

"Yeah, well, she's very aggressive on her clients' behalf—and that's a *good* thing," Jocelyn hedged, unwilling to dis a sister; she approved of Kravitz in theory, hard as she was to take in fact. "But maybe she overcompensates sometimes. Comes on a little too—"

"She's a ballbuster," Flynn cut in.

"Ah, no, no. That's the wrong terminology." Taking the coffee cup, O'Roarke wagged an index finger in the air. "That implies a gender bias on her part. Kravitz didn't give you a hard time 'cause she's some sex-repressed man-hater, Sergeant . . . She's a *cop*-hater. If Mother Teresa wore a badge, she'd bust her chops, too."

"I stand corrected." Flynn grinned as he perched on the edge of his desk. A true Son of the Sod, he appreciated a sense of humor just as Josh appreciated someone who, unlike Judith, got the joke. Sipping their coffee, which was excellent by station house standards, they took a moment to size each other up. In appearance, they were opposite sides of the same Hibernian coin: Flynn was fairly tall with blue eyes and carrot-colored hair whereas Jocelyn was Black Irish all the way.

"Which corner does your family come from?" O'Roarke asked.

"The West. Little town called Maigh Cuilinn." He gave it the Gaelic pronunciation. "Just north of Galway. . . . Yours?"

"Southern tip. West of Skibbereen on Roaringwater Bay—Ballydehob's the name. Two streets and one pub-slash-restaurant. You blink, you miss it."

"Been there, have you?" The Sergeant's eyes brightened with interest.

"Years ago. My mother wanted to see where her mother came from—so I took her." The memory of it made her smile. "I drove the scenic route from Cork, which was gorgeous—though I got lost half a dozen times."

That cinched it for Flynn. Any girl who had taken her mom back to the old country was all right by him. Clucking his tongue in mock sorrow, he said, "Then you forgot to turn your coat inside out to—"

"To fool the fairies," Josh chimed in, then tapped him sharply on the knee. "Now you just think that's an old wives' tale, huh? But believe me, the little people are alive and well and *very* busy with those damn road signs!"

Flynn laughed so hard he slopped hot coffee on his lap and didn't mind the burn. After his set-to with Kravitz, O'Roarke was a welcome relief. But was she also going to be the ace in the hole Zito had promised? Before he could pose the question, Jocelyn arced her empty cup across the room directly into the wastebasket, then looked up and said flat out, "P.J. didn't do it, you know."

Surprised by the quick change, he shuffled some papers around on his desk and cleared his throat officiously. "Yes, well, uh—there's certainly not enough to hold him on."

"As I'm sure Judith pointed out in great detail," Josh agreed.

"Oh, yeah. That she did." He sighed heavily, then straightened his shoulders. "But that doesn't mean he's out of the woods."

"So what would it take for you to see a light in the forest?" Her matter-of-fact tone was belied by the hard glint in her eyes, and Flynn was reminded of Zito's warning: "Whatever ya do, don't try to finesse her. She hates that kind of crap."

Heeding his old friend's advice, Mike came back with, "Another suspect would do. I thought you might be able to help with that."

"Huh?" She blinked owlishly. "You think I know who did it?"

"No, no, of course not . . . but I think you could help me find out." O'Roarke just held his gaze and made no reply. Opening both hands in a cards-on-the-table gesture, Flynn came clean. "Look, this is a very dicey case for us. The Peakmont Playhouse is a local institution with lots of important ties in the community. Know what I mean?"

"Sure—you mean money. That theatre brings in a lot of bucks to the area," she translated briskly. "And I bet the mayor's already been on the blower sayin' stuff like 'Proceed with great discretion' and 'Don't make a bigger stink than you have to.' Or words to that effect."

Left with no bushes to beat about, Flynn just nodded. "You got it. But there's another factor—that place is a closed shop, least as far as we're concerned. Look, your pal Cullen's a perfect example! He was sweatin' his socks off in here but he never said a word to implicate anyone else. Not a word—not to save his own hide! How am I gonna penetrate *that* kind of stonewalling?"

"Unh-uh, oh, no. No way!" Josh writhed in her chair and stared fixedly at her toes. "I see where this is going. Screw Tommy. He set me up!"

"But they'll *talk* to you," Flynn pleaded. "At least they'll tell you more than they'll tell me."

"Not necessarily," she countered. "I know some of the staff but I've never worked there. There's no reason to suppose they'd open up to me anymore than you—"

"Oh, yes, there is," Flynn said firmly. "Tommy told me."

"Told you *what*," she demanded.

"You want an exact quote? He said, 'O'Roarke's like a priest. She slides this invisible little grate open and people pour out their sins to her.' "

"I'll strangle him! That's a *rotten* thing to say—and a gross exaggeration."

"He also said you'd say something like that."

"Ah, Mike, have mercy," she begged, leaning toward him. "Listen, whatever Zito said, divide by five. I can't be some ersatz Mata Hari for the homicide squad. I'm just an out-of-work actor who wants to see her friend cleared. That's all."

"I understand," Flynn said sympathetically. "But it still comes down to—find me a better suspect."

"Aw . . . crud."

"Judith stopped by with P.J.," Jack said when O'Roarke finally emerged from Flynn's inner sanctum. "But when she heard you were still in there, she took off. Said we could take the bus back."

Slipping her arm through his, Jocelyn made for the exit, muttering, "I repeat—aw, *crud*."

8

"Aw, fongoo! Where's that damn forensic report?" Zito yelled at no one in particular. Which was just as well, since nobody in the busy squad room paid him the slightest heed. He had been yelling a lot lately, ever since Gerrard's departure for Chicago, to be exact, and his cohorts had wisely chosen to ignore his outbursts. Sifting through the stacks of paper on his desk like a mad scientist searching for a lost formula, he cursed again, and again got no response. They knew what the trouble was; it was the bane of every cop's existence and they had all been there themselves—Tom was in the grip of paperwork hell. He was backed up on his reports and feeling like a sophomore with two term papers due. Plus his wife was making gnocchi and he couldn't go home until he finished two crime-scene reports, both on straightforward drug-related shootings where the perps had been caught red-handed, but the reports had to be filed before justice could take its course. And where were the damn forensic findings?

"Phil never has this problem. How does he *do* it?" Zito wondered aloud. But he knew the answer: Gerrard, college-educated and concise in thought and speech, could whip out a good report with one eye closed. He had it all in his head before he even sat down at the computer. Whereas Tommy, who thought and spoke always in the vernacular, had to stop himself from writing things like "Then the scumbag punched the poor broad's lights out," and search for a more literary, albeit less apt, description.

The wayward forensic report finally made an appearance (though he could have sworn he'd already *looked* in that top drawer) and Zito settled down to write. But he couldn't focus; his stomach wanted to get home to his wife's gnocchi and his mind was on O'Roarke and had been, at least in part, most of the day.

Jeez, what a welcome home for the poor kid, he thought. Hardly gets her bags unpacked and—boom! A guy gets killed and her gay pal gets pegged for it. Shit. It was greatly to Tom's credit that even in his thoughts he referred to P.J. as "gay," not "faggot," "fairy," "fruitcake," or "queer" as, in the past, he would nave. Before he knew Josh. And it was a testament to their friendship that he no longer used those derogatory descriptions. Though set in his ways, in this one respect he had seen the light—thanks to her.

Several years back, in the heyday of her romance with Phil, they had all gone out to a movie, Josh and Gerrard, Tom and his wife. It was Jocelyn's pick and she had dragged them down to a revival house in the Village to see *Casablanca*, insisting, "I know you've all seen it but when did you last see it on a *big* screen, huh?" And she had been right. To Zito, it had felt like falling in love all over again. Coming out of the theatre, supporting his wife, who had been weeping happily for the last fifteen minutes, he had turned to O'Roarke and said, "Boy, Bogart, man. The great ones only get better, huh?"

"Yup, they're *all* great—Bogie, Ingrid, Lorrie, Doolie. Claude Rains is always to die for. But the one who really, really gets me is Conrad Veidt."

Phil and Zito had both halted in their tracks and exclaimed

as one, "Colonel *Strasser?*" Even Tom's wife had interrupted her lachrymose fest to snort, "That Nazi *pig?*"

"Ah, ah, I'm not talking about the character, I'm talking about the *actor*," Josh had replied rapturously, facing the other three as she walked backward down the street, dancing on the balls of her feet. (Zito remembered thinking that O'Roarke talked about acting—*good* acting—the way he talked about his kids.) "And the thing is Veidt *didn't* play Strasser like a pig. He made him a villain, yes. But a refined villain. Articulate and intelligent. He gave him dimensions. He didn't have to but he did . . . which is amazing, considering his background."

"Okay, I'll bite," Gerrard had said, laughing in that easy, expansive way he'd had back when they were an item. "What's his résumé, Jocelyn?"

"Not his résumé—his history." Suddenly serious, she had planted both feet on the pavement and pulled them up short. "Conrad Veidt was a big star in Germany before the war. Then he got out—in fact, *Casablanca* was one of his first U.S. films. He got out because he was, *A*, a Jew. *B*, homosexual." She had paused to swerve her eyes toward Tommy, adding, "They killed them, too, you know. So he was dead meat on two counts. If anybody had reason to make Strasser a caricature of pure evil, it was Veidt. But he *didn't*. He made him real. Because it was the right choice . . . it's also one of the classiest things I've seen an actor do—ever."

Then she had flushed up in that funny way she had whenever her emotions got the best of her. Zito remembered the way his throat had tightened and the way Phil had looked, for just a moment, so naked and so in awe of her passion. Man, it was just a movie but the way she *cared*. Then his wife had burst out in a fresh onslaught of tears, startling herself and the others so much that all four started laughing. Then they had gone to a great, cheap Mexican restaurant and had a lot of margaritas and fajitas.

And that was when Zito had consciously decided to chuck

the homophobe crap. He didn't make a big deal about it, didn't come down on his fellow officers when they made crude remarks. There would always be that element in the police force, and he wasn't out to reform anybody—except himself. The fact was Tommy Zito was a true Italian Catholic. And the old saying about "the closer to Rome, the looser the Catholic" fit him fine. The Vatican might condemn homosexuals, but he wasn't about to let that interfere with his newfound conviction. And, in his book, Conrad Veidt was a four-star prince.

But it's a bitch Phil ain't here, Zito thought as he plowed through his report. He had faith in Mike Flynn and knew he would get on with O'Roarke since they were both micks and micks hang together. But Flynn, stout Hibernian fellow that he was, still wasn't Gerrard. And the hell of it was Tommy hadn't been able to reach Phil all day to tell him what was up. So he felt that, somehow, he was letting both Josh and Gerrard down. Kind soul that he was, he labored under the misapprehension that he could make other people's lives smoother.

Pausing to store his document, he grabbed the phone and dialed O'Roarke's number. The least he could do was to see if the lawyer had managed to bail Cullen out. The last thing he expected was to hear a man's voice.

"Who's this? Where's Josh?" The easy laugh on the other end only added to his indignation.

"Uh, answering in opposite order, Jocelyn's down at the unemployment office. And I'm Jack—a friend from out of town."

O'Roarke, like most theatre folk, had many actor friends on both coasts as well as in between at various regional theatres. But Zito knew instinctively that this wasn't one of them. *This* was the dread hairdresser she had shacked up with in L.A., the guy with the horses. Zito had never discussed the Breedlove affair with Phil; "least said soonest mended" was his motto. And after all, Gerrard had been engaged to what's-her-face at the time, so O'Roarke had been, in Tommy's humble opinion, entitled to find what comfort she could. But that was then and this was now. And hadn't Phil traipsed up to Corinth to eat crow and help her out with that Tessa Grant business? Didn't the poor guy deserve a break?

Holding the receiver away from his mouth, he muttered some harsh words in Italian that could be roughly translated as: "Frailty, thy name is woman." Then he barked into the phone, "Your name Breedlove?"

There was a momentary pause, then another chuckle. "That's me. Like to leave a message . . . Sergeant Zito?"

"How'd you kn—?" Tommy bit his tongue; he wasn't going to give this putz the satisfaction. Instead he growled something about calling back later and slammed the receiver down hard, hoping to hurt the asshole's eardrum. Shaking his head sorrowfully, Zito went back to his computer and again shouted out to all and sundry, "What's this goddam world comin' to? I mean, you think you know somebody then—*shit!*" A young rookie passing by nearly jumped out of his skin as Tom suddenly glared up at him and added, "She wouldn't treat Conrad-fucking-Veidt like this!"

"Lord, they wouldn't treat a dog like this," the heavyset black woman seated next to O'Roarke sighed dispiritedly. She had been in the unemployment office filling out forms when Josh had arrived, and still hadn't been called to the front counter.

Jocelyn commiserated. "They like dogs better—dogs aren't entitled to benefits."

"Mmm, that's right. And dogs don't mind eatin' outa garbage cans but I *do*." She raised her voice and cast an evil eye toward the civil servants behind the counter, who, having long ago raised indifference to an art form, didn't bother to look up.

It had been a while since O'Roarke had had to apply for unemployment—or, as she liked to call it, "an arts grant from the New York State Department of Labor." If anything, she thought the system was working more smoothly now than it had then, thanks to the sharp rise in unemployment. Practice does finally make perfect, or less imperfect at least. But she wasn't fool enough to point this out to her beleaguered neighbor. She merely put out a hand and introduced herself.

"Jocelyn, huh? Well, I'm Josie—short for Josephine." The black woman gave her a sudden luminous smile. "Mother named me after Josephine Baker."

"You mean the Divine Josephine. Heck, I coulda guessed that. You've got that same kind of smile."

"Yeah? Well, I wish I had that same kinda *body!*" Josie gave one of those deep long laughs that sound like a train approaching as she slapped her knee. "Then I wouldn't hafta be cleaning houses, would I?" She went on to add that the family whose home she had cleaned for the past ten years had just departed the East Side for the wilds of Connecticut, leaving her behind with good references and a bad mink stole. "You know, the kind with them little skanky heads on the ends? Makes me lose my appetite just lookin' at 'em!"

"That's a damn shame," Josh said, and meant it. While she didn't think the awful mink heads would really interfere with Josephine's proper nourishment, she feared joblessness might. Then, rooting through her purse for a stick of gum, she came across a business card, Judith Kravitz's business card, and was struck by serendipitous inspiration. Not allowing herself a second to reconsider, she pressed the card into Josephine's hand.

"Call this woman tomorrow. Use my name," Josh urged. "She needs someone like you."

"She does?" Josie asked doubtfully. "Why?"

"Well, you know, she's one of these fast-track career women. Can't clean, can't cook." O'Roarke went on tap dancing as fast as she could. "Her place is a wreck. She just needs someone to put things right."

"Really? She a single woman?"

"Yeah—so you wouldn't have anyone around to bug you during the day."

"Hey, I could like *dat.*"

Nothing in life is purely black or white and the same applied to Jocelyn's motives. True, she had never set foot in Judith

Kravitz's home but she had seen her car; so she reasoned the apartment had to be nearly as bad if not worse. Judith *was* a slob. So, whether she knew it or not, she needed a housekeeper. Hell, I'd hire Josie if I had the money, O'Roarke thought, in full rationalist's throttle now—and Kravitz does and she's so damned politically correct, she'll *have* to hire her. A distant voice, like an ersatz Jiminy Cricket, whispered, "You're only doing this 'cause she dumped you in Peakmont and you had to take a bus back." To which Jocelyn rebutted, "Who *cares*— if it gets the lady work?" Just then a whey-faced man finally called Josie's name. Hauling her girth out of the plastic chair, she flashed that incandescent smile again, saying, "Thanks. You stay well, hear?"

Josh grinned back and nodded. So shines a good deed in a naughty world or, more precisely, a naughty deed in a good cause. Either way, it cheered O'Roarke up no end. And it had succeeded in taking her mind off grislier matters for a moment.

But that moment was about to end.

"Jocelyn? My God, is that *you?*" A finger prodded her shoulder from behind. Without bothering to turn around, she answered, "Guilty."

"Well, too much, too majorly much." Claireanne Howe shrilled as she *jetéed* around the chair to face her. Claireanne had briefly taken one of Josh's acting classes several years back when she had first come to Manhattan. O'Roarke recalled her first time up in class; she had done one of Maggie the Cat's monologues from *Cat on a Hot Tin Roof,* only it had come out like Maggie the Kitten. Jocelyn had worked diligently with her on it, but the kitten never grew claws. Claireanne's background was in musical comedy and, while many performers with the same background went on to become fine straight actors, Howe was not destined to be among them. Even now every energetic little fiber in her lithe body seemed to shout out: "All dancin', all singin'—*no* actin'!" Still, she was a sweet kid.

After leaning over to give O'Roarke an air kiss, she straightened up and assumed an uncharacteristically grave demeanor.

"Man, am I a jerk or what? You must be so—I dunno—impacted! I heard you were *there* last night . . . at the Peakmont."

"Oh, uh, yes, I was." Jocelyn blinked in surprise; she well knew what a small world theatre was, but still hadn't imagined her presence would have been noted and passed on. "Who told you?"

Claireanne widened her eyes as if to say: "Who told the colonists the British were coming? Paul Revere—*duh!*" Then she hissed, "Amy, of course."

"Amy? Oh—Wendy?"

"Yes! Amy St. Cyr—my best bud. Oh, Jocelyn, she is totally, absolutely *destroyed*."

"I can imagine. It was pretty shocking for everybody."

"But she's not everybody!" Claireanne stretched her dancer's neck to the limit and gasped, "Don't you know? They were *involved!*"

"Um, 'they' meaning . . . who?" O'Roarke asked. It had been a long day, and Howe's breathless reportage was making her feel older by the minute.

"Who? Amy and Richie! Didn't you know they'd been dating?—since the first week of rehearsals."

"You must be kiddi— . . . you don't say," Josh amended. "Claireanne, how old is Amy anyway?"

"Older than she looks. She's almost twenty-two." Howe flung herself into the chair next to Jocelyn's. "Look, I know what you're thinking. It's a big age gap. And Amy *was* concerned about it at first, okay? But after a while—they were just *so* on the same wavelength—it didn't bother her at all. If anything, she said sometimes she felt like Rich was the kid."

"Well, she wasn't alone there," O'Roarke answered vaguely as she studied Claireanne's guileless face, wondering what the younger generation was coming to, and where was their AC/DC detector for chrissake?—that sixth sense she and her girlfriends had developed early on in their careers that told you, at a glance on the first day of rehearsal, who swung in which direction. The AC/DC detector saves a lot of wear and tear on a girl's heartstrings, since there are few things more ego-eroding than being a Jill who discovers her Jack really prefers Bill. Granted, it could fail you sometimes, in which case you called friends and got the skinny.

Poor Amy, she concluded, must be wholly detectorless and, with friends like Claireanne, destined to be left in the dark. But, Jesus, Richie Rafelson was *not* a tough call! How were these two babes going to survive in the gay woods? And what the hell had Rafelson been up to anyway?

Taking her silence as censure, Claireanne grasped Josh's hand. "Listen, it was a lovely thing while it lasted. It really helped Amy grow as a woman and an actress."

"I bet." By which O'Roarke meant she bet their little romance had been Richie's way of getting the performance he'd wanted out of St. Cyr. A crummy thing to do but not out of character; Rafelson had never been an actor's director, as Jocelyn knew from the few times she had auditioned for him. Constantly surrounded by sycophants, he had lacked that essential faith in human nature that allows a director to trust his actors. Instead he would try to manipulate a performance out of them by intimidation or browbeating or, in Amy's case, gross pretense. A seasoned professional would sense it and circumvent it. But someone like St. Cyr, gifted yet naïve, would have been too flattered and too infatuated to see the puppeteer's hand at work. It made O'Roarke seethe inwardly, and she was briefly tempted to tell Claireanne what kind of toad Amy's prince really was. But, since that dangerous liaison was now permanently severed, why cause Amy needless pain?

Then the whey-faced man called her name, giving Josh an easy out. She rose, gripping Claireanne's shoulder. "Tell Amy I'm sorry, will you? And tell her I think she's a lovely Wendy . . . and she'll be a lovely Wendy no matter who's playing Peter."

"Oh! But it won't be the *same* kind of—"

O'Roarke cut her short. "No. But it'll be better, believe me."

9

"Come on, come on. You gotta go!" P.J. wailed into the receiver. "I need the moral support. Plus, I *hate* funeral parlors."

"Oh, whereas I, of course, spend all my free time there just for the fun of it." O'Roarke wiped sleep from her eyes as she dripped sarcasm into the phone. "Is it an open casket?"

"Uh . . . yeah," Cullen admitted. "Rich stipulated that. I only hope he didn't ask for a pin spot."

"Then *forget* it," she snarled. A Catholic childhood had left her with a strong distaste for embalmed bodies wearing bad makeup. "You're on your own, fella."

"What is it? Is the divine Jack there?" Cullen's cloud of anxiety lifted long enough to let a ray of prurient interest shine through. "Is that it?"

"No, he is not. He's at the horse show. Where he would've been yesterday if he hadn't trekked out to Peakmont on your behalf. So show some gratitude, you schnook."

"Oh, I do, I *am!*" P.J. sighed fervently. "I'd give my left ball to be Mrs. Breedlove and so should you, girlie."

"Damn—and I don't even have one," Josh shot back. "However, I will make do without. Just as you will without me."

"But you should be there!" Cullen was adamant. "You might notice something—pick up vibes, clues, subtle shit, you know?"

"Whoa, whoa, that's Flynn's job, not mine," she protested. "As long as you're off the hook, sweetums, there's no need for me to stick my—"

"But I'm *not!* That's what Judith says." He quoted the gospel according to Kravitz: " 'Until a more viable suspect surfaces, you're still in legal jeopardy.' I can't afford that, Josh. It could ruin my career. . . . I *need* you."

Oh, those three little words she feared most and had the least resistance to. She nudged Angus off her stomach and pulled back the bed sheets, grumbling, "Aw right, aw right, I'll be there! But I'm tellin' you right now, I will *not* view the coffin."

Rafelson was laid out at McDermott's, an old undertaking establishment in the West Forties where many actors had made their final appearance over the years. Jocelyn had been there several times before, and was fairly certain that McDermott's was the only funeral parlor in Manhattan to showcase framed headshots of their more illustrious clientele in the large, high-ceilinged foyer. Whether Rich would make it into this pantheon of past greats remained to be seen but, at any rate, he would have been pleased by the turnout, O'Roarke thought, as she propelled P.J. ahead of her into the packed front parlor.

Although the room was already overheated by the crush of people, she didn't mind; at least it provided a comfy buffer zone between her and the dread casket. It was just like Rafelson to have arranged for an open coffin. She supposed cremation hadn't appealed to his love of exhibition or, perhaps, he had feared a crematorium's furnace might give Somebody Up There ideas about his future in the hereafter.

Standing on tiptoe to peer above the crowd, Cullen sucked in his breath and grabbed Josh's sleeve. "My *Lord*—can you see up there?"

"No, and I don't want to."

"Well, I was jokin' before but, swear to God, there is a spot above the damn thing and I think it's *gelled!*"

"Then it's probably a bastard amber." O'Roarke, still refusing to look, referred to the shade of lighting gel commonly used to make actors appear younger on stage. "Why switch now?"

Among those paying their respects, there was, naturally, a large contingent from Peakmont, but Josh noted that Big Al Brenner was not present. Contrary to P.J.'s paranoid expectations, no one was treating him like a leper; either his cohorts hadn't heard about his prolonged tête-à-tête with Mike Flynn or they were happy to give him the benefit of the doubt. Relief brought out the normal social animal in him. He waved to a short, roly-poly man huddled in a corner with a surprisingly dry-eyed Amy St. Cyr. The little man whispered something in her ear, to which Amy gave a curt nod, then he made his way over to Cullen.

"Josh, this is Rex Strauss, our set designer. Rex, Jocelyn O'Roarke."

One of the few things she had liked about *Peter Pan* was the sets, and she said as much as they shook hands. Strauss passed a hand over his thinning dark hair and smiled weakly. "Thanks. I had something simpler in mind originally but Richie put the—" He stopped as a complex mix of embarrassment, sorrow, and something very near spite suffused his features, then went on coolly, "Well, he had grander notions as always."

O'Roarke's gaze drifted back to St. Cyr as she asked, "How's your Wendy holding up?"

"Oh, fine, she's fine," Rex answered vaguely as he and P.J. exchanged quick, nervous glances. "Amy's a rock."

"Yeah, a rock," Cullen seconded, trying to match Strauss's offhand tone.

"Really?" Jocelyn feigned the same degree of nonchalance, but she was ready to reach out and strangle P.J. by his blue and white bandanna. Here he had dragged her out of bed to play P.I. on his behalf, and now the little twerp was holding out on her! Knowing it was neither the time nor the place and not giving a damn, she whispered with pseudonaïveté, "Gee, isn't that something? I mean, considering her youth . . . and the fact that she was *dating* the deceased? I'd say she's more than a rock—she's goddam Gibraltar!"

P.J. gulped and stuck a finger under his bandana to get more air as Rex, sans sangfroid now, blurted out, "Jesus! How did you kno—?"

"Don't. Don't even bother asking," Cullen cautioned. "She does this kinda thing all the time. Picks up news like lint. . . . I'm sorry, Josh, really, truly. I was *going* to tell you but—"

"Well, there's no time like the present."

Turning on her heel, she pushed her way out to the corridor, knowing P.J. would follow. Strauss trotted after Cullen, who gave Josh an aw-shucks grin, which cut no ice, then hung his head. "See, I felt bad about it."

"I did, too, real bad," Rex chimed in, playing Tweedledum to P.J.'s Tweedledee. "It was crummy of Rich to lead the kid on like that."

"Totally shitty," Cullen agreed, inclining his head toward the set designer. "And we wanted to wise her up—we talked about it. But we were afraid of how he'd react. I know it was a chicken thing—"

"You're being too kind," Strauss protested. "We should've outed him. We were gutless wussies, P.J."

"Who wanted to keep their *jobs,* okay?" P.J. glared at Rex, then turned back to Josh. "So we shoulda but we didn't. And I guess we were both feeling guilty about it."

"Well, I won't tell ACT UP if you tell me who *did* give Amy the bad news." Both men gaped at her as if she were the oracle at Delphi. To deflate that impression, she told them of her brief encounter with Peter and Wendy backstage, adding, "And you don't need X-ray vision to see young Amy ain't exactly distraught today, do you? So I figure, not to be too crude, the shit must've hit the fan before Rich hit the floor, right?"

"Actually, that *is* pretty crude," Rex reproached. Then P.J. gave him a shot in the ribs and he winced, "But not inaccurate!"

"Thing is," Cullen said, in the spirit of full disclosure now, "the day before the first preview, Amy caught him playing feely-touchy with one of the chorus boys backstage. At the end of rehearsal, she locked herself in her dressing room and wouldn't come out for notes. You could hear her crying all the way out in the house."

"That's why we feel so bad," Tweedledum reiterated. "I think what you saw that night was Richie trying to put a Band-Aid on a hemorrhage—just to get Amy through the show. Poor baby."

"Uh-huh, that makes sense. I appreciate your candor, Rex," she said evenly. "But, if you don't mind, I'd like a word with P.J.—alone."

Strauss took his cue and sidled back into the parlor. As soon as he was out of earshot, she whipped round to Cullen. "Did you tell Kravitz any of this?"

"Uh, no, not yet."

"What're you waiting for? A written invitation or an *indictment?*"

"Aw, come on, Josh. I can't believe little Amy would ever do anything—I mean, it'd be like Shirley Temple putting ground glass in Bojangles' tap shoes!"

"Jeesh, wake *up!*" She didn't grab his bandanna but she did yank the front of his denim shirt. "Don't make me do the whole Hell-hath-no-fury spiel. What do you think Judith *means* when she talks about finding 'a more viable suspect'? Amy has motive and opportunity."

Looking agonized, P.J. paled under his perennial tan and rasped, "But Amy? I can't believe it—and I don't want to point the finger."

Jocelyn appreciated his distress because she knew that, for Cullen, cast and crew were family. But this was a luxury of sentiment he could no longer afford. Drawing close, she locked eyes with him and said calmly but with utter seriousness, "I know you don't. Nobody does. But, fact is, if you didn't cut that harness, someone else did. And, honey, it wasn't the friggin' one-armed man! It was someone you *know*. That's awful and that's hard but you've gotta face it . . . or it's your ass." She paused to let the message sink in, then added, "Do you know how murders get solved? It's not like Sherlock Holmes or Columbo where the detective whips in, views the scene, reconstructs the crime, and solves it with a flash of deductive brilliance. It's people talking about other people, mainly—until the right name comes up. So if Amy or anyone else in the show had anything like a motive, you've got to *say* so."

Staring hard at her left shoulder, Cullen licked his dry lips and cleared his throat. Forcing himself to meet her gaze, he seemed on the brink of some fresh admission when Nan Semper came in the front door flanked by Arthur Freed and Anthony Romero. The Ocelot, her makeup perfectly in place now, looked much better than she had two nights ago. Of course, she had help; Jocelyn did a quick head-to-toe price check and estimated that Nan's tasteful mourning attire cost roughly the same as O'Roarke's monthly rent. Anthony, on the other hand, looked like hell despite the impeccable cut of his Lagerfeld suit. Well past fifty though you'd never know it, Romero was the Dorian Gray of theatre producers. However, today he looked like Dorian *after* the portrait got slashed. Slack-jawed and red-eyed, he seemed to be leaning on Semper for support. Artie Freed, however, seemed full of beans and ready to run the five-hundred-yard dash. Spotting O'Roarke, he broke away from Nan and Tony.

"Jocelyn—just the person I wanted to see! Can I pick your brain a sec?" Without waiting for a yea or a nay, he took her arm and drew her outside. In their past dealings, Josh didn't recall Freed being so pushy, but this seemed to be a brand-new Artie. As soon as they hit the sidewalk, he lit a Camel and said, "You've worked with Lily Trent, haven't you?"

"Sure. When she was just a baby. We did *Ah, Wilderness!* together."

"Oh, yeah. Eugene O'Neill's one stab at light comedy," he said dismissively. "Who'd Trent play—Muriel?"

"Uh-huh. And she was lovely in the part."

"Sure, sure. But was she good to work with?"

"A dream."

Freed's face lit up, since O'Roarke wasn't one to give accolades lightly; he asked eagerly, "And was she quick on the uptake?"

"For her age, yeah. By now she's probably greased lightning. . . . Why?"

Flicking his cigarette into the gutter, Freed leaned down and whispered, "See, she played Peter last year at the Arena . . . and she's available."

Well versed in the sometimes harsh necessities of show business, O'Roarke was still taken aback by Freed's forwardness. She cast her eyes at the front door of the funeral parlor, then up at Arthur. "You haven't even paid your last respects to the man and you're already looking for his *replacement?*"

"I *have* to, Josh! It's my job. Look, the run's practically sold out. Sure, we'll have to postpone for a week, but, you know, the show must g—"

"Oh, please! Spare me," she begged.

But Artie was too caught up with his casting inspiration and raved on. "But if Lily already knows the part, I can work her in in no time. And she's petite. She'll be so easy to fly. I always thought Trent would be the perfect choice—" Finally Freed pulled himself up short and assumed a contrite countenance. "I must sound like the heel from hell!"

"No, Art, you sound like a nitwit. Stop and think—Lily's agent is Harry Brill." She enunciated the last name with great precision to make sure it sunk in. It did.

"Ohhh . . . as in the Brill That Kills?"

"Yes—if you mess with his clients. So what d'you think the

odds are Harry's gonna let one of his up-and-coming stars fly high in the same production that made a human pancake out of Richie?"

"But—but it wasn't an accident or incompetence or anything," Freed wailed wildly. "It was deliberate."

"And you think that's a *selling* point?" She reached up and tugged on his tie. "Please pick up the white courtesy *clue* phone!"

Seeming, at last, to sense the dimensions of his dilemma, Arthur frowned, kicked a fire hydrant, then sighed. "Damn. And Lily's so right!"

Dimly, Freed heard a muffled rumbling sound coming from O'Roarke's direction, but when he glanced up she was gone.

"Let's see, I'll have corned beef hash with a poached egg on top and home fries on the side. And a large Coke Cola," Cullen said to the peroxide blonde waitress in the Lord Camelot coffee house. She scribbled his order and turned to Jocelyn, who was looking a little bilious.

"What would you like?"

"Coffee and an English muffin."

"That's it?"

O'Roarke looked over at P.J. and asked, "You gonna pour ketchup all over that stuff?"

"Natch."

"Yeah, that'll be all for me," she told the waitress, adding, "Trust me, it's the safe choice."

After spending a decent amount of time at McDermott's, she had hauled P.J. off for further pumping. At first he had resisted, then pled hunger pangs. Knowing that Cullen needed to consume at least his own body weight each day, and that food worked on him the way shopping worked on Cher, she had acquiesced.

Carefully averting her eyes, she waited as he dug into the dog-food doppelgänger on his plate. Then she heard the hum;

P.J. always hummed, mostly show tunes, as he achieved culinary nirvana. When he had finished the first ten bars of "Have an Eggroll, Mr. Goldstone," she broke in on his bliss.

"So who besides Amy?"

"Hmm? Who what?" He tried to distract her by dumping more ketchup on the hash. She snatched the bottle away from him.

"Stop potchkying, Tex. You know what I mean. Who else was Rafelson screwing with—literally or figuratively?"

"Aw, man!" Cullen crumpled his paper napkin and tossed it on the table. "I *hate* this kind of gossip."

This was like Liz Taylor saying she hated weddings, but Josh didn't point out the irony; she merely said, "Close your eyes and picture a state penitentiary. Now picture yourself *in* one."

"Oh, *shit*—uncle!" He shoved his plate away and rubbed his face with both hands. "Okay, okay—you got a pencil? 'Cause you'll need to make a list. First off, I gotta tell you I goddam love Manny Greer. He's a pro, he's a gent, and he's a pisser as Hook . . . but he's gettin' old, Josh. He doesn't retain lines as well as he used to. No big deal but he had some trouble in rehearsals and—and Rich was a swine about it. He'd lay into Manny in front of the whole company—just *humiliate* the poor guy." P.J. half-rose from his seat as his gorge did. "And this is a man who played Polonius at Ontario! Hell, Rafelson only did it 'cause he was worried Hook would walk off with the show and the reviews. And he would've. If I were Greer, I'd've cut that sucker in a second."

Surprised by his own rage, Cullen sank back in his seat and mopped his brow with a fresh napkin, mumbling, "Not that I think Manny really *did*."

"Yes, but that's not the point right now," Josh affirmed, though the bite of muffin she had just taken tasted like ashes on her tongue. "All we're trying to do is establish that you're only one of many with just grievance, okay? Now who else?"

For a moment, P.J. looked close to tears as he stabbed aimlessly at his hash. Then he threw his fork down. "I'm gonna hate myself in the morning—Rex. Rex had . . . issues with Rich."

"Uh-huh, past or current?"

"Both. Rex has been working there for years, even though he's had tons of other offers. It's a love-hate thing, Josh. He hated working for Rafelson—Richie was always buggin' him to do it bigger, splashier, when Rex really likes simpler, more suggestive stuff. He's near genius, you know?"

"Yes, I saw that," she agreed, but persisted. "Where's the love part?"

"Ah, he's had a major Jones for Rich for years. But it was just *never* gonna happen, you know?" Cullen shook his head sadly. "Rex shoulda left Peakmont a long time ago. But Rich knew he had the hots for him and, every time Rex got close to bailing out, he'd give him just enough slap-and-tickle to make him stay. He cock-teased the poor s.o.b. 'cause he knew he'd never find another designer as good."

Drained and too miserable to eat, Cullen slumped back in his chair with his chin on his chest; he looked like a little boy who had just broken his favorite toy. O'Roarke took pity and soothed. "Hey, it's not that bad, Tex. You're right, Manville probably hadn't the time or the strength to cut the harness. And he's been in the biz for ages—he's survived worse schmucks, I'm sure. As for Strauss, well, you say he's been carrying this torch for years. So, unless they had some recent run-in, there's no reason why Rex should all of a sudden go off the deep end and kill the thing he loves, is there? . . . Is there?"

P.J. just gave a hangdog shrug. Beginning to feel like a puppy beater herself, Josh relented. "Look, why don't you give Kravitz a call? Tell her what you've told me. Then do as she advises, okay?"

"Okay." Cullen nodded sullenly as he got to his feet. "You're right—it's the right thing to do. Just don't expect roses or nothin'." With that, he stomped out of the Lord Camelot, and it wasn't until Jocelyn was on her second cup of coffee that she realized he had stuck her with the tab. If it made P.J. feel better after the way she had outraged his sensibilities, that was fine. The only trouble was O'Roarke's cash flow was currently dammed up; she wasn't sure if she had enough to cover the tab.

Visions of an ugly scene with the bleach-blonde waitress, followed by a nasty case of dishpan hands, danced through her head as she scrambled through her purse looking for loose change. Then a cultivated voice broke in, interrupting her frenzied search.

"Jocelyn! So glad we caught you." Anthony Romero and the Ocelot slid into the booth opposite her. "You two haven't met, uh, properly, have you? This is Nan Semper, head of our board of directors. Nan, this is—"

Before he could finish, Nan put out a magnificently manicured hand and gushed in a Jackie Kennedy whisper, "I've heard so *much* about you!"

"Well, bad news travels fast," Josh quipped, returning the handshake and nearly cutting her hand on the rock Nan wore on her index finger. O'Roarke had no idea how much this little bauble cost—clothes she could estimate; after all, she had personal experience purchasing them, but she had never gone shopping for honest-to-God *jewels*—however, she wouldn't have been the least surprised if its price equaled her last year's earnings. "Nice ring."

Mercifully Semper didn't actually say "Oh, this old thing!" but her expression did as she returned the compliment with, "Thanks. I'm *wild* about your necklace!"

"Really?" Fingering the faux pearls she only wore for weddings, funerals, and when she went up for feminine hygiene commercials, she cracked, "Filene's Basement—five ninety-nine."

"Well, anyways, they're *lovely*," Anthony broke in anxiously, then nudged Nan as he gave both women a strained smile. "But we're not here to talk accessories, are we, Nan?"

"Oh, *no*," she exhaled in horror of such frivolity at such a somber time. Turning back to O'Roarke with earnest eyes, she stretched out a beseeching, bejeweled hand. "Jocelyn, we need your help."

"With what?" Josh played dumb for all she was worth.

"This whole horrid *mess!* We have *got* to get it cleared up A.S.A.P." The Ocelot's purr shifted to a soft growl as she looked to Romero for confirmation. "Right, Tony?"

"Yes, I owe it to—to Rich." His eyes clouded and he struggled to keep his voice from breaking. "If we can't open the show, the theatre will be in bad shape financially. He—he wouldn't want it to end like this."

"But you can open the show. Rich had an understudy, didn't he?"

"Of course. Jimmy Treeves." Semper's face lit up as she babbled, "He's quite divine in the role actually. I mean, he's young, he's charming, he's even *short,* praise the Lord!"

"Nan, *please!*" Romero's tone was very sharp, and Josh could see by the startled look in her eyes that Semper had never heard it before. "That's not the point. The point is we need a *name.* Arthur told us what you said earlier, Jocelyn, and I think you're right."

"Totally right!" Nan was going to get her two cents in no matter what. "No one'll touch us with a ten-foot pole until we resolve this . . . situation. And that'll spoil all our plans!"

"What plans?"

Josh saw Tony flinch with distaste, but Semper plowed ahead with schoolgirl enthusiasm. "To move the show . . . to Broadway! You see, we've had some *interest.*"

O'Roarke said not a word, just raised her eyebrows in Romero's direction. She knew, as did every other actor in town, that the Peakmont had long hoped to have one of their productions picked up by a Broadway producer. Aside from the prestige it would garner, it would also earn them some cold hard cash. But it hadn't happened so far, and she found it difficult, nigh on impossible, to believe that *Peter Pan,* with Rafelson in the lead, would have been the show to turn the trick.

Anthony read the disbelief on her face and said, "It's true, Josh. And it was Richie's dream. That's why we need you."

"For what?" She assumed a blank expression; no way was she walking into this one without a fight. Tony saw the signs and balked, but not our Nan.

"You have *experience* in . . . these matters. And you can be discreet. Make inquiries in a sub rosa way, right?" O'Roarke studied her cuticles by way of indicating her manifest disinterest. So Semper dropped the soft sell and fell back on her favorite prop—her checkbook. Drawing it out of her purse faster than Wyatt Earp drew a six-gun, she flipped it open on the table and demanded, "Okay—how much?"

O'Roarke wasn't ready for this one. Much as she wished to keep clear of this investigation, which promised to be ugly in the extreme, there was no denying that her finances were in sorry shape at present. Just as there was no denying that the Ocelot obviously had more money than God, and Josh could just name her price.

"Uh . . . I dunno. I'm not—I've never accepted anythi—" Squirming and waffling, she looked up and saw that Nan wasn't hearing her; she was staring intently out the window. Craning her neck, O'Roarke looked round to see a squad car pulled up at the curb with its patrol light flashing. She laughed inwardly. It was a sure sign, since the siren was silent, of a rookie cop who had recently risen from pounding a beat. There was no purpose to it; it just looked cool as hell. Assuming that Semper feared an outbreak of urban crime, she turned back and said, "Don't worry. It's nothing."

"Well, it's *annoying!*" Tony sprang from the booth and twitched the café curtains closed, cursing, "Why the hell do that for no reason?"

Josh shrugged lightly. "They're boys and it's a new toy, that's all."

"Hmm?" Nan blinked as her pupils adjusted to the dimmed light. "What was I—? . . . Oh, yes, Jocelyn—what figure did you have in mind?"

"If I had my druthers, Geena Davis'. There's a torso money can't buy," she chuckled, glad for the diversion that had bought her time and brought her to her senses. She did not wish to be in their pay. Encountering Tony's and Nan's baffled looks, she expanded: "Look, save your money. I'll do what I can to help P.J. 'cause he's my friend. And to help Sergeant Flynn—'cause he's the law. But I'm not about to ruin my amateur standing and that's all, folks."

"Are you *serious?*" Semper seemed aghast by the prospect that there were actually some things money could not buy. But Tony smiled his first genuine smile of the day as he patted Nan's shoulder.

"Yes, love, she's serious. Jocelyn, thanks for listening and thanks for your time." Just then the waitress dropped the check on the table and Romero plucked it up. "And, please, let me take care of this."

Bowing her head humbly, O'Roarke sighed, "Glad to."

10

"Too many damn *people* here," Jack Breedlove muttered under his breath as he was jostled for the umpteenth time while walking up Eighth Avenue in the late-afternoon sun. He had had a good time at the Garden watching the jumping competition. Though how those poor horses managed to make it around that tight course with all the crowd noise and those bright lights was beyond him. Still they had been something to see, beauties every single one, and the riders had acquitted themselves as well as their mounts.

Jocelyn would have loved it, but she had refused his invitation to tag along, claiming imminent destitution and, hence, the need to seek gainful employment. He only half believed her. Not that she was fibbing about her financial straits; he knew her savings were running out fast. But he didn't think that was the only reason she had passed on the horse show. After their warm reunion the other night, Josh had grown cool.

Breedlove didn't like it but he didn't take it personally, either. He had been down this road with O'Roarke before and her typical gait was always one step forward, two steps back. After wildly spontaneous bouts of lovemaking, she was often visited by a kind of retroactive shyness, brought on, at least in Jack's view, by the sense that she had gotten a bit more naked than she intended to. She also had to get *used* to having you around. Of this he was well aware, and so he had taken no offense last night when, after fixing him a fabulous roast chicken with wild rice stuffing, she had given him a sisterly kiss and sent him off to his hotel. Perhaps if he had given prior notice of his visit, things might have been different. Then again, perhaps not; he had no idea what her current involvement with Gerrard was and didn't much feel like asking. If the two ex-lovers were an item once more, he knew Jocelyn would have already said as much. For the present, he was content with the lieutenant's absence.

He had an hour or two to kill before meeting a sharp Kentucky horse trader for drinks at the Regency Hotel. Jack knew the sly old Kentuckian would have a mint julep waiting for him, but he was hot and thirsty now and in the mood for something more basic, like a nice cold draft in a nice dark bar just seedy enough to be atmospheric.

On West Forty-sixth Street he found what he was looking for; a place called J.R.'s that seemed to have an interestingly mixed clientele. What Breedlove didn't know was that J.R.'s was unique: the only jock/actor hangout in greater Manhattan. The TV sets at either end of the long bar were constantly tuned to the Sports Channel, and actors, like the guys in the Neil Simon show up the block, usually stopped in after performances to trade beers and stats with the rowdy fans, if only to prove to themselves that they were just regular, red-blooded Joes, too.

Jack, red-blooded as the rest, slipped onto a stool and ordered a draft and a pastrami sandwich. There was no game on, but Knicks fever was in the air, and, with the exception of two actors in a corner booth running lines, everyone was glued to an on-air interview with Pat Riley. Seeing Riley's familiar, chiseled features, Breedlove got a little lump in his throat. A Lakers fan of long standing, he missed ol' Pat and felt it had been a black day when the L.A. team owners had let him go. So strong were his sentiments that he couldn't stop himself from saying, "It's a crying damn shame those jerks fired him!"

A huge, burly fellow on the next stool turned to him with bleary but amused eyes and rumbled, "What? You from Lakers Land? Hah! Well, tough luck, pal. Your loss, our gain. That's the way the ball dribbles." He turned back to his drink, not his first by the look of things, with heaving shoulders. "Fired Riley, then got hit with that damn big quake. It was a *sign*, man." Then he downed his drink in one toss and called for another.

Breedlove was rooted to his seat. He *knew* this guy. It wasn't that he actually recognized him but he knew his voice and knew it well. It was a little deeper, a little coarser than he remembered, but so familiar. Gingerly he tapped the hulk's shoulder and got a baleful glance in return.

"Uh, 'scuse me, but . . . did you ever live in California?"

"Me? No fuckin' way!" He drew himself up to his full, towering height and gave Jack a look that said: "You'd better not be a fruit, fella." Out loud, he slurred, "I only go where the ground stays *under* your feet. See, I like ta know where I shtand—while I'm shtill shtandin'." His shoulders heaved again as he savored his little witticism. And Jack grinned and nodded; he had heard that line many times before from one guy only. This man was a far cry from the gawky, pimple-faced kid he had known, but they had to be one and the same.

Leaning over, Breedlove whispered, "And if you're not standing, you're out cold." The big man's head jerked up as he squinted suspiciously in Jack's general direction. Then Breedlove added, "Ain't that right, Bimpff?"

So great was the other man's surprise that he almost sobered up. "Who the hell—? Oh, jeez . . . is that you? Jackie? Outback Jack?"

"That's right, Bimpff—I mean Alan."

"Holy Mudder a' Gawd," Big Al Brenner bellowed as he locked one arm around Breedlove's shoulder, nearly pulling him off his stool, and waved at the bartender with the other.

"Give this man a drink! Weren't for him, I'd still be in friggin' *high* school, man."

"Aw, Bimpff, I just explained logarithms to you—"

"The guy's a *saint*," Brenner announced to the bar at large. Customers indicated with vague smiles and nods that they would be glad to support his canonization, if only to shut Al up. He spun back to Breedlove and demanded, "What the hell're you doin' here?"

"Could ask you the same, Bimpff. Hey, we're both a long way from Vegas and Eisenhower High."

"Thank Christ!" Big Al dropped a heavy fist on the bar and Jack watched all the glasses shudder. "Hey! You ever get your horse ranch?"

"Yeah, yeah, I did. Took me some time to raise the money though."

"How'd ya do it?"

Breedlove mumbled into his beer, "Hairdressing."

"Huh?" Brenner smacked a hand against one ear and guffawed. "Thought you said hairdresser. Hah!"

"I did—I was, Bimpff."

"*No.*" Al shoved his shoulder.

"Yeah, I cut hair."

"No!" This time Jack knocked Al's oncoming hand away.

"Yes, yes, *Alan*, I cut hair and I made a bundle at it, okay?" As this slowly sunk in, Brenner bobbed his head, then leered. "Bet you got laid a *lot*, huh?"

Ignoring the question, Jack laughed and countered with, "I never figured you'd end up in the Big A."

"Nah, I don't live here. I got a house an hour away, near where I work. Just came in for a funeral thing." He stopped to take a swig, then frowned. "But I didn't go. I *hate* those things."

"Yeah, me too." Breedlove felt a faint wobble in his spine. Manhattan was a big place with a ton of funeral parlors; still . . . "So where do you work, Bimpff?"

"Get this, at a theatre," Big Al snorted. "I'm master carpenter at this place, Peakmont Players it's called."

Brenner was too far gone to see Breedlove reel, then regain his cool. After downing half his draft, Jack said, "So you must know P.J. Cullen then."

"Huh? Wha'—you know Tex, too?!"

"Um, yeah, sure." Jack made a quick gut decision to keep Jocelyn's name out of it for the time being. "Met him a little while back. . . . Good guy."

"The best! The *best*—even if he is a fairy." Al called for another round and wiped his eyes on his sleeve, then spoke, as the Skipper might have of Gilligan, "He's my bud and they're tryin' to crucify the poor li'l bastard, Jackie."

"No? That's awful." Jack placed a comforting hand on Bimpff's shoulder. "Wanna tell me about it?"

"If you'll just take a seat, miss, Sergeant Zito will be with you in a minute."

"Sure, thanks." Jocelyn smiled at the desk sergeant and selected the least scarred chair in the precinct waiting room. Ten minutes went by with no Tommy in sight. Never a good waiter, Josh started tapping a fingernail against her teeth. She had called Zito after leaving the Lord Camelot to ask if she could come by. He had sounded surprised (O'Roarke, even when dating Phil, had rarely visited the station house) and a bit brusque, but he had said it was okay.

After nearly half an hour of studying Wanted posters and the pattern of cracks in the plaster ceiling, she decided something important must have come up. Just as she was about to leave a message for Zito, he ambled out to the waiting room. Nodding her way, he jerked a thumb over his shoulder and said, "Come on back," then spun around and marched toward the office he shared with Gerrard. Puzzled, Josh hurried after him. If it had been Phillip giving her the cool cop treatment, she would have understood; he was meticulous about keeping his personal feelings separate from his professional persona, especially in front of his fellow officers. Whereas Tommy, the few times she had come in, usually acted like a proud dad on Daughters' Day.

"What's up, Jocelyn?" he asked as he turned up his shirt-sleeves and turned the A.C. on low. O'Roarke thought this was unnecessary; even though it had gotten hot outside, the temperature around Tom seemed fairly frigid.

Leaning against the wall opposite his desk, she coughed uncomfortably, then began, "I went to Rafelson's what's-it . . . viewing today at McDermott's."

"Really," Zito grunted. "I didn't know he was Catholic."

"He wasn't. Just a devout exhibitionist." She waited for the laugh but didn't get it. Tom was acting like a tough house on a Wednesday matinee. "I just wondered if, uh, you'd heard anything more from Flynn?"

"Not today, no." He sat down and made busy motions with the piles of paper on his desk. "Anything else?"

It took her a moment to answer, so surprised was she by Zito's behavior and how deeply it cut her. If this were Phillip, with whom she had fought many a battle royal, she would know what to do; take her shoe off and throw it against the wall to get his attention, probably. But this was Tommy, her friend and interceder, the guy most likely to be on her side. What was going on here? Finally she said, "Yeah, there's something I've been meaning to ask you. The night Richie died, you said something about Al Brenner being an ex-con. You know that for a fact?"

"Not for certain. But I told Mike it might be a good idea to check him out for priors."

He still hadn't looked up from his paperwork, but she persisted. "How come? Just because he has some tattoos—"

"Not just *some* tattoos, O'Roarke. If those aren't a jailhouse job, I'm a . . . I'm a goddam *hairdresser!*" He slammed his fist down so hard, it made dust motes rise from the desk—which made him sneeze and spoiled the overall effect. O'Roarke blinked but said nothing. Zito grabbed a Kleenex, blew his nose and then his stack. "What're ya, shacked up with the guy again? Huh? Phil leaves town and, soon as his back is turned, you have Mr. Hot Comb move in. That it?"

"No, that is not it—at *all.*" She could have asked him how he knew about Breedlove but didn't bother; some folks have an innate antenna but Tommy had his own satellite dish. "I didn't know Jack was coming to town. He just showed up."

"Yeah? So what was he doin' in your apartment when I called—blow-dryin' your cat?!"

"He was waiting for me to come home and fix dinner—a thank-you dinner. For going with me to get P.J. sprung." Placing both hands on his desk, she leaned down to make her point. "He's my *friend,* Tommy. I don't forget my friends."

Zito acknowledged this with a begrudging shrug, then gave his nose another swipe with the Kleenex and mumbled, "So, what'd you make him for dinner?"

"Oh, for cripes—! . . . Roast chicken."

"With the wild rice?" His face went hard again.

"Yes, with wild rice! That tears it, huh?" She threw both arms up dramatically and hollered, "Well, hell, come on, let's get it over. Just round up all the guys, take me out to the parking lot, and *stone* me to death. Will that make you feel better?"

"Hey, hey, easy, Josh. Keep it down," Tom shushed nervously. Unlike Gerrard, he was unused to fighting with O'Roarke and unprepared for the one-two punch of an Irish temper coupled with a Gallic gift for mockery. Hurrying over to close the door, he feinted with, "I'm not passin' judgment here or anythi—"

"Sure sounds that way to me, Your Holiness," she hissed back, then sighed. "Look, I know how loyal you are to Phillip and I find it lovely. But Phil's not here now and Jack is. And he's willing to help me help P.J., that's all."

"But, chrissake, Josh, he's not one of us!" Zito's voice teetered on the brink of a whine.

"Us? Who's *us?* You, me, and Phillip makes three—like we're musketeers or something?"

Since these were exactly his sentiments, he chose to ignore her sarcasm. "Well, yeah, kinda."

"In that case, Thomas, just think of Jack as d'Artagnan," she countered smoothly. "Someone with a fresh eye and special talents of his own who—"

"Yuh—*right!*" This analogy was a bit more than Zito could bear. "So what's he gonna do if you run up against the perp? Tease the guy's hair till he begs for mercy?"

"Oh, would you stop with the cheap hairdresser jokes? You don't even know the guy." Irked beyond her better judgment, she whipped out her wallet and flashed him a photo of Jack, in swim trunks, on Zuma Beach. "He's six-two in his stocking feet. He handles horses—*big* horses, Tom. I've seen him ride a bronco bareback and stay *on*. The man can take care of himself."

Zito's eyes bugged and he quickly rubbed them. It didn't help; this guy was a god, tall, bronzed, with a devil-take-all grin. Tommy cringed inwardly, imagining what his wife would have to say: "Holy Mother, he's a dream! And not a cop. She's a nice girl, Thomas"—his missus was the only person he knew who resolutely referred to O'Roarke as a nice girl. "She deserves a nice boy in a safe profession, capeesh?"

He tried to sneer and say something real crummy, but, faced with this kind of evidence, he, like little Georgie Washington, could not tell a lie. The best he could do was waffle one hand in the air and sniff. "Yeah, okay. He looks like he's in decent shape. And, maybe, he's not a total moron."

"Thank you." Smiling, Josh put her wallet away and gave him a peck on the cheek. "Now stop worrying about me and Phil."

"Huh? Wha'd'ya—? You two're my friends! I got a right to worry, Josh."

"These things work themselves out, Tom." Then, winking and curling her lip à la Bogie, she lisped, "And, 'It doesn't take much to see that the problems of three little people don't amount to a hill of beans in this crazy world.' "

"Oh, cute, cute." He applauded her impersonation listlessly. "What's that supposed to mean?"

Opening the door, Jocelyn paused to look back and say, "It means, compared to a murder and my present state of unemployment, my love life is the least of my worries and—I say this with deep affection—none of your damn business."

11

"Who? Who is it?" O'Roarke put her ear close to the small metal grate and pressed the listen switch harder; another of the things that had not changed in her absence was the horrible static on her intercom system. Through a fresh burst of hissing noises, she dimly heard a voice slur, "Me. Izz me."

"Me who?" The static broke up, but all she could hear was someone humming what sounded like the opening bars of "Layla." Giving up on the intercom and not about to buzz in a possible mugger, she grabbed her keys and headed downstairs. Through the plate-glass door she saw Jack Breedlove leaning against the brick wall in the small foyer, playing air guitar. This was a sure sign that he had been drinking; whenever Jack had had a few, he rediscovered his spiritual kinship with Eric Clapton. Opening the door, she got a strong whiff of beer and whiskey and a bleary grin.

"Hi there, hot stuff. Guezz wha' I been up to."

"No good."

"No, no—iz good. Very good." He lurched toward her and aimed a kiss at her forehead, missed, and got her left eyelid. "Jack's been a very good boy."

"Really?" He was looking a little wobbly, so she slipped one arm around his waist. "I take it that means you made a deal with your Kentucky colonel or whatever the hell he is."

"Holy *shit!*" Reeling backward, Breedlove grabbed the handrail with one hand and his head with the other. "I forgot all 'bout him! Oh, oh, oh, I blew it. I'm screwed. Totally screwed . . . Gotta call 'im right now."

Pushing him up the stairs, Jocelyn said, "Not a good idea, pal. Not just this second."

An hour later, after a cold shower and some hot coffee, Jack sat in her rocker and watched in fascination as Josh, affecting a fetching Southern accent, drawled into the phone, "So you see, Mr. Sandquist, Ah'm the one to blame here. As his assistant, Ah shoulda called you the instant Mr. Breedlove was taken to the hospital but Ah was just beside myself. . . . No, no, sir, it wudn't anythin' serious. Seems he jist got some bad shrimps somewheres." She even pronounced "shrimps" as "sherimps"; a brilliant touch, Jack thought. "Which is no big surprise to me 'cause mah momma a'ways sez Yankees can't cook shellfish to save their sorry souls." Even across the room, Jack could hear faint echoes of the horse trader's guffaws. Completely in character now, O'Roarke giggled, batted her eyelashes, and went on with deep contrition, "But Ah don't mean to sound flip, sir. Ah know what a busy man you are—how valuable your time is and Ah'm jist purely mortified. Wudn't blame you a bit if you told Mr. Breedlove 'bout this awful oversight on my part. . . . Well, aren't you the dearest man alive. Thank you, Mr. Sandquist. . . . Oh, now stop or Ah'll start bawlin' like a baby. Hmm?—Oh, yes! Ah'm sure tomorrow night will be jist fine with him. Bless you . . . Wha'? Yes, mah word, it'd be a delight to meet you, sir—if Ah'm still in Mr. Breedlove's employ, that is. Ah only hope he'll be as understandin' . . . Yes, you, too, Mr. Sandquist . . . awright—Shelby. You take care now. Nightie-night."

As she hung up the phone, Jack rose to his feet, applauding.

"My God, you are *good*. Blanche DuBois is a charm school dropout by comparison! That was brilliant!"

"Nah, just adequate," O'Roarke said, shrugging off the Southern belle act like an overcoat. "If you'd shared a dressing room with Sadie Sitwell for a year, you could do it, too. Sadie's got more charm than a shark's got teeth. Now, if that'd been *her*, she'd have saved your skin *and* closed the deal."

"Well, I don't care. I'm still impressed. I think you're a real contender for the Bullslingers Hall of Fame."

"Oh, stop, I'll blush," was her dry reply. "Thing is, Jack, you're gonna have to do some tap dancing yourself tomorrow. Shelby wants me to come to your meeting. You'll have to think of a reason why I can't."

"But I can't say I *fired* you. He'd hate me!" Sinking back in his seat, he gave Josh that little-boy-lost look she knew so well, and sighed, "I don't want to sound like a schmuck but I *did* go out to Peakmont with you and—"

"Oh, come on!" O'Roarke huffed, pointing to the phone. "Didn't I just pay that one off?"

"Uh, yeah. But I missed that meeting today 'cause I was doing some investigating for you."

"In a *bar*? Investigating what—how many boilermakers it takes to see double?"

"No. I was talking to Bimpff Brenner."

"Bimpff? You mean Big Al? You met Al?"

"A long time ago, yeah. We went to high school together."

Jack had been waiting to drop this bomb and he enjoyed watching it go off. Jocelyn's eyes almost bugged out of her head as she gasped, "You *did*? Oh-my-gawd, that's absolutely unbelieveab— John Guare just can't do math!"

"Huh? John who?" Not as up on theatre as he was on film, Jack blinked in bafflement. "What's math got to do with it?"

"Guare's play, *Six Degrees of Separation*. The title refers to his theory that there are only six people between you and anybody else on the whole damn planet. Like, say, me and the pope. I probably know somebody who knows somebody who knows somebody else, et cetera, et cetera, who knows the *pope,* see? But I think, if John had been writing just about Manhattan, he'd have cut it back to two, three tops. . . . Jesus, you went to school with Al and you ran into him in a bar?"

"Yeah, place called J.R.'s on Forty-six—"

"Sure. That makes sense, at least. . . . What did he *say?*"

"Lotta stuff. Don't kill me if I can't remember all of it," Jack warned. "He kept buying rounds and I had to keep up. But I think I got the gist."

"Which is"—Jocelyn pulled an ottoman over to the rocking chair and plunked herself down—"what?"

"He thinks P.J.'s innocent for one thing. He says the whole scene backstage was such chaos that, to borrow your analogy, the pope could've waltzed in there and cut the harness unnoticed—if he were wearing that uniform thing?"

"Uh-huh, the blue grease-monkey suits . . . What else?"

"He figures whoever did it, really wanted Rafelson dead 'cause the other harness was okay."

"Other harness? There's *two?*"

"Yeah. Hold on. Let me get this straight." Jack took a sip of coffee and squeezed his eyes shut. "When Peter—Richie—flew *on* stage, he wore a, uh, tumble harness. Bimpff says, if the tumble harness had been cut, Rafelson would've got hurt, sure, but probably not fatally. The *other* rig is called a—a back-point harness. Whole different piece of equipment. And it was only used at the very end of the show . . . when he flew out over the house for the curtain call."

O'Roarke found this painfully ironic. "So, if Rich hadn't insisted on flying out front for his second bow, he'd still be—?"

"Breathing, yeah." Breedlove shook his head, then locked eyes with Josh, adding, "He said something else you're not gonna like."

"Tell me."

"Maybe you know already. When your friend Cullen first went to work there—when? Two years ago?"

"That sounds right. What?"

"Umm, did he ever mention that he had a, uh—thing with Rafelson?"

"A thing?" Josh sprang up from the ottoman. "No, he never—what kind of *thing* are we talkin' here?" She already knew the answer but still had to ask.

"A boy-meets-boy thing . . . briefly, according to Al. And par for Rafelson's course, I guess. But he's afraid it'll come out and make P.J. look—"

"Guilty as sin." Since Cullen's throat wasn't handy, Jocelyn reached for a pencil and snapped it in half. "That infernal fool! He's *still* holding out on me."

"Easy, easy." Jack got up and started rubbing her shoulder-blades; they felt like two steel plates under his hands. "There's more."

"If it's more about P.J., I don't think I want to—"

"No, it's not. It's about Romero. Did you know he had Rafelson insured?"

Josh's shoulders softened as she turned round to face Jack with wide eyes. "Tony took out a policy on Richie? When?"

"Not long before they went into rehearsals." Breedlove paused to pick up his coffee mug and savor the moment. "Seems Romero really wasn't hot to have Rich play Peter."

"Which only speaks well for his taste and sanity," O'Roarke felt compelled to interject. "So?"

"So they had words—loud words. Al said the whole theatre was buzzing about it. 'Cause Romero had never put his foot down before and the crew was really rooting for him. But Rafelson threw a major fit and threatened to resign, I guess. So Tony caved but not before he got Rich to agree to being insured."

"Interesting," was all she said. Breedlove had expected a bigger reaction but, unlike O'Roarke, he hadn't seen how devastated Romero had been at McDermott's. "But who's the beneficiary—Tony or the theatre itself?"

"Don't know," he admitted, then added, "But that's when the 'Splat' jokes started."

"Who started them? Did Al say?"

"Uh, yeah, but only because he was so blasted." Jack shifted his weight uneasily under her gaze. "Bimpff did. . . . He just plain couldn't stand the guy. But Al's just a rough-tough cream puff, Josh, always has been. He'd never *do* anything."

"You sure?" Jack gave her a quick, angry look but something in her face stopped him from speaking. "Do you know what Al's been up to since high school?"

"Not really. Just that he's been working at Peakmont for about five years—started right before they had that big fire. . . . Why?"

"Well, my friend Zito, who's pretty infallible in these matters, thinks Al may have done some time."

"Aw, that's just . . . !" The denial died away on his lips. While it was true that Brenner's bark had always been far worse than his bite, it was also true that, as a teenager, he had been constantly in trouble with the authorities. Any and all authority, in fact, starting with his parents, then the school principal, and finally the local cops, who had caught him joy-riding one summer night with two joints in his jacket pocket and sent him for a brief stay in Juvenile Hall. But that, as he tried to explain to Jocelyn, had just been kid stuff.

Patting his cheek, she said kindly, "Some guys grow up. And some guys just get *taller*, love. They go on doing the same old crap, only in a bigger playpen with bigger consequences. Maybe Al hated Richie 'cause they had that in common."

"Come on, you're just speculating!" Turning away from her, he went to refill his mug so she wouldn't see how disturbed he was. Even when, during the Buddy Banks case, he himself had briefly come under suspicion, it hadn't upset him as much, since he hadn't done anything. The possibility that a friend of his, albeit one he hadn't seen in years, might be capable of cold-blooded murder shook his compass. "I think your pal Zito should check his facts before he . . . Anyhow, even if Bimpff did a stint, I don't see how it ties him to—aw, *shit!*" Pouring hot coffee on his hand, he dropped the mug, which shattered in the sink.

Grabbing his hand, Jocelyn held it under the faucet and ran cold water over it. "I know, I know, Jack. It's scary stuff. Makes you doubt yourself, your perception of people." Wrapping a towel around his hand, she stood on tiptoe to kiss his cheek. "Feels like an eclipse in your heart."

Despite the throbbing in his hand, he felt a bit better. Tilting her chin up, he asked, "Is that how it is with you and Cullen? You don't believe he did it, but maybe, just maybe—?"

She didn't dodge the issue. "Yeah, just . . . maybe. 'Cause, awful thing is, given a particular set of circumstances, we're all capable of—"

"Christ, no! Josh, you can't really believe *that?*"

" 'Fraid so." Leaning her head against his chest, she confessed, "I like to think of myself as a civilized human being, Jack, but I gotta tell you, a niece of mine was attacked once. Not raped, thank God, but he got away, see. So, if I ever got my hands on that fucking animal—I doubt I'd think twice."

"Don't blame you," he said, taking her in his arms. "In fact, I'd help you."

"Ah, but that's the whole trouble. That's what I'm talking about." His heart caught as she looked up and gave him a smile just this side of *La Gioconda.* Pressing a finger against his breastbone, she whispered, "People always say, 'It's a jungle out there.' Truth is—it's a jungle in *here.*"

For a long time, he stroked her hair and her face and said nothing. Finally he asked, "So what do we do about that?"

"To save my soul, I don't know. . . . Maybe we just huddle a little closer round the campfire to stay close to the light."

"Well, I'm all for that." Pulling her close, he bent down to whisper in her ear, "And right now, not to make a cheap segue, sweetheart, you're the one I want to huddle with."

Slipping her arms around his neck, she nodded. "Me, too."

Moments later in Brooklyn, just as Jocelyn was slipping into something more comfortable, Tommy Zito was slipping into his favorite easy chair and staring hard at his telephone. After a brief internal debate, he snatched up the receiver and dialed a long-distance number. On the third ring, a hotel operator answered and connected him to room 936.

"Phil, that you? You sound beat, man."

"Oh, Tom, hi. Yeah, I am. I just got in." Kicking off his shoes, Phillip Gerrard sank down on the sofa. "We're near nailing this sucker but Chicago judges are tough s.o.b.s—it's hell even getting a wiretap here."

"I bet." Zito went on to inquire and commiserate about the case, then, after he felt Phil had had time to blow off enough steam, he said, "Don't suppose you've heard from Josh?"

"Not this week. Last week, she sent me a plant."

"A plant?"

"Yeah, some huge fern," Gerrard laughed as he popped open the minibar. "With a note—'You'll probably be looking at lots of dead things. Thought you might need to see something green and growing.' Meanwhile it's this monster plant, Tom, like out of *Little Shop of Horrors.*"

"Yeah, well, she's a card," Tommy said as Phillip broke into fresh chuckles. "Uh, she, uh, took me to a show the other night—*Peter Pan.*"

"Yes—and?" Gerrard leaned forward in his seat; two "uh"s in one sentence meant Zito's news wasn't going to be great.

"And, uh . . . this guy, Rafelson, playing Peter—"

"A *guy?*" Gerrard knew his theatre lore well enough to be dismayed. "Like a young kid?"

"Uh, no, a guy 'bout your age."

"Jesus—no!" Phillip was appalled but tickled. Compared to his case, this sounded like benignly awful fun and games.

"Yuh, yuh. He was the director-slash-star, see? . . . Guess nobody thought it was a great idea."

"Nobody in their right mind would. So what? He bombed big time?"

"No, he fell—big time." Zito gave the gory details as precisely as possible, ending with, "But Josh's friend Cullen was the guy in charge of the flying gear. So they brought him in for questioning and she's, uh, a little concern—"

"Ah, Christ! She's got herself in the thick of it, hasn't she?" He knew; Tommy was way over the "uh" limit.

"Yeah, I think so. I shouldn't be bothering you with this stuff but I—"

"No, that's okay, I'm glad you told me, Tom." Gerrard grabbed a tiny Scotch bottle and poured its contents over some ice. "Keep me posted, huh? I'm hoping to wrap things up here within the week. So I should be back before she can get into any serious trouble, right?"

"Right." Zito didn't have the heart to tell him that, homicide aside, there was already serious trouble and its name was Breedlove.

12

"Can I get you anything else, Sergeant? A croissant? Some nice pâté?"

"No, thank you, Mrs. Semper, this is fine." Mike Flynn indicated the frothy cup of cappuccino the maid had just brought him. He had asked for black coffee but Nan had insisted he have something fancier. Since "Fancier Is Better" seemed to be the motto of the Semper household, judging from the ornate crystal chandelier hanging over the vestibule and the carpets so thick you could get a nosebleed crossing them, Flynn had tactfully acquiesced.

Tact was the operative word when interviewing the wife of one of Peakmont's wealthiest citizens, Cyrus Semper, who was also one of Peakmont's most itinerant sons. With business interests all over the country, Cyrus was often away for weeks at a time, leaving Nan, who disliked flying, to amuse herself with the Peakmont Playhouse and other toys.

After Jocelyn O'Roarke had called that morning with news of the insurance policy on Rafelson, Mike had felt a chat with Mrs. Semper might be in order. Clearing it with Lieutenant

Holstein, his superior officer, he had gotten permission but with a warning attached.

"Careful with that one, Mikey, she's got eyes."

"Oh, I know. I've seen her. She's the one they call the Ocelot."

"I'm not talking about her mascara, man! She's got eyes . . . for the gents. All ages, all sizes. I don't know if her husband knows but every motel manager in and around town does. So watch your step there."

Happily married and without a shred of male vanity, Flynn had laughed and told Holstein not to worry. "I'm sure her tastes run to those glamour boys at the playhouse. Not some middle-aged flatfoot with adenoids."

Now he wasn't so sure. Wearing toreador pants and some low-slung blousy thing that gave a nice glimpse of her décolletage (though there wasn't much of it, but Flynn was too naïve about ladies' lingerie to spot the augmenting affects of a French push-up bra working overtime), the Ocelot was curled up on a Louis XIV love seat giving him the once-over as well as her undivided attention.

"Please, tell me, how can I help, Sergeant . . . or can I call you Michael?"

"Um, Mike's fine." He coughed nervously, loosened his necktie, and wondered how the hell she got those stripes in her hair.

"Well, Michael, I like to think of myself as a good citizen. I'm at your service. Completely. So don't worry, you can ask me *anything*."

"Thanks, that makes my job much easier. I know, being on the board of dir—"

"Not just on the board," she corrected coyly, waving one jeweled finger in the air. "I'm the chairman."

"Ah, yes, sorry. So I assume you work closely with Mr. Romero?"

"*Very*." She nodded solemnly. "Tone consults me on all major decisions."

"That so? Then did he consult you about taking insurance out on Mr. Rafelson?"

"Oh, no! It was the other way around." Nan straightened up and dropped the Lana Turner pose. "We *insisted* on it."

"Who's 'we' exactly?"

"The entire board. Richie had a five-year contract with the Players, for which he was paid handsomely, believe me." As her mind turned to money, her eyes hardened. "Peter's a risky part. So we stood to lose a bundle if he got hurt and couldn't . . ." Hearing herself, she stopped with a stricken look. "I mean, we never anticipated *death*. Heavens no! But, good God, he was a grown man, Michael. And did you see that harness? Would you want to wear that contraption?" Before Flynn could reply, she snorted, "I don't *think* so. He had to wear maxi pads!"

"Beg pardon?"

"You know, sanitary napkins." Semper feigned embarrassment as she sipped from her iced-tea glass, which Mike guessed had more rye than tea in it, then pointed daintily toward her nether regions. "There's that strap that goes between the legs, remember? Very uncomfy, not to mention the *chafing*. So Richie wore pads. Big ones."

"Uh, I see." Biting the inside of his lip to keep from laughing, Flynn made a mental note to review the coroner's report; the boys in the morgue must have gotten quite a jolt. Finally trusting himself to go on, he said, "Sounds, ah, awkward. But not seriously harmful."

"Oh, but there were so many ways he *could* have been injured—a slipped disc, a pulled groin muscle, a *hernia*. Then he'd've been unable to fulfill his duties as artistic director. Plus we'd end up paying his workman's comp forever and a damn day!"

"I see, I see." Flynn scratched the back of his head and made his voice bland. "Then this was more of an accident-and-injury policy? Not actual *life* insurance?"

"Well, I believe it covered all possible contingencies." Nan smiled, lifted her shoulders, and flashed him a little more cleavage. "You know, in for a penny, in for a pound."

"Sure. Makes sense." Mike returned her smile as his mind raced. "And was there a double-indemnity clause?"

"Hmm?"

He repeated the phrase, adding, "That means the claim would pay double in the event of accidental death. But not at all if it were suicide or . . . murder."

"You know, I really can't remember." The Ocelot was back in her sex kitten mode, playing dumb. "But I'm sure Tone could tell you."

"Of course— Oh, that reminds me. I heard you and Mr. Romero usually watch the first preview of every show. But not this time. You were both up in his office for most of the performance?"

"That's right." For the first time, Semper showed signs of discomfort. Twisting the ring on her finger, she said, "Didn't come back down till the last scene, where Peter comes back to the nursery. We both hated to miss it but, well, duty called. We had some pressing business to discuss."

"For over two hours? And Mr. Romero never left the room once?"

"Nope." Her tone was calm and adamant now. "And neither did I."

He believed her, and Flynn's shit detector was fully operational; whatever she was edgy about had nothing to do with the murder. Maybe, given Romero's Hollywood handsomeness, their pressing business had been of a horizontal nature. Adopting a man-of-the-world air, he gave her an insinuating grin. "Well, I'm sure you have a lot to, uh, *talk* about . . . being so close and all."

"Huh? Oh, my Lord! You don't think we were—?" To his amazement, Semper kicked her heels against the love seat and howled with laughter. It was the first time, since the start of their interview, that she had seemed wholly without pretense.

Trying to catch her breath, she gasped, "Oh, what a scream! Me and Tony? Oh, oh, honey—he's queer as they come. Queerer!" Realizing her elaborate eye makeup was in danger of running, she pulled a hankie out of her pocket, dabbed, then went on matter-of-factly, "I don't mind 'cause he's, you know, *tasteful* about it. Subtle. I bet half the board doesn't even know—but I sure do. Spend any time around actors and you get a knack for spotting the Friends of Dorothy."

"The who?" Flynn tried his utmost not to look as dim as he felt.

Had O'Roarke been present, she would have been more than a little impressed to find that Nan, of all people, possessed an AC/DC detector of such high caliber.

"Aw, that's an old saw." Semper suppressed another hiccup of mirth. "Dorothy in *The Wizard of Oz*, as in Judy Garland, see? Every gay guy in America is—hah!—*queer* for Garland. You go to Tone's house and you'll find every damn album she ever recorded!"

"Got your point." While Nan hummed a few bars of "Over the Rainbow," Mike fell back on official decorum, pulling out his notebook and the silver pen his wife had given him last Christmas. "In that case, could you tell me what exactly you two were discussing?"

In a twinkling, Nan went from glee to gloom. Giving Flynn a severe look, she spoke in her best lady-of-the-manor mien. "I honestly don't see what bearing it could have on your investigation, Sergeant."

"Probably none at all, Mrs. Semper." Flynn flashed her what he hoped was a beguiling grin while insisting, "But I can't know that for sure till you tell me, can I?"

"Well, I suppose it really doesn't matter *now*. But let's keep this *entre nous,* all rightie?" Either his charm was working on her or the rye was; she shrugged, tossed her hair (which tremored but did not actually move), and sighed. "For some time we—the board has been concerned about—how can I put this? About Richie's showboating. Casting himself in starring roles.

Understand, we *loved* him as a director but as an actor, especially the *lead,* well, let's just say he was no Orson Welles."

"No, of course not, Welles would never've gotten into that harness," he mumbled, unable to resist. But his little joke worked wonders on Semper, who cackled and downed the rest of her drink.

"You can say that again! I mean, Jesus—Peter *Pan?* Really! It was gettin' a bit *much,* ya know?"

"So why'd you—I mean, the board let him do it?"

"Because it was Tony's place, as producer, to put his foot down and just say *unh-uh.* But he didn't have the heart. He had such a soft spot for Rich."

"Maybe he was afraid Rafelson would quit?"

"Nah, that was never in the cards. Oh, Rich might threaten to, but, like I said, he had a five-year contract. And it was air*tight.* If he quit, he'd have to buy himself out." Again, as money reared its head, the Ocelot showed her claws. "No way was Rich gonna cough up *that* kind of change. Unh-uh, he was too fond of his wallet by far."

"And that's what you were discussing with Mr. Romero that night?"

"Damn right." Dropping the iced-tea ruse, she reached for a crystal decanter and refilled her glass. "Look, Mike, how do you think an outfit like this makes money—especially after so much of our arts funding's been cut? You hope to God one of the shows is so good it'll get picked up for Broadway. That's how."

"Was that likely to happen with *Peter Pan?*"

"Let's say, we had—have hopes. We got a lot of press 'cause it was the big anniversary show. So we spent oodles on it and you can see every damn dime on that stage. It's a handsome production." All brass tacks now, she lit a Virginia Slim and growled, "But you think any respectable Broadway mogul would move this show with an over-forty male diva in the lead? Hah! Pigs would fly at the Shubert before Rich ever would. So I told Tony fine, let Richie open the show, have his moment of glory. Then let's have him fake an illness or something and get a real *name* in before the New York people come to check it out!"

Flynn, who had wisely taken shorthand in school, wrote so rapidly that the light coming through the huge picture window bounced off his silver pen. "Was this just a suggestion from the board, or an ultimatum? And how did Romero respond?"

"Hmm? What?" Mike looked up to find Semper staring fixedly at his pen. Figuring she was either guessing its value or getting a bit tanked, he put it down and repeated his question slowly. She blinked several times before answering, "Oh, he, um, fought me tooth and nail at first. Got all Italian and emotional. Said we were ingrates and philistines, blah, blah, blah. It got pretty tiring. After a while, when he saw I wouldn't budge, he just threw up his hands, said—'Fine. You tell him. I wash my hands.' But I got a few drinks in him and got him calmed down. Said how much I admired his loyalty but that he couldn't pull a . . . who's-it? A Herod. That it was his sad duty to drop the bomb on Rich. Then, let's see? . . . Then we talked a bit 'bout who we could get to step into the part, yeah, and that's about it."

Recognizing the signs of interviewee exhaustion, Flynn knew it was time to wrap things up. Gently he asked, "And after you finally left his office?"

"We went straight down to the back of the house." Nan stopped abruptly as if watching a replay of a train wreck. Squeezing her eyes shut, she whispered hoarsely, "Just in time to see . . . the finale."

He watched in horror as Semper's shoulders started to heave. But this time the tears were not from mirth and this time she didn't bother about her mascara.

13

"You *slept* with the stiff?" P.J. Cullen, who had excellent hearing and perfect pitch, jerked the phone away just in time to save an eardrum. Keeping his word to O'Roarke, albeit belatedly, he was in the shop of the playhouse making a clean breast of things to his lawyer, Judith the Hun, who was mighty angry and completely off pitch. "When I asked you at lunch to tell me *everything*, what the hell did you think I meant?"

"It was just a little oversight on my par—"

"A damn big little oversight, buster," she fumed.

"But it was over two years ago and it was just a one-nighter." Having had more than the average person's share of one-night stands, certainly more than Kravitz's share he imagined, P.J. was at a loss to explain how, in his world, sometimes, these things just don't *count*; so he blathered, "Before I really *knew* the guy. I mean, if I *had*, I wouldn't have, see? Anyway, I just didn't think it—"

"No-you-didn't-did-you?" Judith spat out each syllable like a nail. "But you know what, P.J.? I don't *want* you to think. Leave that to me, I'm better at it."

"Yes, ma'am, I will." She made him feel like a first-grader

who had just had an "accident" in class. On one hand, he feared and loathed Kravitz; on the other, he was damn glad she was in his corner. "So what do you think I should tell Sergeant Flynn?"

"Nothing just now," was her instant reply. "I'll decide when and I'll do the telling."

"Well, okay. But Jocelyn always says you should—"

"Hey! Who's your lawyer, me or her?"

"You, you are, absolutely."

"Good boy. Now, have the cops been bugging you any-more?"

"Not really." He cupped a hand over the receiver and whis-pered, "They've been hanging around the theatre looking for the, uh, instrument."

"Instrument? What—a cello?"

"No, I mean whatever it was that was used to cut the har-ness."

"Oh, they haven't found it yet?" Judith's voice brightened considerably. "That's good. It's been forty-eight hours already. Means any prints they find can't be considered conclusive."

"Well, they won't find *mine!*" Cullen felt the need to assert himself, however feebly.

"Of course not," Kravitz yawned. "You just lie low for now."

"Sure, sure," he said, anxious to end the conversation. "When in doubt, duck and roll, as Josh says."

"O'Roarke! That reminds me." The lady lawyer's voice rose an octave. "You know what she pulled on me?"

"No." He couldn't, didn't want to, and was afraid to guess.

"Yesterday morning a black cleaning woman shows up at my door—just shows *up!* Says she's out of work and O'Roarke told her I needed help with my 'domestic affairs.' Can you believe that?"

"Um, well, yes, I can actually." P.J. plucked a hammer off a nearby tool rack and lightly bonked his head to keep from laughing. "She's very concerned about the high unemployment rate, Judith. Honest. I'm sure she meant well."

"Like fun," Kravitz barked. "I know the type. She's a mixer. A born mixer-upper. Knows what's best for everybody but herself, I bet."

Feeling his spine stiffen, Cullen riposted, "Maybe. Or maybe she just likes to help people get *work*."

Judith grunted, "Well, you know what you can tell her for me?"

"What?"

"Tell her . . . thanks."

"Huh?"

"You heard me! I don't like her methods, but this housekeeper—this Josie person is a four-star general of domestic engineering." For the life of him, P.J. thought he heard a quaver in Kravitz's voice. "She even does *windows*. Hell, I never knew I had a view of the river."

"Well, I'm glad—for the both of you."

"O'Roarke was still outa line," she huffed, reverting back to type. "But tell her . . . I owe her one, okay?"

"Sure will. That's real nice of—" The receiver buzzed in his ear; obviously Judith hath spake and was done spaking for the moment. Which was just as well since Arthur Freed, having gone from co-director to sole director, had scheduled a full-tech dress rehearsal, except for the flying, to begin in thirty minutes.

While the rest of the cast was keeping to itself in various dressing rooms, Rafelson's understudy, little Jimmy Treeves, paced the floor of the shop in mint-green tights, running lines under his breath. The crew went about their business in a subdued fashion, some pausing now and then to give the anxious actor an encouraging nod or pat. The only people who seemed unaffected by recent events were Freed, who kept flying back and forth from the house to the stage giving notes to the P.S.M. and the sound man, and two guys from the nearby Peakmont Fire Department who liked to hang around the shop on lunch and dinner breaks in hopes of glimpsing babes in underwear.

Since Princess Tiger Lily and her girls were cloistered away like Carmelites, one of the firefighters, a young buck named Glen Kimmons, helped himself to free coffee, then sauntered over to Cullen.

"Hey, P.J., where are the girls?"

Holding up a hand to silence him, P.J. announced over the backstage intercom, "Half hour, ladies and gentlemen. Half hour to places for Act One, please," then turned back to Kimmons. "Having a Tupperware party. Sorry, Glen, no T and A today. I'll be lucky to get 'em out of their dressing rooms on time."

"Poor kids." The horny devil heaved a sigh. "They're probably spooked by these grunts crawlin' all over the place, huh?" *Grunt* was the term of disaffection used by members of the Peakmont Fire Department to describe members of the Peakmont Police Department, who, in turn, referred to the former as "hosers." It was a rivalry of long standing in the town; one that P.J. wisely wanted no part of, so he merely mumbled, "They're just doin' their job, Glen."

"Sez who?" Kimmons cracked. "They haven't found the knife—or whatever was used, have they? Looks to me like the grunts are just spinnin' their wheels."

Cullen kept mum, but a voice behind him boomed, "And you're just lovin' it, aren't ya?" Big Al stood in the doorway, nearly filling it, looking hungover and haggard. "You wanna see them screw up the way you guys did."

"What's that suppose to mean?" Kimmons, who was in superb shape, strode over to Brenner—then strode back a pace; being in shape was one thing, being a human monolith was another. Still, Glen demanded, "How'd we screw up? If you're talking about the fire, there was no *way* anyone could've put that sucker out after the first two minutes. The old playhouse was a damn tinderbox and you know it, Al. Hell, somebody could've lit a fart for fun and—whoosh! Ashes."

"I'm not talking 'bout putting it out. I'm talking 'bout finding how it happened, you moron." Like a pumped-up N.B.A.

player, Brenner bumped his chest against Glen's belligerently. "What did you hosers come up with? Zip, that's what."

Stung, Kimmons looked like David getting ready to clock Goliath. "Why, you dick head, you don't know shi—"

"Hey, quit it!" Cullen stepped between the two men and firmly shoved them apart, much to his own amazement. P.J. disliked violence, especially when it might be aimed at him, but after his dealings with Kravitz, these guys didn't seem so tough and he didn't have time for their bullshit. Raising his chin to Big Al, he ordered, "Go check your presets—*now*."

Brenner looked down at Cullen, saw that he meant business, then back up at Kimmons and barked, "Later."

Waiting till Al was out of earshot, Glen rejoined, "Fine by me . . . What is *with* that guy?"

"Gimme a break!" P.J. blew out his cheeks in exasperation. "We're all a little tense here, Glen, ya know? So, not to sound corny, if you can't be part of the solution, you're just part of the damn problem. So blow, okay?"

"Hold it, hold it." Kimmons danced backward to block Cullen's imminent exit. "Look, I wasn't even with the department when the theatre burned down. But they still talk about it 'cause, well, it kinda haunts us."

"Why?" The distress on Glen's face was enough to give P.J. pause. "Nobody got hurt, did they?"

"No, no, only"—Kimmons checked to make sure no one was nearby—"Only we're pretty damn sure *how* it happened. . . . It was arson."

"It *was?*" Cullen's eyes popped wide but, in one smooth move, he hooked the arm of a passing production assistant and said, "Lora, be a love and call fifteen minutes for me, okay?" As the girl headed for the intercom, he pulled Kimmons into the hallway. "If you're sure, then how come the insurance company paid off?"

"Knowing something and proving it are two different things, P.J." Glen gulped, then whispered, "And this wasn't an amateur job. No V-patterns, nothing like that."

"Whoa! V-patterns?"

"Yeah, you get that with amateurs or pyros. The perp puts some oily rags in a wastebasket and drops a match. But they usually put it by a wall and the flames will make a V-pattern on it, see?" Cullen just nodded and waited for Glen to go on. "Only it wasn't like that. I wasn't lyin' when I said the old theatre was a tinderbox. It was. Still, it went up much too *fast*. Too fast to be from faulty wiring or anything like that. And that alone tells us something. But the bitch of it is, it was so fast and so hot, we couldn't put it out in time to preserve dick as far as evidence. I know it sounds weird, but that's why we think it was a professional torch."

"Shut my mouth!" Which P.J. did as he let out a long, low whistle. Then he squinted and asked, "Glen—how come you're telling me this stuff now?"

"Well, heck, it's a small town, P.J." Kimmons looked over his shoulder then back at Cullen. "I know the grunts pulled you in. But they were just fishing without bait. And, like I said, we talk about that fire a lot . . . and I got a gut feeling about it."

"Like you know who did it?"

"Oh, no, no way. It was a stranger, just a hired gun probably," he answered hastily, adding, "But I can't shake this idea that the fire had something to do with Rafelson's death."

"Huh? How the hell do you figure that?" For the first and only time in his professional career, P.J. didn't give a damn if they went up on schedule or not.

"It's not—I don't *figure* anything." Kimmons squirmed as macho guys will when caught in the grip of what is commonly called feminine intuition. "It's more like a karmic thing. See, if you asked me who was the person most likely to have hired the torch—I'd say Rich Rafelson. Everybody knew he wanted a new theatre. And he got it *and* got made artistic director. That's a little too friggin' tidy for me."

"Yuh, okay." Cullen was intrigued but not buying. "But what're you sayin'? Zeus came down and cut his harness?"

"No! I just think what goes around comes around. Maybe somebody else knew what we knew—that the fire was deliberate. And maybe they pegged Rafelson for it." Princess Tiger Lily came out of her dressing room in her skimpy buckskins but Kimmons barely noticed. "You gotta understand, there're people in this town who really *loved* that old theatre. It was part of Peakmont's history. They didn't want something bigger 'n better. They wanted quaint."

Much as he would have liked to offer the grunts a fresh suspect, P.J. felt Glen's imagination had run away with him. "So—you think the Peakmont Historical Society did him in?"

"Aw, crap, course not! I just think"—Kimmons lowered his head and his voice—"Rafelson had *something* to do with that fire. *Somebody* knew it and decided to pay him back for it."

"But why wait five years?"

Better with a hose and ladder than with hard logic, Kimmons scratched his head and screwed up his face. Then he spotted a Polaroid of Rafelson as Peter tacked on the shop bulletin board. Someone had drawn a scar on one cheek and blacked out his front teeth; on the bottom was printed: PETER GETS MUGGED BY SOME FAIRIES. Pointing to it, he grinned. "Maybe they were just waiting for the right role to come along, eh?"

"Easy to use, gentle. Yet effective. Fem Fresh—so you can feel good about being a woman *every* day of the month."

The lanky guy behind the camera nodded to the svelte young casting director, who turned back to O'Roarke. "Fine, Jaclyn. I think that one had the right mix of confidence and openness. Thanks for coming in."

"My pleasure." Josh didn't bother correcting the red-haired woman in the Versace suit. She merely placed the feminine hygiene product back on the prop table and subtly wiped her hands on a spare makeup towel, thinking Lord, Lord, the things we do for filthy lucre.

Not that she stood a chance of getting the job. It was an unwritten law in the land of TV commercials that any and all products designed to be placed between a woman's legs, like Fem Fresh's new scented douche, should only be promoted by ethereal blondes, refined redheads in a pinch. But never, never brunettes who, in the advertising world, were viewed as too earthy for such ads and better suited for selling things like pork sausage and oven cleaners. Not only did O'Roarke know this, she rejoiced in the fact. The thought of becoming the Fem Fresh lady, despite the tens of thousands it would earn in residual checks, made her shudder, though she had wisely refrained from saying so when an agent friend had called with the last-minute audition. The whole point of this pointless exercise was simply to demonstrate her eagerness to work.

After saying her good-byes and waving her thanks to the cameraman who looked half asleep, Josh went out to the waiting room and instantly pulled the barrettes out of her hair. Is this any way for a grown-up to make a living? she wondered, watching the roomful of auditionees mouthing various renditions of: "Fem Fresh—so you can feel good about being a woman . . ."

Eager to get home and get out of what Breedlove had laughingly called her Marian the Librarian clothes, she hurried for the elevator. Just as the shiny steel doors opened, a young girl jumped up from her seat.

" 'Scuse me, you're—aren't you P.J.'s friend? Jocelyn . . . uh?"

"O'Roarke, yes." Masking her surprise, she put out her hand to shake Amy St. Cyr's. "I was with him at McDermott's yesterday, but it didn't seem the time or place to say how much I liked your Wendy."

"Really? That's so sweet." Amy fairly quivered with delight until her strawberry blonde curls bounced. Josh figured this kid was a shoo-in for the Fem Fresh spot; she had the virginal air of someone who, still in that first rapturous flush of becoming a woman, might actually find douching *fun.* Then she broke the spell by glancing down at her copy and smirking. "Tell me, how'd you get through this dreck without puking?"

"Didn't have breakfast. Never eat before reading for feminine hygiene spots, that's my motto." St. Cyr placed a dimpled hand over her mouth and giggled. Then Josh said, "Isn't there a run-through today?"

"Oh, yeah, but my understudy's doing it. Artie agreed to let me out so I could make this audition. . . . I really need the bucks."

"Don't we all?" Another elevator opened. Josh moved toward it, giving Amy a nod and a smile. "Well, good luck—break a hymen."

"Uh, Jocelyn, can I ask you something?" O'Roarke turned back to the girl as the doors slid shut. St. Cyr drew close, lowering her voice. "This is gonna sound weird, but—what did you think of Richie's performance?"

Since Amy didn't look like someone still carrying a torch, Josh leveled. "I thought it was a travesty."

Digesting this, St. Cyr bobbed her head up and down a minute, then asked, "But did you think it was just bad acting or—or something else?"

"What else? Bad casting?"

"No, more like he was *on* something."

"As in *drugs?*" Amy nodded somberly and Josh had to swallow her mirth. "Richie? I doubt that. From what I hear, his graduating class voted him the person least likely to end up at the Betty Ford Clinic. Plus, he was *flying,* for Pete's sake, and way too smart to—"

"No, I don't mean he took anything." St. Cyr was starting to look a little pale under her blush. "I think, maybe, he was *given* something."

"Why do you think that?" Another elevator appeared but O'Roarke wasn't going anywhere now.

"A bunch of reasons. You could call it nerves but I really didn't think he was himself that night and . . ." Amy plaited and unplaited her fingers. "And there were all those jokes. He never heard them but I did. The tech guys calling him Splat Rafelson and other stuff. The cast got into it, too, even

Man—" She caught herself, but, Josh felt, only because she wanted to be drawn out.

"Manville Greer? What did he say?"

"I'm sure he didn't mean it—Rich was *not* nice to Manny, see? But I was waiting in the wings, during the first preview, and Manny was in a corner with Al Brenner watching Rich do the scene where Tinkerbell drinks the poison. Anyway, I hear Manville whisper to Al—'Pity it's the wrong—'" Here Amy stopped again but not for effect; she grimaced and went on. "'It's the wrong fairy.' Big Al laughed and said something like 'We should fix that.'"

Well acquainted with backstage black humor, O'Roarke shook Amy's arm lightly, saying, "Honey, honey, he wasn't *poisoned*. He was dropped."

"I know, I know." St. Cyr shrugged off her hand. "But what if he was doped up some so—when he got into the back-point harness—he wouldn't *feel* that it wasn't right?"

"Did you mention any of this to Sergeant Flynn?"

"Huh? Me? No—*no!*" Her eyes widened in horror. "I don't want to get anybody in trouble."

"Then why tell me?"

"Because I heard—uh, P.J. says you know how to deal with cops."

It was too bad; Josh was just getting to like the girl. But she didn't like being made a patsy. Jabbing the down button, she said roughly, "So you want me to do your snitching for you? Well, you're out of luck there. Either you're concerned enough to go on record with the police or you're not. Or you're just trying to make smoke 'cause your romance with Rich went sour and everybody knew it." Seeing Amy shrivel up with shock, she softened. "Look, it doesn't make a damn bit of difference how you *felt* about him—even if you wanted to wring his neck. Emotions aren't acts, thank Christ, or we'd all be in the docks. But, if you're clean and you think somebody else *isn't*, talk to Flynn. It'll be better for you in the long run, trust me."

St. Cyr's eyes moistened as her mouth worked soundlessly.

She looked to be on the brink of spontaneous combustion. Just then, the door flew open and the casting agent called, "Amy St. Cyr."

"Here!" Squaring her shoulders, Amy turned away from Josh and walked toward the Versace suit with outstretched hand, trilling, "So *nice* to meet you." Whatever O'Roarke felt about her, she had to admit the kid was a trouper.

14

"You're a lucky man, Jack, havin' this little lady lookin' after your affairs." Stretching out his legs in the bar of the Regency Hotel, Shelby Sandquist put a slightly libidinous spin on the last word as he hailed the cocktail waitress with one long index finger. She came promptly to their table; Sandquist was the type who never needed to raise a whole hand. "We'd like another round here, darlin', when you get the chance."

"Oh, don't I know it," Breedlove agreed as both men favored Jocelyn with patronizing smiles. She blushed modestly, waving the compliment away. Jack knew the blush was as manufactured as her sweetly submissive mien, but he enjoyed it all the same. Her hair piled high with loose tendrils nestled at the nape of her neck, she was wearing a frilly little sleeveless top—much to his delight; he didn't know she owned a frilly, little anything—and a midcalf skirt with an enticing side slit. He couldn't resist patting her exposed knee. "She's the last of the great gal Fridays."

"Aw, go on. You're just funnin' me." Uncrossing her legs as the waitress brought a fresh round in record time, she snuck Jack a look that said his days were numbered, then cooed archly, "Anyhow, Ah don't believe *Ah'm* the filly y'all should be discussin'. In't that right, Mr. Sandquist?"

"Aah-*hah!* Clever girl." Sandquist slapped his knee, then assumed a sorrowful air. "But you call me Shelby, hear? Or Ah'll feel mighty hurt."

"Well, we can't have *that*—Shelby. But you know what ma daddy sez?" She gave him a dazzling smile and a saucy wink. "He sez—a man talkin' 'bout women, when he's really thinkin' 'bout horses, is usu'lly talkin' through his hat and dreamin' 'bout your *wallet*." Sandquist's jaw dropped as O'Roarke rose from the table, daintily smoothing her skirt. "So Ah shall remove mahself to the ladies' euphemism and let you boys git down to cheatin' each other fair'n square."

With that, she sailed through the lounge with Shelby's eyes glued to her back, more precisely to her behind. Not happy with the hungry look on the horse trader's face, Jack was relieved when Josh disappeared from view. Pulling a silk handkerchief from his breast pocket, Sandquist wiped the back of his neck with an appreciative grunt. "Son, you should'na let her leave. That li'l girl could do me out of mah best brood mare if she had a mind. . . . How much you pay her anyhow?"

"Jeesh, even I did not know you were *so* full of horseshit," Josh said to her reflection as she repinned some wayward locks. Lighting a cigarette, she sank down on a settee, tired from her performance. It would all be worth it, of course, if it helped Jack get the horse he wanted at a price he could afford. Still, she felt it was a bit much, having to play Miss Fem Fresh and Miss Lorelei Lee back-to-back. "But, hey, that's what friends're for," she told herself. Then, recalling the night she had spent with her "friend" Jack, she gave a groan laced with pain and pleasure; the latter having to do with his sweet skills as a lover, the former with the guilt it triggered vis-à-vis Gerrard.

Damn Tommy Zito anyway for making her feel like the original two-faced woman! She had made no promises, told no lies. Wasn't she a free agent? Nobody was getting hurt, so—"Aw, who'm I kidding," she said aloud, putting out her cigarette in the pristine sands of the cannister ashtray. It wasn't a question of right or wrong; it was simply a matter of feelings. And Phillip's feelings, if he knew, would be terribly hurt. In the heady days of her dating twenties, O'Roarke had frequently had more than one man around. But that was before AIDS and before Phillip; that relationship, for good or ill (and it had been a bit of both), had permanently altered her sensibilities. She was no longer able to take these matters lightly. Life was not like the movies, and she couldn't reasonably expect Jack and Phillip to reenact *Jules and Jim* for her. The small fact that both men knew she had no yen for formal matrimony still didn't justify her playing both ends against the middle, nor did she want to.

So it was time to face up and ask the hard questions, she decided. Like, why was she sleeping with Jack after keeping Phillip at arm's length for so long? Answer: Because with Jack there was less pressure, less expectations. More pure fun. Less hate . . . and less love, she finally admitted. Jocelyn wholly adored Breedlove. His easy humor, his insouciant charm, and his eternal optimism were qualities she liked and admired. Whereas Gerrard, while not without humor and charm of his own, was intense, skeptical, and, by profession, all too aware of the dark side. But Phillip lived in the same moral terrain as Josh, while Jack dwelt in sunnier climes; this she knew bone-deep.

Just as she knew that, if Jack's fancy were taken by another, she would sorely miss him but survive. When Phillip had gotten engaged, however, it had nearly killed her.

"Eureka!" O'Roarke bounced up and addressed the mirror again. "You yutz, that's why you'd rather sleep with Jack—he can't cut your heart out."

Having made some small sense out of the tangled web of her emotions, she was happy to have done with introspection for the time being, and headed for the pay phone. Her machine picked up after two short rings, which meant she had messages. Punching in the remote code, she waited for the tape to rewind;

it was a long wait. First came a short, succinct message from Mike Flynn: "Josh—I've checked out the insurance policy and it's a no-go. It was a double-indemnity thing. Only pays off on accidental death. So Romero and the playhouse don't get a dime. Call me tomorrow, okay?" Next was a garbled bulletin from P.J., one of the few people who liked answering machines because "they don't interrupt you." He also liked to leave long soliloquies worthy of Samuel Beckett; this particular rendition of *Krapp's Last Tape* made vague, hectic references to Rafelson and fire. Then static broke up the line and she could only hear disjointed phrases like "a horrible mistake" and "he's not that stupid!" before P.J. sputtered off in an urgent chorus of "Call-me-call-me's." Lastly, like a bolt out of the blue, like a judgment, came a familiar baritone: "Josh, it's me. Tommy told me what happened at the Peakmont. I'm sorry you had to see that, love. And I know you're worried about your friend—uh, J.P., is it? But, listen, I'm not saying you should keep your nose clean 'cause I know you won't. Just—just try to stick close to Flynn and hold tight, okay? I'll be home soon as I can. It'd better be soon, your plant's taking up half my hotel room. Be good or, at least, be careful."

"Oh, *ouch*." After the five short bleeps, she hung up the phone and hung down her head. "Does that man have timing or what?"

But, mindful of the task at hand, Josh glanced at her watch and realized it was time to return to Jack and his horse trader. After powdering her nose and freshening her lipstick, she inspected her handiwork and pronounced, "Once more into the breach, dear friends, once more."

And so she marched out of the ladies' room, ready to do Southern-belle battle for Jack and his horse deal—until she spotted Tony Romero at a corner table with a short, bald-headed man and froze. It was a bad freeze, the kind that attracts the eye by its very abruptness. And Romero apparently had good peripheral vision. Even as she tried to lower her profile and slink by, he half-rose from his seat and waved.

"Jocelyn? That you?" Waving back, she gave him a what-a-small-world grin and kept moving toward her table. But Tony started making come-hither motions. "Jocelyn, come, come meet Harry Brill."

Glancing across the room, Josh saw that Shelby and Jack were knee-deep in negotiations, so she quickly weaved her way through the tables. She knew Brill by reputation and had actually met him once during her novice years in New York. A wreath of smoke hung around his head as he switched a long cigar to his left hand in order to shake hers. Brill was famous for his Cuban cigars and his Sad Sack demeanor, which cloaked the heart of a pugilistic counterpuncher. "Nice to meet you, Miss—?"

"O'Roarke. Jocelyn O'Roarke," Romero said, smoothly pulling out a chair for her. "A really wonderful actress."

Tony appeared to be in much better spirits tonight, but the change might have more to do with good business than genuine good cheer. With his seamless charm and impeccable manners, Tony was a natural at public relations; one of those rare sorts who could attend a party with a nasty migraine and still be the life of it. Even as she turned to Brill, O'Roarke wondered why he was so keen to have her interrupt what was obviously a business meeting.

"Actually, we've met before, Mr. Brill, years ago. In your office." Understandably, Harry, having interviewed countless thousands of actors in his office, looked blank as a slate. Much as she disliked name-dropping, Josh jogged his memory by adding, "Freddie Revere sent me to you."

"Of course, *Frederick.*" Brill breathed the name reverently as Tony bowed his head and looked like he was about to cross himself. Choking back a chuckle, she had to admit it was fun being pals with a living legend as she watched Harry's memory banks make the big leap. "But you were an actress then and now you're a director, aren't you? You staged that Shaw revival with him where one of the actors dropped—"

"Yes, that's right." She cut him off quickly—the less said about the Burbage case, the better—and created a diversion by bringing in another big gun. "But I'm still acting. In fact, I was working in L.A. most of last year, thanks to Gabrielle Brent."

"You're one of Gabby's clients?" She had his full attention now. One of the ironies of an actor's life is: You're nobody till somebody *signs* you. Somebody big, that is. And powerhouse agents, like Harry and Gabby, are shameless poachers. They love trying to steal each other's clients, not so much to acquire the actor per se, but for the thrill of one-upmanship. Chomping down on his cigar, Brill smiled the smile of a fox entering the hen house. "How *is* Gabby? I hear she's been away from the office lately."

"Yes, she's in Europe." If Brill didn't know that Brent was on extended sabbatical, Josh saw no reason to enlighten him. "Part business, part pleasure, you know."

"So you're back here."

"For the time being, yes," she answered like a wealthy woman doing some casual window shopping but with no real interest in buying. "Mainly to see friends and plays."

"Not looking for work?" Harry raised his brow quizzically, to which Josh replied with the slightest of shrugs. He made his voice heavy with regret. "But you must miss doing theatre."

"Oh, sure! Like mad. But there doesn't seem to be much going on now—compared to L.A., I mean," she sighed wistfully.

"There is if you know the right people," he insinuated, blowing smoke rings above her head.

"Really? Such as?"

"Tons, tons of things!" Tony broke in a little shrilly. He was too adroit not to see their little courting dance, and he clearly hadn't called Jocelyn over for the pure joy of giving her career a boost. "But, speaking of Gabrielle, didn't you help solve her husband's murder, Jocelyn?"

Oh, thanks a *heap*, she thought, but said, "Not much.

There was a very fine young detective on the case. He did most of—"

"But you *did* help," Romero insisted. "And I know you've been talking with Sergeant Flynn . . . another *fine* detective, eh?"

"Yeah, Mike's a good guy," she replied cautiously, knowing this was leading somewhere but not sure of Tony's destination. "Seems to know what he's doing."

"I'll say!" He laughed as if she had just said Pete Sampras seemed to know what he was doing with a tennis racket, then nodded to Brill. "I was just telling Harry what a great job he's done for us."

So that's what he's after, she realized. He wanted Lily Trent or one of Harry's other hot clients for Peter. And wanted *her*, as some sort of expert witness on theatrical homicide, to assure Brill that all would soon be peachy-keen at the playhouse. The hell with *that*, she thought, then wondered why he had just used the past tense.

"What do you mean *done?* Mike's still workin—"

"Haven't you heard?" Romero, having cast her as a distaff Ellery Queen, was shocked. "Didn't P.J. tell you?"

"Tell me what?"

"They've made an arrest." Seeing her disbelief, Tony nodded firmly, as did Brill, who seemed to have contracted a sudden case of what Josh termed Court TV fever: the frisson created by a vicarious proximity to murder.

Narrowing her eyes, she asked, "Based on what evidence?"

Before Romero could reply, Harry cut in eagerly. "They found the—thing! The murder weapon."

"Murder weapon? You mean whatever was used to saw the harness—a knife?"

"Yes, a hunting knife with a serrated blade." This time Tony beat Brill to the punch, then gulped. "It's such a shame. And I feel so responsible. I—I should have been more thorough when I hired him. But his résumé was good and there was no reason to think he had a criminal record. Still I blame mysel—"

"Hired *who?*" She clamped her hand down hard on Romero's, to stop his dithering. "Whose knife was it?"

"Al Brenner's. He even admits it." His shoulders drooped now that he was done with the high drama of disclosure. He rubbed his eyes, whispering, "And I hired the man."

"So what?" Josh said, bringing both men back to attention. "So he owns it. Doesn't mean he *used* it."

"What're you nuts?" Harry Brill, newly minted amateur sleuth, shook his cigar in the air. "The guy was in jail for aggravated assault! The knife had bits of the harness leather on it. *And* his prints're all over the damn thing."

"Sure they are," she agreed, waving away his smoke. "It's *his* knife. Where'd they find it?"

"In his toolbox," Tony said softly.

"*Brilliant* hiding place, huh?" she scoffed. "Come on! Anybody could've picked up the knife and put it back afterwards. They had to have more than that. Something that showed motive."

"Oh, hell, I didn't want to mention this." Romero gave Brill and Josh a sheepish look. "I was hoping—I still hope we can keep this out of the papers. . . . In the bottom of his toolbox, they found photos, *lots* of photos—of Amy, our Wendy. Seems he had a fixation of sorts."

"Hot damn," Harry gasped. "Like a Hinckley–Jodie Foster thing?"

"Yes. I guess seeing her with Richie—they were, uh, intimate, Harry—just pushed him over the edge."

"Well, hey, a leopard can't change his spots, right?" Brill said philosophically. "The guy was just a walking time bomb."

The two men nodded their heads in accord and it was all O'Roarke could do to keep her peace and her temper. Unlike Breedlove, she wasn't entirely convinced of Brenner's innocence, but she didn't like the smell of this. Granted, Big Al, given his prison record, was the obvious candidate, a little too obvious for her liking. But she didn't want to debate the issue with her two companions; she wanted to get back to Jack and pry him loose from Sandquist. Rising from the chair, she offered disingenuously, "I hope your troubles are over, Anthony."

"Okay, how's this—you knock another two grand off Desert Storm's sale price and I'll give you five percent of all future stud fees."

"Make it fifteen percent and mebbe we'll have somethin' ah can live with," said Sandquist, who enjoyed haggling as much as any Arab rug merchant. Breedlove, having kept count of Shelby's bourbon and waters, to the tune of five now, was impressed; the guy had hollow legs and a good head for business. A lesser man would have been under the table and in his pocket by now, but Shel looked like he was just warming up.

Before he could make a counter offer, Jocelyn reappeared.

"There you are!" Sandquist gallantly got to his feet and pulled out her chair. "Ah was startin' to worry. Thought the white slavers might've got you."

"Ah'm so sorry. It's jist—" Josh stopped, swallowed hard, and blinked back tears. To save his soul, Jack couldn't tell if she was acting or not.

"Sugar, wha's wrong?" Shelby put an arm around her shoulder and lifted her chin. "Tell Uncle Shel."

"Oh, Ah'm such a goose to get so worked up." She smiled up at him bravely. "See, Ah jist called home and Daddy tol' me mah Grandma Tyler's taken a real bad turn. She's near ninety, bless her heart, and we've been expectin' it. Still it's aw'ways a shock, in'it?"

"A' course it is," Sandquist soothed. "There's no way to prepare for these things, darlin'."

Knowing that O'Roarke had no Grandma Tyler, no living grandparents at all, Jack still sensed that she was disturbed about something. But he had no idea what this little improv was in aid of. Then Josh gave him a kick under the table, signaling that the next line was his. Jerking up in his seat, he nearly shouted, "It's a crying shame! . . . Anything I can do?"

"No, no. Ah've awready called the airport. There's a flight to

Baton Rouge at 'leven thirty." She paused to pick up a cocktail napkin and delicately dab the corners of her eyes. "Ah'll jist hop in a cab. And you two can get back to business—"

"Hell, no," Shelby bellowed. "We can't let you go off by yourself."

"*Please.*" Jocelyn grabbed his hand and looked up beseechingly. "It's important to me—after the way ah messed up the other day—for y'all to wrap things up. Ah'll be fine, truly."

"Thunderation, we can do that in two shakes. Ah was jist havin' fun dickerin' with the boy." Grinding out his cigar, Sandquist looked over at Jack. "Ah still want fifteen percent, son. But Ah'll take four grand off the askin' price. How's that?"

Sandquist put out his hand. At first Breedlove was too stunned to move, but Josh gave him another sharp jab in the shins; he jumped to his feet, croaked, "Done," and shook on it. Shelby reached down for his glass, tossed back the last of the bourbon, then said, "Now let's get the little lady to the airport."

Jocelyn protested while the horse trader tut-tutted her. The deadlock broke when the waitress approached to tell Sandquist he had a long-distance call. "Damnation! Ah'd better take this. Jack, can you handle things?"

"You bet." Then Shelby kissed Jocelyn on both cheeks, slapped Breedlove on the back, and strode off. O'Roarke whispered "Thank God," under her breath and, without a by your leave, dragged Jack out of the Regency.

As soon as they were across the street, he spun O'Roarke around to face him. "Don't *ever* do that to me again!"

"Do what?" Jack's temper flared infrequently and always took her by surprise when it did. "You made the deal."

"You conned him, Josh. By playing on his decency. That's not how I do business."

She saw his point, saw that she had let expediency take precedence over fair play, and was not happy with herself. On the other hand, she wasn't entirely unhappy and couldn't help saying, "But you got the horse for a good price."

"Would you *listen* to you!" Jack hopped on the pavement as

if it were made of hot coals. "We were coming to terms—gradually. That's how a man like Sandquist does things and I respect it. I sure the hell didn't need you barging in like Little Eva with your bogus tale of woe. Sandbagging the poor schnook that way—'mah dyin' grannie, bless her heart'—yeech!"

Not bothering to mention that, even on the worst day of his life, Shelby Sandquist could never be termed a poor schnook, she merely said, "I had to, Jack. You two would've gone at it all night. And I needed to talk to you."

"About what?"

"About Bimpff." Quickly as she could, she recounted her conversation with Romero. "So I think we should call P.J. and get his version of what happened. Then, if you want, we can go out to see Flynn tomorrow."

"Yeah, yeah, I want," he mumbled. His brain felt like an oversoaked sponge, but one stray thought managed to surface. "God, lucky thing Shelby got that call, huh?"

"Luck my eye! He's a Southern gentleman. I knew he'd insist on coming along."

"No! You didn't rig a phony page?"

"Jack Breedlove! What do you take me for?" she demanded with hurt pride. "Shelby's no fool and neither am I. I have a friend in Louisville who has a friend on the local paper. And Sandquist is a big deal down there, you know? Well, of course you do. Anyway I got my friend to ask her friend to call Shel and ask for an interview. . . . He'll like that, don't you think?"

Shaking his head, Jack started to chuckle helplessly. Finally he gasped, "You're right."

"Right? About what?"

"About John Guare—he *can't* do math. At least, not where you're concerned."

15
—

"I'm flying!"

Jimmy Treeves flung his arms out wide, cocked his left knee, and floated to the top of the Darling nursery like a dandelion puff while the denizens of the Peakmont Playhouse held their collective breath. Treeves had already flown in through the nursery window on his first entrance, but that was a relatively simple maneuver. The "I'm Flying" number required the new Peter to do a corkscrew twirl midair then sail over to the fireplace stage right and land lightly on the mantelpiece.

The last time O'Roarke had watched this scene, Rafelson, on landing, had bumped his hip against the stage right flat, causing it to shudder and him to nearly slip off the narrow ledge But Jimmy, six inches shorter and lighter in pounds and years than his predecessor, executed the whole sequence with apparent zest and ease. Slipping into the seat next to her, Rex Strauss whispered, "Some difference, huh? Kind of like seeing a *Tristan und Isolde* with a soprano who doesn't weigh a ton."

"Kind of," Josh agreed. In her heart of hearts, she still felt a female would make a preferable Peter, if only to undercut the rarefied strains of misogyny in Barrie's story. But she had to admit Treeves was a major improvement. Around the same age as St. Cyr, Jimmy, with sandy blond hair and a freckled pug nose, read even younger on stage. Helped by a sweet Irish tenor, the diminutive actor hit the right notes and the right balance between boyish bravado and childlike longing.

"*Big* difference." Strauss echoed his previous sentiments as he nudged Jocelyn. "When Rich did this number, we called it 'I'm Flaming.'" He hummed along, then sang, "Look at me. In the air. How's my hair? I'm flaa-ming!"

"*Jesus*, Rex!" She tried her best to sound appalled but the rotund set designer remained unabashed.

"Oh, come on! You saw him, Jocelyn, in that Gwen Verdon wig. Now, be honest, what went through your mind when Richie read that line—'I've lived a long time among the fairies. I know a *million* of them.'"

She tried to shrug the question off, but his evil grin pierced her pretense of good taste. Twirling one hand in the air, she did a Bette Davis. "And they-knew-*you* . . . Okay? Happy now?"

"Well, not happy exactly." Rex finally showed some signs of conscience. "Only—I dunno—it's awful what happened to Rich, just awful. But I don't want to see him Nixonized, you know? All those people, politicians and the press, who'd hated his guts for years, got the guilts and all of a sudden it's, 'Oh, but he was a genius at foreign affairs and so misunderstood.' And all that crap. When Dick was *always* a slick, sick twist and being dead doesn't change that!"

"Good analogy." In the darkened theatre, Strauss couldn't see the fascination in O'Roarke's eyes. If what P.J. had said about the designer's undying lust, if not love, for Rafelson were true, then you'd think Rex would be among the first in line to romanticize the man, if only to justify all those years of fruitless yearning. But here he was making bitchy cracks, adamantly unsentimental about his late, lost love, comparing him to a despised, deceitful pol. Cautiously, she said, "And, yes, Rich's memory is probably in for some temporary revisionist history—but why does that bother you?"

"Because it clouds the issue! Because—" Strauss squirmed in thought in his seat. "Because if Richie's made out to be a saint, then anyone who had a beef with him has to be a—a sinner."

"Or a potential killer?"

"Yes—exactly! And that's ridiculous. He was a goddam diva and he pissed *everybody* off at some point. But the police don't realize that!" Pressing his hands against the armrests, he half raised off his seat. "If they did, they wouldn't have been so quick to arrest Big Al. I mean, did you *hear* what went down yesterday?"

"Ooohh, yes." She nodded wearily. "In spades."

After leaving the Regency with Jack, she had called Cullen and, not finding him at home, had tracked him down at one of his favorite haunts, a cabaret bar called Don't Tell Mama on Restaurant Row. They had found him, on his fourth vodka stinger, weaving and singing "Losing My Mind" along with the drag queen on the tiny stage. And he was; the events of the last few days having taken their toll on his nerves and his sanity. Once his eyes had focused on the two of them, he had hiccuped hello and "*Love* those friggin' boots, man" to Jack, then turned to Josh with an accusatory, bleary glare.

"Know wha' they *did?* They nailed Big Al's ass. Tha's what your buddy Flynn did."

"I know. I heard. But—"

"So why din't you *do* something? I mean, shee-it, so they found some head shots of what's-her?—Wendy. So what!" He kicked his foot against the bar rail, stubbed his toe and winced. This was fortunate as the pain seemed to clear his brain somewhat. "So he had a boner for her. Big Al aw'ways gets the hots for some girl on every show. Is's no big deal."

"Okay, fine. But tell me about the knife and—"

"Aw, knife-schnife! Look, the guy may be a felon but he ain't stoo-pid. He's gonna—what? Saw the freakin' harness with it and then drop the damn thing back in his toolbox?" At this juncture, P.J. slapped his glass down on the bar and turned to the rest of the room with outstretched arms. "We are livin' in a police *state*, people. Is's like *Les Mis* starring Jouvert as Big Brother. Get it?"

While secretly applauding Cullen's drunken defense of Brenner, Jack had seen they were getting nowhere fast and signaled the bartender for some coffee. Meanwhile, O'Roarke had tried to keep the histrionics down to a dull roar by asking, "What was that message you left me? About Rafelson and a fire?"

"Ah, ah! Glad you axed. Tha's another thing." P.J. had given her a sharp poke in the breastbone. "Ol' Glen thinks Richie burned the playhouse down . . . and got whacked for doin' it."

Several cups of coffee later, after Cullen had recounted his conversation with Kimmons, Josh had said, "Look, I'm sorry, even if Glen's right—and that's an enormous if—I don't see what bearing it could have on Rafelson's death. And I also don't see how it helps Al."

"Poor Al." A little saner but still sodden, P.J. had screwed up his face like a stricken six-year-old. "Just 'cause he's got a record, they're gonna make him take the fall."

"Oh, for chrissake, this is not *The Maltese Falcon* and he is not Mary Astor," she had snapped, shaking his arm. "Get a grip, damn it! Tell me about the knife. Who knew he had it and where he kept it? *Think!*"

"Okay, okay, hold on." Cullen had gulped down a half mug of cold coffee and squeezed his eyes shut. When he had finally opened them, they were wide with wonder. "Well, hell, practically everybody—least everybody on the tech staff. See, it wasn't a work knife. It's his hunting knife. Al's a big deer hunter and proud of it. He's not into trophies—heads on the wall, that kinda shit, thank Gawd. And he doesn't gun hunt. Doesn't think it's sporting. Uses a bow and arrow and guts the deer himself."

"That sounds like Bimpff," Jack had murmured, to which Josh had replied, "Lovely. Very picturesque. But why was this common knowledge?"

" 'Cause he'd *kill* you if you touched it," Cullen exclaimed as if she were an idiot. "Lots of guys are finicky about their tools and I don't blame 'em. People borrow stuff and forget to give it back. But Al's not like that. You can use any of his stuff, *except* that knife. He just kept it around as, like, a rabbit's foot, I guess. He'd never use it on a show. And he sure as hell would *never* use it to waste Richie. That'd be a—a sacrilege to him, I think."

Nodding, Breedlove had given her an it's-a-guy-thing look. But O'Roarke, hailing from upstate and having known a fair share of bow hunters herself, had had a different view: Hunters were hunters and the tools they used for one kind of kill, they might very well use for another. Though all she had said was: "Did Flynn make the arrest himself?"

"No, uh—I dunno. It all happened so *fast*. I don't even know how they came across the knife. We'd finished running Act One and I was checking the presets for Act Two, then—next thing I know—two cops are leading Al out the back in cuffs." His indignation roused again, Cullen threw up his hands, adding in an if-things-weren't-bad-enough tone, "Natcherly, the rest of the run-through was a *mess*. We were all so wigged out. Tell Flynn that!"

But she hadn't; when she had finally managed to reach him the next morning, Mike had done most of the talking. "Look, before you start hollering, lemme just say I realize our case is largely circumstantial—for *now*. So far, we don't have anyone who saw Brenner near the harnesses during intermission, but—"

"*I* saw him during the intermission," she had interjected. "We had a smoke in back of the theatre. So doesn—"

"It was a long intermission," Flynn had cut in quickly, then asked, "Were you with him the *whole* time?"

"No . . . but I still say it's flimsy, Mike."

"Well, flimsy or not, Brenner's got priors. And we got the knife and the prints."

"Okay—the knife! Doesn't that bother you? That he'd just leave it lying in his toolbox like that?"

"Not even a little," Flynn had answered with a dry laugh.

"Happens more'n you'd think—thank God!—crooks making real bonehead moves. Few months back we found a stiff in an alley. One of his shoes was missing, so we went looking for it. Found it in a trash can six blocks away . . . along with some of the perp's *junk* mail!"

"No!"

"Yup. That's an extreme example, but I could give you lots more."

"But Brenner's not that stupid," O'Roarke had insisted, echoing P.J.

"Maybe, maybe not. But Jocelyn, master criminals mainly live in comic books," Flynn had said. "My theory is: Most people get *dumber* when they commit crimes, not smarter. Could be from panic or guilt or whatever, but they do not function at warp speed. Makes my job *much* easier."

"Maybe too easy this time." Wanting to shake his cop's complacency, she had needled, "And you've got diddly for motive, Mike."

"Since when is sexual jealousy diddly?" The needle had gone in and put Flynn on the defensive. "He knew St. Cyr was involved with Rafelson and—"

"And he also knew Rich was *gay*." Josh had paused a moment to let that one sink in. "So I seriously doubt he was frothing at the mouth about them."

"Doesn't matter," he had answered, undeterred. "With or without the girl in the picture, Brenner's had a grudge against Rafelson for years. And I've got plenty of people who'll swear to that."

"Oh, well, take a number and get in line," she had rebutted hotly. "So did most of the staff and crew."

"No. It's not the same. They may not have liked the man much. But I said a *grudge*." Flynn had paused as if in silent debate, then added, "See, Josh, I knew before Tommy called me that Brenner had a record. Rafelson told us after the theatre burned down. Seemed Big Al was his pick for the torch. But there was nothin' to tie him to it, and, frankly, I think it was bullshit. Or spite. Whatever it was, he had good cause to hate the guy's guts."

"But why wait five years for revenge?"

"I've known people who've waited longer'n that. We once arrested a woman for killing her husband with a steam iron. When we asked her why, she said he'd slept with her best friend once—twenty years back. I guess, with some folks, these things just fester till one day—"

"Okay, okay, you win," she had sighed, undone by his arsenal of gruesome anecdotes.

Flynn had heard the defeat in her voice and offered kindly, "Look, if you wanna help the guy out, make sure he gets . . . Huh? Who's here?" His hand had gone over the mouth piece but Josh, having a fair idea of what was going on, had checked her watch and nodded in satisfaction just as Mike had yelled, "Aw, Holy Mary! Not *her*."

In the background a familiar female voice had called out, "Flynn, we gotta talk." Kravitz to the Rescue, Part Two. Mike had muttered, "Haf'ta go," and hung up in a hurry.

"So what do you think?" Strauss nudged her again. "How bad does it look for Al?"

"Bad enough," she admitted. "They have no witnesses. But the circumstantial stuff could get them an indictment anyway."

"Oh, it's *too* vomitous," Rex hissed. "And the theatre isn't doing a damn thing for him! Tony just wants it *over*—which I can understand—but Artie is—"

Before he could expand on his theme, the theme strode up the aisle, calling to the sound man, "Dave, I'm hearing static on Hook's mike. Do something." Then he stopped and did a double-take. "Jocelyn?! What're you doing here?"

"Waiting to meet a friend. Show looks good, Artie."

"I know! It's all coming together finally. Funny, isn't it? How it's always darkest before the dawn. . . . Gotta go!"

"A laugh riot," Rex muttered, watching Freed scuttle back to his seat. "The man is a *vulture*. Building his career on death and destruction. Dawn, my ass! Well, sure, Al's in jail, so Arthur's day is bright. Now he'll have no trouble getting a name in—what does he care if the poor man's being railroaded?"

The old saw about not judging a book by its cover came to Josh's mind, along with the conviction that the "fat people are jolly" cliché was a crock. Because here was Rex, looking like a cheery, miniaturized Friar Tuck, while inside his pudgy exterior raged a seething, rail-thin man. Still, he had manners and, as the Act One finale came to a close, he applauded soundly as did O'Roarke and the smattering of people in the audience.

When the house lights came up, she turned to him. "Why're you so hard on Freed? What about Tony? I saw him in the Regency last night with Brill."

"That's different," Rex replied without a thought. "He's the producer. He *has* to keep things going, whether his heart's in it or not. And, believe me, it's *not.*"

"How come?"

"How *come?*" Strauss gaped at her as if she'd just sprouted snakes for hair. "How come! He loved Richie, Jocelyn. I mean, they were 'in love' once, you know. They had an affair before Rich even began working here. Once he did, I guess it was too much of a muchness for both of them. I think it ended by mutual agreement—but not the friendship. Aside from his mom—maybe—Tone's the one person who loved Rich despite his faults, despite everything. Hell, I've spent the last few nights at his place 'cause I'm worried he might—"

Again the set designer had to cease and desist as Jimmy Treeves came pelting up the aisle. "Rex, Rex—how was I?"

"Great. And if you don't believe me, ask her." He jerked a thumb toward Josh and made the introductions. Hearing her name, Jim's eyes perked as he waited for her comments.

"I think you're golden. You've just made your agent a happy man or woman."

"Thanks. You really think so?" Treeves was a trouper, but not seasoned enough to take compliments in his stride. "But what about the 'For Wendy' number? I felt I was kind of flailing around there."

"You were *fabu*lous. Just terrific, Jim." Artie Freed popped up behind his Pan and clamped an arm around his shoulders. "I've got a few notes but they're minute." Then the peripatetic director headed for the lobby with, "You've got nothing to worry about, believe me!"

Once Artie was out of the house, Rex made a gurgling sound in the back of his throat, indicative, Josh supposed, of the bile he was swallowing, while Jimmy gave a short, sarcastic laugh. "Nothing to worry about. Yeah, right! Until he finds a name to replace me."

"Probably somebody red hot like—oh, hey, what's Mary Lou Retton doing these days," Rex asked snidely.

"Still smiling," Treeves rejoined. But before their little bitch fest could get into full swing, Earl, the box office manager, came down the aisle and brusquely handed Jocelyn a note. "Call came for you but I didn't want to disrupt rehearsal," he said with the clear subtext: I have better things to do than play answering service. O'Roarke started to thank him but he testily turned away and trudged back to his sanctuary. Earl was a good example of why a box office has bars on the window.

"Guess I won't be asking to borrow his phone," she said, reading the message. It was from Jack, who was supposed to meet her at the theatre, asking her to call him at the police station. Whatever he had to tell her, O'Roarke wanted to hear in private, not over the pay phone in the lobby or the one in the shop. She asked Strauss if she could use his office.

"Sure, but it's on the top floor and—it's a sty. Tony's not here. Why don't you use his?" Pointing toward a side exit, he said, "Just go out there. It's only a half flight up."

Leaving the two disgruntled lads to continue their own version of Cast in Hell, she followed Rex's directions and found herself inside Romero's lushly appointed, tchotchke-crammed inner sanctum. Even after closing the door, she could still hear backstage sounds and scraps of conversations quite distinctly, thanks to a small intercom speaker mounted in a high corner of the room. Easing into the producer's high-backed leather armchair, she got an outside line and quickly punched in the number.

After the second ring, she heard an efficient female voice answer, "Peakmont Police. How may I help you?"

"I'm trying to reach a Jack Breedlove. Is he still there?"

"Oh, yes." The voice on the other end thawed appreciably. "He sure is. Wait a sec." On hold, Jocelyn studied the four office walls, or rather, the framed posters of past shows that filled nearly every inch of space thereon, and smiled to herself. Whatever was going on at the precinct house, Breedlove had obviously made at least one friend there, which was no surprise. She often thought his surname was all too apt; while he was no lothario, Jack genuinely *liked* women and the feeling was usually mutual.

"Josh, that you?" He came on the line sounding agitated. "I got held up here. But I'm just leaving."

"How'd things go with Flynn and Kravitz?" she asked with a twinge of guilt.

Last night, as they were walking Cullen back to his apartment, Jack and P.J. had hit upon the brilliant ploy of enlisting Judith's aid on Big Al's behalf. While O'Roarke had agreed that Kravitz, if willing, would be a great asset, she had also said, "But you're on your own here, boys. No way am I getting in a car with that woman twice in one week." After enduring their joint protests and pleading, she had shrugged. "So call me pisher. Sorry, I'm just not *that* good a human being." Though she had, by way of appeasement, agreed to accompany P.J. to the playhouse and rendezvous there with Jack.

But now, hearing the strain in his voice, she felt she had left poor Jack in the lurch.

"Not too good," he sighed. "Flynn's got a better case here and knows it. So does Judith. If they arraign Bimpff, she doesn't think they'll set bail—given his record."

"Ah, that's rough," she sighed back, not surprised but sympathetic. "And they've been going at it all this time?"

"Uh-huh. Kravitz left a half hour ago. But they—they let me see Al."

"Oh . . . How is he?"

"How do you *think* he is," Jack snapped back.

"Stupid question. Sorry," she whispered meekly, feeling she deserved that one.

"No, no. I'm sorry. I shouldn't—it's just hard, Josh. Seeing him like that." He swore softly, then, in typical Jack fashion, poked fun at himself. "Actually Bimpff handled it way better'n me. I was like a teary dame in a thirties Warner's gangster flick. But Al said he'd been around this block before. And, compared to other lockups, the Peakmont police offered pretty nice accommodations."

"Well, that sounds good," she said, nervously toying with various knickknacks on the desk. "Sounds like he's keeping his chin up."

"I dunno about that." Breedlove's voice and spirits sank. "I think he was just joking around for my sake. He swears he didn't do it—but he doesn't really expect anyone to believe him—not even me. I could see it in his eyes. He's given up."

"He can't! That's *nuts*." Despondency she could understand, but defeatism made her wild. Snatching up a shiny glass cube, some sort of paperweight, she smacked it sharply on the desk top. It began to tinkle a melody, a tinny version of "You Light Up My Life," as the cube lit up from within and began blinking. Fumbling to find an off switch, she spluttered, "You just—you go back and tell him—tell him I'll slap him silly if he takes this crap lying down."

"Easy, tiger." Jack laughed, his spirits restored by the vigor of her outrage. If O'Roarke became sufficiently pissed off, he thought, Bimpff's chances of acquittal would increase greatly. "Hey, where are you? What's that sappy tune?"

"Oh, just—something Debbie Boone should be *deeply* ashamed of," she muttered, finally managing to silence the nasty thing. Once she did, she thought she heard something and glanced up. The door to the office was ajar now, but Josh, craning her neck, could see no one in the hall. "Forget it. . . . Hey, if Judith's gone, how're you getting over to the playhouse?"

"No prob. Terry—uh, Officer Murphy is going to drive me over."

"Ah! Let me guess, that's Terry as in Theresa and she's the one on the switchboard, right?"

"Clever woman," he replied, hoping that was a tinge of jealousy he detected in her tone. And hoping to capitalize on it, he added casually, "She's a sweet kid. Just out of the academy."

To his chagrin, O'Roarke just chuckled, "Well, love, they do say rookies try harder. But watch out for those handcuffs, okay?"

"You really know how to bust a guy's bubble, you know that?" But Jocelyn had hung up, still laughing, as Terry Murphy sidled up to him with doe eyes.

"Ready to go, Jack?"

From the flurry of noises on the intercom, O'Roarke knew that Act Two was about to begin. After restoring the knickknacks to their original position, she left the office and headed down the long hallway that led to the stairs. But her path was blocked by Manville Greer in full Captain Hook regalia.

"Manville! Don't you have an entrance soon?"

"Yes, but they've just begun the entr'acte and it's rather long. Besides, I heard you were here and wanted to have a word."

"Sure. About what?"

He lowered his black, bewigged head and raised Hook's heavily penciled, sinister eyebrows. "About this dreadful business, Jocelyn. So disturbing! And I heard—well, Amy confessed to me, after they arrested Big Al—she told you about our conversation in the wings. . . . I just didn't want you to get the wrong impression."

The wig he wore must have weighed a ton but, even so, Josh

didn't think it accounted for all the sweat that was running down both sides of his face. She pulled a Kleenex out of her purse to blot him and asked, "What kind of wrong impression?"

"Well, you must know by now, Rich and I had our . . . differences. But I had *no* idea Al was so, well, so on the edge. I'd hate for you to think I'd purposely egged him on in any way."

She let her hand drop and took a step back. "So you think Big Al did it?"

"No judgments! I make no judgments," he answered with both hands raised. "But the evidence seems rather damning and—and I want there to be no question of, uh, collusion, you see."

"Yes, I see." And she did but, at the same time, she was sorry to find that Frederick Revere's old friend was so afeared and so much the lesser man. Then she heard herself say with newfound certainty, "But there's no need to worry, Manny . . . 'cause Al didn't do it."

"You *know* that?" Now Greer took a step back, blinking in amazement.

"I don't know it for sure. But I'd *bet* it." She tugged on his ruffled cravat for emphasis. "And I am not a betting woman."

"Well, well—fine then. Fine." He straightened both his wig and cravat hurriedly as the entr'acte wound to a close. "Glad to hear it. Now, if you'll excuse me"—he made an elegant, courtier's bow. "My dastardly duty calls."

Watching the old pro glide down the hall to the backstage stairs, she had one of those existential actor moments, which came more frequently each year, when she felt herself standing outside her profession, looking in, and wondering: How can people so supremely gifted be so constantly insecure?

But there was no answer. Just as there was no reason why, inversely, someone like Rafelson could assume a role he was so atrociously wrong for with nary a qualm. Go figure.

Turning toward the nearby stairway that led back to the house, she stepped down. On the second step something caught at her ankle. As her body pitched forward, O'Roarke made a wild grab for the handrail, missed, and started falling, headlong, down the stairwell.

16

―――――

"Well, if that don't beat all," Tommy Zito wondered aloud as he hung up the phone. After a moment's consideration, he picked up the receiver again and punched in a long-distance number. "Can I have Phil Gerrard's room, please," he asked the hotel operator and debated, as she made the connection, how much or little of what he had just heard to tell his friend and superior officer.

On the one hand, Gerrard was on a very big case and certainly didn't need any outside worries to distract him. On the other, Phil disliked being kept in the dark about anything, especially anything concerning Jocelyn. It was a fine line to tread, and Zito decided he would work up to it gradually. But he didn't get the chance. Instead of getting Gerrard, he got his voice mail, panicked, and blurted out, "Hey, Phil, it's Tom. Thought you should know—Josh had a little accident out at Peakmont. Nothin' serious! Okay. She just took a header—uh, a spill down some stairs. But she's *fine*. Honest. But, um, maybe—maybe give her a call when you get in. All right? Bye."

Dropping the receiver back in its cradle, he wiped flop sweat from the back of his neck and berated himself. "Cool move, *strugats.* That'll really put his mind at ease." But what else could he have said? Zito hated talking to machines as much as he hated telling half truths. The *whole* truth was: O'Roarke, though not requiring hospitalization, was something less than "fine," and her fall might be something more than "a little accident." At least that was Jocelyn's suspicion, which he had learned courtesy of one Jack Breedlove, who had called him from the playhouse.

Tommy had been dumbfounded to hear his voice on the line.

"Hello, Sergeant Zito? We spoke once before. This is Josh's friend, Jack Breedlove." Coming right to the point, he had described O'Roarke's mishap, quickly adding, "But nothing's broken. She was damn lucky. Took most of the impact on her left shoulder. They've got the house doctor here strapping it up now."

"Uh, I see," Tom had grunted, slightly discombobulated. "Thanks for lettin' me know."

"One thing," Jack had said uneasily. "She's still pretty shook up but—but she thinks it might've been rigged. Her fall, I mean."

"What the hell else would ya mean?" Alarmed, he had shouted at the cowboy, "Did you examine the damn stairs?"

"Sure. As soon as she told me," Jack had replied with manly forbearance. "But I wasn't there when it happened. When I got a chance to check it out—well, a dozen people had been there before me. All I could see were scuff marks. On the second step—each step has a rubber tread on the edge, see?—the tread on that step was coming away from the cement. They think that's what tripped her."

"But Josh doesn't?"

"No. She says something caught her *ankle,* not her heel. As for the loose tread—"

"That coulda been done after," Zito had broken in brusquely. "To make it look—"

"Yeah, I know," Jack had broken right back. "That's why I'm calling."

"But why the hell are you calling me? Sergeant Flynn's the one you should contact."

"No. Flynn's the one *Jocelyn* should contact," Breedlove had whispered. "And she plans to. Once she's away from here. But *this* is my call. She doesn't know about it and I'd like to keep it that way, okay?"

"Why?"

"Why? 'Cause I'm worried about her, that's why!" Finally losing patience, Jack had snapped, "Look, you don't like me—*fine*. I'll live. But you do like Josh and you must know she doesn't imagine things. Which means—somebody's got it in for her. Right?"

"Right. Which is why you should tell Flynn as soon as—"

"Aw, screw Flynn! He's got the wrong guy behind bars so he thinks it's a wrap."

"Hey, listen—Vidal!" Tom had huffed and puffed, "Mike's a solid cop. Don't you go—"

"Hey, I'm sure he's a great guy," Jack had amended, his innate tact reasserting itself. "But, at this stage, I don't have a whole lotta faith in his judgment. I think *he's* gonna think—she just *tripped*. Why not? There's no proof otherwise."

Much as he was loath to, Zito had seen the other fellow's point and grumbled, "So, 'zactly what do you expect me to do here?"

"I dunno. I realize it's out of your jurisdiction. I just thought—" Sounding suddenly out of his depths, Breedlove had let out a long breath, then plunged. "I thought you might want to tell Gerrard about it."

"Come again?"

"You heard me. If she's in real trouble—I think he should know."

Hearing something so sad but so resolute in Breedlove's voice, Tom had had a tough time trying to maintain his mad at the guy. "Yuh, well—Phil's away now, ya know. So there's not much he can do about—"

"Oh, yes, there is," Jack had insisted. "Believe me, I've heard about this man. And—no offense to you, Sarge—he's the sort who can manage things at a distance better'n most of us can up close." Then he'd asked, semi-hopefully, "Or am I wrong?"

"Umm, no, that's pretty much on the money." After hearing this astute homage, Zito had had no choice but to begin liking this guy; so he'd added graciously, "And it's kinda annoying sometimes but the man can't help it. Anyhow, thanks for filling me in. I'll pass it on to Phil. You—you just take care of Josh, okay?"

"I will. Don't worry—and thank you, Sarge."

Doodling at his desk now, Tommy resolved in future to heed his wife's counsel more closely. Just the other night, when he had complained to her of O'Roarke's perfidy, assuming that a woman who had stayed married to her high school sweetheart for twenty years would sympathize with poor Phil, she had shocked him by saying, "Don't be such a baby, Zit. You sound like one a' the kids goin' 'Momma, who do you love best?' It ain't like that. Women've got more—oh, what's that Sally Field movie?—more places in the heart than men. Yeah, they *do*, Tom. And Josh'lyn, for all her smart talk, has got a big heart." He had begun to argue but she had waved a warning finger in his face. "Hey! She aw'ways remembers to send a card for each kid's birthday, right? So don't tell me! If she likes this Hollywood hairdresser guy, then he's worth liking. Period. End of discussion. I'm goin' to bed . . . You comin'?"

"Are you coming?"

"No, actually, I don't think I am. . . . Are you out of your *mind?*" Tottering up the stairs of the St. Luke's Hospice, O'Roarke beckoned to Breedlove with her one free hand. "Oh, come on! It'll only take a minute."

"Perversity, thy name is woman," he muttered, following her through the revolving door. After refusing to go the hospital in Peakmont, she had insisted, once they were back in Manhattan, on making this stopover. As good a Samaritan as the next fellow, Jack had still protested, "Why do you have to visit this guy—Eddie Isgro—*now?* You should be home in bed. It'll keep, Josh."

"No, no, I don't think it will," she insisted, heading for the front desk. "I hear Eddie's not doing too well."

"Has he got—?" He didn't finish the question; he didn't need to.

The anger in O'Roarke's eyes was offset by the despair in her voice. "Yeah, Dave, the sound man, told me today. Ed was just HIV-positive when I left town but he's full-blown now." This was the one bad part of coming back to New York; finding out who had gotten sick, gotten sicker, or died in her absence. On the whole, Jocelyn had been fortunate in that the AIDS epidemic hadn't claimed any of her closest friends—as yet. But she had attended the funerals of far too many peers and professional cohorts, an indecent number, she felt.

After the attendant behind the desk finally divulged Isgro's whereabouts, Josh turned round to find Jack had disappeared. Sickroom-shy herself, she couldn't blame him for wanting to sit this one out. Hell, she thought as she walked over to the elevator banks, Jack doesn't even know the man. Why should he have to go through this wringer. But, just as she entered the elevator, she heard him call, "Whoa, whoa. Hold it!" He slipped in just as the doors were closing, nearly decapitating a bunch of Gerbera daisies.

"Where did you get those?!"

"Gift shop." Running a finger under his collar, he shrugged. "He's probably got a bushel of 'em already. But, hey, they're colorful. And my mother always said you can't show up empty-handed."

Breedlove's mother had been a Vegas showgirl who had loved big wigs, big jewelry, and big men, but she had clearly also known a thing or two about the smaller niceties, and passed them on. "They're lovely." Josh reached out to touch Jack's sleeve, adding, "And you're a good son."

"Yeah?" He searched her face for signs of flippancy but found none. Every once in a while, O'Roarke said something damn sweet and meant it. And it flummoxed him, every time. Squelching a foolish grin, he asked, "So this guy, Ed? You two worked together a lot?"

"Oh, no! Eddie's a gypsy, king of the chorus boys. And, you know me, musicals aren't my thing. But we have a lot of mutual friends so we'd see each other a couple times a year—at opening nights and Christmas parties. Eddie's a—" She got no farther. The elevator doors swished open on the fifth floor and they found themselves directly opposite his door.

Entering the room, they heard a soft voice whisper hoarsely, "My God, is that Rocky O'Roarke? Home from the Land of Nod?"

"That's right, Eddie, 'tis I." Jocelyn threw her free arm out wide and sang, " 'Dolly's come back where she belongs!' "

The rail-thin man on the bed eyed the sling she was sporting and inquired wryly, "Well, is this a social call—or are you just here for repairs, darling?"

"No, Edward, it's a fashion statement." Pointing to the sling, she did a runway pirouette. "*Everyone* in L.A.'s wearing one. It's the postquake look."

Then she drew Jack toward the bed to make introductions. Shaking Isgro's clawlike hand, he murmured some vague pleasantries, inwardly marveling at Josh's drollery. The man in the bed was waxen, with only a patch or two of hair left on his head and large lesions on his arms and chest; a far cry from the chorus king she had last laid eyes on, Jack imagined. It had to be a cruel jolt, but she gave no sign of it. In fact she made no reference to his condition at all; just pulled a chair up to the bed, plunked herself down, and said, "Truth is, Eddie, the sling's a new prop. I had a little accident today—out at the Peakmont."

"*Really?*" Isgro raised himself up a bit and Jack thought he saw a trace of color come into his cheeks. "Well, considering Richie's 'little accident,' I'd say you got off easy. . . . how *are* things at my old stomping grounds—now that, ding-dong, the witch is dead?"

"Um, tense, a tad tense, I'd say. Tenser than an ex-nun at her first orgy, actually."

"Oooh, I bet! Tell me—tell me *everything*."

O'Roarke obliged in spades, giving Isgro an in-depth account of all that had happened during and since the fatal preview performance. Isgro hung on her every word and seemed to gain strength along the way. When she had finished bringing him up to speed, he snuggled into his pillows with a blissful smile and sighed, "Bless you, angel puss. I've been dying to hear the whole poop—no pun intended. But my friends think it might upset me too much . . . Hah! I always said it was only a matter of time before someone took a shot at Rich. . . . Of course, I didn't think it would be such a direct hit."

Somewhat shocked by how blithely a man on death's door spoke of one who had just crossed that threshold, Breedlove couldn't keep himself from blurting out, "Geez, was he *that* bad?"

Isgro gave him a look both figuratively and literally jaundiced, then nodded at Josh. "You tell him."

"See, Jack, Eddie's done—what? Maybe fifteen shows with Richie over the years. Always in the chorus."

"Nineteen shows, to be exact," Isgro interrupted. "It was steady work but it was not *fun*. Dress techs were always a fuckin' nightmare. And Rich treated us gypsies like—well, like gypsies! Like we were just chess pieces he could shove from square to square. I mean, I've worked with the giants—Jerry Robbins and Michael Bennett, God bless 'em! And *they* respected their dancers."

Eddie's cheeks were definitely pink now. Anxiously O'Roarke reached over to pat his arm. "I know, love, I know. But don't wear yourself out, huh? I need to ask you something."

Isgro instantly calmed down. "About what, darling?"

"The fire—the one that burnt down the playhouse. You were working there when it happened, weren't you?"

"You betcha. We were doing—let's see—oh, yes! *Damn Yankees*. I remember. There was a big flashpaper kind of effect when Lola made her first entrance. She came up from a trap door. So, finally, they assumed a stray spark had caught below the stage."

"That what you think?"

"Oh, pumpkin, who knows? It was closing night, see? And the cast party was at this god-*awful* club called Electricity—the kind of place where disco elephants go to die." He chuckled raspily. "You know, neon sculptures on the wall and strobe lights on the dance floor. Only in Peakmont, which prides itself on being behind the times . . . Anyhoo, it was a big bash and we all *got* bashed. So, sweetie, my memory is not the clearest."

"I see. And you don't recall anything about Al Brenner being a suspect?"

"Big Al? No, not at all. But—hold on—there *was* somebody the cops questioned. A new kid. Who was it?" Eddie stopped to wrack his brains as Josh poured him a glass of ice water. Breedlove, who had just put the Gerbera daisies in an empty vase, signaled her to let things rest, but she ignored him. After taking a small sip, Isgro recalled, "Whoever it was went missing from the party for a while. That was it. He'd been dancing with, oh, that rich Stepford wife—the Cat Woman."

"You mean the Ocelot—Nan Semper?"

"Yes, yes! Our Lady of the Eyeliner. The kid said he'd been with her and *she* said she couldn't remember. I chalked it up to Valium or booze. Anyhoo, the cops wisely let it go. . . . Oh, oh! I know who it was—how weird—it was Richie's understudy. Jimmy Treeves."

"Jimmy? You're sure?"

"Jocelyn, I may be dying but I am *not* addled—not yet, anyway." He blinked an eye at her like a wise old tortoise.

"I know you're not, Eddie." She gave a strange, strangled laugh and clasped his hand. "It just seems so far-fetched. If Treeves had just started working at the Peakmont, what possible motive could—"

"But there doesn't have to be a motive, does there? Not if it was a pyromaniac," Isgro said, pulling O'Roarke up short. Pleased by her reaction, he smiled wickedly, adding, "I had this cousin, Tracy. We used to call her the Little Match Girl—when my folks weren't listening. When Tracy was, oh, twelve or so, my poor aunt couldn't leave her alone in the house for two seconds! She was an absolute firebug. Nearly burned their place down *three* different times!"

"You're kidding! A little girl?" Jocelyn's eyes saucered.

"Not so little. Tracy was an early bloomer. Never even had time for a training bra." He *tsk*'ed in mock regret. " 'Course, she was more interested in gasoline than undergarments anyway."

"Eddie, stop! That's terrible," Josh half scolded, half shrieked, which gratified Isgro no end. "What happened to her?"

"Oh, Trace lives in Jersey now. With a hub and two wee ones. She's fine." Seeing the blank disbelief on both Josh and Jack's faces, he nodded. "Honest. Her folks took her to scads of doctors but it didn't seem to help much. Then one day, she just *stopped*. My family never talks about it, natch. Though, last Christmas, I did send her little boy a toy fire truck with a working hose . . . just in case."

Breedlove stood at the foot of the bed, slack-jawed, watching Eddie and O'Roarke dissolve in hoots of hysteria. Seconds later there was a starchy rustle at the door.

"Please! You'll have to keep it down in here," an imposing R.N. hissed at them. Glancing at her wristwatch, she frowned. "Actually, I'm afraid it's time to go. Visiting hours are over."

Chastened, O'Roarke rose quickly but Eddie tried to wave the nurse away. "Oh, come on—ten more minutes! We were just getting ready to play Catch the Catheter."

"Catch the—!" Josh quickly clapped a hand over her mouth to keep from cackling. Then seeing that, despite his high spirits, Isgro was growing weak, she bent down and softly kissed his bony brow. "No, no, we should get going. Thanks for the dish, Eddie."

"My pleasure," he said dreamily. Just as they reached the door, he raised his head and called, "Josh! You'll keep me posted about—you know?"

"You bet," she promised with a wink and a nod.

She and Jack rode the elevator without speaking. Once outside the hospice, Breedlove said one word: "Taxi!" then lapsed back into silence as they sped uptown. As the cab turned on to the Seventy-ninth Street transverse, O'Roarke swiveled around to get a look at his face.

"You all right?"

"Been better," he grunted back.

"I'm sorry, Jack. I hate hospitals, too. But I wanted to—"

"No, unh-uh!" He held up one hand as if to block her from his view. "The hospital's not what I hated."

"Well, I know it's hard seeing someone in Eddie's conditio—"

"Wrong again." Dropping his hand, he turned to her with blazing eyes. "What I hated was *you*, Jocelyn. What you did in there. Here I thought you were on an errand of mercy. Stupid me! You went there to *pump* the guy. I mean, playing detective is one thing. But that—that was just crummy."

"*Jesus.*" When she was seven, she had fallen out of the cherry tree in her backyard and it had knocked every bit of breath out of her; she felt the same way now. Sucking in air, she said, "That's how it looked to you?"

"Hell, Josh, you didn't even ask him how he's doing."

"I *know* how he's doing, Jack! He's dying, okay? And he knows it, too," she rebutted harshly. "So am I suppose to sit there and ask about his cell count? It's boring already."

"Boring! How can you—? God, that is so *cold.*"

"No, it's not," she said, stung. Then she fell back against the cracked vinyl and on hard logic. "Look, if Eddie *weren't* sick, would you still think I was out of line?"

"Of course not! But that's not the point," he protested hotly.

"Yes, it *is*," she insisted. "You're pissed 'cause I wasn't—I didn't treat Ed like he's got one foot in the grave. And you're absolutely right! I didn't. I treated him like he's still got one damn good foot in this *world*. And Eddie's world is all about theatre and gossip and who did what to whom when . . . So sue me." Done defending herself, she folded her arms and turned away from him to stare out at the inky darkness.

Jack shifted in his seat uneasily. The Russian cab driver, whose English was rudimentary but good enough for him to glean that a lady, an *injured* lady at that, had just been insulted, glowered at him in the rearview mirror. Not prepared to apologize as yet, Breedlove finally muttered, "I still don't get why you're so cranked up about a stupid fire that happened five years ago."

"I'm not—P.J. is," Josh said dully. "Some hoser put it in his head that it might've been arson. Even so, I don't see how it connects to Rafelson's death . . . except for the overlap."

"What overlap?" he asked, trying to keep his voice as neutral as Switzerland.

"Well, some people who were around *then* were also around when Richie died. Al had just started working at the playhouse and Jimmy Treeves was there, too. Like Eddie said, it's weird. Too much co-inky-dinky for my tastes."

"But P.J. *wasn't* around then, right?" He gave her a dubious glance. "Maybe that's why you're hot for this theory, huh?"

"No, that's not what I mean. It's—ow, shit!" She winced in pain as the cab hit a pothole, then, gritting her teeth, went on doggedly. "It's something about the chronology of it all. Rafelson's ascendancy at the playhouse began after that fire, see? That's when he was made permanent artistic director. And when we were with Eddie—look, this is gonna sound nuts— but I got this line from a poem in my head and it won't go away . . . 'In my beginning is my end.' "

17

"Okay, once more. From the beginning."

"Ah, crud! Come on, lady, gimme a break," Al Brenner pleaded to no avail.

Judith Kravitz shook her ginger-haired head and tapped a fingernail imperiously on the tabletop in the interview room. "*No*. We have to get all our facts straight before the arraignment tomorrow. If I can't show cause for an outright dismissal, you're gonna be staring at cement walls for a while, fella. Given your record, our chances of getting the judge to set bail are—"

"Rotten, I know," Big Al agreed dispiritedly. "Even if he did, I'd never be able to raise that kinda cash."

"Well, that's neither here nor there since it ain't about to happen," she replied briskly but not without some sympathy. One would have to look hard to notice, but Kravitz was in a kindlier frame of mind of late, due in no small measure to the ministrations of the excellent Josie Jessup. Having a clean, well-kept living space, she had discovered, was a soothing thing. She had also discovered that Josie was a fabulous cook. So they had negotiated a raise in salary, in return for which Judith got to come home to a hot meal every night. For the overworked attorney, it was like a dream come true; she had finally found what she had always wanted: a wife. Flipping to the front of the police dossier, she repeated, "Once more with feeling, Al . . . Why all these photos of St. Cyr?"

"I *told* you," he groaned loudly, "I just thought she was real cute, that's all. Skippin' around in that little white nightdress, you know?" Big Al squirmed in the metal chair that barely held his girth. It appalled him to be discussing such things with a woman, but he had no choice. "Look, some guys're into the high-heels-stockings-and-garters thing. Not *me.* I like girls to be, uh, girlie." Catching the sour expression on her face, he added vehemently, "We're not talkin' short eyes here, okay? Nuthin' like that. Those kinda guys make me puke!"

"I understand, Al," Judith assured him, adopting a Dr. Joyce Brothers air. "You just prefer grown women with a gamine quality."

"A what?"

Dropping the clinical act, she barked, "You like 'em to at least *look* like virgins. Right?"

"Oh. Uh, yeah, I guess. . . . But anyhow, those pictures. They're just extra production shots. They were lying all over the theatre so I picked a few up. That's all."

Brenner, hot under the collar and perhaps in a few other places, let out a long breath and hung his head in embarrassment. For her part, Kravitz was feeling a little overwarm as well.

O'Roarke had been right in telling Flynn that Judith was no generic man-hater. In fact, she liked men quite a lot, more than she ever let on in her professional guise. And she liked Brenner, both as a man and a client; liked his big size and big muscles and was pleased with his no-bull approach to his defense. That was the nice thing about dealing with ex-cons, she thought; they know the drill and don't waste time protesting their innocence.

At their initial meeting, Al had shook her hand and grunted, "I didn't do it but I know you don't give a shit 'bout that."

"You're right, I don't," she had rejoined. "What I do give a shit about is—their case has more holes than a golf course. Everybody and their Aunt Fanny wanted to take a pop at this putz, it seems. Cops picked you as the fall guy 'cause it's the easy way. But I'm gonna make it *much* harder for 'em."

"But what about P.J.?" Brenner had asked anxiously. "Is this gonna, like, hurt his case?"

"Pfft! What case?" Kravitz had waved a dismissive hand. "It was weak as water to begin with. So don't worry about his ass. Just worry about yours."

At the moment, however, Judith was worried about more than Al's ass. Or rather, she was worried about the effect that said ass, along with other parts of his burly physique, was having on her powers of concentration. Supremely professional and used to bullying her clients, she was baffled and distressed by the instincts, maternal and otherwise, that Brenner brought out in her; not the least of which was a strong urge to shred the shots of little Amy with her bare hands. These were emotions common to ordinary women but not to Judith Louise Kravitz, attorney at law!

To her credit, Al had no inkling of the tempest he had stirred in her teacup and she was determined to keep it that way. Casually leafing through the photos of the nubile ingenue— How do you *get* tits like that? she wondered—Kravitz coolly inquired, "And you didn't mind it? Amy having an affair with Rafelson?"

"Well, no and yes, I guess," Al muttered uncomfortably. "It's not like I was *jealous* or nuthin'. Richie was gay as a goose. I knew she'd figure that out sooner or later. But I didn't like him stringing Amy along the way he did. Just to get a performance outa her. That pissed me off."

"Must've pissed her off more—when she found out, I mean."

"Oh, sure. She was plenty upset. Wouldn't you be?" Brenner appealed to her with puppy-dog eyes and Judith felt her knees knock. "Walking into the wings and seeing him hit on one of the frickin' pirates! That hadda be a real—wha'd'ya call it?—a trauma for the poor kid."

"She's over twenty-*one*, Al," Kravitz hissed, letting a little asperity leak out before adding, "So, okay, St. Cyr finds out her Peter's a pansy and goes to pieces in her dressing room. But how was she the night of the preview—*before* the shit hit the floor?"

"I dunno. We said hi when she signed in. But she just seemed real quiet and she went straight to her dressing room." The tender look on his face made Judith meshuga. "After, things got pretty busy. I never saw her again, 'cept on stage."

"That so?" Kravitz quickly consulted her notes. "Not even during the intermission? In the hall or the scene shop, maybe?"

"Lemme think." Jutting out his lower lip, Brenner squinted, then said, "Nope. I guess she just stayed in her dressing room the whole time."

"Is that what she usually did? Is she one of those performers who isolate themselves so they can stay in character?"

"Amy? Shit, no! She ain't no Method freak." Al smiled for the first time in their brief acquaintance and Judith's heart stopped as she helplessly wondered how she could be so turned on by a man who used double negatives. "Amy likes to hang out in the shop and joke with the guys. Plus, we got a set in there and she likes to catch Geraldo."

Scribbling "ST. CYR = CULTURAL MORON" on her legal pad, Kravitz asked obliquely, "Does Amy share a dressing room?"

"Hell, no. Rich made sure she got a single."

"Uh-huh. And she doesn't have a big costume change between acts or anything?"

"Nah, she just adds a shawl for Act Two. Her only big change is before the final scene and it's done in the wings." Al paused and leaned toward her across the narrow table. "Why'd you ask?"

Keeping her tone as neutral as possible, Judith observed,

"Well, it's always interesting when people deviate from their normal pattern, isn't it? Especially when, in this case, it creates a window of opportunity for Ms St.—"

"Now just wait a goddam second," Brenner bellowed. "You gotta be out of your frickin' gourd to think Amy coulda had *anything* to do with this!"

"Oh, for cryin' out loud, what *is* it with you people?" Kravitz threw her Marks & Spenser pen down in exasperation. "You're as bad as Cullen. He holds out on me because he doesn't want to implicate anyone. *You* don't want to say a word to implicate him, either. Then you bite my head off when I so much as suggest that—"

" 'Cause it's a cruddy suggestion is why! Amy was just feelin' blue that night. Don't try to make a federal case outa it."

"Look, mister, that's my *job!* What you call 'feeling blue,' I call possible motive," she volleyed back. "And whether you like it or not, the hard fact is *somebody* cut that harness. You say it wasn't you. Fine by me. But you can't pretend it was done by gremlins. You can't have it both ways, Al! As it stands now, I can't claim your innocence without implying someone else's guilt . . . and Amy's a contender."

"Well, I won't help ya." Brenner folded his arms across his massive chest in a show of recalcitrance. "I'd sooner fry."

"Oh, *really?*" Judith jumped up so fast her chair tipped over. "Then get yourself another mouthpiece, Al. Because it is simply not possible for me to save your hide and protect all your little playhouse pals at the same time. You could call Alan-damn-Dershowitz and he'd tell you the same. Somebody's gonna hang for this. And if you are so goddam besotted as to sacrifice yourself for a possible—just possible, okay?—murderess, then I'm wasting your money and my time." Having had her say, Kravitz demurely uprighted her chair, resumed her seat, and faced Brenner with hands neatly folded on the table. "So what's it gonna be, Al? I know you're a loyal guy . . . but you gotta give up somebody."

For a long moment Brenner stared at the small square of

window above Judith's head. When, at last, he dropped his eyes to meet hers, Kravitz thought she detected some moisture around the rims. Her heart wrenched as he gave a hollow sigh and said, "You're right."

"Right here is our smoke house."

"Really? I'm guessing it's not for curing hams, huh?"

Standing in front of a small, gray cement building, Fire Marshal Rick Heppel smiled thinly at Jocelyn. "Good guess. This is where we conduct the final test for all our rookies. We pump it so full of smoke you can't see your hand in front of your face. Then we send 'em in in full gear to see if they can hack."

"Ah, their trial by smoke, so to speak."

"So to speak. Only it's not real smoke anymore." Heppel's mouth pursed in annoyance. "Couple years back the E.P.A. got on our case—said we were polluting the air."

"No!" Glancing at the heavy, exhaust-laden air on either side of the narrow island, O'Roarke clucked sympathetically, "What a crock."

"I know. Compared to the toxic emissions coming off the Throgs Neck Bridge *alone,* it's a drop in the bucket." Heppel shook his head sadly. "And, thing is, the fake stuff we hafta use now—just doesn't give a true sense of the claustrophobia, the intensity of the real thing. Most of the dropouts in each class would happen after the smoke test. And it was probably for the best. Now . . ." His voice trailed off in regret. Then he grinned and pointed to a big bird that had strolled out from behind a hedge. "Look—a pheasant."

"Well, I'll be damned," O'Roarke exclaimed. "How'd that get here?"

"Oh, there's a whole flock of 'em on the island."

Randalls Island, situated in the East River, was the home of New York City's Fire Academy, where fledgling firefighters are educated in all manner of things incendiary. The smoke house was only one of several buildings designed for that purpose. There was another building used solely for the purpose of teaching rookies how to execute window rescues, a very difficult and dangerous maneuver, according to Marshal Rick. Firemen working in one of the world's largest cities with a busy seaport and a gargantuan mass transit system also had to know how to extinguish boat and subway fires. To that end, the academy had one building with an interior that was an exact replica of a ship's, and several M.T.A. subway cars that trainees had to learn every inch of *blindfolded,* since power is always cut during track fires.

All of this, thanks to Heppel's concise and colorful descriptions, Jocelyn found informative and fascinating. None of it was what she was after, however.

Earlier that morning, after swallowing her pride along with some extra-strength Advil, she had put in a call to Tommy Zito. Anticipating a frosty reception in the wake of their own little conflagration, she had been surprised to find him cordial and concerned.

"Hey, Rocky! How ya doin'? Heard you took a fall yesterday."

"Yeah. Just a short one though. I'm achy but okay . . . Who told you anyhow?"

"Ah, you know—heard it through the grapevine," he had answered vaguely. She had let it go at that, assuming Mike Flynn had got word of her accident and passed it along. Nor had she mentioned her suspicions about a trip wire. Where his friends were concerned, Tommy was a world-class worrier, and she hadn't wanted him confiding those worries—which might well be groundless, though her sore ankle said different—to Phillip, who had more pressing matters to attend to.

"Look, Tom, about the other day—"

"Oh, Josh, do me a favor, huh? Just erase the tape. I was bein' a jerk. Stickin' my nose in where it don't belong," he had offered in contrition. "Mea culpa, 'kay?"

"Forgive you? Who me? Ms Meddlesome Fool." She had laughed. "Gee, that'll be real tough. Silly man. It's forgotten."

"Thanks . . . I owe ya."

"Lucky me then," she had chirped back fast. " 'Cause I'm calling to ask a teensy favor, Tom . . . You got any friends in the fire department?"

"Wha'?" After patiently explaining to her that, while cops and hosers were uniformed birds of a feather, they did not tend to flock together, Zito had finally admitted, "I do know one guy—Ricky Heppel. He teaches at the academy. Also does lots of P.R. and liaison work for 'em. I s'pose you could call him. He ain't a *really* arrogant asshole like some."

Fortunately, Heppel held Tommy in the same grudging regard and had agreed to meet with Jocelyn. Unfortunately, his teaching schedule kept him tied to Randalls Island for the day. So Jocelyn had made the long schlepp out to the academy.

Now, not wanting to waste any more of Heppel's time or hers, she sidled up, crablike, to her objective. "I don't know if Tom mentioned it, but I'm an actor and I'm—"

"Ac*tor?*" The fireman raised an ironic brow. "Not *tress?*"

"That's right," she replied firmly. "I think an ac*tress* is just an actor with really long hair. And, believe me, not all of them are women. Okay?"

"Hmm, yes. Point taken." Heppel, a highly dedicated professional, recognized and respected that attribute in others. "So, don't tell me. You're here to do research?"

"Right. I'm up for a part in a new play called"—she fudged furiously—"called *Fire at First Light.* So I need to find out all I can about arsonists and pyromaniacs. And I wondered—do you do what the F.B.I. does with serial killers, say? Like personality profiles?"

"Absolutely. Come on, I'll show you." Turning away from the ersatz smoke house, he led her toward the main building. "But I'll tell you right now—there's a lot of diversity in types."

"What types?"

"Well, an arsonist versus a pyro, for one. You must know that," he chided affably. "An arsonist's a pro. A torch for hire, period. A pyro's a sociopath, pure and simple. Then there's the other thing."

"Other thing?"

"Well, I don't want to raise any feminist dander here or anything," Marshal Rick joked, turning around to face her, walking backward toward the academy as easily as if he were facing front. Zito was right, she thought, these guys are cocky, but, damn, they're agile. "But there *are* some big differences between male and female pyros."

"Really? Like what?"

"The men, once they start torching—they *never* stop. Clinically speaking, they're almost untreatable. One-hundred-percent hopeless, most of 'em. Total obsessives."

"And the women?"

"*Whole* other ball game," Heppel said, warming to his topic. "For instance, women set fires in and around their home environment. Men tend to go out of their neighborhood."

"Hmm, interesting," O'Roarke murmured, remembering times when, rather than undertake spring cleaning, she had briefly considered incinerating her apartment. "What's the other big diff?"

Holding one finger aloft, Rick grinned mysteriously. "Unlike the gents, the ladies start—then stop."

"Yeah?" Since this gibed with Eddie's tales of Cousin Tracy, Josh asked, "So does that mean women are more treatable—or just less obsessive?"

"Umm, I dunno. We're just not sure," Heppel admitted ruefully. "It's real strange. See, a female pyro usually begins torching during puberty. Once her hormones settle down, it seems to abate."

"Oh, well, *sure!*" This made absolute sense to O'Roarke, who had once, during a very cold winter and an onslaught of P.M.S., hacked up a straightbacked chair and tossed it into her fireplace. "But what do you mean 'seems'?"

"I mean—it can start *again* . . . later."

"Like when later?" she asked, wondering if an emergency call to Eddie might be in order.

"Around menopause. Ain't that a kick?" Rick, pleased as

punch with himself, chuckled. "Male pyros are perennials. Women just do it during their, uh, big changes."

"Remarkable." She bridled. There was something in Heppel's tone that seemed to suggest that the hormonal, on-again off-again female pyro was somehow more disturbing than her male, depend-on-me-to-torch-till-I-drop counterpart. Still O'Roarke stuck to her theme and asked, "Any other disparities?"

"Yeah—one," Heppel said cautiously. "I know you're in the theatre and you must know a lotta—theatre types. But, fact is, most male pyros are queer."

"Oh, come *on!*"

"No, really!"

Taking her into the archives, he showed her various documents and crime-scene reports that backed up his theory, among them dossiers that confirmed that David Berkowitz, the Son of Sam, had been a long-term pyro before he began his killing spree. Still O'Roarke snorted. "I think you guys've confused sexual dysfunction with homosexuality. I mean, from what I'm reading here, these sickos couldn't get it up for *anybody*—male or female. Doesn't mean they're gay."

"Well, I have to disagree with you there," Heppel said brusquely. "I have to go with the statistics."

"All rightie. Swell. Fine," Josh said, swallowing a bit of bile. "How 'bout arsonists? Do you have psychological profiles for them?"

"Unh-uh. They're criminals—not necessarily sociopaths. Money's the main thing. Insurance fraud, all that stuff. So they tend to be faster and more efficient than pyros. And harder to catch. A really good torch can make a building go up so fast, the scent of kerosene's gone before the first truck pulls up, and so are any decent clues."

"So how do you catch them? The really good ones?"

"We don't always," Rick admitted. "A lot of times, we *know* it's arson but can't prove it. So we look for the money. *Somebody* hired the torch and those guys don't come cheap."

"What if the money's hidden," O'Roarke asked, "or too well laundered?"

"Then we lose." He gave her a wry smile. "And everybody's insurance rates go up."

"Next up, ladies and gentlemen, is Roy Laker on Hot Tamale."

A sandy-haired youth on a pinto pony waved his hat to the crowd in Madison Square Garden, then hunkered down to business as the buzzer went off. Two chutes opened at opposite ends of the arena; Roy and the pinto burst out of one just as a big steer charged out of the other.

Leaning forward in his seat, Jack Breedlove kept one eye on the action and one eye on his watch. Hot Tamale made a clean, sharp turn right in front of the steer and young Roy got his lasso around its neck on the first throw, but he had a ways to go to beat Texas Pete Taylor's best time.

"Why do they always have names like Roy or Tex?" P.J. Cullen crabbed at his side. "I mean, it's been *done* already."

"Don't know. Now shut up," Jack ordered. The cowboy was off his horse now and the steer was on its side. But Laker was having some trouble getting his rope around the back legs. Hot Tamale was doing his bit beautifully though, adjusting his position to keep the rope taut. Roy succeeded in cinching all four legs together and shot his right arm up in the air to signal the judges.

"Close but no cigar," Breedlove said as they waited for the official announcement. "The kid's good though—but the pinto's better. Cool as a cucumber." He kept his eyes glued lovingly to the horse as it trotted out of the ring. P.J. thought, Christ, that's how I look when a new trick walks in the bar. . . . Straight guys are strange. But what he said was: "Thanks for asking me along, Jack. I've never been to a rodeo."

"Huh? P.J., you're from Texas!"

"Yep. But somehow I just didn't *blend* with the rodeo crowd."

Cullen gave him a look of such mock mystification, Jack

broke up. "Boy, am I an idiot! Here I thought it'd give you a chance to visit your old stomping grounds."

"Well, if I *had* gone to one of those rodeos back home, I woulda been stomped—into the ground. So you're not too far off," P.J. quipped campily, sending Jack into a chortling, choking fit.

When he caught his breath, he said, "Sorry, sorry. You must be bored stiff."

"Oh, no! It's like a whole new kind of absurdist theatre," Cullen assured him with great sincerity. "Cowboys in Manhattan—I love it! Plus, their outfits are *fabulous*. I mean, the boots alone!" Fearing he'd taken his feyness, not to mention his footwear fetish, too far, he added, "But I hope you didn't leave Josh home on my account?"

"Huh? No, not at all. She's been to the rodeo. I took her once when we went to Texas. She thought it was a hoot—the announcers and the corny spiel they do. The clowns and the whole crazy hoopla." Nodding toward the arc-lit arena, he said, "Makes this show look like a tea party. But Josh isn't wild 'bout steer roping. She tends to root for the steer."

"Well, she's got a thing for underdogs, bless her," Cullen said. "Anyways, it's best she stay home and nurse that shoulder."

"You nuts?" Breedlove gave him an incredulous look. P.J. had known O'Roarke longer than he had. How could he imagine she would do something so safe and sound? "She's not home. She's out—somewhere." He waved a hand in the general direction of the greater cosmos. "Talking to some arson expert."

"She *is?*" Cullen was agog with admiration. "Jumpin' Jehosephat, she just doesn't quit, does she? Even after that little spill yesterday."

"It wasn't so little and it may not have been a spill," Jack said uneasily. In the interests of full disclosure, he told Cullen that Jocelyn's accident might not have been an accident after all.

"Christ!" P.J.'s eyes widened in alarm as he croaked. "But I—I don't see why the killer would go after her."

"I do," Jack answered instantly. "Jocelyn radiates a certain kind of skepticism. She *never* takes things at face value—which is what the guilty party wants us to do. So she's a magnet for trouble."

"God, I feel awful, just *sick*," Cullen moaned.

"How come?"

" 'Cause I *saw* something yesterday—jeez, Jack, I just didn't think at the time!—but I went by the foot of those stairs where she fell. Right after we called places for Act Two. And I saw someone at the top of the landing. Just a glimpse, then he took off down the back hallway."

"*He?* He who?" Over the loudspeaker, the announcer asked the crowd to warmly welcome the next roper, but Breedlove barely heard him. "Who was it, P.J.?"

"I'm not sure! I only saw him from behind. It could've been anybody."

"Come off it! You must've seen a shirt, slacks. Something that'd differentiate them—"

"No! Whoever it was, was wearing a monkey suit. That overall thing they've got us all in. Hell, all I saw was the back of a head—briefly—and it coulda been male, female, or animal. But there *was* someone there, outside Anthony's office. And whoever it was probably was eavesdropping."

"And if they didn't like what they were hearing," Jack interjected, "Would they've had enough time to rig a trip wire?"

"Sure. The playhouse is better'n a hardware store," Cullen said. "But, before we get into Watergate paranoia, let's pause a sec. . . . Josh was on the phone in Tony's office, right? So I'm wondering, who was she talking to and what was she saying that'd put the killer's knickers in such a twist?"

"She was talking to *me*, P.J. About Bimpff. So I don't see how that could—"

"Bimpff? Who's Bimpff?"

Once Breedlove had recounted his past with Brenner,

Cullen gasped, "You and Big Al? In Vegas, in high school? Bite me!"

"Um, no thanks. But it's true. . . . And knife or no knife, I don't think Al did it."

"Me either! I know he hated Richie's guts but, heck, I saw the big slob mist up watching *Old Yeller* once. That part where Tommy Kirk has to shoot—"

"Stop!" Jack yelled, then shook his head to dislodge the image. "Sorry. I still get worked up just thinking about it. Disney, man, they really knew how to traumatize a kid. . . . But I don't think we can build a defense around *Old Yeller*. P.J., tell me something, you say Bimpff hated Rafelson's guts. More than the other guys on the crew?"

"Like me, you mean?" Cullen gave him a shrewd look.

"No, no! I'm not trying to suggest any—"

"Why not? Hey, *I'm* the one who had the big fight with him, right? That afternoon, I'd say I won the Can't Stand the Star contest hands down," P.J. said candidly, then shrugged. "But Al's been there longer than I have, longer than most of the guys, except maybe Art Freed. So I figure he had a bigger backlog of resentment."

"Yeah, but how does Romero fit in that equation then? He knew Rafelson longer than anybody," Jack pointed out. "And Josh says the man's all torn up."

"Well, as ol' Yul used to say, it is a puzzlement." Propping his feet against the empty seat in front of him, Cullen scratched his head. "Tony can hardly bear to be around the playhouse ever since—didn't even show up to watch Jimmy yesterday. Which I thought stunk, actually. But, yeah, he doted on Rich all right. I can understand it on a professional level. To give the devil his due, Rich was a royal pain but he did know how to deliver an Ed Sullivan."

"A what?"

"You know." P.J. hunched up his shoulder, pursing his lips. "A reely big shew. The kind the matinee ladies love. In that sense, he'll be awful tough for Tone to replace."

"What about Freed? Isn't he a candidate?"

"Artie the ass-kisser? In his mind, maybe. And he's been givin' a way-cool impersonation of the heir apparent lately." Cullen chuckled dryly, pointing the toe of his boot toward the luckless roper in the arena whose lasso had just missed the steer's head by a mile. "But I'd say that guy stands a better chance of gettin' the job. Art was Rich's toady too long. I don't think Tony sees him as leadership material." Abruptly dropping his feet to the floor, P.J. declared loudly, "You know who *should* get the job?"

"Who?"

"O'Roarke, that's who! When I worked with her, do you know? She got the final dress tech down by *ten thirty*. Heck, the Peakmont crew would *love* her."

Pleased by P.J.'s enthusiasm, Jack still felt compelled to interject a note of reality. "But Josh has never done musicals, has she?"

"No, she hasn't." Cullen sighed blissfully. "It'd be a real nice change. And they could always job another director in to do the musicals—like Rich jobbed in people to do the straight shows." Then his shoulders slumped and he sighed again, sans bliss. "Never happen though."

"Why? 'Cause of the Burbage Theatre thing?"

"Ah, phftt! Ancient history. No, it's 'cause she's a woman."

"And Romero's a sexist?"

"No, not Tony. He's always liked her a lot. No, it'd never get by the board," Cullen intoned solemnly, then grumbled, "i.e.—Nan Semper. The Ocelot ain't a feminist. She likes to be the only cock-tease on the walk. If Nan had her way, we'd be back in Shakespeare's time, with boys playing all the women's parts. And it's only getting worse, what with her Big Change comin' down the track. Or should I say tubes?"

"P.J., get out!" Jack scoffed, smelling a little gay bitchery in the air. "How can you tell she's menopausal? I'm sure she didn't whisper it in your ear."

"No, but I know all the signs, believe me," he insisted as a new horse and rider entered the ring. "Saw my mother go through it big-time. I can spot a hot flash at forty paces. . . . Oh, hey! Look at the buns on *that* one. Can I borrow your binoculars?"

18

"Whoa, whoa, back up a bit. During the intermission, you went out behind the theatre and had a smoke with this guy, Big Al. But your friend Cullen wasn't around? You never saw him?"

"No. But that's not unusual." O'Roarke, with cordless phone wedged under one ear, sloshed iced tea into a tall tumbler. "As A.S.M., P.J. had a lot to do between acts. Like check the fly harnesses for one thing."

"I see. And he swears all the harnesses were in perfect working order when he did?"

"Absolutely. The three Darling rigs and both of Peter's."

"Darling rigs? Is that a technical term?"

"No! Darling as in Wendy, Michael, and John." Jocelyn laughed. "Silly wabbit."

"Oh, gosh, a thousand pardons. But with a profession that uses words like fresnels, panilight, and schelpitchka, you can never be too sure."

"Touché, monsieur." Lifting up the tumbler, she accidentally sloshed some iced tea on Angus' head, prompting the indignant animal to glare up at her accusingly. "Whoops! Sorry, Angus."

"What—the fur bag gets testy now if you speak a foreign

language?" Phillip Gerrard asked, only half joking; he wouldn't put anything past Jocelyn's cat.

"That's right. He's recently developed a virulent case of feline xenophobia," she quipped giddily. "Just yesterday I found him shredding old issues of *Paris Match*."

Coming home from Randalls Island, Josh had just reached the first floor landing when her phone started ringing. Rushing up the second flight, she had searched clumsily for her keys with her one free hand. By the time she had succeeded in unlocking her door, the answering machine had already picked up and Phillip's sonorous voice had filled the room. "Hey, Rocky, heard you took a dive. Just called to see how you're doing. I'll try back later."

For a moment she had stood stock still, torn between her delight in hearing from Gerrard and her dread of telling him about Jack's unexpected arrival. But delight had won, and she had snatched up the phone, gasping, "Don't hang up! I'm here. Just walked in the door."

After assuring him that she was bruised but unbowed, O'Roarke had been relieved when Phillip had immediately begun peppering her with questions about the Peakmont case. She had attempted to reciprocate by asking a few questions about his own special investigation, but Gerrard had shrugged them off with: "I just want it *over*. I'm ready to blow the Windy City."

Now that they were done joking at poor Angus' expense, he got back to business. "So, Josh, don't bite my head off but—how certain are you about your friend's innocence?"

"I'd say P.J.'s like Ivory soap. Ninety-nine point nine percent pure," she answered mildly. In the old days, O'Roarke might have flown off the handle, but time and hard experience had taught her better. Now she admitted, "Of course, there's always that niggling tenth of a percent of doubt. And, frankly, if it had been the *tumble* harness that was cut, the percentage would be higher."

"Uh, I'll take a gamble here 'cause I'm pretty sure there's no

Mr. Tumble in *Peter Pan* and ask—What the hell's a tumble harness when it's at home?"

As best she could, O'Roarke gave him a brief description of the differences between tumble and back-point harnesses in construction and use, winding up with: "So, if the tumble rig had been cut, Rich would've fallen on *stage*, see? Now he might've broken something but it wouldn't have been his neck!"

"I get it," Gerrard said. "So he'd be out of the show but still amongst the living."

"Right. And, while I can imagine P.J. being pissed off enough to want to shake Rafelson up good and, yes, maybe break a limb or two, I can't see him deliberately killing the man, Phillip. . . . He doesn't hate that hard."

"Okay, he's clean then." In earlier days, Gerrard would have felt compelled to play devil's advocate and point out that a man who has had his livelihood threatened might suddenly develop a big enough hate to do the deed. But he knew by now what an excellent judge of character Jocelyn was. Her loyalty to her friends didn't blind her to their faults and foibles. If she said Cullen was innocent that was good enough for him. "Which means this guy Brenner doesn't *need* an alibi for the intermission."

"Really?" Josh spilled some more iced tea but Angus jumped clear in time. "How do you figure that?"

"Do the math, darling. It's like one of those if a equals b and b equals c equations."

"Uh, gimme a hint here, Phil," she groaned. "It's been a long time since I took algebra."

"It's simple, sweetheart. The a factor is: Cullen's telling the truth and the harnesses were all fine when he checked them. While you were having a smoke with Brenner. So b is—correct me if I'm wrong, but didn't you say the house lights started blinking before you got back to the lobby?"

"Yes, that's right!" Putting the tumbler down, Josh smacked her forehead soundly. "Damn, I gotta stop taking those Stupid

Pills. Of course, *b* is: Al didn't have the *time* to saw through the harness. Intermission was almost over! So *c* is: If P.J.'s innocent, so's Al."

"Uh, *nooo*, not necessarily," Gerrard corrected carefully. "*C* is: Brenner couldn't have done it during the intermission. I think that rig had to've been cut later."

"O'm'god, *yes!*" O'Roarke felt like a woefully dense child who had finally found where Waldo was. "That makes so much more sense. During intermission, the work lights are on backstage. Other than P.J., *no* one could've spent that much time at those harnesses without being noticed. But once Act Two starts, the wings are dark. And with a show that size, all the commotion—"

"Sure. I bet even a crazed Mary Martin fan could have strolled backstage unseen and done it," he jested.

"Well, yes, I could have," she cracked back, but added seriously, "But that *would* be seen. The Peakmont's gotten very careful about those things. Seems that's why the crew's in uniform these days. If you weren't in costume or one of those grease monkey outfits, you'd be spotted for sure."

"But can't you narrow it down some? As far as time and opportunity?" he asked. "How long into Act Two before the—what's-it?—center-line harness is used?"

"No, see, that's the problem," Josh said, massaging her wrenched shoulder. "It's only used once . . . at the curtain call."

Phillip let out a low whistle. "So we're still stuck with most of the cast and crew as possible suspects."

"That's right," she agreed morosely. "And what we've got now—thanks to your brilliant reasoning, my dear—is a much longer time frame. Hence, a larger window of opportunity for the killer."

"Hmm, that doesn't bode well for Brenner, I'm afraid."

"Why not?" O'Roarke demanded. "Sure, Al could've done it. But so could a slew of other folks, all things being equal."

"Only they're not equal," Gerrard interrupted gently. "Al's the one with a record and the one who owned the murder weapon. In Flynn's eyes, that's enough to give Brenner the big edge . . . and I can't say I blame him, Josh."

"Well, that just *sucks*," O'Roarke protested, though with less vehemence than he expected, then lapsed into a sulky silence.

Even though the Chicago P.D. was paying for the call, Gerrard didn't feel it was right to spend taxpayer money on dead air, and asked, "Is the shoulder bothering you much?"

"Only when I move it," she muttered. To test her claim, Josh lifted the shoulder up an inch—then shrieked. Phillip flinched away from the receiver.

"What'd you do for chrissake—move it?!"

"Yeah, just checking. Hurts like hell," she said, but her tone was downright cheery.

"This *pleases* you? I hope you're not developing a masochistic streak."

"Nope. It's just sometimes excruciating pain can clear the mind wonderfully," she chirped. "Like that apple braining Newton."

"You mean you've *just* discovered gravity this second," Phillip teased.

"Stifle thyself, sweetie. I've just come up with an equation of my own."

"Do tell—but don't holler again, okay?" he asked, switching the receiver to his remaining good ear.

"All right, it's the *a* equals *b* bit again," Josh began eagerly. "This time *a* is: my accident was no accident. You okay with that?"

"Fine." Not only did he trust her hunch, Phillip had once seen O'Roarke negotiate a particularly slick and icy piece of Columbus Avenue in two-inch heels while other more sensibly shod pedestrians, himself among them, were going down left and right that windy December day. Thanks to an upstate childhood, she was as nimble-footed as a mountain goat. "You didn't fall, you were tripped. What's *b*?"

"*B* is: I was tripped by the killer. And *c* is: Al was already in custody! So he couldn't have done it—so he's not the perp."

She ended on a triumphant note, only to hear Gerrard groaning on the other end. "Why so glum, chum? Makes sense, doesn't it?"

"Yeah, that's what I don't like," he answered, then asked hopefully, "You weren't, perhaps—and I realize it's *so* unlikely—being unusually obnoxious that day, were you?"

"No! I was being a *lamb,* I swear," she swore, then paused. "Well, I did piss off the box-office guy a bit. But not enough to make him get off his fat duff and rig a trip wire. . . . Come on, Phil, it *had* to be the perp."

"Most likely," he demurred. No other woman in his acquaintance—hell, in the *world,* he thought—would sound so jazzed by the notion that a killer was after her. "I want you to call Mike Flynn right *now,* Josh!"

"Aw, phooey, what's he gonna' do? Nothing, that's what." She could hear Phillip building up steam but overrode him. "Look, I'll call, all right? And I'll tell him everything we've discussed. But, honey, Mike's not *you.* He's a good cop but he doesn't trust my judgment the way you do. Why should he? And you said it yourself—Al's his boy. And I had a little fall, nothing more, that's what he'll think."

They both knew she was right; a detective with a viable suspect, especially one as viable as Al, holds on to him the way a pit bull hangs on to another dog's throat. It was the way of the law enforcement world, and the reason why Gerrard always waited to make an arrest until he was damn sure; he, too, never wanted to let go but, even more, he never wanted to make the wrong man swing. Still he insisted, "Call Flynn anyway. If only as a courtesy."

"Sure t'ing, Lieutenant," Josh said with a Runyonesque accent. "Youse know I aw'ways cop-perate with da pole-ice."

"My ass! Just *do* it, Josh," he bellowed at the top of his voice, getting revenge for her piercing scream. Then a new thought struck him. "Hey, hold on. If you weren't making any waves that day, why would the perp go after you?"

"That's what I can't figure. It was such a potentially dangerous move. Not to mention plain stupid," she mused. "Here Flynn's got Al locked up, so the heat's off—why risk rocking the boat?"

" 'Cause you did *something* that panicked 'em," Gerrard said with a sudden certainty, getting that familiar tickling in the nostrils that came with his particular brand of intuition. "If it wasn't something you said or did downstairs, then it was something you said or did in the office."

"You're right." Remembering that sound at the door, O'Roarke shut her eyes and tried to picture what the killer had seen or heard. "Honest to God, Phillip, I *wasn't* snooping. Just sitting at Tony's desk, fiddling with a paperweight and talking on the phone." As soon as the words were out, she wished them back but it was too late.

"To whom? About *what?*"

"Nothing . . . nothing that had any bearing on the case—"

"Let me decide that," he preempted. "Who was it?"

"Jack Breedlove," she blurted. "See, he's an old friend of Bimpff's—I mean Al's." Then she explained, in as cool and matter-of-fact a manner as she could muster, why Jack happened to be in town and how he had gotten involved in the Peakmont mess, all the while trying to make it sound as if his presence was of no great consequence. It was the only bad performance Phillip had ever heard her give. Though he sensed she wasn't lying about the essential facts, he knew she was lying in her heart, and that was worse. "So, whether I like it or not, Jack's in this up to his neck. He believes in Bimpff."

She waited in dread for she didn't know what: accusation, recrimination, or simple hurt, which would be worst of all. She was wrong. The worst was the sound of Phillip's voice, far removed and neutral to the *n*th degree, asking, "Getting back to my question—what were you two discussing just then?"

"Oh, Christ! I don't—" Josh stopped, swallowed a sob, and tried to speak calmly. "We talked about Al. How he was holding up and his chances for bail—slim or none, we figured. Really, that's all I can think of," she fibbed. She'd see herself in hell before she'd bring up their silly bantering about Officer Terry.

"Well, think harder. 'Cause it's your ass on the line now," Gerrard said coldly. "I don't think it could have anything to do with Breedlove. He's too far out of the loop. It's *you*. You did something to rouse the beast, Jocelyn." She wondered if that last phrase was meant as a dig but couldn't tell. Phillip, when he wanted to be, was more oblique than the tip of an obelisk. And she couldn't call him on it; she had no right. "Try your damnedest to figure out what it was, okay?"

With that cheery advice, he hung up. Jocelyn spluttered, "But—but—" into the buzzing phone, then replaced the receiver dejectedly. Why didn't *Martha Stewart Living* cover this sort of thing? Probably because men were a lot more stubborn than grease stains. But how was a single adult supposed to handle her affairs in the nineties?

Jocelyn wasn't one of those women who wanted to have it all; she had never really believed in that concept, even in the eighties. If anything, her wants were rather modest: work, family, friends, and a longtime companion. Gay men got to have one. Why not straight women? But it seemed her simple wish to remain unmarried complicated matters, making her relationships with men somewhat amorphous. And men—more than women, she felt—needed clear categories, needed to know where they stood. O'Roarke, a big fan of clarity herself, still felt that this need stemmed from the days when women were chattel. "Either you are mine or you are none of me" seemed to be the underlying principle behind it.

Or maybe she had been a free agent too long to accept an exclusive contract.

"Balls! That's not it," she said aloud, giving Angus a good belly rub. For the two years she had been with Gerrard, she had never looked at another man or cared to. For that matter, the six months she had spent with Jack in L.A. had gone unmarked by any outside interests as well. In no way, shape, or form was O'Roarke a playgirl; she wasn't even a good flirt, except when a role required it. By all rights, Josh was the last woman in the world who should end up at the apex of a romantic triangle; she just wasn't cut out for it. She couldn't take the guilt, the feeling that she was playing fast and loose with someone else's emotions, when all she wanted ... "Well, there's the rub," she told Angus wryly. "What the hell do I want from these guys? And what do they want from *me*, huh?" The cat yawned with such elaborate disinterest that she burst out laughing. "And what does all this have to do with the price of Friskies, right?"

Deciding that action was the best antidote and God help her if she didn't keep her promise to Phillip, she reached for the phone and punched out the number of the Peakmont police. While the number rang, she wondered if, maybe, her problem lay in the fact that she found it difficult at times, especially on days when the news was full of massacres in Bosnia and cholera in Rwanda, along with myriad horrors at home, to take her romantic life all that seriously. This philosophical mood was shattered as soon as Flynn picked up the phone and barked, "Kravitz—that you?"

"Kravitz?" She could hardly hear him over the din in the background; other phones were ringing and frenzied voices shouted back and forth. "No, Mike, it's Josh O'—"

"Can't talk to you now," he broke in. "You'll have to call back. We've got a little crisis here."

"Wait, wait!" Before he could hang up, she asked urgently, "Whatever's going on—what does Judith have to do with—?"

"Judas Priest, Jocelyn! I can't go into it now," Flynn yelled, then lowered his voice to a whisper. "But if she contacts you, I wanna know *pronto!*"

"Contacts me? Why? Where is she?"

"That's what we're trying to find out." Mike swore under his breath, adding shakily, "Seems she's been—uh—abducted."

"*Seems?*" O'Roarke sat up so fast she jerked her shoulder sling but barely felt it. "You mean you're not sure?"

"That's right—we're *not*," he said through gritted teeth. "She may be a hostage—or she may be an accomplice. It's too early to tell—"

"Sweet Jesus! Don't tell me," she gasped in disbelief and fell back on old movie dialogue. "Al made a break for it?"

"Okay, I won't tell. . . . You'll hear it all on the news tonight anyhow."

19

"Ack'ally, it's not so much like he *escaped*," Tommy Zito said between sips of beer. "It's more like they . . . mislaid him."

"Tommy! How could they?" O'Roarke asked in amazement. "It's not as if Al's a little guy."

"Yeah. Go figure." Zito shook his head in sorrow over the ineptitude of his Peakmont peers. "From what I hear, your boy Brenner had 'em snowed. Model prisoner—course, he had practice—cooperative. Joked around with the guards. Never complained 'bout the food or nuthin'. So, well, they got to liking him."

"So they turned a blind eye?"

"*No.*" The little Italian snorted indignantly, but Josh thought he just might be covering a chuckle. "No, the arraignment was over. The judge *did* set bail, by the way, but it was way too steep for a working stiff. Anyways, they're outside the courthouse with him and his lawyer and there was some mix-up about the police van. It was supposed to be waiting for 'em but it wasn't there." At this point, Zito could not keep himself from pulling a face. "*So* one a' the two guards goes to the car radio to check on the van. Next thing you know—and I really can't fuckin' believe this!—Brenner's got his cuffs right round the little lawyers throat, see? Screaming that he'll snap her neck in two—which I bet he could do easy."

"Like a twig," O'Roarke agreed with a shudder, recalling those massively muscled arms. "Then what happened?"

"So he backs up to the lawyer's car, using her as a shield." Tommy scowled briefly. "Gets a little vague here . . . *Somehow* he manages to get her in the driver's seat with him in the back—still with the cuffs choking her. And they peel outa there!" Throwing his arms up in disgust, he exclaimed, "Feebs, the both of 'em! Jeez, Brenner's tall, the attorney's tiny, right? So they musta had a good shot at his head and upper body. That's what I'd've gone for if I'd been there."

"Then thank Christ you weren't," Jack Breedlove said fervently. Jocelyn held her breath, watching both men bristle.

Too impatient to wait for the evening news after hearing Flynn's bombshell, she had immediately phoned Zito and begged him to meet her for drinks as soon as he got off work. She knew that, by then, the cop grapevine being what it was, Tommy would have more and better info than any of the TV stations. Her mistake, she now felt, had been allowing Breedlove to come along for the ride. Not that she had had much choice. After the rodeo, Jack had called her from Madison Square Garden and, once she had foolishly let the cat out of the bag, had insisted on accompanying her. Tommy, while surprised to find Breedlove sitting next to O'Roarke in the booth at Barrymore's, had accepted his presence without comment, merely giving him a cool nod after Josh's introductions. For his part, Jack had been a model of decorum, ordering the drinks but keeping mum while Josh quizzed her friend.

But Zito's bit about taking a shot at Bimpff's head had pushed him past tact and tolerance.

"You got a problem with that, Mr. Breedlove?" Zito asked with ill-concealed scorn. "A police officer doin' his duty—trying to halt a fleeing prisoner *with* a hostage?"

"Call me Jack." Breedlove gave him a tight smile, adding,

"And, yeah, I do. When the supposed felon's a friend of mine . . . but I'm just silly that way."

"There's no supposed about it, pal," Tommy smirked. "Your buddy did time."

"For aggravated assault—when he was a dumb kid," Jack pointed out heatedly. "That's a far cry from premeditated murder, Sergeant. And I don't think he *did* it."

"Ah, call me Sarge," Zito mocked, making Josh want to punch him. "But it don't make a damn bit of difference what you think or what I think. Even if your friend *was* innocent before, he sure the hell ain't now. Forget escaping arrest—kidnapping carries almost as much time as manslaughter."

"But are they sure it *was* a kidnapping?" Josh interjected, trying to calm the male hormonal storm brewing. "You said you don't know how Al got Kravitz into the car. Maybe she was helping."

Zito drained his mug, then admitted, "Yeah, there's speculation 'bout that. But I don't know this dame. . . . Wha'da you think?"

Jocelyn and Jack exchanged looks, then turned to Tom as one and shook their heads. O'Roarke said, "She's a good, tough lawyer. Very aggressive on her client's behalf. But, like Rick in *Casablanca*—she sticks her neck out for no one."

"Well, fine." He nodded toward Jack. "Then your friend's fucked."

"Just wait a goddam minute," Breedlove bellowed with atypical outrage. "Let's put Al's past record out of our minds. Let's forget the friggin' knife thing, okay? Even in light of what he pulled today, where's the *hard* proof, huh?"

"Jack, Jack, take it easy," Jocelyn murmured. "Tommy's only telling you the way he sees it."

"Uh, yes and no, Josh," Zito amended mildly. Then he did one of those about-faces that always took her by surprise. "He's an escaped ex-con and prob'ly a kidnapper, too. I dunno if he's the perp, though."

"You *don't?*" O'Roarke asked the question since Jack's gaping jaw was temporarily immobilized. "Why?"

"Couple a' things," he offered offhandedly. "About the hunting knife for instance."

"What about it?" she asked eagerly.

"I can see the guy using his own knife and even leaving it in his toolbox," Zito said with a scowl. "It'd be a ballsy thing to do but he coulda got away with it easy enough—if it weren't for those bits of leather on the blade. Now lotsa bum-fuck felons would be too dumb to wipe the blade clean but not a bum-fuck who *hunts.*"

"Sure," Josh agreed instantly. "Never happen in a million years. Even in the dark, in a hurry, he'd wipe off that blade. It's second nature to a hunter."

"Right. Then there's the fingerprints on the handle."

"They're not Al's?" Jack asked expectantly.

"Dream on. Course they're his," Zito snorted, shooting Breedlove the kind of look Moe gives Larry. Then he relented. "But I hear they ain't 'zactly pristine. Mike got the results back this morning—before all hell broke loose—and even he said they're sorta smudged. So I'm thinkin'—"

"Gloves," O'Roarke filled in fast. "The real killer wore gloves and didn't bother wiping the blade 'cause he/she wanted to set Al up."

Holding thumbs and index fingers at right angles, Breedlove made a box around his face and demanded, "Isn't that what I've been saying all along? Bimpff was *framed.*"

Jocelyn patted his back as Tommy shrugged and said, not unkindly, "Yeah, maybe. Still, sayin' it and provin' it are two different things. But right now your pal's on the lam with a possible hostage. And the Peakmont boys've got enough egg on their face to make an omelette. So you'd better pray his lawyer brings him in. 'Cause they'll—"

"Don't tell me." Breedlove had seen enough gangster films

and spent enough time with Zito to fill in the rest. "Shoot first and ask questions later. Right?"

"You got it."

"Al, you've gotta give this up," Judith Kravitz hissed in the dark woods, sucking her right shoe out of a muddy patch. "It's crazy! You're gonna get us both *killed*."

"Me, maybe. But you'll be fine, Jude," Brenner said soothingly as he pulled her along behind him. "I promise. And I'll make sure they know you were—uh—coerced."

"If you get the *chance*, you mean," she pointed out anxiously. "Ow!" A low branch snagged her hair and Big Al turned round to untangle it.

Kravitz, Manhattan-born and -bred, had spent little of her life in the great outdoors, and now she knew why. It was terrifying, especially at night. The solid silence cracked intermittently by sounds the likes of which she had never heard, the dense, musky smell of the earth and the unbroken blackness all around her converged in a sensory nightmare that made her long for the nice, squalid comfort of, say, Rikers Island. She never would have guessed that the sunny suburb of Peakmont had so much woods around it. And Brenner seemed to know them, even at night, like the back of his hand. For such a large man, he moved surely and softly through the rough terrain. She could sense he wasn't just fleeing blindly. He had some destination in mind.

"Al, please, can we stop a sec?" she heaved. "I'm about to drop."

"Oh, sure," he answered, instantly repentant. "Sorry, Jude. I don't want to wear you out."

"What a prince," she cracked, only half in jest.

The ironic fact of the matter was that—except for the small faux pas of abducting her outside the courthouse—he had been a perfect gentleman all day, even going so far as to risk a short stop at a 7-Eleven to buy hot dogs and sodas before abandoning her car on a back road and heading into the hills. For a kidnapper, he had very nice manners, she thought. But this prompted Judith to ask herself if Al was really a kidnapper at all. Hadn't there been a moment—a nanosecond, maybe, when he was herding her into her car—when she *could* have broken free? No, impossible, she insisted inwardly. Her professional ethics would never allow such a slip, whatever her personal feelings.

Then again, her feelings had taken a deep plunge when the judge had set Brenner's bail at the quarter-million mark. At that point, Al had sucked in his breath as if he'd just gotten a sharp shot in the groin, and sighed, "That's it. I'm screwed." Judith had insisted otherwise, but he had gone zombie-like, not seeming to hear. She had kept up the pep talk all the way out of the courthouse, trying to shield him from her own keen disappointment. Given Al's appearance of total abstraction, she could understand why the cops had been off guard. As she had been, and she was no suburban rube. One moment Brenner had seemed like a man in a muddle; the next instant he had turned into the Incredible Hulk.

Still, she had to admit, it had been kind of thrilling. Even while pulling the chain of the cufflinks across her throat and facing down the cops, Big Al had whispered, "Don't worry. Just keep still. I'll take a bullet 'fore I'd hurt ya, Jude."

Kravitz couldn't help but sigh at the memory. Idiotic and sad as it seemed to her now, as she traipsed through a primeval forest, it had been the high-water mark of her romantic history; as near as she would ever get to being Maureen O'Hara in those pirate flicks with Tyrone Power or Douglas Fairbanks, Jr. It's all frickin' O'Roarke's fault, she cursed silently, watching the muscles under Brenner's shirt rippling in the moonlight. In the space of a week, she's turned my whole goddam life upside-down. New client, new housekeeper, new infatuation. And, gee, let's not forget, new chance for disbarment here. I really should thank her—or kill the interfering bitch.

But Judith knew she was soundlessly whistling in the dark. Reaching out to tug Brenner's shirt, she said, "Listen, as your attorney, I'd kind of like to know where we're headed. . . . if that's not asking too much."

"Oh, shit, I thought you *knew!*" Al spun round to face her with hands clapped to his cheeks apologetically. "I told you, Jude!"

"If you did, I forgot," she hissed. "But then kidnapping does weird things to my short-term memory."

"Aw, gee, I wish ya wouldn't call it that—kidnapping." He shivered with distaste, shifting his weight from one foot to the other like a lumbering, dancing bear. "Yeah, okay, I meant it to *look* that way . . . but I thought maybe you wanted to come along."

"What—for the *ride?*" Drawing his head back as if she had just smacked his nose with a rolled-up newspaper, Al looked so stricken Kravitz felt like putting her arms around his big, broad shoulders, but she fought the urge valiantly. "Look, either leave me here now—No! I take that back. Leave me by some road, with lights and traffic and stuff. Or tell me what the hell you think you're up to."

"Well, it's not so much a plan really," Brenner confessed, scratching his head. He paused to pluck something from the nape of his neck and flick it away.

"What was that—a tick?" Judith asked, then moaned, "Oh, God, we're both gonna get Lyme disease!"

"No, no, it was just a burr, honest," he said soothingly.

But Kravitz, despite all her tough talk, was starting to cave. Fear, exhaustion, and hunger ganged up on her, making her legs wobble and her throat constrict. She heard a whimpering sound like the cry of a small woodland creature caught in a trap, then realized in horror that she was the woodland creature and the whimpering was coming from her. Brenner, almost as horrified as she, held her gingerly as the whimpers escalated into sobs. One of those men who had the good sense to keep mum and let a lady have a good cry when she needed one, he still grew anxious as Judith's waterworks kept gushing and growing. What poor Al didn't know was Kravitz hadn't had a really decent wail in years. She had permitted herself a sniff here and a tear or two there, usually while watching some soppy Hallmark commercial, but never a genuine, no-stops blubber. Now the dam had burst and he was caught in the flood.

Never a smooth talker where women were concerned, Al had no idea how to coax or cajole her with words. Instead, rocking her back and forth awkwardly, he started to sing off key, "Hey, Jude, don't make it bad . . ." He kept singing and rocking until the tiny lawyer relaxed in his arms and even hummed along on the chorus. "Na, na, na, na, nanna-nah na. Nanna-nah na . . ."

They were doing a little, shuffling two-step now, both lost in the moment and completely oblivious to the absurdity of it. Then, as they wound up for the big finish, Brenner did something he had never done before in his whole life—he *dipped*. Surprised and delighted, Judith threw her head back and giggled like a schoolgirl, and kept on giggling, unable to stop herself. As with crying, she hadn't allowed herself a really rib-aching guffaw for far too long. But, hey, she figured, when you find yourself dancing in the dark with an escaped prisoner who makes you so giddy you don't give a damn about your precious career, it's time to "laugh, clown, laugh."

Grinning with relief, Al asked, "So you okay now? Want me to take you to the nearest intersection? There's a gas station where you can call—"

She nixed the notion with a wave of her hand and said with a levity that was wholly unlike her, "Forget it. I've come this far. Besides my shoes are already shot and I'd never get home in time to catch *Headbangers Ball*."

"You like that show, too? Jeez, I'd never guess." Even in the dark, she could see his eyes light up. "Who's your favorite grou—"

"Uh, Al, let's talk rock and roll another time, huh?" He was cute as the dickens, she thought, but not the canniest of creatures. "So where are we headed?"

"It's not far, Jude." He jerked a thumb up and to the left. "Just over this next ridge here."

"Oh, great. Just another quarter mile *uphill.*"

"I could carry ya! Want me to carry ya?"

"No . . . but you're an angel to offer," Judith cooed coquettishly, then wondered, Christ, who am I? Ann-Margret, all of a sudden? Lowering her voice, she added, "Lead the way, *mon capitain.*"

"Peakmont police found the abandoned car on a back road around five p.m. Sometime before, it seems, the escaped prisoner and his hostage stopped in a 7-Eleven for—um—hot dogs and sodas." The local news anchorman with the bad toupee coughed discreetly, then continued, "Since then there have been no other sightings of the two." Grainy, black and white images of Brenner and Kravitz popped up on the TV screen. Al's was a mug shot. Judith's looked like an old yearbook photo. "Though Brenner is presumably unarmed, he is assumed dangerous. Police advise Peakmont residents to take extreme caution and phone 911 immediately if—"

"Oh, Lord! I can't listen to anymore." Hitting the mute button on the TV remote, Anthony Romero rubbed his eyes with the heels of his palms. "This is a total *nightmare.*"

"Ah, come on, Tony," Rex Strauss cajoled, helping himself to more of Romero's malt whiskey. "It could be worse."

"Worse! *How* worse?" Romero nearly rocketed out of his recliner. "Harry Brill hasn't returned any of my calls today. With Al on the loose, there's absolutely no way we're gonna get a big name to step into that role."

"But you don't *need* one," Rex insisted, topping up Tony's glass, too. "That's what I keep telling you! You should've seen Jimmy the other day. He's gonna be great as Peter."

"So what? So was Richie." Romero choked up and took a sip to clear his throat. "It still won't help move the show to Broadwa—"

"Oh, yes, it *will.*" For emphasis, Strauss dropped a chubby fist on the coffee table. "Okay, you can hate me for saying this but—hard fact is—it was a lousy show with Rich in the lead.

He was too fey for days, Tone, and you know it. At least, with Treeves, it *works*. And the big money can see it works. They'll put their own star in later."

"I don't know, I don't know," Tony whispered. "I just feel like it's all been such a miserable waste."

"Oh, hey, you and me *both!*"

The two men bolted up as the French doors on Romero's veranda suddenly shot open and they were confronted with the sight of Al Brenner nudging the small, ginger-haired lawyer they had just seen on TV in front of him. She seemed to have something digging into her back, what they couldn't tell, and a look of frozen supplication on her face.

To ease their minds, Al said, "Don't worry, guys. I ain't out for blood—just information."

"Aw, Al, for chrissake," Rex erupted, "This is nuts! You're only making it worse for yoursel—"

"Rex, stuff it! Okay?" Brenner growled. "You got no damn idea what *worse* is for an ex-con. I didn't off the twerp and I can't go back *in,* see? So I'm just taking my best shot here while I can. And I'd really, really 'preciate it if you guys would help out."

Feigning acute terror, Judith smiled tightly and whispered, "I think he's got a point, don't you?"

Using her as his faux shield, Brenner circumnavigated the room and unhooked the phone. Then he turned to his employer with a sheepish grin and said, "Hey, Anthony, I'm sorry but we're starved. You got anything in the fridge?"

The four of them sidled awkwardly as one into Romero's large country kitchen. Once there, Al detached the wall phone while Tony began making focaccia sandwiches. Rex Strauss, feeling more curiosity than fear, uncorked a bottle of pinot noir and, nodding in Judith's direction, asked, "Al, why the hell'd you do it? You figured she couldn't handle your defense or what?"

Kravitz bristled but before she could speak, Brenner bellowed, "You just leave her the fuck outa it, okay! She's one damn fine mouthpiece. But she can't bust a frame-up all by herself."

"Frame-up?" Romero looked up from his sandwich-building. "Al, honestly, it's not that I think you did it. But how can you think someone deliberately set you up."

"I'm the one with a record. It was my knife they used." Brenner snatched up a sandwich and devoured half of it in one bite. Chewing ravenously, he mumbled, "Call me paranoid."

"Call you dimwit is more like it," Strauss snapped at his cohort, to Romero's acute discomfort. Tony didn't think a kitchen filled with sharp instruments was a wise place to harangue a desperate man.

"Rex—*please*," he hissed. "The man's been through an ordeal."

"Of his *own* making," the set designer shouted in exasperation. "For pity sakes, why didn't you just sit tight, Al?"

"Why don't *you* sit tight and shut up for a minute?" Brenner clapped a hand on the diminutive man's shoulder and shoved him down onto a stool, then turned his gaze to Romero. "I need to ask you something."

"Sure," he said, handing around the plate of sandwiches. Romero was the sort who, in dire straits, might lose his reason but never his manners—and he was, after all, the host for the evening.

"That night, when you were up in your office with the Ocelot?" Al paused until he got a nod from his employer. "She never left *once*? Even for a minute, to take a leak or somethin'?"

"No!" Tony's eyes widened with surprise. "Why do you ask?"

"Well, see, I went by your office during Act One and I heard you two in there." Embarrassed, he looked down at the stone floor. "I, um, heard her rippin' you a new asshole."

Rex smiled sweetly at Judith and confided, "That's our Nan."

"Well, I wouldn't go *that* far," Romero protested mildly. "But, yes, we were having an argument about replacing Rich. Though I don't see what that has to do with—"

"Lemme me tell ya what I *see*," Brenner broke in. "What I've been seein' for years, okay? And that's—whatever the Semper bitch wants, she gets. Only one who could hold a candle to her on that score was Rafelson and that's why she hated him. And if she doesn't get her way and it's *your* fault she doesn't . . . watch out. Somethin' bad'll happen."

"Like what?" Anthony asked with polite skepticism. "Give me a for instance."

"For instance—your theatre burns down."

"Whaaat?" Rex bounced off the bar stool, goggle-eyed.

"Now, *really!*" The outrageousness of Al's remark made Tony tsk sadly. "No offense, but I think you're grasping at straws. Richie wanted the new playhouse, not Nan. You forget."

"Unh-uh. *You* forget, Anthony," Brenner insisted. "I remember it like yesterday 'cause I'd just started workin' there. The Ocelot just didn't wanna *pay* for a new building. And the way it worked out—she didn't hafta. The insurance company did."

"Good Lawdy, Miss Maudy, what a *scream!*" The other three looked on in dismay as Strauss did just that, then laughed so hard he had to hold on to the counter to keep from falling. Catching his breath, he mugged dramatically. "Can't you just see it? Little Nanny backstage in the dark in her best de la Renta, popping Valium and desperately trying to ignite an old flat with her Cartier lighter! Oh, oh, what an image, I *love* it."

"Hey, moron, I ain't sayin' she did it herself," Brenner said, taking great umbrage. "She'd be too afraid of breakin' a nail. But she coulda found somebody."

"How—through the *Peakmont Pennysaver?*" His patience and good breeding almost exhausted, Romero rebuked, "I've never heard such bilge. You'll have to do better than *that.*"

"Okay. How about her and Jim Treeves?" Al jogged the other men's memory with a piercing look. "He was the new boy on the block then. And at that cast party, she glommed onto him like an octopus in heat all night. But it was no dice, Jimmy told me so himself. Then the cops come round checkin' everybody's alibi and, all'va sudden, the Ocelot can't recall bein' with the guy. Don't tell me *that* wasn't payback time!"

Romero said nothing, merely wrinkled his nose and started slicing more focaccia. But Rex tapped his arm and said, "There's something to that, Tone. You know she's got a vindictive streak wider than I-90. . . . Makes you thank Christ you're queer, doesn't it?"

"Ah, *va fan cul*," Tony swore savagely, throwing down the knife, which skidded across the counter. Out of the corner of her eye, Judith saw Brenner quickly pocket it for insurance since, unbeknownst to the other two, he had merely been holding a nail file she had supplied to her back all this time. Romero raged on, "So the woman's a horny rich bitch—so *what!* This town's packed to the rafters with 'em. So she made a play for Treeves and was too bombed to remember it the next day. Big damn deal."

"No, unh-uh. There's a pattern here," Al said softly, taken aback by the producer's outburst. "See, I think she pulled the same shit on me."

Romero froze but Rex, all agog, swiveled around like a lazy Susan. "My, my, still waters still do run . . . Spit it out, son."

"Well, it's like this." Brenner coughed and took a deferential step away from Judith as if trying to shield her from possible contamination. "Show before this—at the cast party again—I, uh, I guess she musta run outa fresh meat."

"Uh-huh, yes," Strauss concurred. "*The Boyfriend* was very fairy-friendly. . . . So?"

"So she hit on me that night," Al half-barked, half-wailed. "And it was just—creepy! I hadda be polite, right? But she was, like, rubbin' up and—and gropin' me. I didn't know what to do. I just felt—"

"So *cheap*," Rex asked archly.

At which point Kravitz dropped her hostage demeanor and snarled, "Have you ever *considered* joining the Carmelites, Mary? 'Cause it'd be a relief to the rest of us." Romero choked back a laugh as Strauss' pupils spun like gyroscopes. For his part, Big Al looked down at Judith and, despite the flakes of dandruff he saw on her scalp, thought: What a bitchin' broad —Without realizing it, he fell in love with her that second. Tilting her head up at him, she prompted, "What were you saying?"

"Huh?—Oh, yeah. She was all over me and I didn't know what to do. So, finally, I tell her my mom's birthday's coming up and I say—'What should I get her?' Semper bats those dead mink things on her lids and sez—'Why ask me?' I go—' 'Cause I think you're 'bout the same age.' "

Strauss and Romero, both gay men of a certain age, winced in unison. Rex croaked, "Smooth move, Al. What did she do then?"

"Went to the john. Never spoke to me again, that night or since." Brenner rubbed two fingers between his brows. "I thought I got off easy till this shit happened."

"Oh, Al, Al, Al," Tony moaned. "You can't seriously think Nan killed Richie just to get back at you?"

"Hell, no." He sighed. "She killed him 'cause she wanted him *out*. Gone. But she framed me 'cause I'd pissed her off . . . and I had the record."

Romero stretched out a hand, palm up, across the counter and said earnestly, "But Nan didn't *know* you had a record, Al. What's more, she had no reason to kill Richie. She'd already won that fight—the whole board was behind her—we were going to replace him. And last but not least . . . I swear to you on my mother's grave, Semper *never* left my office."

"Oh." Al's "oh" sounded like a balloon deflating and Judith felt her hopes deflating with it.

But Rex Strauss lifted his head and her spirits by exclaiming, "Still it's weird about yesterday. O'Roarke taking that spill down the stairs right after she came out of your office. . . . You hear about that, Tone?"

"No! Was she hurt?"

"Wrenched a shoulder pretty bad. But don't worry," Rex assured his boss. "Josh won't sue. She's not the litigious type."

Kravitz, being the litigious type, said, "She *should*. Especially if the injury causes her to lose gainful employment . . . and if the handrails aren't up to code."

"The handrails are *fine*," the set designer insisted. "Besides O'Roarke thinks maybe somebody rigged a trip wire. And I *did* see Nan's BMW in the parking lot yesterday."

"Horse shit. The whole thing's total horse shit," the producer declared with supreme disdain. "What could she possibly have against O'Roar—"

"*Quiet,*" Judith bellowed, snapping the three men to attention. "Listen."

At first Al heard nothing and had to strain his ears. But he had to hand it to her, his attorney's hearing was as sharp as her tongue. From far off came the faint wail of a police siren, and it was getting louder.

20

"Is everybody *happy?*" Richie Rafelson's leering face filled the small TV screen in Eddie Isgro's tiny Chelsea apartment. "It's party time!"

"*Gawd,* this is too creepy!" Ensconced in an overstuffed armchair, P.J. groaned and covered his eyes. "I don't think I can watch."

"Then don't. Just keep still so I can," O'Roarke ordered as she adjusted the volume. "You didn't have to come, you know."

"Well, I thought it'd be a kick," he said, peeking through his fingers at Rafelson gyrating on a brightly lit dance floor. "And it is—in the gut."

"Shh," Jocelyn hissed as Eddie, grinning devilishly and glowing with health, stepped up to the camera, jabbed a thumb in Rich's direction, and yelled over the pounding music, à la Robin Leach, "Yes, folks, it's the fabulous *Damn Yankees* cast party. Here at the fabulous club, Electricity—Donna Summers' retirement home!" Looking over his shoulder at Rafelson doing a rather grotesque imitation of John Travolta circa *Saturday Night Fever,* Isgro sighed and said, in his own voice, "Christ—someone give that boy a long scarf and a Bugati."

O'Roarke couldn't help herself; unseemly though it was, she hooted with laughter. Cullen gave her a puzzled look. "Huh? I don't get it."

"What? You've never seen *Isadora*? With Vanessa Redgrave?" P.J. shook his head and Josh sniffed. "Ignoramus."

The camera, whether by design or accident, cut away from Isgro and swept around the room, taking in the flashing lights, the spinning mirrored ball, and the generally garish decor as P.J. asked, "So was that your friend? The one who's got—?"

"Yeah, that's Eddie," she answered quickly, swallowing a sudden lump in her throat. "King of the gypsies."

"What a goddam shame," Cullen said sadly. "And he's the one who made the tape?"

"Well, yes and no."

In point of fact, Ed hadn't made the tape. It had been shot by his boyfriend of the moment, a video buff whom Isgro had given a camcorder that Christmas. As Eddie had explained over the phone early that morning, "Hector wasn't in the biz and he was very shy, didn't like to mingle much. But I dragged him along to the party and he taped it—his way of being a part of things without actually having to talk to people, see?"

"You always did like the strong silent type," Jocelyn had said brightly, stifling a yawn. He had phoned at seven thirty, sounding alert and eager, so she hadn't wanted him to know that she had been up until nearly two, scanning the late news to no avail for any reports of Al and Judith's whereabouts, and was now only semiconscious.

"Well, dear Hector was a little *too* silent. Put a wig on him and he'd have made a swell Johnny Belinda. So, since I do like to hear the occasional monosyllable, we soon parted company. I forgot all about the tape till after your visit." Eddie paused to get his wind back, then said, "I thought maybe you'd like to go over to my place and take a peek at it? My neighbor can let you in."

"Yeah, that'd be great," Josh had answered instantly, not because she seriously thought the video would contain anything germane to Rafelson's murder but because Eddie had sounded so pleased and perked up; disappointing him had been completely out of the question. And what the hell, she had thought, dragging herself into the shower. Can't hurt.

Wrong again, O'Roarke, she told herself as her gaze drifted around Isgro's memorabilia-filled home. One wall was completely covered with snapshots of him over the years in sundry shows: Eddie mugging with Chita Rivera, Eddie sticking his tongue in a grinning Liza Minelli's ear, Eddie bumming a cigarette from Bob Fosse . . . It hurt like hell.

And all the while she could hear his running commentary, though the sound was tinny and diffused, as the camera zoomed in on various revelers. At one point the screen showed a young chorine, twitching and twirling by herself on the dance floor, gazing up at a mirrored ball, mesmerized, as Isgro whispered confidentially, "Either our Mandy has had one tequila sunrise too many or she has suddenly contracted Mary Hart syndrome."

"Huh? What's he mean?" P.J. asked, once again breaking his vow of silence. "What's Mary Hart syndrome?"

"Don't you know?" Chuckling, O'Roarke pointed at the TV. "Right around then, there was this news story about a woman somewhere in the Midwest, I think, who went into a kind of seizure whenever she heard Mary Hart's voice on *Entertainment Tonight*. Ol' Mary, true humanitarian that she is, even apologized about it on the show one night."

"Oh, you are making this *up*," Cullen cried. Josh raised her hand in an honest-injun gesture, prompting P.J. to snort. "Well, it had to be a put-up job!"

"Uh, actually, no," she answered, still watching the screen. "I remember talking to my brother about it. My brother the—"

"The *doctor*," he intoned with mock solemnity. "Yeah, so?"

"So it seems that woman had some rare nervous disorder that could be triggered by certain sounds." Out of the corner of her eye, she saw the patent disbelief on his face and quickly nodded, "Really! It can be sound or a visual pattern that triggers it."

"Oh, *yeaah?*" Cullen wasn't from Missouri but he did have to be shown. "So what's the actual medical term for it then?"

"Uh, what'd he call it?" Squinting at the screen, trying to make out some blurry images in the background, Josh shook her head. "It was—I dunno—a something something partial something . . . a type of epilepsy."

"Great—now can you sell me some real estate in the Everglades?"

"Can I get you to just shut your trap?" she retorted. "That's the real question. Come on, P.J., I'm trying to *watch!*"

Knowing he had better behave since Jack Breedlove, mightily concerned about ol' Bimpff, was out renting a car to take the three of them to Peakmont in an hour, and Jocelyn, if pushed too far, was very apt to get spiteful and make him take the bus, he wisely decided to cease and desist. But no sooner had he settled back to watch than he spied a familiar figure and shouted, "Look—there's Tony way in the corner."

"Yes, that's who it is! I wasn't sure." O'Roarke made a mental note to get her eyes examined, then asked, "Who's he talking to?"

"Uhh, I can't tell," Cullen said, leaning in. "A tall guy. Might be Art Freed. But I've never seen Artie in a suit that good." Even on a small screen with fuzzy images, P.J. could spot style. Then he hiccuped, "Hoo-ee, look—there's Jimmy and the Ocelot!"

"God, you're good." O'Roarke spotted Treeves but, given the strobe light effects going on the dance floor, could barely make out the woman soldered to his side. "How do you know it's Nan?"

"The *streaks,* honey chile," P.J. said as if it were as plain as the nose on Streisand's face. "In the hair. It's the Semper frost, trust me. Everybody else stopped doin' it in the seventies but not Nan."

"You sure?" As if on cue, Jimmy swayed to one side, revealing the Ocelot's uplifted face as the camera came in and Isgro's voice with it, whispering, "Now here is our ever lovely, ever lusty Nan Semper with her newest boy toy . . . and our heart goes out to him. Mercifully, though, she's looking a bit too zonked to make the Big Score *ce soir*."

Then the camera jiggled, thanks to a weaving passerby, and swung to the left. Josh jerked up and pointed to a gray-haired man in the far corner of the screen. "Hey, eagle eyes—look over there! Am I nuts or is that—?"

"Manville! Yeah," P.J. confirmed, sitting straight up in the cushy chair. "He wasn't in that show. What the hell was he doin' there?"

"Beats me." Then the picture suddenly became sharper, as if dear Hector had finally gotten the hang of things, so they could see Greer's expression clearly. And it looked like the wrath of God.

"What's he so pissed about?" Cullen wondered.

"I'm not sure. But look." Jocelyn grabbed the remote and pressed pause, then went up to the screen and drew her finger from Manville at the far left to the far right, where his awful glare was directed. And there was Rafelson, in his glory and in his cups, holding court with a gaggle of chorus boys.

P.J. gulped, then said, "Holy shit. I thought it was just recent. But looks like he's hated Rich for *years*, huh?"

"Looks like." O'Roarke nodded—then, releasing pause, sighed, "Lord, I wish Freddie wasn't still in England! He'd know what the back story was."

"*Freddie*," Cullen mimicked with a sour puss. He was deeply envious of Jocelyn's friendship with the legendary Revere. "Shee-it, can't you at least call him Frederick? Show some respect, girl."

"Oh, he gets nothing but respect," she retorted, smiling fondly. "Poor thing, he says it makes him feel like he's surrounded by a sea of kid gloves."

Struck by the note of tenderness in her voice, P.J. looked up and saw that tenderness mirrored in her expression. It occurred to him that he had never once heard Josh, a woman as hard on her friends as she was on herself, say anything remotely critical about Revere; so he had to be one hell of a man. Switching from reproof to supplication, he wheedled, "Well, why don't you introduce us sometime, huh? Maybe a little dinner at your place? Just the three of us? I'll call him Freddie. I can be disrespectful, too, ya know."

"Oh, honey, no you *can't*," she chided affectionately. "You'd go all awe-struck and food would dribble out of your mouth."

"Would *not*," he cried in outrage.

"Would too. Remember, I was with you at that AIDS benefit when Liz Taylor showed up. She bumped into you and said 'Oh, pardon me.' I nearly had to give you C.P.R."

"No, you didn't. You put an ice cube down my collar," he corrected, roused by the memory. "Anyway, I *told* you—it was those eyes. They really are violet!"

"Whatever." She shrugged as the intercom buzzed, signaling the arrival of Jack and the rent-a-car. Stopping the tape, she hit eject. As Cullen scrambled out of his seat and grabbed his backpack, she put the video into its plastic case and slipped it into her shoulder bag.

Watching her, Cullen asked, "You're taking it with you?"

"Yeah, I want to watch the rest of it later. Eddie won't mind."

Once out on the thruway, after a brief debate between the two men over who would drive (P.J. maintained that he knew the best route while Jack maintained that all Texans drive like maniacs so O'Roarke broke the impasse with a coin toss, which Breedlove won), Cullen, in the passenger seat, gave directions while scanning channels on the radio, trying to find further reports on Big Al's escape. In the backseat, Jocelyn watched in amusement as the two men bickered to and fro like an old married couple; apparently they had bonded that afternoon at the horse show, to the extent where they were now comfortable enough to bust each other's chops.

"Could be, we might actually hear something if you'd stick to one station for more than two lousy seconds," Jack groused.

"Just drive, hot shot," Cullen returned in kind, still channel surfing. "There's always news on somewhere. . . . Next exit, next exit!"

"I know, I know! You've told me twenty times already."

"Play nice, children," O'Roarke murmured wearily. Staring out at the swiftly passing scenery, she tried to conjure Frederick in her mind. What had he told her about Greer? After a minute or two, Revere's voice came back to her, velvety and confiding: "Manville's really very good on stage. Wonderful technician. I always felt he should have gone farther and he might have—if it weren't for his aversions. To gay men, mainly."

"He's a homophobe you mean?"

"No, not *exactly*. And it doesn't apply to all the lads." "Lads" was Revere's own euphemism for homosexuals, and Jocelyn thought it dear. "Just the very promiscuous, whatever their sexual proclivities. He was always rather Victorian, even as a young man. Whereas I was, I blush to say it, a bit of a rake back then. Of course, that was before the lovely Lydia came along and settled my hash for fair." The mention of his late wife had brought a beatific smile to Frederick's lips, then he had pursed them. "But not Manny. Oh, my dear, the sexual revolution was a *very* distressing time for him as I recall. He abhorred all that indiscriminate canoodling! Especially when it came to—what's that sports term you use?—oh, yes, switch-hitters. Bad enough to sleep around with one gender. *Unforgivable* to mix and match, that was his view."

Freddie's voice and face faded, only to be replaced by the image of Greer glowering across the discotheque at Richie and his ring of "lads." Rafelson's freewheeling sex life had been a known fact in the theatre community for years, and, O'Roarke felt, an understandable one. In Rich's position as an artistic director of importance and influence, true love would be an especially difficult commodity to come by. How could the poor putz ever know he was wanted for himself, not his clout? And then, good God, to be surrounded by a legion of sycophants and fame-fuckers, all of them up for grabs and at your beck and call; it just didn't make for lasting attachments. You took your comfort where and when you could, Josh supposed sadly. But Rafelson's wasn't an isolated case, and certainly no reason for Manville to turn into a homicidal angel of vengeance. Unless—unless Rich's affair with Amy St. Cyr had pushed the old thespian's sense of moral rectitude to the breaking point. To Jocelyn, it seemed as insane as antiabortionists gunning down doctors to preserve the "sanctity of life," and she didn't want to believe Greer was that sort of mad dog.

"Wait, wait, I think I got something," Cullen shouted, turning up the volume and causing Jack nearly to swerve off the exit ramp. A bland male voice announced: "After being alerted, police discovered that escaped murder suspect Alan Brenner appeared last night at the home of Anthony Romero, his employer and head of the Peakmont Players. According to Romero's statement, Brenner was holding his attorney, Judith Kravitz, hostage at knifepoint but did not appear disturbed or violent. After demanding food and money, Brenner left on foot with his hostage. Peakmont Police are now combing the area with helicopters, but no further citings have been reported as yet. Residents are advised to call 911 if—"

"Crap! I can't believe he's doin' this," P.J. wailed, stabbing the off button viciously. "Why'd he hafta take Judith? Anything happens to her and he's finished—kaput!—for good."

"He won't let anything happen to her," Jack said with perfect calm. "Don't worry."

"Don't *worry!* How can you—?" Cullen made a strangling sound, then hollered, "You're crazier than an armadillo crossin' the freeway, you know that?"

"Speaking of crossing freeways, pal," Jack yelled back, ready to jettison P.J. from the moving vehicle, but, catching O'Roarke's harried look in the rearview mirror, he relented. "Relax. Bimpff would never in a million years hurt a woman."

"Great. It'd be nice if he had that kinda time," Cullen

humphed, pointing to an unmarked road on the left. "Turn here. It's a back road up to the playhouse. No lights."

"Fine," Breedlove hissed, yanking the wheel so sharply that Josh nearly fell to the floor. "Oh, sorry, love. You all right?"

Rubbing her bad shoulder just enough to give both men a pang of guilt, Jocelyn quoted pointedly, "Can't we all just get *along?*" After that, silence prevailed and Jack drove slowly up the long, twisty hill. Which was a lucky thing. Coming over the top of a steep rise, he had to swerve quickly to avoid hitting a short, bedraggled figure standing at the side of the narrow road with outstretched thumb.

"Jesus! What a damn fool place to be hitchhiking," Jack swore, pulling the car back into the right lane shakily and hitting the gas. "I coulda—"

"Stop," Josh shouted, peering out the rear window. "Now!"

Breedlove followed orders so instantly that Cullen, despite his seatbelt, nearly hit the dashboard. "Christ on a crutch," he barked, "what's the big—?"

But O'Roarke was already out of the car and running back down the road. Too surprised to move, both men watched in the rearview mirror as she approached the hitchhiker while awkwardly untying the sweater round her waist with one hand. After exchanging a few words, she helped the forlorn figure into the sweater and waved to Jack to back up.

As the car drew abreast of the pair, Jack and P.J. goggled in amazement. There, under the matted hair and the dirt-smudged face, were the red-rimmed but piercing eyes of Judith Kravitz. Leaning against O'Roarke, she pushed a thick, wet strand of hair off her cheek, gave them a loopy smile, and croaked, "Thanks for the lift, fellas."

Then she proceeded to faint dead away.

21

"How could you do it! Let him get away like that?" Nan Semper raged between cigarette puffs as she paced Romero's office. "What're you, men or mice?"

One hand over his mouth, Rex Strauss started making squeak-squeak sounds, but Anthony silenced him with a look. Dog-tired after spending hours with the police and getting scant sleep, he was in no mood for the set designer's shenanigans or Nan's hysteria, but, as always, he played the diplomat.

"We really had no choice at the time," Tony explained patiently. "Al had a hostage and a weapon so—"

"Christ, what a *crock*. Some hostage, his lawyer! Some weapon." She sneered sarcastically, "A Diamond Deb nail file. How truly pathetic."

"Hey, we didn't know that *then*," Strauss protested defensively. "We still can't be sure."

"Oh, yes, we can, Rexie-Pooh." The Ocelot gave him a sugary smile. "I have friends in the police department and that's what Kravitz said it was. . . . You must've been *terrified*."

Strauss had never hit a woman in his life, never hit anyone for that matter, but that didn't mean he couldn't learn. Wrestling his rotund body out of an easy chair, he muttered, "You know what you need, Nan? A good—"

"Please! Both of you, calm down," Romero pleaded, then turned to Lady Chairman. "The point is, dear, we simply couldn't take that risk. Big Al's, well—big. Weapon or no, he'd be more than a match for us. *Someone* would've got hurt. Hurt needlessly . . . since I knew the police would be coming soon."

"You did?" Semper asked in surprise. "How?"

"Well, darling, I may not have Jackson Pollocks on the wall like you." The irony in his voice was so faint only dogs could have heard it. "But my home *is* my castle and I protect it same as you do."

"You mean you've got a security system, too?" Smiling, Romero nodded as Nan regarded him with a new respect while Rex gaped, for once, in silence. Sergeant Flynn had questioned each of them individually, so Anthony's revelation was news to him as well.

"That's right. Brenner triggered it when he opened the sliding doors. You see, there was no need for strong-arm stuff." Feeling the worst was over, Tony added, "All we had to do was keep him talking long enough."

"But you *didn't*, did you," the Ocelot howled, signaling that the worst was yet to come. "You couldn't even do that much!"

"Hey, it wasn't Tony's fault, okay?" Strauss butted in. "That lawyer has ears like a hawk!"

"Eyes, Rex. It's 'eyes like a hawk,'" Romero mumbled hopelessly.

"Whatever! She musta heard the sirens before the squad car even left the parking lot. So what does she do?" Rex asked rhetorically, then imitated Judith gasping and widening her eyes like a silent movie queen. "Well, hell—Al's dumb for sure, he may even be a bit deaf but he's not *blind*. That little charade tipped him." Struck by a new thought, he turned to Tony and demanded, "What the hell were they doing with the sirens on anyways? Pfft! That's real *stealth* for you, huh?"

"Well, even professionals make mistakes," the producer said

mildly. "I hear it was just one car—an overanxious rookie. Sergeant Flynn was not pleased about—"

"Who gives a damn about Flynn!" Wild with frustration, Semper jumped up and down like Rumpelstiltskin. "What about *me*? *My* husband's out of the country. That—that *maniac*'s still out there on the loose. The cops are complete incompetents. Who's going to protect *me*?"

"Why does li'l ole *you* need protecting, Nan?" Rex kept his tone bland as he tried to catch Tony's eye. After hearing Al's story last night, he found Semper's paranoia awfully interesting. "I mean, what do you—as opposed to all the other fine citizens of Peakmont—have to be so afraid of?"

Seeing the Ocelot's eyes flash like the fat diamond on her hand, Romero sank into his chair with a soft, "Oh, God" and buried his head in his hands. Stalking across the room, she glared down at Rex and spat, "Exactly what are you implying, you wormy little *gnome*?"

"Easy, easy, Nannie. I just think you're overreacting," the set designer said. All innocence now, he reached out to give her a reassuring pat. "See, I *really* don't think Big Al did it. So you really don't have anything to worry about. Unless . . ."

He cast the last word out like a lure and Semper took the bait. "Unless *what*?"

"Oh, lemme see." He sat up straight and pantomimed writing a list. "Unless Al, for some reason, thinks you've got it in for him and maybe helped set him up. Unless you've been withholding somethin—Ow!" She slapped at his hands then stepped back, pointing a manicured finger at him.

"I see what you're doing, you snake! You're just trying to cover your own sorry ass. In case Brenner is cleared." Looking over her shoulder at Anthony, who was stroking the small glass cube on his desk as if it were a magic lantern that might mercifully produce a genie to whisk him far away, she crowed, "*He's* the one who's got something to be afraid of. Right, Tony? You and I were here the whole time—but where the hell was old Rex? I mean, considering he's no taller than a hydrant, who'd spot him slipping backstage with Al's knife in his fat little fist?"

"You rotten, lying bitch!" This time Rex had no problem getting out of the chair; he popped up like a jack-in-the-box with one palm raised, ready to strike his first female, as Noël Coward put it, "like a dinner gong." Romero rose up in alarm just as the door cracked open and Arthur Freed stuck in his head and crooned, "We'll be starting in a few minutes, folks."

The others froze instantly, creating a fine Grecian tableau of the Three Furies, which Freed managed to completely ignore. In a supreme show of opacity, he turned to his producer with a chiding grin and said, "Tone, I'd really like you in the house. So would Jimmy Treeves. Don't you think, despite all this mess, you owe the poor guy?"

"I'm sorry. Deeply, truly, sorry," Amy St. Cyr said, sounding nothing of the sort as she puffed on a cigarette bummed off the prop master. In her first-act nightie with her hair in ringlets, Amy, cigarette dangling from her pearly pink lips, looked like an angel just recently fallen. "I never thought I'd ever say this but—I really don't think I can go on."

"Aw, shit," P.J. sighed softly. After taking Kravitz to the police station, he had barely gotten to the theatre on time; what with Sergeant Flynn, in an understandably filthy mood, wanting to know in minute detail how, when, and where they had found the lost lawyer. Finally Jocelyn, displaying diplomatic skills to rival Romero's, had finessed Flynn into letting Jack take Cullen up to rehearsal by agreeing to stick around and help with Judith, who had been Ping-Ponging alarmingly from tough gal to weeping waif ever since they had arrived.

Once at the playhouse, Cullen had been busier than a one-armed paperhanger, doing his presets, checking the harnesses, and, lastly, collecting the cast's valuables. That was how he came to find Amy/Wendy in her dressing room in a stew. The cigarette was the first tip-off; St. Cyr had a sweet soprano voice that she coddled diligently, popping throat lozenges and sipping tea with honey at the first signs of strain. Now she was dragging on the cigarette like a latter-day Bankhead, pleading with Cullen, "Please, P.J., please tell Artie I just *can't.*"

"Uh, hon, he's gonna want a reason. What's wrong?"

"I'm a *wreck,* that's what's wrong," the ingenue cried, dropping the butt in a cup of cold tea; the hiss it made echoed her sentiments. "I didn't get a wink of sleep last night. God, now I know how poor Jodie Foster felt."

"Huh?" It took Cullen a second to get the comparison, then he asked, incredulous, "You—you think Big Al's your own personal Hinckley or somethin'? Oh, get a grip, girl."

"Hey, it happens every day, P.J.! He's already kidnapped one woman, hasn't he?"

"Which means his dance card's pretty full for now," Cullen reasoned dryly; he'd be damned if he'd add fuel to her fire by mentioning Judith's return. Besides, he thought St. Cyr was off her nut. "Besides, I think you're—overreacting just a tetch. A couple a' crummy photos doesn't make Al some kind of stalker or—"

"It's not just the pictures! I'm afraid that—" She bit her lip, looked down at her lap, then up at Cullen with stricken eyes, and whispered, "I'm afraid he did it for *me.*"

My, my, don't we fancy ourself, P.J. thought, but said, "I wouldn't worry about that. Al's the real horny type, Amy, not the real jealous type."

"No, no, that's not what I mean!" St. Cyr pounded her fists against her knees. "I think it was something I said that Al . . . well, he might've taken it the wrong way." Cullen didn't prompt, just waited for further details. Tossing her ringlets back, she gave a dramatic groan. "It was *that* day—after I caught Rich with the chorus boy—when I finally left here, almost everybody else had gone. But Big Al was in the shop and, as I went by, he kind of shuffled his feet and asked if I'd like a lift to the bus. Which was sweet, since I'd missed the van. We hardly spoke in the car but when we got to the bus stop, he said something about how sorry he was about what happened."

"We all were, Amy," P.J. reassured her. "It was a lousy thing Rich did. Making you think he was straight when——"

"Oh, *that.* Feh!" She lit another scrounged cigarette and french-inhaled, looking more like Tallulah by the second. "How dumb do you think I am? I *knew* he was gay, for cripes sake. And I knew why he was coming on to me, too. Which was silly 'cause I can act this sucker in my sleep. But that was Richie, always pulling strings. Just wouldn't trust actors to come up with the goods. Probably because, deep down, he didn't think *he* could. As a performer, he was awfully insecure really. That's why he pushed too much." Nothing can distract actors from their problems like analyzing the problems of other actors; delicately plucking a shred of tobacco from her lips, St. Cyr smiled slyly, "It was kind of funny, actually, 'cause there he was, thinking he was *romancing* a good performance out of me, when, really, I was giving him notes. And I was *very* subtle about it, if I do say so myself."

"So you knew all along?" If you had walked up to P.J. and smacked him between the eyes with a two-by-four, he could not have been more stunned. "So why were you so shook up about the chorus boy?"

"Well, I was and I wasn't," she hedged. "See, I was more pissed off than hurt. I mean, I was going along with his big true-love act. The *least* Rich could've done was stay in character till we opened. Not humiliate me, make me look like a darn fool in front of the entire company! Boy, did I wanna kick his butt. But I couldn't, could I? So I cried instead . . . I knew it would look better for both of us."

"*Why?* Why did you even bother to——"

"Hey, Beautiful Dreamer, wake up!" Amy leaned forward and snapped her fingers under his nose. "You don't say no to a guy with as much clout as Rich. And you don't let him see you could care less if he's played around on you. I want to work here again, P.J.—so much that I even let that jerk try and make up with me the next day while I did the wounded Wendy bit."

"Uh-huh, I see." What Cullen saw was a Medici whom he had mistaken for a mere Darling. Realizing that they were well into the pre-show half hour, he shook himself and asked, "But what about Al? What did you say in the car?"

"Oh, right." All the cockiness went out of St. Cyr as her face and voice sagged. "Well, after Al said how sorry he was, I went into some cosmic karma rap about Rich. About how the crap you deal out in life always comes back at you in spades. Then I said—'I just hope I'm around to see it when that bastard gets his.'" Then Amy shut her eyes and took a long, nervous draw.

"And? And?" P.J. pointed to his watch and yelped, "Hell, it's fifteen, Amy. If you want your understudy to go on, speak *now*."

"And Big Al said—'Don't worry. You'll be around to see it. I promise.' Then the bus came."

"Well, hello there!" Jack Breedlove stopped flipping a silver dollar through his fingers and looked up to see a pencil-thin woman with streaked hair (too thickly streaked in his expert opinion) and a Dior outfit sauntering toward him. Whipping off her sunglasses, she gave him a Theda Bara smile and he knew at once, from O'Roarke's vivid descriptions, that this *had* to be Nan Semper, a.k.a. the Ocelot. "I'm Nan Semper. Chairman of the board." She extended her hand, trilling, "I don't like to say 'chairwoman' or 'chairperson.' Sounds too clunky, too not-nineties. Are you on the crew?"

"No. Only friend of crew," Jack answered, shaking her hand. "I just dropped off P.J., P.J. Cullen."

"Oh, yes." In the bright sunlight flooding the side patio of the playhouse, Nan squinted inquisitively. "A *close* friend?"

"A recent friend," Breedlove replied, stifling a grin, knowing full well he was being carded for his sexual I.D. "We're mutual friends of Jocelyn O'Roarke's. You know her?"

"Of course! Who doesn't? Theatre's a very small world, Mister—?"

"Oh, sorry. Jack—Jack Breedlove."

"Hmm, divine name," Nan twinkled. "As I was saying, Jocelyn's very well known, for her acting, of course. Not to mention her other exploits with that dishy policeman—what's-his-name?"

"Gerrard, Phillip Gerrard," Jack supplied blithely; he wasn't about to let her get a rise out of him. "Hell of a cop. Working on a big case in Chicago right now."

"Really? How nice—for all of you," she said suggestively, but Jack let it go at that. He knew a female barracuda when he saw one, and Nan definitely was one, but he didn't hold it against her. By nature and inclination, Breedlove liked most all women, not as a womanizer but as a connoisseur of the female sex in all its infinite variety. While harboring not a whit of lust or longing for La Semper, he could still enjoy her style. Like an ersatz Mrs. Robinson, she was as arch and artificial as Jocelyn was earthy and direct. While he infinitely preferred the latter, he was rather fascinated by the former's blatant vamping. The way she shook her streaked hair back to gaze up at him through narrowed, steamy eyes reminded Jack of Anne Baxter; not the Anne Baxter of *All About Eve*, where she had a good director who wouldn't let her chew too much scenery, but the later Baxter who murmured huskily to Chuck Heston in *The Ten Commandments*, "Moses, Moses, my lips are like pomegranates." Nan's lips looked more like figs but the line reading was similar as she cooed, "So where is Jocelyn? And why has she deserted poor you?"

"She's, um, assisting the police in their inquiries, as they say." Jack paused for effect, giving Nan a sidelong smile. "Isn't that what you wanted her to do in the first place?"

"Well, yes." Semper stepped back, batting her lashes in dismay. "But that was *before*. When we didn't know who the culprit was."

"So you think the cops have—well, had the right guy?"

"Oh, absolutely! I just pray they find him fast," she gasped and grasped his wrist. "You have no idea what a big brute he is."

"Uh, I do actually. I grew up with Al," Jack said mildly as he disengaged his wrist. "He was a big guy even back then—but he was no brute."

"No, I'm sure not," Semper said weakly. This tête-à-tête wasn't going at all the way she wanted. As Jack started flipping the silver dollar through his fingers again, she heaved her artfully arranged bosom. "It's terrible what prison can do to people, isn't it?"

Breedlove made no rejoinder; he wasn't about to waste his breath trying to defend poor Bimpff, everybody's favorite scapegoat, to the likes of the Ocelot. Trying to move on to friendlier ground, Semper nodded at his small display of legerdemain and purred, "Well, well, Jack be nimble, Jack be quick. Where did you pick that up?"

"Hanging around the strip in Vegas," he said as the sun made fiery glints on the flashing coin. "In my younger days, I liked to watch the old magicians. Guys who played the lounges, not the big rooms. They had no big tricks, no disappearing tigers or any of that Siegfried and Roy stuff. Just nice, clean close-up work, which is really tougher to do. In a lounge, the audience is right on top of you, so you've gotta be good." Warming to his subject, Jack increased the speed of his fingers as Nan looked on in apparent fascination. " 'Cause you're working with small objects—cards, rings, coins. If you ask me, it's the real art of the craft. Some of those old guys were just amazing. But TV kind of ruined things for 'em. Now people just want to see David Copperfield levitate an elephant. . . . It's terrible what television can do to people, isn't it?"

Jack glanced sideways at Semper to see if she had caught his little dig, but it didn't look like it. From the blank expression on her face, it didn't look like she had heard a word he'd said, which Breedlove found odd. Mature women on the make are usually among the world's best listeners. Figuring he had bored her to distraction with his ode to old magicians, he quickly pocketed the coin. The Ocelot blinked her kohl-rimmed eyes in momentary confusion as if Jack had been performing hypnotism rather than sleight of hand. Catching his look of puzzlement, she smiled anxiously.

"I'm sorry. Did I phase out for a sec there? It's just—I've been under so much stress, you understand." She fished a cigarette out of her purse along with a slim, gold lighter. Her hands seemed unsteady so Jack obligingly took the lighter and did the honors. Nan stared intently at the small, blue-yellow flame as she drew on the filter. Exhaling heavily, she pulled out a linen hankie and dabbed the nape of her neck. "Christ, it's beastly hot, isn't it?"

Actually, it was quite balmy and there was a nice breeze to boot but Jack, sensing she was asking for some sort of reassurance, said, "Yeah, broiling."

"Judas Priest, it's hot in here!" Mike Flynn loosened his collar as he walked over to open a window. O'Roarke was reminded of the Dorothy Parker anecdote recounted by Lillian Hellman, who had been visiting Dot and her husband Alan Campbell when the latter had had a nasty row upstairs with his mother. Slamming out of the room, Campbell had rushed downstairs and burst into the parlor where Parker was knitting and chatting with Lillian, and had uttered roughly the same words as Flynn's. To which, without looking up from her knitting, Dorothy had replied softly, "Not for us orphans." But Jocelyn, knowing Mike wouldn't see the humor, refrained from paraphrasing "Not for us civilians."

After listening to Judith's account of her quasi-abduction, O'Roarke was more convinced than ever that Brenner was innocent. A guilty man would have ditched her as soon as possible and headed out of state, then out of the country if possible. The fact that Al, despite the risk, had chosen to stick around and seek out Romero told her he wasn't fleeing justice; he was trying to clear himself. Flynn thought it a minor miracle that Brenner had evaded capture this long, but Josh, though she didn't say so, was less surprised. Al was a hunter, and hunters know the countryside with an arcane intimacy that defies description. Even with dogs and helicopters on his tail, Bimpff could probably keep himself hidden for a little while longer.

Certainly Judith, whether by design or genuine ignorance, hadn't helped the search any. Against the battering ram of Flynn's interrogation, she had maintained, tearfully but obdurately, that it had been dark, she had no friggin' sense of direction, and, after they had left Tony's house, Brenner had led her to a roadside where he knew she would be found, and melted into the early dawn. Nothing would shake her from her story, and Josh felt it was nine-tenths true. The other one-tenth, she sensed, had more to do with feelings than facts.

At one point during his questioning, when Kravitz had broken down in sobs and hiccups, Mike had softened somewhat, asking, "Judith, are you holding back 'cause you're afraid? Did he . . . do anything to you? 'Cause, if he did, we have people here to help—"

"*No!*" Swinging back to bravado, she had thrown up her hands to make erasing motions. "Nothing, nothing like that." O'Roarke wasn't sure but she thought she had heard Judith add, under her breath, "Don't I wish." Part of her said it was a preposterous notion: the canny Kravitz in thrall to her hulking ex-con client. Another part of her said: Stranger things have happened and do. *You* fell in love with a cop and a hairdresser. Who'd give odds on that?

At the moment, Judith was in a holding cell, not because she'd been formally charged with anything as yet but because, after giving her statement, she had been exhausted beyond endurance and badly in need of rest. Flynn knew, as he stood sucking in fresh air, that Kravitz wouldn't have been able to give a coherent statement if Jocelyn hadn't been there to cajole and calm her. And O'Roarke knew he knew. So, as he turned from the window and announced, "I've got to get back to the search parties," she fixed him with a gimlet gaze and said, "Mike. A favor?"

"Aw, hell. What?"

"Nothing major. I'd just like to look at the reports on the playhouse fire, that's all."

"*Why?*" She had already told him about her suspicious fall at the theatre and her subsequent conversation with Gerrard, neither of which he took into much account in view of his present problems. But why did she want to dredge up old history? Still, he owed her one. "Okay, just ask Terry. She knows where the files are. Though, for the life of me, I don't know what you hope to find."

"A pyro, maybe," she said softly but firmly, watching his expression closely. Flynn rubbed his unshaven jaw contemplatively and seemed about to confide something. Then his beeper squawked, bringing him back to the unpleasant present.

"Crap, Josh, I don't have time for this," he growled, slipping his gun into his shoulder holster as he reached for his coat. "Look at the reports all you want. You'll find what we found —insufficient evidence."

"Fine, fine. That's fair enough." Josh plaited her fingers, raised them above her head in a long stretch, and added with a wink, " 'Cause I know, proof or not, you have an idea who did it but, what with professional ethics and all, you really can't say and I can't ask. See, I understand the rules, Mike . . . So I'll just read the statements and draw my own conclusions, okay?"

"Okay," Flynn answered warily as he headed for the door. "But don't jump to any. I know you're clever but it's trickier than you think, Josh."

Two hours later, sitting in a cramped corner of the precinct records room, O'Roarke realized Flynn had been right on both counts: there was no hard evidence, and, given one or two startling facts contained in one of the statements, it was *much* trickier than she had imagined.

22

"Don't *bother*," a voice behind P.J. hissed so vehemently he nearly dropped the harness in his hands. Then it was snatched from him by a fuming Arthur Freed. "You don't need to check it. In fact, you can cut it into a thousand tiny pieces if you like." Throwing the harness to the ground, Artie kicked it into a corner.

Having noticed Tony whispering into Freed's ear at the end of the first-act run-through, Cullen wondered if the producer had had a few harsh notes for his director. All in all, despite the fact that they had gone up late because Amy had required much mollycoddling to persuade her to perform, P.J. thought Act One had zipped along nicely, thanks to Jimmy Treeves who improved with each rehearsal and had taken out most of the dead air that Richie's interpretation had let leak in. But maybe Romero thought differently.

"What's the matter, Art? Didn't Tony like it?"

"Oh, yes, he liked it all right. And he knows Jimmy's a big improvement—though he won't *say* so." The tall man grabbed a handful of his crinkly hair and yanked at it, causing it to pop up from the top of his head, adding several inches to his already considerable height. "What he *did* say was: No more back-point harness! He says Treeves can fly *on*stage for the curtain. But he doesn't want him flying out over the house for the bows. Can you believe it?!"

Cullen not only believed it, he silently applauded the decision. The one time they had run the full curtain call, there hadn't been a stomach in the house, save for Artie's, that hadn't flipped over as Jim reenacted Rich's fatal flight. Masking his relief, he said, "It ain't the end of the world, Artie. Come on, it's the show that counts, not the bows. And don't you think the adults in the audience might find it just a smidge tacky? Or downright grim?"

"But the kids, P.J.! The kids would *love* it," Freed cried, looking like a very big one who had just dropped his lollipop in the sandbox. "We're gypping them. And for what? I mean— shoot, nobody's gonna drop Jimmy!"

For a moment, despite their great physical dissimilarity, Arthur looked and sounded exactly like Rafelson, and it made Cullen cringe. The way his voice had risen, his face flushed, and the cords on his neck stood out was so like Rich when things weren't going right; or when someone had the temerity to tell him no, as P.J. had during that awful argument. Shaking off the memory, he also shook off Artie and his tantrum by walking away, saying he had to check the stage-right props. Which he did, efficiently but mechanically, wondering all the while how Freed, with so much hidden ambition seething, had managed to play Mr. Smee to Rafelson's Captain Hook for so long.

"*Psst!* P.J., over here." Manville Greer beckoned from the side door. "What sayeth our Romero about Act One? I didn't want to ask Arthur. He's looking rather dyspeptic. I hope it's only indigestion."

"No, it's the curtain. He's havin' kittens 'cause Tony nixed the back-point harness," Cullen whispered back. "That's all. Tone liked the first act fine."

"Well, praise the Lord on both counts. I, for one, never liked that second bow. Took forever," the old actor said with a smile.

"People can only clap so long before their palms get sore . . . besides, it's just too damn macabre now."

"Yeah, I tried to point that out to Art but he's not buying."

"Hmmf, not surprised," Manny sniffed, then unknowingly echoed P.J.'s thoughts. "Arthur was waiting in the wings, metaphorically, for a long while. I don't know how he stuck it out because, you know, he's not really the patient sort. Never was."

Cullen cocked his head to one side in surprise and asked, "How long've you known him then?"

"Oh, for ages. Right after he graduated from college, he wrote me a fan letter because he'd seen me do Jacques at the Arena. Got very nice notices for that," Greer reminisced, absently twirling a long lock of his Hook wig. "Anyway, when he started working here, they were about to do *Inherit the Wind* and Arthur thought I'd be perfect for William Jennings Bryan. So he brought me out to meet Rich but . . . well, let's just say it wasn't an auspicious first meeting."

"*Inherit the Wind*, huh?" Cullen's mind ticked backward; along with being an excellent A.S.M., he was also a walking-talking compendium of theatre history, especially the history of the Peakmont Players. He knew the chronology of their past productions almost by heart. "That was the show that *didn't* go on, wasn't it? It was set for the slot after *Damn Yankees* but then there was the fire."

"Yes, yes, you're right. My word, P.J., so old a head on so young a body," Greer borrowed from Shylock as he edged out of the wings. "Now I have to make a quick call before—"

"So *that's* why you were at the cast party!"

"What?" Manville froze in the doorway. "How do—what're you talking about?"

"The cast party for *Damn Yankees*. I just saw a videotape of it a pal of Jocelyn's made," Cullen explained with a disingenuous grin. "We wondered what you were doing there. . . . So that was when Art brought you out to meet Rich?"

"Uh, yes, perhaps, if memory serves, and mine is not the best. But you may be right." Then he hit the side of his forehead with the heel of his palm, as if jogging said unreliable memory, and added brightly, "Of *course*. I remember now. That's why it was such a disaster. The awful music, all those flashing lights, and Rich—well, he was rather stewed, I'm afraid. And far more interested in glomming on to any passing fairy—sorry, fancy —than in me. It was just very bad timing and best forgotten. . . . Which I entirely *had* till now, you see?"

"Sure. Just one of those go-sees from hell." Nodding, Cullen poked a finger at his own chest and declared, "Been there!"

"Haven't we all, haven't we all," Greer chuckled as he slipped out the door and out of sight.

"Crap! If I had a cow, I'd *punch* it," P.J. swore as he checked his watch. There were only five minutes left before the start of Act Two; not enough time for him to contact O'Roarke. Fond as he was of Manny, he felt the old guy was stonewalling, and he knew O'Roarke would want to hear about it—and about the major curve St. Cyr had thrown him earlier. Dashing out the door, he looked up and down the corridor and sighed with relief when he spotted Jack Breedlove leaning against the pay phone.

Rushing up to him, P.J. tugged his sleeve, saying, "You gotta call Josh! I have heard some *hairy* shit today and she should—"

"Can't," Breedlove broke in, nodding toward the pay phone. "I just got off the phone with her a second ago and—"

"Well, call her back, man!"

"Can't," Jack repeated. "She's gone."

"*Gone?* What d'ya mean, gone—gone where?" he gurgled.

"Gone as in departed the police station," Jack said calmly. "Gone as in back to Manhattan."

"Wha'? Why'd she do *that?*"

"Because her work here was done, son," Breedlove joked, squeezing Cullen's shoulder, like Van Heflin in *Shane* telling his boy that Alan Ladd had moved on. But P.J. didn't get the old movie reference or the humor, so Jack added, "Josh just finished reading some old reports that Flynn let her see. Then she checked her machine and found out she has an audition today. At four. I caught her just as she was running out to get a bus back to Manhattan."

"An audition! For what?"

"Uh, I'm not positive—we were both talking so fast—but I think it's for diapers."

"*Diapers?* For diapers, she friggin' bails out on us while we're here tryin' to—"

"Bails *out!*" Jack's hands latched onto the front of the smaller man's work shirt and hoisted him eye-level. "Did it ever cross your little pea brain that Josh has been running her ass off for you and your little pissant theatre while she's got no *job?* She's no cop, no detective. She just has a natural gift for nosing around. Which you've been exploiting, pal. But it doesn't pay her rent or her groceries. Ever think of *that?*"

"Well, now that you *mention* it," P.J. gulped, feeling like Sylvester the Cat just before the big bulldog compresses him into a manhole cover, "I guess I have been hoggin' her time some."

"Some?"

"And I feel lower'n a possum's belly 'bout it, Jack." The intimidated Texan groveled convincingly. Fortunately for him, the intercom announced places for Act Two, so Breedlove released his hold, grumbling, "You should."

"I do. Oh, I do," Cullen promised, massaging his aching armpits and checking for rips as he walked backward, away from O'Roarke's knight in faded denims. For a lanky-looking guy, Jack had arms like iron rods; P.J. thought he might be in love. Wisely keeping the thought to himself, he raised crossed fingers, saying, "And I hope she nails the diaper spot!"

Breedlove's temper cooled as quickly as it had flared, and he grinned back. "I just hope she doesn't nail the baby."

"That's why I use Super Kuddles . . . because the bottom line is your baby's bottom." O'Roarke looked into the camera with a beatific smile just as the infant on her lap placed his chubby hand directly over her mouth and nose. To keep from cracking up, she crossed her eyes and snuffled through his sweaty, little fingers, "Okay, Mommy'll shut up now."

The young casting director, who looked closer to little Eric's age than Josh's, leapt from his chair, applauding. "Terrific, terrific! Jocelyn, that was pure, fuckin' *gold*."

"Hey, watch it," she rebuked, clamping her hands over the tot's ears. "And you wanna kill the lights, please? Eric's overheating here."

The boy's mother, holding a silver and gold pinwheel in one hand, rushed over to retrieve her son, murmuring to Josh under her breath, "Thank you, thank you. That guy's a total ass."

"Uh-huh. And there's thousands more just like him," she whispered, giving Eric a farewell pat. Catching the woman's eye, she added pointedly, "Makes you think twice about a career in showbiz, doesn't it?"

It was one thing, O'Roarke felt strongly, for adult actors to voluntarily subject themselves to the indignities of commercial auditions, but there was no earthly reason to drag innocent children into it. And poor, pink-cheeked Eric had been literally dragged into the room, squirming and fractious. For a moment there, after the tiny guy blew two takes with his antics, it had looked as if the casting director was going to scratch him. Seeing the stricken expression on the mother's face, Jocelyn had gone against her better judgment and salvaged the situation by picking up the pinwheel from the prop table and handing it to the other woman. "Look, just stand behind the camera and blow on this. Maybe it'll keep him distracted."

It had. And on the third take, O'Roarke had rattled through the copy letter-perfect and little Eric had stayed still, mesmerized by the twinkling, twirling spokes.

Now everybody was happy—except Josh; like Fran Leibowitz, she thought using babies in commercials bordered on the obscene. She could only pray Eric's mom was here, like herself, out of pecuniary necessity, not blind, vicarious ambition.

Nodding her customary thanks to the cameraman, Josh gathered up her things and started for the door. But the wunderkind casting director bounded up to her in his designer Adidas sneaks and whispered confidentially, "I shouldn't say this now but—well, I know the client's gonna cream over that last take —so keep tomorrow open, okay?"

"Sure, no sweat," she said, edging toward the door. Josh felt the way Eric looked—in need of a nap. "Just call my agent."

"*Ciao* for now, babe."

"Yuh—*ciao* right back at ya."

As soon as she hit the pavement, she burrowed in her bag for a cigarette and hailed a cab, too beat to face the subway. A taxi pulled up to the curb and she leapt inside. After giving the cabbie her address, she asked, "If I roll down the window and hang my head out, can I light this sucker? It's been a long day, see?"

With the inimitable savoir faire that comes with having a hack's license, the driver shrugged and said, "It's your lungs, lady. Just don't leave no ashes."

"Perish the thought."

As the taxi took the Sixth Avenue entrance into Central Park, O'Roarke puffed and sighed with relief. In an ever-changing world filled with small wonders and large woes, the park remained the park, the jewel in Manhattan's crown. Taking in the beloved, familiar view, she put her brain on hold. All the nagging questions tugging at her mental sleeve—Where was Big Al now? Who rigged that trip wire and why? What, if anything, did a suspicious fire have to do with Rafelson's death? What was to become of Baby Eric?—she shunted aside. For the moment, it was bliss to be alone, driving through Central Park, watching bare-chested boys scud frisbees across the Sheep Meadow for their dogs to catch.

"When I get home, I'm gonna feed the cat. Take a bath and have a drink," Josh said, unaware that she was talking out loud.

"Yeah? Well, have another one for me," the cabbie replied mournfully. "I don't get off till midnight."

"Deal," Josh answered, feeling suddenly blithe and breezy. "I shall drink to you with mine eyes, okay?"

"Eh, whatever," he grunted, not exactly on her poetical wavelength. Jocelyn didn't care. She was going to have a night off, to herself. Earlier, she had encouraged Jack to do the same. When he had called her at the Peakmont station and recounted his odd encounter with the Ocelot, ending with, "So one minute, she's drooling all over me. The next—she's lost in space. Totally gone. Then—poof! She's back," O'Roarke had replied, "I know what you mean. I saw her do the same thing in the coffee shop, when she and Tony were trying to hire me. I don't think it's drink but it may be drugs."

"Like what? Valium doesn't make you *that* loopy."

"Hey, I'm not a pharmacist. How do I know what new happy pill's out there?" At the time, she had been checking her watch, worried about missing the bus and the audition. "Though it doesn't sound like she's listening to Prozac, does it? Anyway, tell P.J. why I had to leave. Then give yourself a rest, love, okay? As it stands now, there's nothing we can do for Bimpff."

"Maybe, maybe not," Jack had muttered cryptically and rung off with, "I'll call you in the morning."

Which was just fine and dandy with O'Roarke, who wanted nothing more right now than to sink into a bath, then her sofa, and vegetate. It wasn't much to ask for.

But it wasn't going to happen.

As the cab pulled up in front of her stoop, she saw a familiar figure sitting on it, basking in the late-afternoon sun. Shoving dollar bills through the plastic cubby hole, too flummoxed to ask for a receipt, Josh muttered, "Keep the change" as she flung open the door.

"And so returns the conquering hero?"

"I don't know about conquering or about the hero bit. But the return part's right." Phillip Gerrard squinted up at her. "Speaking of heroes, where's your Lone Ranger?"

"Uh, out on the prairie, so to speak," Josh answered lamely. "He's in Peakmont right now."

"Good." Gerrard got to his feet, lightly brushing the seat of his pants; not that he needed to. Phillip possessed a kind of sartorial magic that kept lint from clinging to his wool suits, creases from coming out of his slacks, and food from falling on his favorite ties. It wasn't because he was the finicky sort, O'Roarke knew from experience; certain people just had it. Audrey Hepburn, Jackie Onassis, Cary Grant, they could walk through a wind tunnel and come out the other end unrumpled with every hair in place. Whereas she could take a blouse out of the dry cleaner's bag, put it on, and have wrinkles by the time she was done buttoning it. This was why Jocelyn did not own a linen suit, while Gerrard had two hanging in his closet. Looking down at her, he repeated, "Good. 'Cause we need to have a talk, Josh. So while he's out there keeping his ol' buddy Bimpff company, let's you and I—"

"Keeping Bimpff company! Hasn't Tommy told you—? Don't you *know?*"

"Know what? Look, for almost fifteen hours I've been holed up in a dark office with three other cops, two D.A.s, and a judge, listening to tapes," he said, massaging a crick in his neck. "I wouldn't know if the stock market had crashed. I went straight from the public prosecutor's to O'Hare. I fell asleep soon as I got on the plane—so now my neck feels like a bent twig and I'm in *no* mood to play guessing games. What's happened?"

"It can wait." He started to protest but she shook her head and pushed him up the steps. "First let me give you a beer and a neck rub—you're gonna need it."

An hour later Phillip lay on her sofa with a cold Rolling Rock balanced on his midriff, weary but relaxed. However mixed his emotions were regarding O'Roarke, of one thing he was still sure: she had great hands. Small but nimble, they could seek and destroy knots he didn't even know he had. Sitting him in a chair, she had worked on his neck, shoulders, and back for forty minutes without saying a word. The only sounds had been his occasional grunts and groans of pleasure as she had drawn the tension out of him with her healing fingers.

Toweling off her hands, she came out of the bathroom and asked, "Feeling better?"

"I'm halfway to human, yeah." Sitting up, he sipped his beer, then said, "So what's the skinny on Brenner? Shoot."

"He's escaped." Straightening out her middle and index fingers, she cocked her thumb at him and whispered, "Pow."

"You're joking!" He knew damn well she wasn't, but had to ask. "How the hell did it happen?"

Grabbing a beer for herself, she plopped down in the rocker and recited the story of Al's escape with Judith in tow, his appearance at Romero's home, and the recovery of Kravitz that morning. Phillip took it all in silently, without asking questions. He didn't need to; Josh had always possessed an excellent eye and ear for details and, over the years, had developed a cop's feel for what was pertinent and what wasn't. Besides, she was a born storyteller and he didn't want to interrupt a good yarn.

After describing Flynn's interrogation of Judith, she spread her hands and said, "So that's where things stand now."

"You mean, they haven't found him *yet*? That's incredible!" Killing his beer, he stalked over to the refrigerator and pulled out another. "They should've picked him up by now. What's Flynn using—a damn Ouija board?"

"Don't get all in a lather. You'll reknot your neck," Josh warned, aware of what a low threshold he had for police incompetence. "Look, you've been working with an elite task force for weeks. Mike's only got a handful of men. Plus, Big Al's a hunter, so—"

"So *what*? So they can't spot him 'cause he's wearing camouflage?" Phillip sneered in disgust. "Christ, Peakmont's not exactly Sherwood Forest."

"How would *you* know?" Josh shot back. She realized he was tired and disgruntled but she also knew he was no woodsman. "Look, if he's in the woods, helicopters are no good. Dogs can only cover so much ground, and I bet Al's been crossing creeks and streams every chance he gets. I'm sure he knows how to forage, so he doesn't have to come out in the open for food. Hell, if I were in Flynn's shoes, I might try a Ouija board."

"Still, it's absurd." The mad dog in Phil wasn't quite ready to let go of the bone, though he admitted to himself that Jocelyn, with all her deer-slaying relatives, was in a better position to judge. "He should never've gotten away in the first place. Who did Flynn have guarding him—Barney Fife and Gomer? It's—"

"Uh, Phillip—shut up," she broke in kindly but firmly. "You're tired, you're cranky . . . and you're upset with me. So you're venting it on the poor Peakmont squad. Don't, okay?"

"Okay," he agreed, coming to stand in front of her. "You're probably right. So let's talk about us."

"No, let's not. Not right this minute." She looked up at him with a rueful smile and pleading eyes. "First—let's talk about the fire. Please?"

"P.J., P.J., *help*," Princess Tiger Lily hissed in his ear when she came off stage right after her "Ugh-a-Wog-Wha" number, stabbing a finger toward the stage-left wings. "I screwed up—left my tommahawk on the other prop table. And I need it, you know, for the big fight on the ship!"

"Aw, crud," Cullen groaned. "Can't you make it over there and back before—"

"No! I've got a *costume* change," the nymphet actor gasped as if he were suggesting she miss an audience with the pope. "Can you?"

"Yeah, yeah." He got on a headset and told the P.S.M. where he was going, then ran out the back exit. The bitch of it was, thanks to Rafelson's grandiose vision and Rex's accommodating set design, there was a mammoth cyclorama stretched across the back wall of the stage and bolted to the floor. This meant that neither cast nor crew could cross behind the set unnoticed during performance. You had to go through the scene shop or down to the basement below the stage. Most everyone went via the well-lit shop as opposed to the dark, dank basement, but

Cullen, who had eyes like a cat's, took the route less traveled. It was quicker for him since he was less likely to be waylaid by anxious actors or frenzied techies.

Placing both hands on the stair rails, he sailed down the short flight then plucked a penlight out of his shirt pocket as he rushed across the wide, cement floor. He was running so fast, the beam of the small flashlight slewed back and forth across the basement. A shoelace on his Reebok came loose and nearly tripped him. To regain his balance, he had to windmill both arms. The tiny torch bounced rays every which way.

Then they caught something that reflected back. Something that made P.J. stop and suck in his breath. Slowly turning the light to the far left, trying to keep his hand steady, he saw it again; the whites of a pair of haunted eyes.

"Wanna kill the pin spot, P.J.?" Big Al said, coming toward him, blinking. "I been down here for hours. It's blindin' me, pal."

23

"So I can go?"

"Yeah, just go quick, okay." Mike Flynn was exhausted, hungry, and frustrated as hell, but it was some comfort to him that Judith Kravitz looked about as bad as he felt. "Just keep yourself available, counselor. I may need you back here in a hurry."

"Of course. Naturally," she demurred, behaving wholly unlike the contentious attorney he had first met. Edging toward the door of his office, she hesitated. "I know I shouldn't ask but—have you got a lead on him yet?"

"No, you shouldn't," he agreed immediately, then relented. "And no, we don't. We found your tracks going up to Romero's place. But it was wet last night, then it got sunny and dry this morning. After Brenner left you by the road, he must've gone back into the woods. The dogs lost the scent though. It's freaky. He's like the man who never was or something."

"Well—sorry I couldn't be more help," Judith said meekly, then raised urgent eyes to his, and added, "He didn't do it, Mike. I mean *really*, he's clean."

Unswayed but struck by her sincerity, Flynn lowered his face to hers and said softly, "If you really believe that, I'm asking you, off the record and for the last time—Is there *anything* you're not telling me?"

"Come on, Mike, you know I can't violate client privilege," she rebutted, sounding like a ghost of her former feisty self. "But I *will* say this, since it has no direct bearing on the homicide or Al—my client's escape—Brenner thinks he knows who set fire to the old playhouse. . . . No, don't bother with the disclaimers, please. So—you wanna hear it or not?"

"Aw, what the hell," he sighed, sliding out a chair for her with his foot. "I got nuthin' better to do."

Judith slumped down in the chair and reeled off Al's version of the events surrounding the fire like an automaton. When she finished, Mike scratched the side of his nose and said, "Well, it's a pretty theory. And I'll admit, we had some doubts about Semper back then. But that's *all* we had. And you're right, it has *no* bearing on Rafelson's death. The lady's got an ironclad alibi. So—sorry. Your boy's still number one on my Hit Parade."

Flynn expected some kind of outburst, but Kravitz just shrugged and hauled herself out of the chair, saying, "Then we're deadlocked and I'm dead on my feet. . . . Can I call a cab or something?"

"You don't have to." Feeling a twinge of compassion, Mike jerked a thumb over his shoulder, toward the precinct parking lot, and said, "Your chariot awaits you, counselor."

Judith didn't bother asking who the chariot driver was, because she didn't much care. All she wanted right now was to be back in her own apartment with a stiff drink in one hand and a leg of Josie's fried chicken in the other, and even if it was her awful aunt from Queens, Aunt (Why-Aren't-You-Married-Yet?) Sylvia, she would accept the lift and the lecture humbly. Of course, she told herself giddily, I can always say, "Relax, Syl. I've finally found a man. A former felon, yes, and currently wanted by the police—but, hey, he's *single.*"

Hiccuping again with laughter that was on the edge of hysteria, she stumbled out to the dark parking lot and peered into the car waiting at the curb. The driver leaned over to pop open the door for her and she fell into the passenger seat, giggling with relief. "Thank God! You're not Aunt Sylvia."

"No, not now, nor have I ever been," Jack Breedlove answered, a bit bemused. "You okay, Judith?"

"Uh, let's just say I'm bowed but unbroken."

"Well, here." He handed her a paper bag. "I thought you might be hungry. Hope you like pastrami on rye."

"Oh, I *do*." The sandwich was still warm in its wrapping paper and there was a cold can of Heineken to go with it. Tears of gratitude pricked her eyes as she sniffed, "This is so—so kind. Thanks, Jack. You didn't have to—"

"Hey, you're not gonna get all weepy on me, are you?" Breedlove cut her off, making his voice brisk. He realized what a rough time of it Kravitz had had, and figured her overworked tear ducts needed a rest. " 'Cause this ain't no errand of mercy. I wanted to get away from that damn playhouse and . . . I also wanted to ask you something."

"Sure, fine," she mumbled as she chewed. Pausing to lick some mustard from the corner of her mouth, she swallowed and said, "Ask away."

"I know I've got no right to ask, and feel free to tell me to fuck off," he prefaced, not wanting to take advantage of her sorry state. But she was halfway through the sandwich now and looking less sorry with every bite. "But I'd like to hear what Bimpff told—"

"Bimpff? Who's Bimpff?"

"Al . . . That was his nickname in high school."

"Aw, that is so *cute!*" Jack thought she was being sarcastic but, glancing at her sideways, he was jolted by the dreamy look in her eyes. It was the sort of look one would expect from a sweetheart gazing at a photo of her beau as a baby, naked on a bearskin rug; it was unlawyerly in the extreme. Then Kravitz burped softly and it was gone. Popping open the beer can, she guzzled down half of it, burped a little louder, and said, "Sorry. You were saying?"

"I was wondering what, if anything, Al told you about the fire at the playhouse."

"Why do you want to know?" she asked cautiously.

"Well, see, Jocelyn has a hunch it ties in with Rafelson's murder."

"Really? How?"

"I'm not sure. Don't think she is, either. But I trust her instincts."

"So do I," Kravitz said quickly, balling up a paper napkin. "How fast can you get us to her place?"

"Uh, forty minutes if I stay within the speed limit."

"Screw that," Judith said, tossing the crumpled napkin over her shoulder. "Do it in thirty. I'll pay any fines."

"Fine." Breedlove grinned, pressing the pedal to the metal.

"Well, thiz is a fine howdy-do," Nan Semper slurred aloud as she killed the engine of her BMW and glared out at her palatial home. As was her custom when her husband was away, and to take her mind off her worries, she had gone from the playhouse to have dinner and drinks with friends at the Peakmont Country Club. The country club was a favorite hangout of hers since it was only a mile and a half from her house; an easy drive to negotiate even when half-crocked, as she was now.

"Did it again, Agnes, you dum'bitch," she cursed her housekeeper. "You're gonna *pay* for this." The living room lights were on but, contrary to Semper's standing instructions, the long veranda which fronted the house was completely dark. "If I tol' you once, I tol' you a hunder times—turn on the goddam porch light! Lazy slut."

Struggling out of her seat belt, Nan kicked open the car door with a spiked heel. She took a deep whiff of the cool night air to clear her head, then wobbled her way to the head of the gravel driveway where there was a small spill of light from the windows. But the Ocelot did not see all that well even in the semidark, and fumbled with her key ring, trying to identify the latch key. "Shouldn'a had that last stinger," she muttered, listing in the breeze, then giggled. "Where're ya, ya li'l piggie? I gotta go wee-wee-wee."

Then a soft click echoed in the darkness, followed by the hum of an engine. Nan gasped and looked up, only to find herself caught in the headlights of the BMW. Before she could make a move, the headlights began to blink rhythmically, on and off, on and off. Semper stood, rooted to the spot like a redwood as the motor roared louder.

Then the car leapt forward.

"So? What do you think?"

Scooping up the last forkful of O'Roarke's Kung Pao chicken, a new addition in her culinary arsenal and a winner, Gerrard swallowed and said, "Wow!"

"You think I'm right?"

"No—I just ate a red pepper," he gasped, reaching for his Kirin. "Hoo! I'm wide awake now."

"Good." Jocelyn had added extra peppers hoping for just such a reaction. "So what sayest thou?"

"I sayest, it's a nice theory with no backup." He blotted his watery eyes with a napkin, nodding. "Yes, Rafelson probably knew who torched the theatre. And yes, he could've been blackmailing the perp. But since there's no proof of arson—"

"But we don't have to *prove* arson—Flynn already knows it was. We just have to show that Richie was putting the screws on somebody and it wasn't Al."

"Well, has Flynn examined Rafelson's bank records? Looked for the odd, fat cash deposit?"

"Um, I doubt it." Before Phillip could fly off his proper-procedural handle again, she raised a hand and said, "But I don't think he'd've found anything there. Honest. Rich made a very handsome salary and he had a cushy life. I can't see him blackmailing for money—I *can* see him blackmailing for power. Or to get his own way. That was more his style."

"Too bad. Money's easier to trace."

The intercom rang and O'Roarke, assuming it was the liquor

store delivering the bottle of Martell's she had hurriedly phoned for (since it was Phillip's favorite after-dinner drink, which, in earlier days, she had always kept on hand), did something out of her New Yorker norm. She pressed the buzzer without checking the intercom first.

Bad move.

Opening the door with cash in hand, she was greeted, not by gap-toothed Juan from Wines and Spirits, but by Jack and Judith in a sweat and in a hurry. Kravitz burst through the door first, with nary a glance at Gerrard, yelling, "Where's your can? I'm about to bust." Breedlove brought up the rear, then was brought up short when he saw the striking, well-dressed man seated at O'Roarke's dinner table. He didn't need a program to know this player; he had seen photos of Gerrard before. And Jack wasn't all that shocked to find him in Jocelyn's apartment; he had known the man would turn up sooner or later. What hurt was: The guy looked even better in person.

"Well, gee, what a surprise," O'Roarke said lamely, wondering where Noël Coward was when you really needed him, and if she should just whip out her *Design for Living* script and have a group read-through. "This is—this is, uh—" She was interrupted by loud flushing noises from the bathroom. "Well, I think that about sums it up."

Rising from his seat, Phillip put out his hand. "Hi. Phil Gerrard."

"Right. I figured," Jack said. (The guy even had a great handshake.) "I'm Jack Breedlove."

"That was my guess," Gerrard nodded, smiling thinly as he tried to gauge to the nearest centimeter how much taller than he the other man was. "Nice to meet you."

"Same here."

The two men were a study in contrasts; one compact and intense with black hair and fair skin, the other long and lanky with a golden tan and laid-back charm. Standing toe to toe, they made a handsome picture and it was a pity Josh was too sick with nerves to take it in.

" 'Allo. Liquor store." Juan stuck his face in at the open doorway. "Delivery."

"Thank *God*," O'Roarke said, shoving bills at him with one hand as she snatched the bottle with the other. "And not a moment too soon. Keep the change, Juan. . . . Phillip, will you do the honors?" She gave him the brandy and hustled off to get glasses as Kravitz emerged from the john and noticed Gerrard for the first time.

With her usual tact, she asked, "Where the hell did you come from?"

"Chicago," Phillip answered, then introduced himself.

Kravitz, like any other criminal lawyer in any of the five boroughs, recognized the name at once and lit up like a roman candle. "Holy Moly, it's kismet! You turning up now. Pure kismet. We can sure use your help. . . . Isn't this *great*, Jack?"

"Stupendous." Towering over the tiny attorney, he gave the lieutenant a rueful smile and Gerrard found himself returning it. Jocelyn caught the exchange and blessed Judith for her absolute obliviousness to the group dynamic. It broke the tension and made O'Roarke suddenly gay and reckless as she handed out the snifters and said, "Then let's have a toast, folks. To . . . to . . . ?"

"To new friends and old." Phillip said, shooting her a wicked look as he hoisted his glass. "Whether near or far."

"*Perfect*," Judith sighed mistily as she clinked her glass to his. "I always heard you were the *one* good cop in town and it's true."

"Stop. I'll blush," was Gerrard's dry reply to her acutely left-handed compliment, but Kravitz was too buzzed to notice. Before Judith could wedge the other foot in her mouth, Jocelyn said, "Not to break the magic of the moment or anything, Judith, but—exactly why the hell're you here?"

"Oh, geesh! Right." She gulped down the rest of her brandy, which wasn't wise since it muzzed her already weary mind and made her babble. " 'Bout the fire. Jack sez you think it ties in with the murder."

Ignoring Phillip's skeptical gaze, Josh nodded. "Yes, I do. Why?"

"Well, Al knows who did it!" Checking to make sure all eyes were on her, Kravitz assumed a Sherlockian stance, which isn't easy when you're five-one, and piped, "It wuz—the Pussy Cat!"

Jack and Gerrard simultaneously hid grins in their brandy snifters as O'Roarke corrected gently, "You mean the Ocelot? Nan Semper."

"Right," Judith crowed, stabbing a finger in the air.

"Wrong," O'Roarke answered. "Though I thought for a while she might've. I thought she might possibly be a pyro but—"

"Hey, sounds good to *me*," Kravitz interjected.

"But it won't wash. Despite her little memory lapse during the cast party, she *was* there the whole time."

"You can't be sure of that," the demi-dervish shouted. "The cops don't even know for sure."

"The cops don't have *this*." O'Roarke reached over to pluck her shoulder bag from a wall rack and yanked out Isgro's videotape. "Pull up a chair, kiddies. It's show time."

Two hours and two cups of black coffee later, Kravitz rubbed her bloodshot eyes and cried, "Uncle. You're right. Al's wrong. She never left the damn joint."

"Not long enough to get to the playhouse and back anyway," Jack observed. "It's lousy camera work. All over the place. But Rafelson, Romero, Freed—they're all there, all right."

"No. *Somebody* left," Gerrard countered, sensing for the first time that Josh was on to something. "A man in a black suit. Well cut."

"Really?" Breedlove hadn't even seen the guy, but trusted Gerrard's eye for good tailoring. "Who is he?"

"Nobody—that's what's interesting." Phillip looked over at Jocelyn. "He doesn't fit in with that crowd at all. They're at play and he's at work. Right, Josh . . . Josh?"

"Hmm?" O'Roarke had missed the whole exchange and was rewinding madly. "Who?"

"The guy in the black *suit*," Judith bellowed as if she were addressing her Aunt Sylvia, who was stone deaf as well as a noodge. "You saw him."

"Sure, sure," she mumbled absently. "He's fishy . . . but he's not what's worrying me."

"Then what *is?*" Kravitz kept up her stentorian technique, making the two men wince, but Josh hardly seemed to hear. When the tape wound back to Treeves and Nan swaying under the strobing lights, she pressed pause and pointed to the screen, saying, "Look at that! Just like little Eric."

Judith caught Jack's eye and twirled a finger by her temple, but Phillip, pragmatist though he was, could still recognize a leap of deduction when he saw it. Keeping his voice low, he leaned toward O'Roarke and asked, "So who's little Eric, hon?"

"A kid I auditioned with today. Poor mite was all wound up at first," she answered as if on a different planet. "The schmuck director was about to eighty-six him but we got this little pinwheel going and he vegged on it. Completely gone."

"Uh-huh," Gerrard prompted gently, sounding like Heidi's grandfather. "Which means *what?*"

"Which means I . . ." She paused and bit her lower lip, staring hard at the TV screen. With sudden alacrity, Josh jumped to her feet, killing the tape. "I'd better call Flynn."

"Why? What're you gonna' tell him you can't tell us first?" Kravitz demanded to know, like a child afraid of being excluded from the grown-ups' game.

"I'm not telling, I'm asking," O'Roarke said as she reached for the handset and punched in the number. The attorney's cheeks puffed in indignation but, before she could launch a fresh protest, Jocelyn leveled her with a look. "No offense, but you're beginning to bug me, Judith. So don't even start, okay."

"Well, I . . . okay." Kravitz, chastened, sank back against the sofa cushions.

The line seemed to ring forever but finally a harried voice answered.

"Hello, is Sergeant Flynn there? This is Jocelyn O'Roar—"

There was a hurried babble on the other end. Josh listened intently, nodding. "I see, I see. So where is he now? . . . Yes, naturally. Of course, he is. . . . No, that's all right. I'll call back in the morning. Thanks." Putting the handset back on its base, O'Roarke rubbed her aching shoulder and mumbled, more to herself than the others, "Dumb cluck! Shoulda seen this coming."

"What?" Judith leaned forward, alert and adult again. "Seen what?" But Phillip overrode her question with one of his own. "Where's Flynn at this hour?"

"At Peakmont Presbyterian. The emergency room—trying to get a statement."

"Oh, no! *Nooo*," Judith wailed and rose to her feet unsteadily. "It's Al! They caught Al, didn't they? And *shot* him—the lousy, stinkin' . . ." Her voice cracked along with what was left of her composure as she buried her face in her hands, weeping and moaning. "Poor lamb."

Bewildered by this outburst, Phillip looked first to Josh, who was, for some reason, yanking an ice cube tray out of the fridge, then to Breedlove, who helpfully pointed to Kravitz and hummed the opening bars of "Lawyers in Love." Agog, Gerrard raised his brow and mouthed back silently, "Really? . . . With Brenner?" Jack nodded and gave him a "go figure" shrug. Continuing their little pantomime act, Phil raised both hands, shaking his head in amazement.

After a certain number of years on the force, cops reach a point where they think they've seen it all in the way of human behavior—then *kapow*. People get even stranger, he mused, feeling jet-lagged and loopy. Take Josh, for example, who had just walked over and dropped two ice cubes down Kravitz's collar.

The smaller woman jumped and yelped, "What the—! Why'd you *do* that?"

" 'Cause you were getting hysterical, okay?" O'Roarke said, not coldly but very businesslike, as Kravitz danced around trying to wiggle the cubes out of her clothing. "And I really didn't wanna have to slap you. Too melodramatic. And we haven't got time for—"

"Oh, yeah?" Overwrought and obviously feeling that time was not of the essence, Judith melodramatically rabbit-punched Josh in her bad shoulder. Before either man could react, O'Roarke, wincing, sighed, "Aw, *shit*," as she backhanded Judith squarely across the left cheek; a hackneyed gesture, she felt, but it seemed to do the trick. "There. Happy? Now that we've done the cat fight bit?" Breedlove didn't know about Judith, but he was awash with guilty pleasure and wouldn't have missed this scene for the world; it was so Joan and Bette. And he had a sneaking suspicion, even as Phillip moved between the two women, that the lieutenant had kind of dug it, too.

"Come on, ladies, cool it," Gerrard said with a twinkle in his eye. "Or I'll have to haul you in."

"Oh, stuff it, Phillip," O'Roarke rasped, sensing the two men's amusement and none too pleased about it. "Look, Judith, I'm very sorry. It's all my fault. I thought you were too upset to listen. And I've got good news and bad news. The good news is—it's *not* Al in the hospital."

"It's not?" Tears and temper evaporated like dew on a cactus. "He's safe?"

"I don't know about safe. But he's still at large."

"Then *who's* in the E.R.?" Jack asked.

"Nan Semper." O'Roarke's answer was greeted with a round of whats and whys. She sliced the air with her hand to silence them and said, "Someone tried to run her down tonight. With her own car. In her own driveway. The bad news is—they think it might've been Al."

24

"And on top of everything *else*, I hear my snakeskin shoes are *ruined*, completely," Nan Semper moaned on her bed of pain, buzzing the nurses' station for the second time in less than a minute.

"Yes, I know," the long-suffering Sergeant Flynn murmured, having seen the mashed remains of one of the said stiletto-heeled shoes, the kind his wife called arch enemies. "If it's any comfort, I think they might've saved your life. From the marks on the driveway, it looks as if you turned an ankle and pitched to the right before the car reached you. Probably lost your footing in that gravel. We found the left shoe under the front tire." He didn't add that the shoes were probably responsible for her broken ankle as well, since there was no evidence that the BMW had made any contact with her whatsoever.

"Well, thank *God* for Evan Picone," she said, and not for the first time, as a pretty young nurse bustled into the private room, the largest one Peakmont Presbyterian had to offer. Pointing at her elevated foot, Semper snarled, "Where the hell're my pain killers? It's *throbbing!*"

"I'm sorry, Mrs. Semper, but you've already had your morning medication. Your next one's at three."

"But it *hurts*," she whined, then turned to Mike. "Can't you do something?"

He gave a helpless shrug, mumbled something about doctor's orders, and was secretly thankful. Last night, by the time he had reached the hospital, Nan had been too doped up to see, much less talk straight. He needed to get her statement now and he needed her lucid.

"Is there anything else I can get you?" the R.N. offered. "A magazine?"

"Only if you have *Town & Country*, *Harper's*, or *Vanity Fair*," Nan rattled off quickly, adding, "And only if they're the latest issues."

"I'll see," she said, giving Flynn a pitying glance on her way out.

"Now, Mrs. Semper—"

"Nan."

"Right. Nan. About last night—I know it's difficult, but try to think back and tell me everything that happened from the time you left the country club. Can you?"

"I don't know, I don't know," she sighed Camille-like, brushing a hand across her forehead. "It's all a blur. A horrid blur."

"Yes, I'm sure." And he was; he had seen her admittance chart and knew a good part of the blur was eighty-proof. "But try."

"Well, all right, Michael. For you." She gave him a smile that was half Christian martyr and half come-hither; he had to hand it to her, even in traction and looking like hell, she kept pitching. "It must've been nearly eleven when I left the club. It's just a skip and a hop from my place, you know. So I probably pulled in the drive around five after . . . I remember being annoyed about something—Oh, yes! Agnes. She forgot to leave the porch light on again. I tell her and tell her and still—"

"Uh, she didn't actually," he interrupted. "Forget, that is. We checked. The light was smashed. Your housekeeper says she never heard a thing—until the car hit the garage door, of course. Which makes sense since her room's way at the back."

"My Lord, how cold-blooded!" What little color she had drained from her face. "That maniac. He must've been watching the house!"

"Easy, Nan. Let's not get ahead of ourselves," Mike soothed. He didn't want Semper working herself into a state, so he summoned up a smile that said "My, but you're lovely when you give evidence," and asked, "About the garage door? It's electric. So why didn't you use the car remote and just drive in?"

"Oh, I never do. I hate that damn door," she said peevishly. "It's a piece of crap. Last year, I was pulling into the garage and it came down on the back of my old Caddy. Smashed the rear window and scared the living daylights out of me. That's when Cyrus bought me the BMW. And I wasn't going to risk . . ." Her face suddenly clouded with concern as she looked up at him. "Oh, no! I forgot—how bad is it?"

"You'll need a new fender, new grillwork. But the engine's running fine." He patted her hand comfortingly and forged ahead. "Okay, you get out of the car and you're standing at the head of the drive. Doing what?"

"Let's see . . . Oh, of course. Looking for my house key. But it was so dark and I was tired . . . and just a tinch squiffy." She pursed her lips into a shamefaced little girl pout that faded swiftly as she recalled what came next. "Then I heard a noise and turned round. The headlights came on and . . . that's all. I'm sorry. The next thing I remember is Agnes picking me up. Well, trying to. I couldn't stand, of course. My stockings were in shreds and I was bleeding—do you know they had to *tweeze* the gravel out of my *legs*?—so I didn't even see that bastard Brenner run off."

"Uh-huh." Flynn, not liking what he heard, exhaled heavily. "So how do you know it *was* Brenner? You couldn't have seen him behind the wheel. Not with those headlights on."

"No, not then. But, but . . ." The Ocelot's eyes, for once free of kohl liner and mascara, darted back and forth in naked alarm. "But I think there was a second or two before the lights came on when I saw his face through the windshie—"

"Nan, come on," Flynn chided gently. "It was so dark you couldn't find the key in your purse . . . but you could make out a face six yards away? I don't *think* so."

"But, goddam it! Who else *could* it be," she cried frantically, pounding the sheets with her fists.

"I don't know." And he wished to God he did. Lying awake last night beside his softly snoring spouse, he had prayed that Semper would be able to give him a positive I.D. on Brenner. He had also, fair cop that he was, contacted the hotel in Seattle where Agnes had told him Cyrus Semper was staying, because you just never knew with these high-society marriages. But Cyrus was there all right. The hotel registry said so, and so did Cyrus' secretary, who had been his roommate for the night. So Flynn was beginning to understand Nan's compulsive coquetry and how alone she must feel. But he didn't have much comfort to give at the moment. All he could say was, "Look, if it was Brenner, we'll know soon enough. It doesn't look like he's left the area, so it can't be much longer before we pick him up."

"How comforting," she sneered with a trenchant nod toward her ankle. "It's been too damn long already."

"You're right," he admitted frankly. "But I want you to know, from now until we have this whole thing cleared up, there's going to be an officer outside your door, Nan. Twenty-four hours a day. Okay?"

Just then the nubile nurse reentered the room with magazines and an apologetic air. "Sorry, Mrs. Semper. All we have is *McCall's* and *Redbook*."

The Ocelot looked at the nurse, then up at Flynn through narrowed slits that did not bode well for his future on the Peakmont police force, and acidly pronounced, "Peachy!"

Several awkward minutes later, Flynn fled out into the corridor only to find the pretty R.N., her back to him, blocking the person she was chatting with, saying, "So I say, when they catch the creep who ran her down—best punishment they could give him would be: 'You broke her. You keep her.' Now *that* would be justice!"

As the nurse chuckled over her own witticism, another familiar voice drolled, "No, no. I call that cruel and unusual."

Knowing the conversation had to be about Nan, and feeling accountable and oddly protective, Mike stalked over and said, "Keep it down! She might hear. . . . O'Roarke! What're you doing here?"

"Mike, hi! I've been calling the station," she replied as the young girl scurried off. "But they said you were incommunicado. So I thought I might catch you here. How's Nan doing?"

"Like you *care*," he snapped sarcastically.

"But I do. Honest. That's why I came."

"Yeah, sure. That's why you were just trashing her, huh?"

"No. But I get the poor kid's point," Josh said, nodding in the direction of the departed R.N. "I can't see Nan as the ideal patient . . . plus, I gotta admit, I was trying to pump her. To no avail."

"Why? About what?"

"In a sec," Josh said, holding up a hand, then pointing it toward Semper's room. "First, are you putting a guard on her?"

"Sure! Christ, wha'd'ya take me for? A fool?"

"No, no. Sorry. Just checking," she placated, then asked, "Did Semper peg Al as the assailant?"

"Uh, not exactly," he hedged. "She thinks so but she really can't remember enough—"

"I'm not surprised," Josh said with a quick nod as she drew Flynn off to a side lounge. "Look, I know you must've seen the E.R. report but—has her personal physician been here yet?"

"No. He's on vacation in the Bahamas."

"*Damn!*" O'Roarke stamped a foot in frustration, then regrouped and asked, "Mike, listen, is there *any* way you could get a hold of her full medical history?"

"Yeah, maybe. But I might need her permission and I sure as hell need a good reason." He shut one eye and glared at her through the other. "What're you driving at?"

"I'm not sure yet. But I need you to do it, Mike. Really. It's important."

"How? Important to the case or important as a way to clear your buddy Brenner?"

"Both, if I'm right. If I'm wrong, well—then I'm out of ideas and Al's out of luck."

"Not good enough, O'Roarke," the beleaguered cop rebutted. "I need hard reasons, not hunches here."

Jocelyn had a little of both but not time to outline them. So she fell back on her least favorite ploy: name-dropping. "Sure, Mike. I understand. It's just—when Gerrard came by last night and we were discussing the case—he thought it might be worth looking into, that's all."

"He *did?*"

"Well, yeah. Just as a side thing. In case—"

"Wait here," Flynn ordered, squeezing her elbow. "I'll be right back."

"Hey, P.J., you got a spare sandwich in there?" Arthur Freed asked, eyeing the large deli bag in the crook of Cullen's arm. "I'm famished."

"Uh, sorry, Artie," Cullen said, backing away from his director. "This is—it's for the crew. The guys are sick of pizza, so I took orders and ran out to Abernathy's."

"Well, you might've asked *me*," Freed whined woundedly. "I love their egg salad and I haven't had a thing all day. . . . You got an egg salad sam in there?"

"Nope, unh-uh. No egg salad." P.J. smiled a wan apology as sweat ran down the back of his neck. Artie stepped closer, sniffing the air like a bloodhound. The nervous Texan, paranoid now and fearing Freed might make a grab for the bag, tightened his grip and blathered, "Anyway, you—you should go *out* for lunch. Get away from this place. Breathe some fresh air. 'Cause, frankly, Art, I'm worried about you. I think you've been over-doing it late—"

"What choice do I have? Tonight's the first—well, second preview. I have to come up with a new finale—since Tony *still* won't let me use the back-point harness," the director railed, rolling his eyes upward, toward Romero's office. "And you want me to go *out?* That's nuts! There's too much going on to—"

"Nah, not really. You got everything under control." Cullen tried a little flattery where reason had failed. "The show's in much better shape *now* than before."

"I'm not talking about the *show*," Artie hollered, though his eyes lit up with gratification. "Jesus Christ, haven't you *heard?*"

"Heard what?" P.J. didn't know how he managed to get the question out with no air in his lungs, thanks to the big boulder he felt pressing down on his chest.

"About Nan. She was almost run down last night. On pur-pose!" He gave P.J. a brief description of the incident, sounding more as if he were discussing a messed-up light cue than an attempted homicide. "So I've been huddled with Amy for over an hour. She's a total *wreck*. Smoking like a chimney. I told her, 'Honey, onstage is the safest place for you'—until they pick Al up—but she's so—"

"Al! Al tried to—? You're sure of that?"

Freed scowled at P.J.'s incredulity. "Who *else?*"

Then Artie spotted Romero at the far end of the corridor and, hunger pangs forgotten, darted off to make one last plea for the back-point rig. P.J., alone and aghast, steeled himself and headed for the basement, feeling as guilty and scared as he had when, at the age of ten, he had found a stray mutt and hidden it in his bedroom. His mother, fearing germs and dis-ease in general and rabies in particular, had banned pets on the premises. However, Cullen, man and boy, had always had a weakness for strays. Slipping down the stairs to the basement, he pulled out his penlight and prayed that his latest mutt didn't turn out to be rabid after all.

"Al? Al?" he croaked. "You there?"

"Over here," Brenner whispered back, stepping out from behind some flats once used in a production of *Chicago*. P.J. swung his torch toward the voice and gasped to see Al in front of painted prison bars, depicting Roxie Hart's cell. "Didn't you hear my stomach rumbling? Shit, I'm starvin'!"

Handing over the deli bag, Cullen, whose Texas dialect always got thicker under duress, twanged, "Thank *Gawd*. I—I thought you mighta lit out."

"Wha'? And leave these *dee*-luxe accommodations?" Brenner managed a weary grin, even with his mouth full of roast beef on rye. "Geez, this tastes great."

"And you didn't—?" P.J. gulped and began again. "You were here all night long? You didn't go out and—?"

"Do what—pick up a six-pack?" He shook his shaggy head and started on his second sandwich. "Hell, no. You nuts? I snuck out once, around two. Took a leak in the parking lot."

"And came *straight* back?"

"Sure." Brenner paused to swallow half a sandwich whole, then asked warily, "Why? What's buggin' you?"

"Well, see, thing is . . ." Cullen stalled, wondering how to broach the topic tactfully. For a fugitive from justice, Al seemed fairly calm and forthright. But P.J.'s daddy had always told him a rattler looks real lazy right before it strikes. Still, it was a swift death, he decided finally, and blurted, "Someone tried to run over the Ocelot last night and I just wanted to make sure you—"

"Wha' the fuh—fuh . . ." A piece of beef lodged in his windpipe and Al had to swig half a can of Coke to dislodge it. Coughing, he said, "How? When?"

"Around eleven. With her own car. In her own driveway." Seeing the stricken look on the huge man's face, he added quickly, "But she only broke an ankle. So it's okay."

"Nah, nah, it's not okay." Despondent, Brenner slumped down against the painted bars. "I'm screwed. I'm screwed for sure now. . . . I'm *history*."

"Hey, jist quit that talk! Look, I'm sorry I even asked where you were las—"

"Aw, hell, it's not *that*. If it makes ya feel any better, I didn't even know where the broad lived. Honest," Al said, rubbing his beard. "If I had, yeah, I mighta tried to—not *hurt* her—just go over and have it out. 'Cause, see, I thought for sure *she* did it. But now—hell, she couldn'a faked something like that! I was wrong. All wrong." He looked up at Cullen with extinguished eyes, bereft of hope. "And the heat thinks it was me, huh?"

There was no way to duck the question, and P.J. didn't even try. "That's the rumor. But it's *only* a rumor. Sounds like Semper was sloshed and can't remember much."

"Typical," Brenner grunted as his lips twisted ruefully. "Man, they don't make 'em dumber than me, P.J. I coulda made a run for it, ya know? Mighta made it out of state. Maybe even outa the country. But, no. I had this dumb-fuck idea I'd be Harrison Ford, see? Nail the real perp myself. What a goddam joke! It's just—when I got outa stir—I made myself a promise. I was *not* gonna be another two-time loser. I was gonna turn my life around."

"And you *did*." Cullen squatted down and placed a hand on Al's shoulder. "Listen, for what it's worth, I'm behind you. And so's O'Roarke and Jack *and* Kravitz."

"Yeah, she's somethin', isn't she?" Brenner said with a glimmer of life.

"Yes, she is," P.J. concurred. "And she's a hell of an attorney. She can help you—"

"No, nix! I dragged her through too much shit already," Al said, waving both hands in front of his face. "And I blew it when I broke out. She can't have nuthin' to do with me now. It'd look bad for her."

"Well, I wouldn't worry so much about her ass when yours is—"

"But I *do*," he cried out fiercely. "She's got a life and a big career ahead of her. Me, I'm finished. I just gotta do something first—like write it all out. So they'll know she had no part in any of it. . . . Then I won't mind so much."

"Mind what?" Cullen asked, his throat suddenly dry and tight. "Giving yourself up?"

Al gave him a long, steady look as he slowly moved his head from side to side. "No way, José. I'm never goin' back inside. That's another promise I made myself. Swore I'd die first . . . and it's lookin' better by the minute, little buddy."

P.J. felt his stomach flop with fear but, before he could speak, another voice echoed out of the darkness.

"Good grief, Bimpff, don't be so goddam hammy. I mean, what's with this 'Good-bye, little buddy' crap? You sound like the Skipper bidding Gilligan a fond farewell." The two men jumped up and spun round like twin tops as Jack Breedlove strolled toward them down the narrow passageway, thumbs hooked in jeans pockets. "Hey, I'll admit things look tough, Al. But, as Josh would say, that's *no* excuse for overacting."

"Where'd you come from?" Cullen cried as Al hissed, "How'd you *know*—?"

Addressing P.J.'s query first, Jack thumbed over his shoulder. "Saw you go down one stair. Knew there had to be another exit." To his old friend, he said, "Every time you got in trouble in school, you'd sneak down to the boiler room. Well, school's out. So it took me a while, Bimpff, but I finally figured out what the adult equivalent of the boiler room would be for you."

Despite himself, despite his misery, Brenner chuckled. "You sly son of a bitch!"

Breedlove took a bow, then straightened up and snapped, "And you're a stupid son of one! Do you know, you have messed up my entire trip to New York? So if you think you're going to check out permanently before I check out of my hotel, think *again*, pal. For one thing, you got a little Jewish lawyer crazy in love with you. For another—"

"No shit!" Suddenly looking far from suicidal, Al asked, "You really think—?"

"Later, Lothario," Jack inserted severely. "For another—and

you don't deserve this, you really don't, when I think of the *bone*head moves you've made—O'Roarke thinks she knows a way to flush out the real killer."

"She *does?*" Cullen bounced up and down on his heels. "Why didn't she tell me?"

"Why didn't you tell her you were harboring Bimpff?" Jack shot back. "Tit for tat, little *buddy.* Just be glad I didn't share my hunch about Al with Josh or Gerrard."

"Gerrard? *He's* back?" P.J. asked sourly.

"Yes, and we've got 'im," Breedlove quipped, then frowned at Cullen. "For which we should give thanks. Really. The guy knows what he's doin'."

"But he—you can't tell him about me," Big Al cried, grabbing Jack's arm. "You can't! He's a cop. He'll turn me in."

"Ow! Would you just—let go!" Breedlove wrested his arm free and tried to massage some feeling back into it. "And lighten *up.* Did I say anything about telling him? No. So drop the John Garfield act, huh?"

"Okay . . . but what about O'Roarke? You gonna tell her?"

"Uh, that's another matter." He paused to exchange grimaces with P.J.; neither man wanted to contemplate what Jocelyn would say or do if she were told later rather than sooner. "Maybe we should. She might be able to help."

"How?" Al asked uneasily.

"Well, Bimpff, you can't stay down here forever—playing Phantom of the Peakmont, right?" Jack addressed his mammoth friend with delicacy and reason. "And you can't get away. Believe me, they've got state troopers all over the place. Driving out here, I saw 'em everywhere. Now Josh seems to have a good relationship with Sergeant Flynn, so maybe she could sorta feel him out. Smooth the way for you to—"

"*No!* I can't. Honest. I *can't.*" Brenner's voice shook as his eyes pleaded with his old school chum, filling him with pain and pity. "Just walk away. Please? Pretend you never saw me. I swear I won't do nuthin' bad—to me or anyone else. I'm beggin' ya, Jackie."

"Ah, Christ on a crutch." Breedlove kicked the bottom of a flat, sending motes of dust spiraling upwards. Knowing he was about to join the ranks of the severely bone-headed, he jerked his head up and down once and said, "Okay."

"Taxi, lady?"

"Jack?" Shielding her eyes from the bright sun as she walked out of the hospital, O'Roarke peered down the steps at Breedlove leaning against his rent-a-car. "What're you doing here?"

Opening the passenger door with a flourish, he waved her over. "I've realized my true destiny in life is to spirit feisty females away from large institutions. So—hop in!"

"You drove all the way out here just to give me a lift?" she asked, coming down the steps.

"Why not? You can't afford to be cabbing all over the place," he answered lightly, handing her into the car. "You're a starving actor, remember."

As he shut the door and loped around to the driver's side, Josh sniffed the air and studied him closely. Something didn't smell right to her. Not that this generous gesture was out of character; it was exactly the sort of thing the big-hearted guy was apt to do. It was the *way* he was doing it; blithe and breezy as was his wont, yes, but he had answered her question with a question, and, knowing his candid countenance so well, she thought she saw something veiled behind those normally lambent eyes. Of course, it might have to do with finally meeting Phillip, she supposed. Then Jack opened his door and dropped into the driver's seat and she got a whiff of something real and unmistakable. The musty, dusty odor of old sets and stacked flats that had sat in storage a long time; it was a unique scent and one she would know blindfolded. Looking down, she saw dust on one boot tip; looking up, she spotted a cobweb clinging to the back of his cambric shirt.

"So, how'd it go? Dig up any dirt on Nan?"

"Some," she said casually as she reached over to pluck off the cobweb.

"What're you doing? What was that?"

"Just a piece of lint."

"That figures. Messy ol' me." He gave her a sideways smirk. "Not like your immaculate lieutenant, huh?"

"He's not *mine*. But, yes, he *is* immaculate. Always. I find it truly disgusting."

"Well, hey, let's bomb him with paint balloons sometime. Just for the heck of it." Her laughter made his heart leap and gave him the nerve to ask, "So what'd you two do after I took Judith home?"

"Absolutely nothing. The man was dead on his feet. He finished his drink and went home to bed." This was not precisely true, as Gerrard had stayed on nearly half an hour, rewatching parts of Isgro's video while quizzing her. But since nothing of a carnal nature had occurred, and since Breedlove was clearly holding out on her, she felt he deserved to be kept in the semi-dark for now.

"That's nice," Jack said with a vague smile. "I'm sort of surprised he didn't drive you out here."

"I'm not. He's got a ton of work to catch up on."

"Sure. And that comes first with him?"

"Before me, you mean?" Josh turned sideways in her seat to face him. "Yes, it does, Jack. And I'm *glad* it does. . . . That what you wanted to hear?"

"No, actually, I was hopin' for something more specific," he said through clenched teeth, lead-footing the gas pedal. "Like —I don't mean to be pushy or anything—but where the *hell* do I stand here, Josh?"

"Jack, watch it," O'Roarke warned, eyeing the speedometer. "You're going too fast."

"Yeah? Well, you're going too slow," he rebuked. "Stop stalling."

"Fine! Wanna know where you stand? Emotionally, you stand *here*." Jocelyn pressed a finger to her heart. "You're about the loveliest man I ever met and I adore you, okay? *Geographically,* you stand"—she swung the finger out wide to the right

—"you stand there—in California. On your ranch with your horses. And I think that's wonderful! But I . . . can't be there with you. It has nothing to do with Phillip, love. It's just me —I nearly died of homesickness out there, Jack. I could swing it maybe a couple months a year, in pilot season. But my work's here, my family's here—well, upstate—and my friends. And you, you deserve better than a sometimes sweetheart."

"Maybe you should just let me decide that," he muttered softly, daunted by her sound reasoning. The damnable thing about O'Roarke was: though passionate by nature, she was antithetically unromantic. For her, happy endings only happened up on the silver screen; she neither sought nor expected them in real life. Breedlove still did, but he didn't know how to make his case. Instead he said, "Meanwhile—where are we headed? Back to the city?"

"No. I want to stop by the playhouse."

"Huh, why?" He coughed to cover his sudden anxiety.

"I need to talk to P.J."

"Jeez, Josh, I don't think that's a good idea." He feigned a doubtful look. "This is their last run-through before the preview tonight. . . . He's goin' crazy up there."

"Jeez, Jack," she mimicked back, "how would you *know?* Unless you've been there already?" Staring pointedly at his dusty boot, she added, "Poking around some old scenery, perhaps."

"Ah, shit on a stick," he sighed with guilt and relief. "Don't know why I even tried to—"

"It's okay, love," she coaxed, rubbing his back by way of dispensing absolution. "Just spill it . . . then we'll both feel a lot better."

"Sez who?" he snarled.

25

"You're telling me that you've *lost* the murder weapon?" Gerrard's voice was low and calm but Tommy Zito and the uniformed cop standing opposite the lieutenant's desk saw the telltale lines at the sides of his mouth deepen and droop.

"No, sir. I mean . . ." The young officer licked his lips nervously. "Not *really*. It's around here somewhere."

"Uh-huh, well, so's Lincoln Center but I can find it if I need to." Phillip leaned forward with a dangerous glint in his eyes. "Can you say the same, Landrine?"

"Right this second, no. But soon." Poor Landrine, flop sweat beginning to bead his temples, looked into Phillip's eyes as if he were looking down the barrel of a .44 Magnum, and begged for mercy. "See, it was a busy night, Lieutenant. We covered a robbery and two shootings, almost back to back. So we bagged three different guns. I'm sure we just tagged two of 'em wrong. That's all. Once I check my reports, it should be easy to—"

"It should never have *happened* in the first place," Gerrard roared, rising to his feet. "I don't give a good goddam how many crime scenes you covered that night! That's no excuse, officer. Now fix it—*fast*."

"Yes, sir, Lieutenant." Bobbing his head, Landrine backed toward the open door. "Right away." The next instant he was out the door and all the way down the hall, like a gazelle fleeing from a cheetah. Following his progress, Zito chuckled, "Jeesh, watch Willy run. The kid's fast, I'll give him that." Happy to have Phillip back where he belonged, Tommy was even happier to relinquish his position as precinct predator and return to his usual genial self. So happy that he added kindly, "Willy's not a bad cop, Phil. Just a little green."

"I know that. But it's better in the long run to scare the shit out of 'im once than have him screw up twice," Gerrard said without a trace of temper now. "Twice—I'd have to put it on his record. And I don't wanna do that."

"What a guy! I'm gettin' misty here," Zito cracked as Phillip slouched back in his seat wearily and kneaded his eyes with the heels of his hands, groaning, "Ah, stifle yourself. . . . Man, am I bushed. It was nearly two when I left Josh."

"Really!" Perking up like a hunting dog when a pheasant breaks cover, Tommy said, "Had a little reunion last night, did ya?"

"That's right." Dropping his hands from his face, he gave his stocky sergeant a curdling look. "Just me, Jocelyn—and several of her dearest friends. Like the tall and tanned Mr. Breedlove."

"Oh" was all Zito could manage for the moment. Having met the guy himself and found him—though he'd take a bullet before he'd tell Phil—pretty all right, he didn't have much to offer by way of comfort. Feebly he asked, "So? Who else was there?"

"Who else?" Phillip laughed abruptly, grinning at his cohort. "That lawyer, Kravitz. The two of 'em showed up out of the blue. We had a few drinks, watched a video. It was—*nifty*."

"I bet." A long, awkward moment passed. Despite their long friendship, Zito remained hesitant when it came to quizzing Gerrard about his love life; as hesitant as a man crossing a minefield. With a guy like Phil, proud and private, you never knew when you might trip and he might blow. But Tom didn't like the look of resignation on his friend's face, and, frowning, said, "So what're you gonna do about it?"

"Nothing. There's nothing *to* do," he shrugged. "She's a free agent."

"So? That don't mean you hafta sit back and let him pick up her option." Getting in a lather over Gerrard's ennui, he leapt to his feet, yelling, "Mother a' God, Phil! She's a *woman*, not some damn football star. Why don't—why don'tcha punch the guy's lights out?"

"Nah, it's been done." Gerrard, recalling last night's all-girls bout, surprised Zito by breaking into fresh guffaws before he added affectionately, "Tom, no offense, man. But you haven't dated since high school. Believe me, it gets trickier as you get older."

"Don't see why," the small Sicilian huffed. "And I don't understand you just throwin' in the towel like this."

"I'm *not*," the lieutenant shot back, needled at last. "Just call it a waiting game, okay?"

Before Zito could call it anything, Gerrard's phone rang and he reached for the receiver, saying, "And this may be the call I'm waiting for—Lieutenant Gerrard speaking. . . . Yes, thanks. Thanks for getting back to me. I know you're up to your ears right now. . . . Yeah, sure, I would be, too. Puts you in a hellava spot." Tommy was making mad gestures, indicative of his seething need to know who was on the other end, but Phillip turned his back and continued his conversation in tactful, reassuring tones. "Right, I heard. She called me before she left the hospital. And I agree, it's not conclusive—but it's damned suggestive. Look, Mike, last thing I wanna do is stick my nose in where it's not . . . Well, sure. It's fine with me if it's fine with you. . . . Great. See you later then."

"Who waz-zit, who waz-zit?" Zito demanded, dancing on his toes. "Waz-zit Mike Flynn? About the Peakmont case?" Phillip nodded and Tommy exploded, "Well, wha'-the-hell's goin' *on*? You two been cookin' somethin' up? How come I don't know? He's *my* pal for chrissake."

"And always will be. Don't worry." Gerrard walked over to lay hands on his sergeant's twitching shoulders. "We haven't *been* cooking anything. That was the first time I spoke to him. I wanted to keep you out of it till I was sure."

"Sure a' what?"

"That he'd go along with something a . . . a little unorthodox," Phillip answered with a slight frown. Zito saw it, saw the light and said, "It's something *O'Roarke* cooked up, huh?"

"Well, yes and no. I helped. It's something we discussed last night. But I said it was still half-baked. And she said—"

"Aw, jeez. Aw, no. Don't—don't tell me, Phil. I can guess. She said . . ." Assuming a Delphic air, he pressed thumb and index finger to his temples. "Something 'bout turning up the oven?"

"Boy, Tom, I think you're clairvoyant!"

"Tony's being a total schmuck about the harness. So I'm out one damn good curtain call. What the hell would *you* do in my shoes," Artie Freed asked in desperation.

"Hmm, that's a tough one," Jocelyn said, shaking her head in sympathy. It wasn't tough at all, but it suited her purposes to let him think so. Feigning deliberation, she tapped a finger against the side of her forehead then let her face flood with bright hope and chirped, "I know! Use that big mirror ball. The one Rich got for *Follies.* Hang it midway above the house and—when Jimmy comes out for his second bow—he can throw some of that sparkly fairy dust stuff out over the audience . . . I know, I *know*, it's not as good but—"

"But it'll play," Freed agreed begrudgingly. "And they can rig it up in time for tonight. . . . Yeah, yeah, it'll do till something better comes along." Without so much as a by-your-leave, the anxious Arthur stalked off in search of his P.S.M.

"You're quite welcome," Josh said to thin air. Not that she cared; she had bigger hurdles ahead of her. She and Jack had arrived at the theatre shortly after the end of the run-through. Breedlove, by prior agreement, had disappeared into the bowels of the building while O'Roarke had sought out Artie for a little chat.

Entering the auditorium, she hustled down the center aisle and peered down into the orchestra pit. Immensely relieved to find the conductor, Bruce Kallen, still potchkying at his podium, Josh said, "Yo, Bruce! How's it going?"

"Good grief, O'Roarke!" The startled, sweaty musician looked up amazed. "What're you doing here? What is any *sane* person, who doesn't *have* to be in this hellhole, doing here?" Kallen had worked with the Peakmont Players, fairly steadily, for over three years, and the strain was starting to show. Though the money was decent, Bruce hated the schlepp from his East Side apartment and longed to be back on the Great White Way, Jocelyn knew; well, hey, who didn't?"

"Looking for a favor."

"Oh?" Looking dubious, Bruce dabbed a handkerchief around his receding hairline. The sort of favors actors asked him for usually involved a part they were "*so* right for" in the next musical and could he put in a word with the director? Since the next show he was slated to do at the Peakmont was *The King and I,* he feared that the unemployed O'Roarke might have her sights set on Anna. "You going up for musicals these days?"

"Who—me? Nah, I only sing in the shower." She smiled to see the relief on his face, then smiled wider as inspiration struck. "Oh, hey, speaking of musicals, Peter Morrance is bringing in a new one this fall."

"No kidding!" At the mention of Morrance, Josh's longtime friend and crown prince of Broadway P.S.M.s, Kallen perked right up. This was O'Roarke's second big name-drop of the day and she felt slightly shabby about it, but not enough to let it get in her way. "Cripes, I've been stuck down in this stupid pit for so long, I haven't heard the buzz. What is it?"

"An original. I think it's called *Apple Annie.* Those hot new guys Castle and Zesch adapted Capra's *Lady for a Day.* They're workshopping it now down in Louisville. Only thing is"—Jocelyn grimaced with pseudo regret—"Peter says the conductor they've got is—"

"Who? Who is it?" Bruce asked instantly.

"Um." Terrible with names as a rule, O'Roarke shut her eyes, trying to recall her brief conversation with Peter. Fortunately, exigency sharpened her rusty memory. With a snap of the fingers, she said, "Chris Drassner! That's it."

"Aw, crap! For cryin' out loud—the guy can't even keep *time.*"

"No, but he can *make* it, all right," Jocelyn said, her voice dripping with dish as she beckoned Kallen over with one finger. "Seems he knocked up a local girl. Seems her daddy owns a shotgun."

"O'm'God!—he *shot* Chris," the conductor gasped, eyes agog but far from grief-stricken.

"Unh-uh . . . but the happy nuptials will be taking place any day now. Before the bride starts showing. And her father doesn't want his little girl livin' up here." Jocelyn grinned, remembering Morrance's colorful description. "His creed is: 'Two places I never wanna go—hell and New York City!' So Drassner has a new address."

"So he's not coming in with the show?" Bruce was almost breathless with joy.

"Not with a baby on the way. He's still doing the workshop, of course. . . . But Peter has to find a replacement for Broadway."

"Praise the Lord! Oh, Jocelyn, Josh—Joshie," Kallen wheedled, finding the begging shoe suddenly on the other foot—but it fit and he was ready to wear it. "I really *hate* to ask, darling—but if I have to do one more creaking revival out here, I'll—I'll throw myself on my baton, I swear! Do you think you could put in a word with Peter for me? Pretty, pretty please?"

"Oh, sure. No problem." And it wasn't, since she knew Kallen was good and easy to work with. But fairness quelled her scheming long enough for her to add, "I'd be happy to, Bruce.

Though I can't make any promises. Peter always calls his own shots when it comes to making recommendations."

"Of course. Certainly. I *understand*," the musician said mellifluously, knowing full well that O'Roarke and Morrance had worked together often and a good word from her would carry weight with Peter and, hence, with the producers. But his fervor made him forgetful, causing him to add unwisely, "It's just, well, every little bit helps, eh? And that's what we're here for, isn't it? To help each other. So if there's ever anything I can do for . . . you." Realizing his gaffe too late, he stopped and swallowed, feeling her hook lodge firmly in his gullible gill.

"What a sweetheart!" Jocelyn leaned over the rim of the pit and gave him a peck on the cheek before she began the reeling in. " 'Cause, like I said, I *do* need a favor. . . . Now, it's gonna sound a little bizarre, Bruce, but bear with me . . ."

As soon as she finished outlining the nature of the favor, Kallen shrieked aloud then stuffed his handkerchief in his mouth, mumbling, "Ah ou mah?"

"Didn't quite catch that, hon." She leaned down and yanked the hankie out. "Come again?"

"I said—are you *mad*," he spluttered. "As in stark raving? I can't do *that*. I—I could lose my job!"

"Hey, it's better than committing hara-kiri with that long chopstick," she reminded him, tapping on his baton. "And, Brucie, honest, I don't think it'll come to that."

"Bu—but I can't just futz with the score like that! What'll I tell the musicians?"

"Like they'd *care*." Josh snorted. "Long as they're getting their paychecks, they'll play 'Waltzing Matilda' if you say so."

"But *why*? Why on earth would you want to—?"

"I'm sorry, sweetie. You're gonna have to trust me on this." Cupping his quivering chin with one hand, she said simply, "It's important . . . very."

Weighing a steady salary against a possible Broadway berth, he eyed her closely and asked, "And you'll really tell Morrance I'm good?"

"As gold. Or may I spend eternity in a stuck elevator with Muzak playing." Josh crossed her heart lightly, then said serious, "I don't welch, Bruce."

"I know, I know. Lord, I must be loony." He sighed and stuck out his hand. "You're on."

26

"Places, please. Places for Act One. . . . Have a good show, boys and girls." The stage manager's dulcet tones were in marked contrast to the buzz of voices in the hallway as the actors swarmed into the wings, exchanging kisses, hugs, and odd variations on the old standard, "Break a leg." In light of recent events, no one felt comfortable using that exact phrase; instead one of the pirates told the poor little guy playing Nana, and already perspiring profusely in his dog costume, to "Stub a paw," while Mr. Smee told Princess Tiger Lily to "Bust your buckskins," and so on.

As Jimmy Treeves walked into the wings, looking like the spitting image of a young Mickey Rooney, albeit a grim one, hands reached out to pat his back or rub his shoulder. Nodding his thanks, he marched purposefully over to the two stagehands who held the tumble harness ready.

Before taking his place, Manville Greer, resplendent in Mr. Darling's crimson smoking jacket, slipped over to whisper in his ear, "Don't worry, son. The role was meant for you. So have no fear."

"Fear? Heck, no." Treeves looked up at the old actor with a

sickly expression. "I'm too busy being nauseous. I know this is only a preview, Manny, but my stomach thinks it's opening night."

"Well, that's probably a good sign. After all, the Divine Sarah puked before every performance." Pumping Jimmy's hand, Greer offered a final piece of advice. "Just remember, 'tis better to blow your lunch than your lines."

It seemed that Treeves' intestines were not alone in regarding the performance as something more than a mere preview, judging from the excited hum coming through the curtain from out front. As before, the audience was largely an invited one, only tonight's crowd was strictly S.R.O. There was not a seat to be had, and the standees were elbow to elbow across the back of the house.

Standing in the lobby as more and more people poured into the theatre, Artie Freed rubbed his hands together and flashed his Cheshire-cat grin. "God, look at 'em all! This is great, huh?"

"Great? It's disgusting." Rex Strauss lifted his snub nose disdainfully. "These people are *ghouls*. Buzzards. The sort that slow down to gawk at fatal collisions on the freeway. Right, Josh?"

"Hmm?" Having listened with only one ear, she turned back to the two men with a shrug. "I dunno. Some are, sure. They're jazzed to see the scene of the crime."

"Yes," Freed broke in with a hiss. "And they're going to be *so* disappointed at the curtain call."

"You make me *sick*," Rex shouted, giving Art the evil eye. "What've you got in your veins? Vichyssoise?!"

"Why you little twerp, you," the director blustered. "I *saved* this show—"

"Keep it down, boys," O'Roarke cautioned quickly. "No brawling in front of the guests. The voyeur contingent would *love* that." She reached over to pat Rex's chubby red cheek soothingly. "But the rest wouldn't. Look, schnooks, human nature being what it is—good, bad, and everything in between—

you just can't fret about what motivates people. Mainly, they're just plain curious. Which is fine—better than having them shun the show, isn't it?"

"I guess," Rex admitted dourly. Then his eyes lit up as a new face appeared in the crowd. "Well, bless my soul! If it isn't the poor man's Patty Hearst. Done with your deprogramming so soon?"

"You're about as funny as a canker sore, you know that?" Judith Kravitz shot back with a scowl as she wedged her way between Jocelyn and the two men. Tugging O'Roarke's sleeve, she added under her breath, "Can we step outside? I gotta ask you something."

Hoping that Kravitz wasn't just looking for a rematch, Josh let herself be drawn through a side exit onto a small flagstone terrace. As soon as they were alone, she said, "What is it you want to know, Judith?"

"Nothing much. Just—what the hell am I doing here?" the tiny attorney demanded. "I get home and get this weird message on my machine from Jack saying *you* said it'd be a good idea for me to come out here tonight. *Why?*"

"Look, Judith, I know you're gonna hate this," Jocelyn began awkwardly, taking care to put herself beyond the other woman's arm and fist reach. "But I just can't tell you right now. It—it wouldn't be fair to you if I did."

"Fair to me?" Kravitz was annoyed, as she always was when anyone held out on her, but something in O'Roarke's tone and careful phrasing quelled her ire and alerted her legal instincts. Peering up at Josh, she asked softly, "Does it have anything to do with . . . Bimpff?"

"Don't ask," Jocelyn answered adamantly. "Just believe me when I say it's important that you stick around. Okay?"

Though hers was not a trusting nature, Judith realized that she had reached one of those awful moments in life where it becomes necessary to place one's faith and fate in the hands of another person. And much as it went against the grain, from what she had seen thus far, she knew O'Roarke was the right person. To Jocelyn's relief, she dipped her head once and grunted, "Okay."

The sound of footsteps coming up the terrace steps made the two women break apart. Reaching the top, Anthony Romero put a hand against a pillar for support and said, "Jocelyn! I didn't know you were here. . . . Oh, and Ms Kravitz, too. How—nice." As ever, his words were cordial, but his expression was pained and his voice blurry.

"Just here to lend an applauding hand." O'Roarke got close and got a whiff of his breath, which held a trace of gin. Since this was not Romero's pre-show style, she asked, "Everything all right, Tony?"

"Oh, yes. Show's in fine shape," he said with a smile that buckled, then came apart at the seams. " 'Fraid I'm not, though. Sweet Jesus, Josh, I have to go in there and make some sort of speech. It's expected, under the, uh, circumstances. I—I'm not sure I can face it."

"You'll do fine," she said, placing a hand under his elbow and gently leading him toward the doorway. "You always do."

Twenty minutes later, sitting on a folding chair next to the sound console, Judith poked O'Roarke's rib and whispered, "The man's amazing. . . . You'd never know he was schnockered."

Straining to catch the end of Anthony's speech, Josh shushed her companion.

"So, on behalf of the Peakmont Playhouse, I thank you all for being here tonight. For us, this is more than a preview, more than a performance. It's an abiding testament to the talent and vision of Richard Rafelson, who wanted—more than anything in life—for the show always to go on!"

Coming from anyone else, it would have sounded corny, but Tony's pain and passion made it work, and the audience burst into immediate, deafening applause. Glancing behind her, Josh saw a sour look flit across Artie's face. Romero had only acknowledged him in passing and his disappointment was palpable. Then Romero raised an arm in the air, crying, "Curtain up!" The first bars of the overture swelled up from the orchestra pit and Freed swelled with happy anticipation. Clearly, he felt the production was a testament to him and no one else.

The music held little charm for Kravitz, who found show tunes sappy. She nudged Josh again and asked, "Where's Jack? I thought he'd be here."

"He is." Before the lawyer could whisper "Where?" O'Roarke put a finger to her lips and said, "Don't ask."

This was the mantra she kept repeating as Judith kept asking questions, not about Bimpff and Breedlove, but about the show itself. Not much of a theatre-goer, Kravitz's memory of *Peter Pan* rested solely on the Mary Martin television version, so she was perplexed by some of the "innovations" in the Rafelson/ Freed production. Among other things, she couldn't understand why some of the pirates were wearing lamé and why the male Indians all looked like Chippendale's dancers. O'Roarke could have explained that what they were watching was not, as in the old TV rendition, a child's vision of Never Never Land, but that of two middle-aged homosexuals, who firmly believed that nothing succeeds like excess. But she was more interested in watching Jimmy Treeves fill Richie's forest-green slippers.

Though she still felt the role was better served by a woman, Jocelyn had to admit Treeves wasn't half bad. He didn't have Rafelson's singing voice, but, since the part really called for a soprano, it didn't make a hell of a lot of difference. And, being far younger than Rich, his performance was far more believable. Also, Jimmy was hands-down a better actor than his predecessor; he was neither coy nor cloying and he didn't *try* to charm the audience or milk their emotions. Instead he let his tough-guy swagger, by its very adamance, point up Peter's vulnerability. Despite his youth, Treeves had already learned one of the secrets of good acting: Don't push. Let the audience come to you. It was something that required faith in yourself and trust in the folks out front. O'Roarke felt it infinitely sad that Rich, for all his tricks and technique, had never acquired that particular piece of wisdom.

Judging from the rousing applause at the end of Act One, the audience was coming round to Jimmy in a big way. As the crowd filed out for a drink or a smoke, O'Roarke caught a few comments that confirmed what she was thinking: if the show moved to Broadway and Treeves with it, his star would ascend rapidly. Even Judith, Mary Martin maven though she was, grunted grudgingly, "Not too shabby—for a guy," prior to making a dash for the ladies' loo before the line grew too long.

Relieved to be alone, O'Roarke slipped out a side exit and headed toward the back of the theatre. P.J., waiting by the scene dock, saw her and started shaking in his western boots. "You're pissed at me, huh? How pissed?"

"Right now, not at all. *Later*, however, when all this is over, you will be verbally drawn and quartered," she said swiftly and softly. "Meanwhile, did Jack explain everything?"

"Yeah, yeah—you think it'll work?"

"Lord, I hope so."

Cullen, who was hoping for something a bit more reassuring, started to shiver again. "If it doesn't . . . what'll happen to Bimpff?"

Sick of the sound of it, O'Roarke repeated her "Don't ask" mantra, adding, "Now—don't you have something for me?"

"Oh, right, right!" Cullen took a small object swathed in a piece of cheesecloth from his jacket pocket and handed it to her. "Good luck."

Coming back in by the front of the house, Josh strolled by the apron, then turned up the center aisle. Sitting on the end of the row in the reserved section, a recovered Tony Romero spotted her and said, "Say, where are you sitting, Jocelyn?"

"In the back. You know, the folding chairs near—"

"Oh, the sight lines are lousy there! Look, the seat next to me is empty. Since Nan can't be here. So why don't you—"

"She can't? Then who's that coming down the aisle—her twin?"

Twisting around in his seat, Tony saw a small triumvirate breaking through the milling bodies; the Ocelot, resplendent in a Donna Karan dress, walking cane, and foot cast, was being escorted down the aisle by two ushers. Romero leapt to his feet and cried, "Nan! Good God, how—what're you doing here?"

Happy to have all eyes on her, Semper trilled bravely, "Darling, I felt I *had* to. Whatever the cost. My place is with *you* tonight, Tone." Once ensconced in Romero's aisle seat, she added sotto voce, "And I damn well wasn't about to spend another night in that wretched. place! The service was *awful*. And the food! Soup-kitchen slop. Some hospital."

"Well, heck, let's burn it down and build a new one then," Rex Strauss chirped sardonically, having returned in time to catch Nan's tiny tirade.

"That is *not* funny. Not even a little," she seethed, giving Rex a look that would have frozen the blood of a hemophiliac. "Why don't you go—go suck an egg—or whatever it is you do suck—"

"Know what? I can hardly see a thing where I'm sitting," Josh broke in with forced cheeriness. Romero's spirits were sinking again under the weight of his cohorts' joint bitchery. O'Roarke didn't think he could stand the strain of sitting next to the pair of them for the whole of Act Two. Turning to Rex, she cajoled, "Be a sport and swap seats with me, huh? You must know the show by heart. Please?"

"My *pleasure*." Strauss' line reading indicated that he had just been spared a horrid fate. "It's all yours and welcome to it."

His pleasure dimmed, along with the house lights, when Jocelyn informed him that he'd be sitting with Judith. Choosing not to be thrown from the Semper frying pan into the Kravitz fire, Rex walked straight out of the auditorium and up to his office, where he kept a bottle of Glenfiddich, and, unbeknownst to all others, a framed photo of Rafelson in his bottom desk drawer. After a drink or three, he unlocked the drawer and pulled out the picture. Tapping the glass over Richie's smiling face, he sniffed mawkishly, "You were a tease and a prick and a constant pain in the butt, Rich. I—I miss you, you bastard. So, don't you worry. I'm not gonna let that bitch *win*."

With drink in hand, he locked the photograph away, then weaved his way up to the light booth, perched high at the back of the balcony, to watch the end of the show. With a huge production like *Peter Pan*, hung with hundreds of traveling spots, Lekos, and specials, and with light cues coming one right on top of another, George and Mac, the two guys in headsets working the lighting board, closely resembled the space launch crew at NASA. Intent on their task, they didn't even look up as Rex slipped through the door and whispered, "How's it going?" They didn't turn around, merely gave him a thumbs-up signal.

Sinking into a padded folding chair, Rex sipped his Scotch and squinted down at the stage. The scrim was down for the crossover scene preceding the big battle on Hook's ship. Down front Jimmy/Peter was leading his merry band across the apron while the pirate ship was being flown and rolled into place behind the opaque scrim. Alone on stage with Tinkerbell, who was expressing her anxiety over Peter's safety by blinking madly, Treeves looked up at the colored light as if it were, indeed, his best friend in all the world and spoke with artless awe. "Oh, but, Tink, to die will be an awfully *big* adventure!"

"Oh, Christ," Rex hissed, squeezing his eyes shut but not in time to stop two tears from trickling down his cheeks. The techies, busy with the next set of cues, said nothing but both felt something dark and cold seep into the cramped booth.

Onstage, though, it was all color and light. Jimmy, who had studied fencing in college, was adept at comedic dueling, even in harness. And Manville was being brilliantly inept. Stabbing Mr. Smee instead of Peter, he paused just long enough to give the wounded Smee an arch "you *ruined* my thrust" look.

Then the battle was won. The Darling children, Lost Boys in tow, returned home. And, finally, grown-up Wendy was back in the nursery with Peter. Whatever demons were plaguing Amy St. Cyr these days, she gave no sign of them now. Playing the scene with a yearning poignancy, her Wendy was large-hearted and heartwrenching as she let her daughter take flight with Peter.

Scotch and sentiment left Rex in a flood of tears he couldn't stem. As the "Never Never Land Reprise" came up and the lights faded, the house went wild. They applauded as if their arms were pistons, which was fortunate, since the curtain call as blocked, as was typical of Richie, and hence Art, was about as long as the Book of Genesis.

The clapping rose to crescendo as Jimmy flew onto the stage to take his solo bow. When he extended both arms to link hands with Greer and Amy for the full-company bow, the large mirror ball suspended over the house began to spin, flecking the dark auditorium with whirling shards of light. Just as Treeves stepped forward for his second solo bow, someone else entered the light booth.

Strauss and the tech guys hardly noticed, because something strange was happening with the orchestra. They had to strain their ears to hear over the applause, but still they could tell that the conductor had deviated from the show's score. Instead of playing a reprise of "I Gotta Crow," the orchestra slid into another tune.

"Holy shit, what does he think he's doing," George croaked dumbfounded. "What the hell *is* that?"

"Shh! Let me listen," Mac ordered. After a moment, he wrinkled his nose in distaste. "Aw, puke! It's—ugh—'You Light Up My Life.' "

"It's *insanity*, that's what it is," Rex cried, watching the entire cast, stepping forward mechanically to take the second company bow, stare down at the orchestra pit in blank amazement. "Bruce must be drunk—or on drugs."

"No, he's not." A deep voice reverberated in the small

booth. The three men jumped, then froze as Big Al walked over to the light board and gently nudged Mac aside with a polite " 'Scuse me."

Strauss wet his lips, to no purpose since his vocal cords were paralyzed, while George and Mac, gazing at Brenner as if he were Marley's Ghost, stayed rooted to their seats.

"Hey, Georgie, where's that strobe special?" Al asked mildly. "The one we used for *Mack and Mabel*? You know, when they did that Keystone Kop chase through the house." George, too scared or stunned to argue, pointed at a small red switch. Just as the confused cast came to the very edge of the stage to fling fairy dust out over the audience, Al hit the switch.

Then all hell broke loose.

Just as in *Mack and Mabel,* the strobe special turned the auditorium into a scene from a silent movie. The audience, thinking it was part of the show, still clapped, though a little uncertainly. Pressing up against the glass, Rex saw the cast, shell-shocked by now, take a final bow and flee for the safety of the wings. Then he spotted one small white face, head tilted back, staring straight up at the flashing ball. It took him a second to realize that the slack-jawed zombie lost in space was Nan.

Anthony was shaking her but to no avail. Then O'Roarke tugged his arm as she drew something—Rex couldn't make out what—from her purse and held it out to him. Romero raised a hand and swatted it out of O'Roarke's grasp and into the aisle.

"Oh, fuck. Look," George yelled, pointing down. "Tone's goin' ballistic!"

"Can you blame hi—" Mac stopped when he saw the producer leap to his feet, shouting and cursing. "Holy mother! What's goin' *on* down there?"

Romero was trying to get out of the row, but Semper, oblivious and immobile, with her plastered ankle stuck out in the aisle, was too great an obstacle. Jocelyn was on her feet, too, pleading with him. Romero shook her hand off his shoulder and attempted to climb over Nan. But her cane caught his foot and he fell sprawling into the aisle.

Cold sober now, Rex felt an acrid taste in his mouth as he realized what was happening; he couldn't bring himself to look to Al for confirmation. In a bizarre reenactment of the Keystone Kops chase, two uniformed officers appeared out of nowhere, lifted Romero up, and, for expediency's sake, led him toward an exit near the front of the stage. The orchestra had stopped playing, but Tony was still babbling. As they passed by the apron, one of the floor mikes picked up a fragment of his screed: "But you don't *understand*. It's all a mistake! It was so dark back there, I couldn't see. And I—oh, God help me—I cut the *wrong* harness!"

As they whisked him away, Nan Semper continued to gaze, unblinking, up at the dancing lights while Rex Strauss stared down at the small, shiny cube blinking away like a lonely beacon on the floor of the aisle.

27

"Okay, here it comes," Mike Flynn alerted the visitors sitting in his office as the Ocelot and Treeves appeared on Eddie Isgro's video. "Watch when the camera comes in on them."

When it did, he pressed pause and Judith Kravitz groaned, "Damn, why didn't I see it before? She's not drunk—she's light-years away. I must've been totally fahtootzed that night at O'Roarke's."

"And then some," Jack Breedlove said before turning to Flynn. "Tell me again—what's the medical term for it?"

"Semper's a photosensitive, partial complex epileptic," Mike repeated carefully. Having just boned up on the topic, he elaborated smoothly, "In plain English, an epileptic who goes into a quasicatatonic state when overstimulated by a light source. And, of course, the music can enhance it. That's why she couldn't verify Treeves' presence at the party. She had no memory of it."

"Lemme get this straight," Judith said. "The lights go on and she goes out. Then the lights go out and—bingo—she's back, not knowing she's been *away?*"

"Pretty much. I mean, she'd know if she found herself in completely different surroundings," Flynn amended. "But, yeah, she can phase out for five, ten minutes and never know it. The fact that Semper's in total denial about her condition, according to her physician—well, that helped Romero a lot."

"Well, hush my mouth, as my housekeeper says. . . . How the hell did O'Roarke put it all together?"

"Beats me. I'm still not sure." Flynn looked inquiringly over at Gerrard, who, not wanting to steal the other cop's thunder, had been keeping quiet.

He smiled at Jack and Judith and said, "It was the diaper audition that did it. Hypnotizing that little kid with the pinwheel. When she re-watched the tape, she remembered that—and the way Romero jerked the curtains closed at the coffee shop when Nan started staring at the squad car's light."

Breedlove frowned and asked, "So she *knew* that night we were all watch—?"

"No—she *guessed*," Phillip broke in tactfully. "There's a difference, Jack. She doesn't like to talk about hunches until—"

"But she told you," Jack broke back. "Didn't she?"

"She *had* to," Flynn said, not sure what all the fuss was about, but wanting to get on with the story. "I never would've gone along with her cockamamie plan if the lieutenant hadn't backed her up."

"What cockamamie?" Kravitz protested, wholly certain that Jocelyn O'Roarke was worth more than Flynn and his precinct put together. "It *worked*, didn't it? She saved your sorry bu—"

"Judith." Jack reached over and squeezed her hand gently. "Shut the hell up, please? . . . I'm still not clear on why Romero did it."

" 'Cause he was in a corner," Flynn answered readily, as he pressed the rewind button, then pointed to the TV screen. "See that guy he's with in the black suit? That's the torch. Let's just say he's an Italian friend of an Italian friend of Romero's. . . .

Rafelson wanted a new theatre and Tony saw that he got it."

"And Rich knew about it." Breedlove was catching on quickly.

"Right. According to Tony's statement, he's the only one who did," Mike said. "It was their secret—until Semper and the board wanted to yank Richie out of the show. Since he had no real connection with the arson, he told Romero he'd squeal if Tony let them replace him."

"Oy! What chutzpah," Judith gasped. "Not to mention idiocy. The guy was beggin' for it."

"No, I don't think so," Phillip said. "He knew Romero was the one person in that whole damn place who really cared about him."

"Well, he had an odd way of showing it then," Kravitz cracked.

"Judith, don't you get it?" Jack asked, now that *he* did. "It *was* a mistake. That's why Romero went to pieces and fessed up after Josh whipped out that cube last night. He'd only wanted to cut the what's-it?—the tumble harness. The one Rafelson used on stage. That way, at worst, he'd break a leg, not his neck!" He glanced up at the other two men, who nodded their confirmation. "But he's a producer, not a techie. In the dark, in a hurry, he cut the wrong rig."

"That's right. And that's what confused Josh for so long," Phillip said. "She knew he wasn't faking his grief. Plus, at first, he seemed to have an ironclad alibi."

"But after she took that spill down the stairs, she started to get suspicious," Mike interjected eagerly. "After all, she had been in Romero's office but all she did was talk to Jack on the phone while she fiddled with that little light cube. Now, supposedly, Tony wasn't around the theatre that afternoon. But, Judith, *you* said that Rex saw Semper's car in the parking lot. So we checked it out. . . . Anthony's car was in the garage that day so he'd borrowed Nan's."

"Hey, speaking of Semper and cars," Judith said. "What

about that attempted hit-and-run? Don't tell me he was just trying to *scare* her some."

"Uh, no. You're right there," Flynn admitted. "He had a twofold objective. He wanted to tighten the frame on Brenner, and—he wanted Nan dead. See, he blamed her for Rafelson's death. Felt she pushed him to do what he did."

"Male logic strikes again," Judith muttered, but Jack spoke louder. "So, have I got this right? Romero's in his office, going at it hammer and tongs with Nan, then—at some point after the start of Act Two—he flicks on the Debbie Boone cube light."

"Yes. A gift from Rafelson, by the way," Flynn pointed out.

"Well, I guess he who lives by kitsch dies by kitsch," Breedlove quipped. "But, if Nan was so secretive about her condition, how did Tony know it would work?"

"Because he did a test run first," Phillip answered. "Remember, he and Semper were having lots of private discussions about the show in his office. And, ever since her memory lapse at the disco, Anthony had a hunch what her problem was. So he turned the cube on one afternoon and it worked like a charm. She went into her trance and, when he shut off the light, he picked up the conversation right where they'd left off. Semper never knew."

Breedlove let out a long whistle. "And that's why he flicked the headlights at her, huh? So she'd freeze long enough to get flattened."

"That's right," Mike said. "And it's all in his statement."

"So I guess Mr. Romero will be going away for a spell then," Jack said.

Before Flynn could reply, Judith, index finger in the air, piped up, "Ah, not necessarily. He could always turn state's evidence. Right, Mike?"

"You mean, with the arson?"

Kravitz nodded as Flynn and Phillip exchanged rueful looks. Then Mike shrugged. "Yeah, maybe he can cut a deal."

"A *deal!*" Jack, an innocent when it came to the politics of criminal law, looked around the room wildly. "Are you sayin' —the man whacks one guy, tries to frame another, attempts vehicular homicide, *plus,* let's not forget, nearly breaks Josh's neck—and he's gonna give up some pissant arsonist and *walk?*"

"No, not just some pissant arsonist, sweetie," Kravitz corrected, patting Breedlove's arm consolingly. "A *Mafia* pissant arsonist. Big diff, see?"

"Yes—it is," Flynn agreed. "If Romero's willing to give us some names—the *right* names—well, he'll still do time but far less than—"

"Well, that's goddam swell! Just hunky-dory," Jack shouted. Gerrard, well acquainted with the realities of plea-bargaining, smoothed away a smile with his fingers. But the fact was he thought Breedlove's outrage, naïve though it was, did him credit. And he found himself liking the guy, even as Jack turned to Judith and snarled, "So—lemme guess—you're going to defend the schmuck?"

"No, I am not," she replied, primly smoothing her skirt. Then she grinned, adding, "Not that I wouldn't like to. Should be a very high profile case. . . . But I'll be too busy to handle it."

"Doing what?" Mike asked as the faint sound of footsteps echoed from far down the corridor.

"Planning my wedding," the sharp-eared attorney chortled, popping out of her chair as she fluffed up her hair. "Boy, my Aunt Sylvia's gonna *plotz* when she hears."

In the plotzing department, Mike, Jack, and Phil had a big lead on Aunt Sylvia. They looked like a tableau vivant of the Three Stooges in shock. Breedlove unfroze long enough to croak one word: "Bimpff?"

"That's right—but shush. He doesn't know yet." Looking darn near radiant, she gave them a saucy smile. "Poor baby, huh? Thinks he's free at last. Hah!"

Then Big Al stood in the doorway, flanked by one of the cops whom he had given the slip at the courthouse. After turning himself in at the theatre, Brenner had been kept in custody overnight in order to give his deposition. Despite his recent transgressions, there was no way the Peakmont police could bring charges against a wrongly accused man; not without looking like total pricks. The officer at his side knew this but was none too thrilled about it. Propelling Al into the office with a short shove, he muttered, "Here. He's all yours."

Walking over to link an arm through Al's, Judith looked up at the disgruntled cop and cooed, "You better believe it, pal."

"I can't believe it! You believe it?" Flynn asked Gerrard shortly after Judith had hustled her unknowing intended out of the building. While Kravitz was telling him that she was taking him back to his place for a shower, a shave, and "a good hot meal," Brenner had been a man in a daze but a happy man, Phillip thought, judging from the addled grin on his puss.

"Yeah, I do," he said. "She's made up her mind to it. . . . He's a goner."

"Well, I guess there's some justice in the world after all!" Mike, loopy with relief now that the whole ordeal was over, nearly busted a gut laughing. When his mirth was spent, he finally thought to ask, "Hey, where's Jocelyn? I thought for sure she'd be here."

"Who knows?"

"Beats me."

Gerrard and Jack spoke in tandem, then looked at each other and raised their shoulders in mutual, mystified resignation. Breedlove found himself grinning at Gerrard as he plaited his fingers and mimicked Peter Graves gravely. "Seems she had an important mission. Our instructions, should we choose to accept the assignment, are to meet her back at my hotel at—" He glanced down at his watch and gasped, "Oh, shit! An hour from now. Come on, Phil, let's book."

The two men drove in companionable silence for most of the ride back to Manhattan. But as Breedlove entered the Lincoln

Tunnel, he cleared his throat and asked, "What do you think is gonna happen to Jocelyn—once the whole story gets out?"

"Happen? In what sense?"

"To her career."

"Oh . . . I don't know," Gerrard answered uneasily. "I don't see why it should have much effect one way or the othe—"

"Aw, get real, Phil! You *know* it will," Breedlove retorted. "This—coupled with the Burbage thing. If the Peakmont Playhouse goes under, she'll—she'll become Josh the Giant Killer!"

"I don't think that'll happen," Gerrard said stubbornly. "And even if it did, it's not her *fault.*"

"It wasn't her fault *last* time, either," Jack pointed out brusquely. "But it still stopped her career stone cold, didn't it?"

"That was . . . a different situation," Phillip said, trying to contain his temper. "The real facts never came out. So she got blamed."

"And she'll get blamed again," Breedlove insisted. "Look, I know the business, Phil. It doesn't matter that she did the right thing. It's image—like the camera commercial says—image is everything."

"Yeah, and it's a disgusting slogan if you ask me."

"Sure. No question. But it's the way of the world." Jack softened somewhat and said, "And Josh's image is gonna be shit. Someone who makes trouble. Hell, she'll be the Jimmy Carter of Broadway. Does good but is *not* a team player. Come on, you know what I mean! I bet it happens on the force all the time."

"Yes, you're right," Gerrard said, acknowledging but hating the accuracy of Breedlove's logic. "I know what you mean—but I don't know what you're driving at."

"Just this—I think she'd be better off coming back to L.A."

"Ah! And you say this out of pure altruism, eh?"

"Hell, no! I want her back. I miss her," Jack offered frankly. "But I also want what's best for her. Honest. Now, if it's not too much to ask . . . tell me what you want."

Gerrard gave Jack a long, hard look and found he was no

longer angry with his rival. Placing a hand on the other man's shoulder, he said, "You know, when it comes right down to it, Jack, it doesn't make much difference what *I* want or what *you* want, really. . . . She'll do as she pleases."

Coming out the other end of the tunnel, Jack sighed and smacked his palm against the steering wheel. "Yeah, I know. You're right. . . . Have any idea what that might be?"

Phillip smiled and shook his head. "Not a glimmer."

"Me, either . . . but I think it's about time we asked."

"Yeah—maybe."

But when they got back to Breedlove's hotel, there was no O'Roarke there to confront. Only a message from P.J. Cullen to call him at an unfamiliar number. Jack pulled two beers out of the minibar as Gerrard phoned. A husky voice at the other end answered, "Joe Allen's."

"Hello. Is P.J. Cullen there?"

"Oh, brother, is he," the voice replied before yelling, "Peeje! Phone!"

After a long moment, Cullen came on the line, slurring, "Hi. Who's-it?"

"P.J., it's Phillip Gerrard. . . . Is Josh there?"

"Yup, she's with me, all rightie."

"Can I talk to her?"

"Um—bad. Bad idea just now."

"*Why?*"

The cold timbre in Gerrard's voice seemed to sober Cullen up a bit. Phillip heard him ask for a cup of coffee before he answered, "She's a li'l polluted a'tha moment."

Breedlove, who had picked up the extension, said, "She's *drunk?* At two in the afternoon?" Phil was just as surprised as Jack, since O'Roarke rarely took a drink during the day, and even more rarely did she show the effects of it.

"She's *stinkin'*, fellas," Cullen said. This was confirmed by the sound of Josh's voice in the background crooning a woozy rendition of "Amazing Grace." P.J. hiccuped, "Shee's had a bad day, guys."

Knowing that Jocelyn was apt to feel an irrational remorse at the end of a case, Phillip asked, "Because of Romero?"

"Huh? Tony? Nah, screw 'em," P.J. spat. "He dunnit deserve—aw, forget it. Anyways, it's nothin' to do with him."

"P.J., listen to me," Jack ordered sharply. "What happened? Where'd she go this morning?"

There was a very long pause now as Cullen's coffee arrived. Jack and Phillip could hear him slurping it down. Then he belched and said, "She made a promise, see? Told her friend Eddie—guy who made the tape—told him she'd keep him posted. So she goes to the hospital first thing this morning—'cause she wants to let him know the tape was like, you know, the smoking gun. And she was just so hot to tell him, she flew by the front desk. But when she got upstairs, see, the bed was empty. Eddie, uh . . . he died last night in his sleep. . . . Aw, crap, I'm sorry—I didn't even know him—but I'm losin' it here."

Listening to Cullen sniffle over the line, Jack and Phillip locked eyes across the room and waited patiently. When P.J. finally got himself in hand, Phillip said softly, "So how bad is she?"

"Pretty bad. Not at first. Not when she came by my place and told me," Cullen croaked. "So we came down here for a stiff one—but I don't think she ate any breakfast—and after a while, she's leaning against the bar, asking poor Will, the bartender, 'Why do people bother killing people? It's redundant. We're all dying *anyway*.' Stuff like that . . . Will's gettin' real depressed, by the way."

So were Jack and Phillip. It is always easier to bear one's own pain, no matter how keen, than to see someone you care about in an agony you cannot spare them.

Cullen, even in his cups, felt it, too, and said, "I dunno what to do, guys. She's—she's like fuckin' Antigone or something. It's scarin' me."

"Listen, we'll be there in a few minutes," Gerrard said. "Just sit tight."

"Oh, heck, no problem," P.J. said soggily. "I'm already sittin' and I'm tighter'n a ant's fanny." Cullen hung up and slid the bar phone back over to a misty-eyed Will as he looked around the near-empty room. "Hey! Where'd she go? Where's Josh?"

"Back there." Will waved a dishrag toward the back hall as he thumbed one eye. With the other, he gave P.J. an accusatory look. "Poor thing. While *you* were yakking away, she got on the pay phone. Then she made a dash for the can . . . I think that last margarita did it."

"Oh, no."

Cullen ran to the door of the ladies' room just in time to hear O'Roarke retching. Then there were flushing noises followed by the sound of faucets running. He waited a minute, then tapped on the door gingerly.

"Josh? Josh—you all right in there?"

Flinging the door open, O'Roarke, face damp but eyes back in focus, stepped into the narrow hall, wiping a hand across her mouth. "Jeez, it's been *years* since I've done that."

"What? Got so plastered you puked?"

"No. Induced it." She held up her index and middle finger. "You know, the ancient Roman method. God, can you imagine—they did it all the time! At those big orgies. Yeeck! No wonder the empire fell." With that little history lesson in the origins of bulimia, she walked over to the bar and handed Will two twenties.

"Hey, this is too much," he protested.

"No. Keep it." She leaned over to pat his cheek. "You earned it."

"Josh," P.J. whispered in her ear, "you can't afford—"

"Aw, sure. I'll write it off as therapy," she kidded. "Look, P.J., much as I hate to hurl and run, I've gotta go."

"Go? No! You—can't," he squeaked.

"Why not?"

"Because, well, because Jack and Phil are on their way here," Cullen blurted, then flinched, expecting a tongue-lashing.

"Oh, hell. I forgot I was supposed to meet them," she said

without rancor. "Well, tell them I'll call when I get back. Okay?"

"Back from *where?*"

"J.F.K. Bye."

When Breedlove arrived with Phil to find Cullen had let their wounded dove fly the coop, he was not at all pleased, and he let P.J. know it in clear and colorful terms, winding up with, "For crummy sakes, P.J.! You kept Bimpff in a basement for two whole days. And he's—what? Six-three, over two hundred pounds. But you couldn't keep a five-foot-five woman still for a few minutes?"

"Well, what was I s'pose to do?" Cullen asked indignantly. "Make a flying tackle? Brain her with a beer mug?"

Gerrard gave a short, sharp whistle. "Break it up, boys, break it up. I think what we need is a little lunch."

"Lunch?"

"You wanna eat *now?*"

"Yeah, and I want a nice, tall draft, too," Phillip said, rubbing his hands in anticipation. Seeing the other two men eye him as if he were the coldest fish in the sea, he added, "Don't worry. I think I know where we'll find Josh. Later. But food first."

After what turned out to be, all things considered, a surprisingly convivial meal, despite Gerrard's refusal to discuss Jocelyn's whereabouts, they all piled into Jack's rent-a-car, with Phillip at the wheel this time. As he drove down Lexington Avenue and past Twenty-third Street, Cullen caught on to their destination and gasped, "The Players?"

Gerrard nodded but said nary a word, and Jack didn't press; old movie buff that he was, he could always sense when the big payoff was coming, and he enjoyed the build up.

As soon as they entered the foyer of the Players Club, Phillip approached the porter while Jack and P.J. gazed and gawked at the vast array of vintage theatre memorabilia that graced the walls. Nodding his head, the porter pointed to two large pieces of ancient but elegant luggage behind his desk and said, "Yes, he just got back a few minutes ago. Went straight downstairs to the bar."

Signaling his companions to keep mum, Phillip led them down the short flight to the bar lounge. The bar was near the middle of the long, low-ceilinged room, with café tables and chairs to the right and a pool table surrounded by a wrap-around banquette to the left.

Sitting in the far corner of the banquette, with tea and scones on a tiny table nearby, was O'Roarke, eyes closed, resting her head against the tweedy shoulder of a stately, silver-haired gent. Cullen, awe-struck, sucked in air and said, "Holy cow, that's *him,* huh?"

Breedlove didn't need to ask who *him* was; he knew at a glance. Watching the older man raise a languid hand to take a puff from a trim cigar, he felt himself grinning from ear to ear. "Frederick Revere. Son of a gun. I always thought Josh was exaggerating. But, boy, that is a goddam *star* if I ever saw one."

"And then some," Phillip affirmed softly. "Freddie's the real goods. All others need not apply."

Even from across the room, Revere's sonorous voice carried easily as he lullabied Josh with idle gossip. "So I got back to London in time to see Maggie Smith do Lady Bracknell in *Earnest*. My dear, she was shameless! Beyond hammy—I *adored* every second of it."

"I bet." Eyes still shut, Josh smiled as though she was having a sweet dream. "Did you go backstage after?"

"No. She met me back at my hotel and we jabbered like magpies till dawn."

"Gloriosky, I can't believe it! This is *great,*" P.J. burbled. "I finally get to meet him!"

Cullen took one step down, only to have Gerrard grab his collar and yank him right back up. "Oh, no, you don't."

"Wha'? Why *not,*" Cullen hissed. "Why the hell did we come here then?"

"Just checking, just checking," Phillip murmured. "To make sure she's in good hands. Which she is."

"Aw, come *on*. Josh won't mind," P.J. pleaded. "This might be my only chance!"

"You know, Peeje, I don't think you'd recognize a tender moment if it bit you on the butt," Jack said as he took Gerrard's cue and slipped a hand under the Texan's armpit. "Right now, we are as the French would say, *de trop*."

In unison, Phil and Jack lifted Cullen a half foot off the ground and carried him back through the foyer and out the door, his feet pedaling fruitlessly as he spluttered, "But it's just not *fair*."

Breedlove shot the lieutenant a wry look and said, "So what is?"